ASP

D0616042

PS 3507 .O726 A93 1992
H. D. (Hilda Doolittle), 1886-1961.
Asphodel

ASPHODEL

H.D.

Edited with an Introduction and Biographical Notes

by ROBERT SPOO

Duke University Press   *Durham and London 1992*

PS
3507
.O726
A93
1992

© 1992 Duke University Press
Previously unpublished material by Hilda Doolittle is
copyright © 1992 by Perdita Schaffner; used by permission
of New Directions Publishing Corp., agents.
All rights reserved
Printed in the United States of America on acid-free paper ∞
Library of Congress Cataloging-in-Publication Data
appear on the last printed page of this book.

Contents

Acknowledgments

I wish to thank Perdita Schaffner and the New Directions Publishing Corporation for permission to publish *Asphodel*. I also wish to thank Mrs. Schaffner and the Yale Collection of American Literature, Beinecke Rare Book and Manuscript Library, Yale University, as well as the Rosenbach Museum and Library in Philadelphia, for permission to quote from unpublished H.D. material in the Introduction and Appendix.

Any serious editing project is a collaborative effort, and I have benefited from the advice of many persons within and outside the community of H.D. scholars. From the start, the wisdom and support of Susan Stanford Friedman and Louis H. Silverstein have been invaluable; they read drafts of the introductory material and made suggestions about problematic details in H.D.'s text. I am also grateful for the kind encouragement of Perdita Schaffner.

I would like to thank D. Thomas Benediktson and Eileen Gregory for information about H.D.'s classical allusions; Corinna del Greco Lobner, Jane Nicholson, and Vibeke Petersen for advice about H.D.'s use of foreign languages; and Louis H. Silverstein, Charles Timbrell, and Caroline Zilboorg for biographical information about H.D. and her friends. Thanks also to Joanne Cornell, Michael Davis, Lars Engle, Norman Grabo, Monty Montee, Mary O'Toole, and Omar Pound for reading portions of this text and providing helpful criticisms. It was Gary Burnett who first made me aware of *Asphodel*; our early conversations about H.D. were an inspiration and a spur.

Thanks also to Diana Collecott, Joseph A. Kestner, David Kramer, A. Walton Litz, John Logan, Claus Melchior, Adalaide

Morris, Lawrence Rainey, Caroline Rittenhouse, Kathy A. Sears, and Patricia Willis. I would also like to acknowledge the valuable assistance of Steve Jones and the staff at the Beinecke Rare Book and Manuscript Library, Yale University; Sidney F. Huttner and the staff at Special Collections, McFarlin Library, University of Tulsa; and Leslie A. Morris and the staff at the Rosenbach Museum and Library in Philadelphia.

I also want to express my gratitude to Duke University Press and its editors for their excellent work. This edition would not have been possible without the advice and sensitive collaboration of Joanne Ferguson, who supported this project from its inception.

Special thanks to the owners and proprietors of Silverleigh for their friendship, hospitality, and conversation, and to Monty Montee for his patience and refreshingly ironic smile.

A National Endowment for the Humanities Summer Stipend in 1989 provided a crucial early impetus and allowed me to travel to archives.

Introduction

H.D.'s *Asphodel* is a work with a strangely disembodied reputation, a sort of phantom novel that makes frequent appearances in the criticism on H.D. yet, until now, has had no public, practical existence. Although it has occasioned important exegesis,[1] *Asphodel* itself has remained unpublished since its completion in the 1920s, a modernist text akin in its experimental form and spirit to Woolf's *Jacob's Room*, Stein's *The Making of Americans*, and Richardson's *Pilgrimage*. Its absence from the canon has created a significant historical and aesthetic lacuna, impeding a full appreciation of H.D.'s life and work. Although most serious students of H.D. can outline the plot of *Asphodel*, only those who have read the manuscript at Yale University know more of the actual text than the fragments reproduced in the criticism. It might have intrigued H.D. to learn that this novel of lesbian and heterosexual love would one day have a status curiously similar to that of the poems of her beloved Sappho.

Along with *Paint It To-Day* (written in 1921), *Asphodel* represents one of the earliest surviving examples of the sustained experiments in autobiographical fiction that H.D. began in an effort to free herself from "an old tangle"[2] of troubled thinking about the events of her past—in particular those of World War I—and to move beyond the "H.D. Imagiste" role which seemed to tighten about her after the publication of her first volume of poetry, *Sea Garden*, in 1916. *Asphodel* is in many ways the aesthetic antithesis of the crystalline imagist poem: quirky and nebulous rather than tightly focused and exquisitely controlled; repetitious and recursive instead of immediate in its effect; intensely personal and psychological rather than "objective" in its dramatization of the perceiving mind. Like H.D.'s later

prose writings—but perhaps even more broodingly and insistently—
Asphodel repeats charged images and idées fixes, altering them incre-
mentally as the narrative proceeds, pushing them painfully and re-
luctantly toward what Susan Stanford Friedman has referred to as
"the analytic clearing of understanding and control,"[3] or what the
novel calls, more skeptically perhaps, those "fields of asphodel" not
met with on this side of the grave. Gertrude Stein described a related
process in *The Making of Americans*: "Always repeating is all of living,
everything that is being is always repeating, more and more listening
to repeating gives to me completed understanding."[4]

First composed in 1921–1922 and probably revised a few years later,
Asphodel is, from one perspective, an early version of the quite different autobiographical novel H.D. completed decades later under
the title of *Madrigal* (published in 1960 as *Bid Me to Live [A Madri-
gal]*). H.D. considered *Madrigal* the final, most satisfying version of
her "story of War I," a story she had been evolving for decades: "I
had been writing or trying to write this story, since 1921. I wrote in
various styles, simply or elaborately, stream-of-consciousness or
straight narrative. I re-wrote this story under various titles, in London and in Switzerland."[5] In 1959 she told her friend and literary
agent Norman Holmes Pearson that "[*Madrigal*] Phoenix-ed out of
Asphodel that was put far away & deliberately 'forgotten.'"[6] Her
retrospective characterization of *Asphodel* as an early "version" or
"edition" of *Madrigal*, together with her belief that it lacked the
latter's "daemonic drive or . . . *daemon*" (one of H.D.'s words for
"genius"),[7] made her reluctant to preserve copies of *Asphodel*. In 1949
she asked her companion Bryher (Annie Winifred Ellerman)—
somewhat tentatively—to "destroy" the copy of the manuscript in
her possession;[8] a decade later she wrote Pearson: "If carbons [of *Her*
and *Asphodel*] ever turn up, please destroy them."[9]

Fortunately, for us and for H.D., one copy survived, despite the
fact that its title page also bears the instruction "DESTROY"
scrawled in H.D.'s hand. It is true that part of *Asphodel* overlaps with
the period covered by *Madrigal*—the later years of World War I—
and both novels contain characters based on H.D.'s husband Richard
Aldington and her lover Cecil Gray. But much of *Madrigal* focuses
on the D. H. Lawrence figure, Rico, who never appears in the earlier
novel; and *Asphodel*, which traces H.D.'s life from her departure for
Europe in 1911 to the birth of her daughter in 1919, has a temporal

scope and a range of characters *Madrigal* never attempts. Like Lawrence's *Sons and Lovers* and Bryher's novel-sequence *Development* (1920) and *Two Selves* (1923), *Asphodel* is an autobiographical bildungsroman, a work whose fidelity to the actual events of H.D.'s life, while it should never be taken entirely for granted, is on the whole remarkable. She explained in 1925 that "the things I write are all indirectly (when not directly) inspired by my experiences."[10] (See the Appendix for capsule biographies of the persons behind the fictions of *Asphodel*.)

Asphodel follows Hermione Gart (the H.D. figure), Fayne Rabb (Frances Gregg, H.D.'s friend from Philadelphia), and Fayne's mother, Clara, on their trip to Europe in 1911–1912,[11] first to France and then to London where Hermione contends with the domineering George Lowndes (Ezra Pound), the young American poet to whom she had been engaged for a time back home and who now introduces her to his circle of literary friends in London. *Asphodel* is a valuable and intimate account of female expatriation, a portrait of young artists whose experiences are very different from those of their male counterparts. More vulnerable than men to familial threats and manipulation, deracinated female artists feel a correspondingly greater pressure to marry and legitimate their expatriation, to purchase freedom with yet another compromise with patriarchy.

Rather than succumb to this pressure, Hermione urges Fayne, who is planning to return to America, to live with her in London in a bohemian ménage of their own fashioning. The impassioned speech in which Hermione affirms her love for Fayne ("'I, Hermione, tell you I love you Fayne Rabb'" [p. 52]) and defends the lesbian lifestyle she imagines for them is the climax of part 1. Despite her eloquence, however, she fails to persuade the defensively spiteful Fayne, and her shock is soon compounded when Fayne writes from America that she is going to be married to a respectable lecturer on literature. Part 1 of *Asphodel* ends with the ominous suicide in Paris of a friend of George's, an unmarried American expatriate named Shirley Thornton (based on Margaret Cravens, who killed herself in June 1912) who had come to France to study piano. The final paragraphs of part 1 hint at Hermione's temptation to avoid Shirley's fate by marrying a young English poet she has met, Jerrold Darrington (Richard Aldington).

Part 2 jumps ahead to 1915. Now married to Jerrold, Hermione is recovering from the stillbirth of her child. The war has been raging for some time, splitting consciousness into what Hermione calls "pre-chasm" and "chasm" thinking, a fissure that is dramatically figured by the temporal gap between parts 1 and 2. Like Rose Macaulay's *Non-Combatants and Others* and Rebecca West's *The Return of the Soldier*, *Asphodel* is in part a war novel that focuses on women's lives at the home front. It also traces, as other works by H.D. do, the transformation of the Aldington figure, after his enlistment in the army, from androgynous "faun" and poetic brother into a jaunty, lascivious Mars who is unfaithful to Hermione. It seems to Hermione that Jerrold's civilian self—the person who had restored her confidence in her writing—has been buried beneath a lava flow, along with other prewar treasures like art, beauty, and love; life is now a matter of zeppelin raids, tabloid jingoism, and "guns, guns, guns, guns." Estranged from Jerrold, Hermione joins Cyril Vane (the Cecil Gray figure) in Cornwall and soon learns she is pregnant with Vane's child.

Inspired by legends of Druids and Phoenicians, Hermione fancies herself a "Morgan le Fay" and her child the product of a visit from the god Helios—a private myth that gives Hermione a kind of Madonna/witch identity, restoring to her some of the playfully subversive innocence she had enjoyed with Fayne. (George had said in part 1 that she and Fayne would have been "burned in Salem for witches" [p. 50].) Hermione decides to keep the baby and, following a period of solitary self-communion, meets the wealthy but troubled Beryl de Rothfeldt (the Bryher figure), who helps her during the later stages of her pregnancy. After a frightening encounter with a jealous, vengeful Darrington back from the trenches, Hermione succeeds in breaking away from him and establishing with Beryl the very ménage that Fayne Rabb had earlier renounced, except that this one is augmented by Phoebe, Hermione's daughter, whom Beryl promises to take care of as if the child were a "puppy." Salvation is mutual at the end of *Asphodel*: Hermione has escaped a series of destructive relationships, and Beryl has promised to stop threatening suicide.

Even so brief a synopsis as this suggests that *Asphodel* is less an early version of *Madrigal* than a snugly fitting sequel to H.D.'s autobiographical novel *Her* (written in 1926–1927 and first published by New Directions in 1981 as *HERmione*), the story of Hermione's life in Philadelphia in the period before her departure for Europe.

H.D. herself called *Asphodel* "a continuation of HER,"[12] and there is evidence that she revised *Asphodel* around 1926–1927, possibly to recast the 1921–1922 version as an aesthetically consistent sequel to *Her*.[13] *Asphodel* completes the Ezra Pound and Frances Gregg stories begun in *Her*, and extends and consummates that novel's madrigal-like rhythm of relationships, the weaving in and out of variations on the beloved. The ambiguous image of Fayne Rabb waiting alone in Hermione's "little workroom" at the end of *Her* is clarified in *Asphodel*, where Fayne indeed continues to blight Hermione's artistic hopes and her emotional life, just as George Lowndes has done. It is not until Beryl arrives on the scene that Hermione can begin to connect her art with her emotional and domestic needs. Hermione's lonely walk through the snow at the end of *Her* is rewritten at the conclusion of *Asphodel* by a new domestic economy that converts the demoralizing love triangles in which she has been enmeshed into the "triptych," to use the novel's phrase, of Hermione, Beryl, and the infant Phoebe, an unlikely holy family but a mutually supportive one. In this sense, the *Her-Asphodel* sequence is an extended tribute to Bryher. That *Asphodel* has a candid lesbian theme may have been one reason that H.D. wanted typescripts of the novel destroyed; that it is the story of H.D.'s journey to a life with Bryher probably made the two women reluctant to put a match to all copies.

In terms of aesthetic construction, *Asphodel*, like many works of high modernism, reveals a dual impulse toward strong formal control and experimental abandon. For example, the two parts of *Asphodel* are almost geometrically balanced, each containing fifteen chapters of comparable dramatic and thematic development. Yet the writing style is dense, elusive, digressive; paragraphs are unusually long, more like movements of a musical composition than units of narrative; dialogue is expressively congested and often not clearly attributed. Authorial voice and point of view are generated almost entirely from Hermione's perspective, from her intense, sometimes feverish stream of consciousness. *Asphodel* is an important experiment in "stream-of-consciousness" technique, yet H.D. adopted neither the psychological immediacy of Joyce's "interior monologue" nor the authorially mediated, third-person-limited voice of Woolf, but rather a fluid, shifting combination of these modes, a style capable of veering in the space of a few pages from third-person-limited narration ("she was somehow dehumanised and he was seeing it" [p. 141]) to a generic, historical "you" ("Wine went to your brain and you knew there was no division now" [p. 142]) to first-person memoir ("We were two angels with no wings to speak of" [p. 142]) to sudden, visceral interior monologue ("God sends things to people" [p. 143]).

This kaleidoscopic (or perhaps cinematic) effect is occasionally punctuated by passages of direct, urgent authorial address to the reader, particularly when war is the subject: "some god had set a head there in a restaurant (imagine it but I know you can't quite realize it) in that odd 18, 18, 18. Do you know what I mean? In 1918 there was one head. . . ." (p. 141). These oscillations of authorial voice reflect the uncertain boundary between autobiographical fiction and personal memoir, between the writing subject and the self as a projected, dramatized "other."[14] On the whole, H.D. moves skillfully between these narrative positions or stances of the self, so skillfully that she seems to fulfill one of Baudelaire's conditions for modern art: "Qu'est-ce que l'art pur suivant la conception moderne? C'est créer une magie suggestive contenant à la fois l'objet et le sujet, le monde extérieur à l'artiste et l'artiste lui-même."[15]

This unfettered authorial voice, with its variety of moods and inflections, is well adapted to a story that proceeds by repeated motifs and situations. An especially insistent pattern is that of the woman endangered by a hostile, uncomprehending society. From Hermione's doleful meditations on Joan of Arc and Marie Antoinette to the very real perils besetting her relationship with Fayne Rabb, to the suicidal thoughts of Shirley Thornton and Beryl, women in *Asphodel* frequently feel threatened with some form of punishment or death, especially if they are "odd" visionaries with artistic inclinations ("Shirley was like Cassandra smitten by the sungod" [p. 103]). Hermione experiences guilt after the death of Shirley, for she feels that she might have averted the tragedy if she had reached across to "this authentic sister, tangled in a worse web than she was" (p. 105). Yet Hermione's failed friendship with Shirley at the end of part 1 is structurally balanced by the sisterhood she achieves with Beryl at the end of part 2. Like Shirley, Beryl is a thwarted artist who contemplates suicide; both women have wide, staring eyes filled with pain and private obsession. Hermione's offer of love together with the opportunity to care for her baby cures Beryl's frightened eyes, restoring them to "child's eyes, gone wide and fair with gladness" (p. 206).

Beryl represents the happy culmination, the telos perhaps, of a long series of love affairs in Hermione's life, each an approximation to the ideal but not its realization. Together, *Her* and *Asphodel* offer a variegated pageant of beloveds: George Lowndes, Fayne Rabb, Jerrold Darrington, Cyril Vane, Beryl. In a moving passage in *Asphodel*, Hermione thinks of her lovers as flowers woven into "a veil, the veil of Aphrodite" (p. 136). This "veil of Loves," a product of imagination's triumph over personal hurt, is fashioned so as to exclude no one, for "one flower cannot disown another" (p. 136). This strange, generous fabric is an image of the *Her-Asphodel* sequence itself, a figure for H.D.'s textual weaving and reweaving of her past. Despite her intense, demanding nature, Beryl comes to occupy a privileged place in Hermione's veil of Loves, offering an end to torment and the beginning of a new domestic and artistic life in a financially secure relationship. The Bryher figure would not fare quite so well in H.D.'s fiction of the later 20s and 30s—H.D.'s veil of Loves was as honest as it was inclusive—but here at the end of *Asphodel* flaws and inadequacies are lost in the glow of Beryl's eyes, "the eyes of an eagle in a trigo triptych" (p. 206).

Asphodel is unashamedly about pain and suffering. The novel's deceptively idyllic title actually implies the very opposite of contentment and easy optimism, as the epigraph taken from Walter Savage Landor makes clear: "There are no fields of asphodel this side of the grave." In Landor's imaginary conversation "Aesop and Rhodope," the aged fabulist lectures the young slave Rhodope on the advantages of an early death:

> Laodameia died; Helen died; Leda, the beloved of Jupiter, went before. It is better to repose in the earth betimes than to sit up late; better, than to cling pertinaciously to what we feel crumbling under us, and to protract an inevitable fall. We may enjoy the present while we are insensible of infirmity and decay: but the present, like a note in music, is nothing but as it appertains to what is past and what is to come. There are no fields of amaranth on this side of the grave: there are no voices, O Rhodope! that are not soon mute, however tuneful: there is no name, with whatever emphasis of passionate love repeated, of which the echo is not faint at last.[16]

H.D.'s substitution of "asphodel" for "amaranth" is typical of her quotational style and may have been unintentional.[17] The entire passage from Landor is relevant, for it contains several themes that haunt the pages of *Asphodel*: premature death; the impermanence of love and of the beloved; the elusiveness of the present moment and its lack of meaning apart from what precedes and follows it; the desire to transcend pain in the here and now tempered by an awareness that no such transcendence is possible this side of eternity—except perhaps in the activity of the artistic imagination, as Landor's rich cadences suggest, and as Hermione herself concludes at one point: "Imagination is stronger than reality" (p. 136).[18]

Aesop's sobering counsels about the inevitability of suffering represent one aspect of *Asphodel*. But this modern bildungsroman is also about a woman's realization that undeserved agony must end before a productive life can begin: "You suffer toward sea-change but there was an end to legitimate suffering, this suffering of Hermione's was illegitimate" (p. 199). The pun on "illegitimate" hints at one source of Hermione's pain—Jerrold's refusal to register Phoebe as his child—but this same infant, while it drives a wedge between Hermione and her husband, helps solidify the bond between her and Beryl: a little child shall lead them. By the end of the novel Phoebe has become an outward and visible sign of Hermione's inward and spiritual rebirth, her emergence from the cocoon of her past. *Asphodel* takes H.D.'s life up to 1919—a crucial year in her personal fortunes—halting just short of one of the most prolific decades of her artistic life, the decade that gave birth to *Asphodel* itself.

A Note on the Text

The sole extant version of *Asphodel* is a typescript of just under 400 pages at the Beinecke Library, Yale University; no draft material or notes have come to light, and references to *Asphodel* in H.D.'s letters are rare and of little use for textual editing. The typescript is a complete, legible carbon copy on ordinary typing bond; no ribbon copy has survived. Various statements by H.D. suggest that *Asphodel* was first composed in 1921–1922 and then revised a few years later, but the precise date of the surviving typescript is uncertain, as is the identity of the typist.[19] While part 1 has a few revisions in H.D.'s hand, part 2 contains none; minor corrections are typed over erasures on the carbon throughout. It is not clear how polished a draft this typescript represents, but the large number of spelling and typing errors suggests that this copy did not receive the usual scrutiny and revision that late typings of other works by H.D. reveal. It is possible that changes made to the lost ribbon copy were not transferred to the carbon copy.

As the Beinecke typescript was the sole possible basis for this edition, the usual avenues of editorial problem-solving, such as collation of editions and comparison of alternative manuscript readings, were closed to me.[20] Total authority for editorial changes brings with it total answerability for those changes, and I have tried to exercise caution for H.D.'s sake and for my own. Whenever possible, I consulted other published works by H.D., in particular lifetime editions, for analogous or related textual details, although I regarded these peripheral texts as heuristic rather than binding. Occasionally the typescript contains a word or phrase that seems garbled; in these cases I have relied on my judgment, taking care to avoid over-ingenious solutions.

H.D.'s spelling offers a special challenge. She frequently misspelled both common and uncommon words, including foreign words, which she sometimes rendered phonetically. She was aware of this tendency and expressed concern over it, writing Marianne Moore as late as 1952: "I still have a sort of Puritan complex, I must spell correctly."[21] I have corrected approximately 300 misspellings (around 170 different words) for this edition. I have retained certain unusual spellings, however, either because they are attested variant spellings or because they are especially characteristic of H.D. and appear in other texts by her (some published during her lifetime): "blurr," "hybiscus," "hypatica," "cotton wadging," "baptismal fount," "carn," "unwieldly," "etherialized," and others. Although British spelling predominates in the typescript, certain words fluctuate between British and American spelling ("realised" and "realized," for example); I have not altered these spellings, regarding them as a significant manifestation of H.D.'s expatriate temperament.

Due to H.D.'s spotty revision of the typescript, some proper names and place-names waver in spelling ("Hermione"/"Hermoine"; "Lowndes"/"Lowdnes"), or appear in variant versions ("Captain Tim Kent"/"Captain Ned Trent"); I have regularized these spellings and variants. In general, I have treated misspelled names as ordinary misspellings, changing "Shelly" to "Shelley," and "Houkashi" to "Hokusai," for example. I have occasionally allowed the external, historical referent of a name to determine spelling when it seemed clear that H.D. had that referent in mind. For example, I have altered "Milais" to "Millet" (the painter of the *Angelus*); "Sir John Sloane" to "Sir John Soane" (the founder of the Soane Museum in London); "Cryseus" to "Chrysis" (the character in Pierre Louÿs' *Aphrodite*); "Quai des Fleus" to "Quai aux Fleurs"; "Monte Solario" to "Monte Solaro." But even this category contains exceptions. For example, in part 2, Hermione thinks of General Trent of "Ladyburg," and though she clearly means the famous siege of "Ladysmith" during the Boer War, the possibility of comic wordplay made me reluctant to interfere. In certain cases, H.D. intends a name or place-name to be typical rather than historical, as when she gives "Krissenden" and "Chissingham" as towns in Buckinghamshire. I have not tampered with these names.

Literary quotations and allusions in *Asphodel* are often free and imprecise, and I have made no changes in these passages except to correct spelling and other accidentals. As noted above, the title of the novel itself is the result of "misquotation," and the line between error and creativity in such cases is hard to draw. Occasionally H.D.'s citational habits produce an awkward phrase—as when, recalling Poe's "To Helen," Hermione thinks of "those Nemean barks of yore" instead of "those Nicean barks of yore," or when Jean Valjean is referred to as "Jean Jean"—but such "errors" are allowed to stand.

Similarly, I have made relatively few alterations in H.D.'s punctuation. To grant H.D. her punctuation is to respect her syntax, the special rhythms and "voices" of her text. Her use of commas is loose and impressionistic, a practice appropriate to the free, experimental style of *Asphodel*. The narrative has a fluent, intimately "spoken" quality, and commas often indicate a voice pause or an emotional hiatus rather than a division of syntax; in this they are not unlike Emily Dickinson's dashes. Only in cases of unusual awkwardness—about two dozen in all—have I added or subtracted commas.[22] H.D.'s liberal use of hyphens ("scape-goat," "super-natural," "cock-tails"), along with her related tendency to split certain words into two ("court yard," "any more," "al fresco"), has been retained almost without exception. H.D.'s form of the dash—a single hyphen flanked by spaces—has been altered to American style. Dialogue passages in *Asphodel* are long and complex, occasionally blurring the distinction between speakers. H.D. (or her typist) evidently had difficulty with these passages as well, for quotation marks are omitted or misattributed in about ninety places. These I have corrected, taking context as my guide. Except in instances where hasty typing and inattentive revision resulted in obvious errors, I have retained H.D.'s italicization and capitalization. At this period she tended to italicize quoted phrases and passages, especially of poetry, but usually left foreign words and phrases unitalicized. Accents in foreign words have been added or corrected where appropriate. H.D.'s intricately rambling paragraphs and her spacing between chapter sections are reproduced exactly as in the typescript.

In general, I have proceeded in terms of a flexible notion of H.D.'s "sensibility," a heuristic concept that has allowed me to accept a traditional model of authorial intention while remaining alert to the exigencies of an experimental modern text and sensitive to current theories of feminine writing. My decision to correct H.D.'s spelling but to leave her punctuation virtually unaltered—to regard the former as error and the latter as creative idiosyncrasy—is of course artificial to a certain extent.[23] But the resulting text is, I believe, one faithful to H.D.'s intentions, insofar as these can be inferred or reasonably posited, and to the spirit of her prose writing as registered in the typescript of *Asphodel* and other published and unpublished works by her.[24]

R.S.

Notes

1. See especially Susan Stanford Friedman, *Penelope's Web: Gender, Modernity, H.D.'s Fiction* (Cambridge: Cambridge University Press, 1990), ch. 3 ("Madrigals: Love, War, and the Return of the Repressed").
2. H.D. to John Cournos, July 9 [ca. 1920–1921?], in "Art and Ardor in World War One: Selected Letters from H.D. to John Cournos," ed. Donna Krolik Hollenberg, *The Iowa Review* 16(1986): 147–48. This letter may have been written in 1918 or 1919.
3. Friedman, p. 141.
4. *Selected Writings of Gertrude Stein*, ed. Carl Van Vechten (New York: Vintage Books, 1972), p. 276.
5. H.D., "H.D. by *Delia Alton* [Notes on Recent Writing]," ed. Adalaide Morris, *The Iowa Review* 16(1986): 180.
6. H.D. to Norman Holmes Pearson, October 14, 1959, unpublished letter, Beinecke Library, Yale University.
7. Ibid.
8. H.D. to Bryher, from Lausanne, April 18, 1949, unpublished letter, Beinecke Library.

9. H.D. to Pearson, October 14, 1959. Even as she urges Pearson and Bryher to destroy "carbons" of *Her* and *Asphodel*, she indicates that there are "MSS." of the novels in her possession. She seems to have been worried about the existence of multiple copies and obsolete versions, but there is no indication that she wished to destroy *all* copies. The letter to Pearson reveals that she had her own typescript of *Asphodel* as late as 1959, two years before her death.

10. H.D. to George Plank, March 31, 1925, unpublished letter, Beinecke Library. For a detailed account of the complexly interrelated novels of H.D.'s "Madrigal Cycle" (*Paint It To-Day, Asphodel, Madrigal*), see Friedman, ch. 3.

11. H.D. and the Greggs left for France in the summer of 1911; *Asphodel* is less precise about this date, at one point suggesting that it may have been 1912.

12. H.D. to Bryher, April 18, 1949.

13. See Robert Spoo, "H.D.'s Dating of *Asphodel*: A Reassessment," *H.D. Newsletter* 4(Winter 1991): 31–40.

14. Cf. Friedman, pp. 107, 171–72.

15. From "L'Art Philosophique," in *Oeuvres complètes* (Gallimard, 1961), p. 1099. "What is pure art according to the modern conception? It is the creation of a suggestive magic simultaneously embracing both object and subject, the world external to the artist and the artist himself" (my translation).

16. Walter Savage Landor, *Imaginary Conversations: A Selection*, ed. Ernest de Sélincourt (London: Oxford University Press, 1937), pp. 13–14.

17. The covering sheet and title page of *Asphodel* contain three versions of the title, all based on the quotation from Landor: "Asphodel," "Fields of Asphodel," and "This Side of the Grave." The last mentioned was struck out by H.D., leaving the first two as options. I have chosen "Asphodel" because it is the title H.D. used most often when alluding to the novel in letters and memoirs. "Asphodel" probably also refers, as Friedman points out, "to Odysseus's descent to the Underworld, where he sees the shade of Achilles stride off into 'fields of asphodel,'" and to certain early poems by Aldington (p. 386n.). H.D. used the title "Amaranth" for one of the trilogy of poems she wrote in 1916 about her relationship with Aldington.

18. William Carlos Williams also noted the interdependence of love, death, and the imagination in his late poem "Asphodel, That Greeny Flower."

19. H.D.'s composition process typically began with rough pencil drafts in notebooks, followed by her own typed draft of the material she had written. She then had her typist prepare a fair copy. The typescript of *Asphodel* may be the work of her typist.

20. Two small exceptions should be noted. The typescript of *Asphodel* contains two versions of page 147 of part 1; both are carbon copies on identical typing paper, one page containing a sentence which the other omits. I have retained the sentence. Also, a short selection from chapter 15 of part 1 was published in an appendix to *Ezra Pound and Margaret Cravens: A Tragic Friendship, 1910–1912*, ed. Omar Pound and Robert Spoo (Durham, NC: Duke University Press, 1988). I have taken this published excerpt into account and have departed from its text (which I also edited) in a few minor readings.

21. H.D. to Marianne Moore, January 19, 1952, unpublished letter, Marianne Moore Papers, V:23:33, Rosenbach Museum and Library, Philadelphia.

22. Late in life, at the urging of Norman Holmes Pearson, H.D. went through her published and unpublished writings and attempted to regularize comma usage and other accidentals, though at times she found the task uncongenial and left it to Pearson. I have decided not to impose this late practice on a work H.D. produced in the 1920s, when her creative assumptions and attitudes toward publishing were different.

23. Readers may wish to compare this edition of *Asphodel* with the text of the first four chapters of *Paint It To-Day*, edited by Susan Stanford Friedman and Rachel Blau DuPlessis and published in *Contemporary Literature* 27(1986): 440–74. With some slight differences, they implicitly make the same distinction I have made between H.D.'s orthography and her punctuation.

24. A comprehensive list of significant editorial changes to the *Asphodel* typescript will be published in the *H.D. Newsletter*, ed. Eileen Gregory (Dallas Institute of Humanities and Culture).

ASPHODEL

*"There are no fields of asphodel this side
of the grave."* W. S. Landor

PART I

1   France. France swirled under her feet for now that the boat
was static it seemed, inappositely, that the earth must roll,
revolve and whirl. Hermione clutched the railings of the
stairs and the broad flight of stairs leading upstairs whirled and
turned with her as the narrow cabin step ladder of steps leading
down into the sordid ship's belly had never, it appeared, even in its
worst days, done. The memories of sea storm were pacific compared
with this thing: stairs that inappositely whirled under her and a bed
that when she flung herself upon it, heaved and swayed under her,
heaving and swaying and swaying with the heave and sway of faded
rose buds in loops that was the almost effaced but still reliable
pattern of the salmon-coloured paper of the wall she stared at. Stairs
in her imagination heaved and sank under her. She seemed about to
float away, lax, bodiless.

"There is nothing wrong with you." Madame Dupont, their boat
acquaintance, had stayed with them, had the room down the corridor
one remove from the rooms of Hermione and the two Rabbs. "There
is nothing wrong with you." Hermione managed to heave aloft on
one elbow and by a determined and valiant effort keep the bed steady
under her elbow while she listened. "There is nothing wrong with
you." A dark figure stood in the doorway. It drew nearer. It was
clothed like a sister of charity in black, it had a black hat pulled over
its eyes, the very hat they had all so bargained over this morning,
shopping in Havre with Madame Dupont. Madame Dupont, had
insisted on it. "My sister and my brother-in-law will be so shocked
to see me back from New York without the proper black things. I
didn't get them in New York as they are so expensive." Madame

Dupont had arranged her mourning to suit her purse and her convenience. Was it French simply? Putting on black when she got to Havre, saving her best black, not wearing black on the boat. This mourning de convenance seemed suddenly to Hermione inconsolably amusing. She would begin to laugh and laugh and laugh. She would never be consoled. Imaginez vous, buying the things in Havre where it was cheaper . . . cheaper for someone you cared for, but Madame Dupont hadn't even cared for her mother. Said so. Told them frankly "you see . . . he was a very old man. But even that . . . in France . . . But you see . . ." and she had whispered the tale of her *dot*-less marriage with a rich old man who had (whispers) and her mother knew it. French. France already on the boat had come true . . . just that horrible story, *true*. Things happened out of de Maupassant, any de Maupassant story might come true, Boule de Suife, fat pretty cocotte in the railway carriage going to bed with the Parisian officer (Bouile de Souife was it?) and then everyone cutting her afterwards . . . *that* was France, de Maupassant was true. Literature was true. If de Maupassant was true then life and letters met, were not sub-divided, hermetically shut apart. *Helen thy beauty is to me* was still hermetically sealed and a star, but de Maupassant in one terrible instant became real, a reality. Terrible and strong. They said it was Flaubert's illegitimate child. Writing. How marvellous. Writing. She must write. Hermione must write. She must write this: salmon-coloured wall paper . . . faded; elegant Louis Seize gilt clock (on the elegantly empty mantel piece) that doesn't go; standing in the door-way a grotesque figure, stiffly erect, in the correct posture of her new cheap mourning, Madame Dupont saying, "but there is nothing wrong with you."

Hermione's elbow kept the bed quiet for a moment. The bed for a moment, was forced, by her effort, to rest firm and four-footed on the floor. "But Madame Dupont, I never said there was." "No, Madame Rabb tells me. You think you are suffering from the effects of the boat. You are not." "I don't think anything—" "Don't interrupt. You think, owing to erroneous impressions, that you, having kept well on the ship, are now ill. The people who thought they were ill on the ship are now well. Is this some sort of punishment for my arrogance, you may well think. But you need not. God in his goodness will eradicate this error from your mind—" O God, Hermione would begin to laugh and laugh and laugh. Her elbow could not now keep the bed from wobbling. The bed itself capered on one foot, on three feet, up—down— "O, O, thank you." If she had known Madame Dupont was a Christian Scientist she would not have wasted Eau de Cologne on her on the boat. If she had so known. Should Hermione remind Madame Dupont of those sunny, dazzling, sick sterile days when everyone said that they would so much rather the boat went down? Or those terrible intense days of baffling salt-whipped storm when there was no one to talk to and only she and Fayne Rabb had survived the mêlée? She had not then said to Madame Dupont "you are not sea-sick" though Madame Dupont kept on now insisting "you are not land-sick. There is, I assure you, nothing wrong. Mrs. Rabb, who persists in error, says you had better rest here. We are going out for lunch. But I persist in this. You will be all right for dinner."

"Brrrr sous la livre. Brrrr sous la livre" went on and on and on. A raucous voice persisted that something was some number of sous (brrrrring over it) the livre and what was a livre anyhow. Livre, livre. A book. A book. It was all a book. They had wandered out of a world into a book. They were dream people and they were wandering in the pages of a book. They were like black flies and they crawled across the print . . . no, it was not print, it was a hard cobbled street winding a little and leading to a shrine. The street climbed the hill and the cobbles hurt the thin soles of Hermione's still seaworthless feet. Climbing the street toward a door—a cathedral was it—the voice going on and on making long echoes like some voice "off" in some obvious stage set. The scenery was worn out, obvious. This was never true, could never have been. Livre. "But a livre is a book isn't it? What is a livre anyhow? Where is that hateful old Dupont creature? She might make herself useful for once. But what a mercy anyhow she's left." She was gone, for the nonce (shopping again?) Madame Dupont, cheap mourning and another half-mourning hat (still cheaper) with a spray of artificial half-mourning wheat sheaves on it. They had themselves bought hats, Hermione and the two Rabbs, were now wearing them, Fayne and her mother, Clara they now called her, Clara Rabb and Fayne Rabb and Hermione had bought hats, wonderful hats, soft about their faces, without linings, not so expensive—sans doublure—no, the bigger one.

Madame Dupont had helped them, helped them buy exquisite wide straw hats for something about three francs, very extravagant Madame Dupont had said, harrowing the dumpy little milliner's assistant who might have been Boule de Souife come to life only she had such odd tobacco coloured eyes and such white skin, somehow dumpy but with white skin like a magnolia. A common girl in a little back-water of a shop, draper's assistant and the masts of the boats showing through the uneven squares of the narrow window over the counters of cheap calico and bunches of artificial cherries and plum and magenta ribbons. Boule de Souife. Hermione had whispered "Boule de Souife" and Madame Dupont had dropped the bunch of magenta bignonias she had almost bought instead of the half mourning wheat sheaves to exclaim, "what, but Mademoiselle, you don't know what you're saying." "I wasn't saying anything. Only remembering—" "You picked up strange ideas in your French studies. You seem to have been oddly coached." Coached. Where had she got that word? Her husband the new American-French one, had learnt his English in Oxford. Coached. "You mean—taught?" "Taught. Yes. What did I say?" "I don't know—please don't be upset, Madame Dupont. It's France simply." "I can't see that there's anything for *you* to get upset about in France. You have your good home and your good parents to return to." Why must she so spoil everything? Black beetle, frog, horrible black beetle French-American frog, getting the best you can out of everyone, out of every country. Sending me back or wanting to. "Can't you see, frog, black beetle" Hermione almost shouted at her "that I adore your country?" Country. Country. Boats bumped up narrow salt canals and there were women in little flower bonnets, white wings to their bonnets like gull wings. Bretons, Madame Dupont told them.

Havre. This was Havre, Havre. Havre. Small boys looking like thin anaemic little girls dressed up in tight short hideous unbecoming little trousers, with curls (some of them) shouting after them, "Engl-eesh. Engl-eeesh. Beef-steak." "O Clara they think we're Engl-eesh." The little boys had persisted and shouted until Hermione had *had* to turn, stick her tongue out at them, thank them, Messieurs for their hearty welcome to their beautiful patrie where in America they were all taught *French* children were so *polite vous savez* till they disappeared and the market was a mass of wine coloured carnations, what were they? "O yes, thank you, Madame Dupont, oeillets, we want some, bunches." "O God, stick your face in them Fayne Rabb. Where have they come from? Wine, wine, they smell of wine, sops-in-wine." "O God Clara look, look they're wet and *smell* them and how cheap, nothing, all these for only (work it out) about ten cents" and Madame Dupont was scolding "you are always so—extravagant. It is extravagant reckless Americans like you Mademoiselle Hermione who *spoil* our people." Sops in wine. I shall go mad with it. Yes, I know I'm too hot and the heat loves me. My head is still going round and round and the salt is sweet from the little clean tide washed canals. They are dreams these Breton women. They are gulls. French. Not frogs. Not hawks. Gulls. Sea-people with wings. How can I ever go further than this? "Can't we have supper on that same little pavement, O damn Madame Dupont. No, we simply can't trail all that way back to meet her, in order to save a half a franc on the dinner and couverts (all the bread you can eat) compris. I'll pay the extra. What did it amount to anyhow? The four of us about fifty cents a piece and she said it was too much. I'm too tired. I'll stay here alone. Let me die here. O yes bring me an omelette like last night. Merci, you are so heavenly to understand my French. How kind of you to understand my French. How heavenly of you to understand. O like last night, exactly, like last night—last night—"

The sunset even like last night, faint flamingo rose touching the sails in the little clean salt-water canal like roses on snow. And the Breton hats, children even, little girls in gull-wing hats. They must wear them. They must wear them. They say it's for good luck. Someone had told her. Where? Was it Pierre Loti? Something had come true again anyhow, something one had read came true . . . Pierre Loti most likely, even the little girls, babies even, wear the gull winged bonnets for good luck.

Sailors like Pêcheur d'Islande with red pom-poms so odd on their blue tam o'shanters that they call berets. O France let me die here, let me die, press me to you, beautiful book, a flower's leaf floated here by chance, a moth with dried wings spread out . . . between your vivid pages.

"Did she die here?" O, but she couldn't, she couldn't have died, the smoke wreathing in its hideous obscene whirl upward across these (perhaps) very roofs. "I can't believe that she died here." But O horrible, horrible suppose it had never happened. Suppose that it was going to happen. For it never could have happened, but it was true. But it could never really have happened. O it was only a story they told us like old King Cole and the Seven Sisters and the prince who turned into a frog. Frog. Frog. It was only a frog story without even the Black Forest intense wood-reality of Grimm's tales. It was not even a legend out of the woods, not a real fairy-story. Something made up and French story books were never any good. So it wasn't true. It was a bad story. On the floor. Here, here it was they *burned* . . . no, no, no, no, it wasn't true. Hideous smoke wreathing up. "I wish we hadn't come to Rouen." "What?" "I don't know. So tired, all these cathedrals. Saint Ouen. How about going back there?" "But it was you who said you wanted—" "O don't say it. Don't say it. Don't say it was I who wanted to come, to come here, to come even to Rouen. O it was the Fennels at the Art Academy, friends of Mrs. Anderson (she wanted me to meet them) who put me up to it. He had made a lot of drawings of the rose-window in the Cathedral and the South Kensington (I think they call it) Museum in London bought them. They put me up to it. Everyone *has* to see Rouen."

And Madame Dupont, saying good-bye at Havre, said they must come here, putting them on the boat, the river boat, because it was cheaper. For one had to see something. One came to France to see something—but why this? Why had she come to France? It was only a story like the Seven Sisters or was it the Seven Brothers turning into Swans; it was only a story like the little Mermaid who wanted feet. O God, God and she died for it wanting feet. O God don't you see, it was something real that happened. It was written on the pavement with the date, a circle and the French words. One dared not read them. Not even herself *there*. She had gone away into the air and she was a Spirit and she was France. O book you are worse than Saint John. I could never read those terrible words and here it is written, all written on the pavement and it happened like the Crucifixion. But one can't. One can't think of it. Here eyes looked out under a hat wreathed with corn flowers, a soft hat like they were wearing and her body was strong and small and like Fayne Rabb's. O don't, don't let's talk about it. Get them away from it. Hermione had spoiled the afternoon (but how much more devastatingly had everyone, had everything spoiled hers) for people had to come, had to stoop over the pavement to see the words written. But it was impossible. It was out of a book. Horrible long pages of French History crowded in between Physical Geography and the Latin or Geometry . . . it was only French history, tiresome out of a tiresome book and the print bad and she had wanted to crown the king at Orléans. And they had caught her. Caught her. Trapped her with her armour and her panache and her glory and her pride. They had trapped her, a girl who was a boy and they would always do that. They would always trap them, bash their heads like broken flowers from their stalks, break them for seeing things, having "visions" seeing things like she did and like Fayne Rabb. This was the warning. Joan of Arc. O stop them. Stop them. They're hurting her wrists. God in Heaven. It was Saint Margaret that she called to. Saints all around Rouen, saints standing rather faint and tenuous on faint long feet. Come down, walk down, see—stop them. Saint Margaret. Saint Michael. Streets and the heat coming back and the reality and Clara reading, "visitors would do well to profit by the neighbourhood—br—br—br—" Hermione could not hear her. Clara was reading out of another book, the wrong sort of book. O France, France, terrible book. Like the revelations. It was like the revelations. Someone had given her a little book and said "eat it." She must eat the little book. Not scan it like other people. O it wasn't a question of scanning the little book, France. She must eat it, eat it, honey and worm-wood. "It's not far. Hadn't we better see the tower where they imprisoned her?" O God more horrors. Turn away. The English soldier was crossing the two sticks and the thin saint's hand was reaching for the cross. The cross was in the hands of the witch and people were shouting, "crucify Him, crucify Him." The witch was very tired and sick with all the noise and sweat of people. Her people. His people. Not that I loved Caesar less—red anemones. Corn flowers. O funny mad moth. O moth with blue wings. They have caught you moth, moth with blue wings. The black smoke shrivels your blue wings. People are shouting, blasphemy. They curse the witch of Orléans. The witch of Rouen. Going. Black. "O don't touch me. This heat. Get out. No. I am rather disappointed in it. Let's get back to Saint Ouen where it's cool anyhow and leave alone these ugly tourist centres." Tourist centres. O let me find lilies. "Yes. Clara. Thanks ever so much. We didn't have enough lunch. My fault. Idiot. I wanted to stay in Ouen. Yes. I know I'm fretful. No, I'm not disap-

Asphodel

9

pointed. It was (wasn't it) our *duty* to come and see the spot. It said so in the guide book." No monument. Nothing. France was all her monument. O queen, Artemis, Athene. You came to life in Jeanne d'Arc. She's a saint now. I'd be a saint if I let them get to me. So would Fayne Rabb. I don't want to be burnt, to be crucified just because I "see" things sometimes. O Jeanne you shouldn't ever, ever have told them that you saw things. You shouldn't have. France. You loved France. But it was a story. Something out of a book. "Yes, Mrs. Rabb . . . Clara. Let's go back. We had to see the place, certainly. Let's get out of this heat anyway."

Heat roasting from the pavement. Heat with black devil wings to catch her. Christ in Heaven keep Jeanne d'Arc safe for ever.

Christ in Heaven, Christ in Heaven, reconcile these things in our hearts. Christ in Heaven stoop low and shelter Athene who is after all only a girl and the Corinthians spoke of idols of silver, idols of gold, O Christ, Christ let me bring you every conceivable kind of lily . . . "Yes, Mrs. Rabb . . . Clara. I do think the baptismal fount is lovely and the Fennels, you know of the Art Academy (yes he is *the* Fennel) told me I must be sure to look in the fount at the odd angle, I don't know what the odd angle is but you must walk round and round and try it. The Fennels said nobody would mind as everyone does it and you see the whole cathedral reflected in a tiny space, all upside down with all the windows. Fennel's wife had to drag him away, she said, and everybody laughed (because he is so dignified) by the coat tail. No they don't mind our whispering. It's not like our *churches*. And you do get it a little (I see what they mean) from this angle. See it's like a shell, not such a big one either and the whole of the church is reflected. It's like some Hokusai drawings I saw once (you know seeing Fujiyama) a hundred views and the same idea. The painter with a little cup or bowl, I suppose and the reflection of the mountain in the bowl. It's oriental I suppose" . . . Christ in Heaven, Christ in Heaven. I suppose this is your church. I suppose it is. I don't think it's like you. It's like the woods simply, tree trunks in long rows and the shade and coolness of the woods. I don't think this is your temple but they say so so for God's as for Christ's sake (but you are Christ and I shouldn't swear and blaspheme) keep Jeanne d'Arc—
"O Fayne Rabb come and look at this. Funniest thing. A sort of little

alcove to the Thief. I suppose the repentant one. What happened to the other?" Christ in Heaven is this your temple? Maybe it is. It's the first temple I've anyhow seen and "who was Saint Ouen? Have you the guide book, Mrs. Rabb. Clara. Here's actually a bench to sit on like an art gallery. That's all it is after all, isn't it? I'm glad we came in now, all empty. I hope they won't begin mumbo-jumbo. No. I don't mean anything. Clara. I didn't mean to be *irreligious*." Christ in Heaven let me fling myself down, something, somewhere, something, some expression of something but not this, not this. This is all trying to make us forget. It's like a wood where one is lost, singing going on somewhere, some sort of chant to keep us from being afraid. But Beauty is Fear. This says fear is to be numbed but I don't think really that was your doctrine . . . long shafts of light from the pool set slant wise in the wall, set slant wise, a pool defying laws of gravitation and dripping ruby colour. The Holy Grail. A cup to take and to forget, to forget—but not this. This classic thing, this action during the soldiers, rough treatment, no kindness, daring to be herself, like Athene, like Artemis. Love in her heart too that led her on for France. Fleur de lys. White lilies. I would find you white lilies like the lilies of Helios. White lilies for you and for Jeanne d'Arc fleur de lys. Of course. Fleur de lys. Blue and gold and white too. A soft cream gold white blue—Jeanne d'Arc. They grow in the meadows and your feet sink in to the ankles. Never mind wet shoes. Your own mired in filth, dragging through mud. They insulted you. But who, who did? They put a crimson robe and a reed, no a sword and they dragged your armour from you. You died defenceless in a white robe. No in no robe. They parted His garments . . . and the soldiers laughed but it wasn't they that slew you. "I know I'm irreligious." "What Hermione?" "I said. I know I'm irreligious but don't you find all this—this—broken line—you know what I mean, a little ginger-bread-y?" "Ginger—? What?" "Ginger-bread. You know. Too much decoration." "What are you trying to do, Hermione? Trying to show off? Pretending you don't care? Pretending not to care? Really caring awfully." "No. Not as you think. Not as you think. I do care. It's looking back, walking off one's own shelf of life, sliding off like sliding off a raft, a float—" "Perhaps. You swim then?" "Well. Not exactly. Yes. I do swim." "Thinking of your *vacation* in your precious Jersey mud flats?" "I hadn't. I wasn't." "This is a little bit of a comedown, Miss Expensive?" Christ in Heaven. Why is Josepha so ill-natured, so perverse? It meant everything getting away with her and she goes on this way. I suppose we're all dead and tired with sights. Why is she so destructive? What's wrong with her anyhow? "Do you believe in this—ah—you know—" "What, Josepha?" "Are you, I don't believe I ever asked you, a—a Christian?" "What is—that, Fayne Rabb?" "What is what?" "A Christian?" "A Christian is a person who goes to communion. Do you? I do every Sunday, ever since I can remember or Madre would sulk. Do you go to communion?" "I used to. I taught some filthy children who called poppies 'coloured rags' and I thought that was better than communion—" "Was it?" "I don't know. It was, while I loved them. But I got sick with them, disgusted . . . their voices, the impossibility of *doing* anything." "What *did* you do? This is a new phase, little smug Miss Settlement Worker." "I took them roses. All I could get, borrow or steal." "Well?" "I could never get, borrow or steal enough. There was one filthy brat with its nose running—" "Dear me, not in a cleaned up college settlement?" "There was always one filthy one, a girl or boy. They were all the same. (They were immigrant class.) There was always one there wasn't a rose for." "Well what about the ninety and nine?" "It wasn't worth it. I always remembered the filthy dirty one, I hated that there hadn't been a rose for." "What a sweet picture." "Yes. Isn't it? As like as not with scabs and they always had a patch of something, colour, or bright blue patches on the seat of their pants—" "Pretty. You should have been an art student at the academy—" "Yes. Shouldn't I? Art—Beauty. What's the use of art and art and Beauty when there's one filthy brat with a running nose that you hate anyway who cringes at you and leaves finger marks on your summer clothes and says 'but sister' (they called me sister. I suppose they never saw anyone but a Catholic sister at a funeral who had flowers) 'but sister. Isn't there one *dirty* broken one left for me—not even any pieces.' Pieces of a rose." "You seem unduly sensitive." "Pieces of a rose. I ask you. Pieces of a lily. He meant petals I suppose. Scrapings. Sweepings. With a filthy face and as like as not some hideous inherited affliction. That's the Church. Have all the children. Suffer little children—" "So, I presume you are not, Miss Wrath of God, a Christian?" "Not in your sense. I'm going over to look at that Lady Chapel—they're going to begin some hocus-pocus. O go get Clara's guide book. She'll put out her eyes reading in this gloom. And it's my fault asking for details. Tell her I don't care." Get away. Get away. Get away. O let me alone. Don't follow me. Don't let me slip O Christ into this pool of numbness, of death in life. A cold place but I am not a hospital patient, a convalescent. O Christ in Heaven— Mea beata . . . gratia mea . . . domina . . . regina . . .

Lady if you are a lady though they said you had one illegitimate child whom they called God, listen to me. Are you really a creature to bring and alleviate people's odd numbing blackness? Are you really a mother and would you really understand? I always think the most awful thing in the world to be would be to be the mother of God. But maybe that's because I'm afraid. George said there needn't be any children. Must I ever, should I ever have one? George Lowndes said I would look like Maria della something or other, he was always rubbing in his filthy old Italians. Italians crowded the steerage of rotten second class boats . . . but they aren't the same. Something tells me, Lady mea gratia, beata or whatever they are calling you that in Italy the mother of God is different. George . . . pearls on her gown. It is hemmed and she wears pearls. Florence is (Browning says orris root or doesn't he?) and pearls are wound round and round the diadem of the baby that hadn't even the dirty ragged pieces of a rose. Not a petal of a rose. Is that what you are meant for, beata domina regina or whatever they are calling you? Incense to numb out your pain but Christ wouldn't take the sponge (O why, why didn't he?) they offered Him. Chloroform I read in the Materia Medica doesn't always help though sometimes—don't let me scream. Don't let me die. Perhaps it's my Hell and must we all pass through it to get to meadows thick with water lilies? Meadows, thick with iris, *I search the meadows for the mirrored iris.* I don't think Fayne Rabb realized . . . how I love her. Christ would understand. Jeanne d'Arc was more beautiful than Fayne, though I'm afraid her hands weren't pretty. Couldn't have been tending the swine or sheep or whatever it was she tended in Arc wherever that was or could ever have been. George said I was like the Madonna something or other della something and that all I wanted was a halo, a thin ring, he said of gold thread though that didn't go with Undine. Undine, mother, lovely Nereid . . . "Sleeping?" "I don't know." "Crying?" "I don't know." "Praying?" "I don't know . . . Josepha, you can't whisper with this singing going on." "Well, everyone else is. Shuffling their feet, blowing their noses on their petticoats." "Where? What do you mean?" "There's a crowd of gargoylesque, Rabelaisian peasants with market baskets and cheeses who have come to see the spectacle." "What spectacle?" "Whatever it is that is going on here. Let's get out." "Why get out?" "Mother's waiting outside in the sunshine. What's the matter anyhow? Pretending? Showing off? Being emotional, hysterical, artistic? Being temperamental?" "A few of those things. Can't you let me alone. You and your mother as thick as thieves, always crowding together and poking fun at me and then saying I'm not appreciative. Well, I am appreciative, damn you. Let me alone. This is my cathedral. Didn't I get you to come here. Would you ever have heard of it if I hadn't known Clifton Fennel?" "*The* Fennel, I think you told us. And if it hadn't been for madre and me you would be now sunk in your New Jersey mud flat, swamped by your mangy relatives and eaten by mosquitoes." "Well let's call it quits then. Go away anyhow—" "Sulky. Pretty Miss Sulks who adores sentiment, hysteria." *Nereid, lovely mother . . .* "I'm tired. You tire me. You wear me out. Can't you *let* me alone. Kill me, do what you want with me, then leave me?" "Sweet perverse adulteress. It was you who started it." "Started?" "Children, come outside. What are you quarrelling for? I've found a new sight—" Sights, sights. Sights. Sights. The clock so huge, the narrow arch and the cobbles that burnt and hurt the soles of her unsuitably clad feet. Court yards that had to be peered into. A little lunch room where a robust sophisticated creature (how did he get there) eyed Hermione and Fayne Rabb. "You girls—attract—attention." "Well, it isn't, is it, our fault, Clara." "You don't seem to have any—sense—of—proportion." Whatever did she mean? Trudging along, meals at any hours. Sleep broken. Bugs in the bed. Having to get up and row the hotel people (they made Hermione do all the rowing in her sparse French) and people looking at them as much as to say well if you look like that and are off a transatlantic liner, why don't you go to another, different hotel? Madame Dupont had given them a list of cheap hotels up the Seine all the way up the Seine even in Paris. Names of hotels, the kind French people go to, "don't Mrs. Rabb let them cheat you," *just* so much and *just* so much and *just* so much and don't go over it or they'll know you are foreigners though how anyhow could they help knowing it? "Pretend to be English. An English lady with daughters learning French. English people do. English people won't let themselves be put on like you careless Americans." Bugs in the bed. Huge room with heavy velvet curtains and they so tired eating plums out of a bag of plums for a few cents and that was what a livre was, a *pound* of plums not a book of plums. Going on and on. "And this is where *Flaubert* lived." "Never heard of him." Flaubert. Flaubert. Going up the Seine like the Sentimental Journey. Salammbô with ostrich feathers and a little person in tight silk drawers who danced but that was a little story in the Trois Contes. "Yes. He was the adopted father of de Maupassant. You know what I mean. I mean he *made*, de Maupassant—Guy his name was. How wonderful to be called Guy, you know Guy de Maupassant. He must have come here. I mean Flaubert lived here like a recluse and he taught Guy de Maupassant how to write. Boule de Souife. All ironical. Ironical. George Lowndes helped me to get books—" "O it was *George* Miss Showoff. You got it all out of *George*. Picked his brains and now pretending to know so much. Hateful little prig." "I don't. I didn't. But how could one ever forget the woods burning and the smell of the smoke as the woods burnt—" "What woods burnt? Where did you see woods burnt?" "The woods you know. The tables were all laid for the banquet—" "Settlement Sunday School?" "No. No. No. No. No. I mean the banquet in Salammbô where the woods burnt—have another plum. No, there can't be bugs in the bed. I never saw one *in* a bed though they always told me that was where to find them. And the clock on the mantel-piece actually is going but it can't be half nine, we haven't had our supper and they're sprinkling the streets below, can you hear them." "*Don't* lean so far out of the window." "What is it a little balcony high up over a street can do to one? It's like a play. A scene in a play. Come look, Clara. All a little triangle and our clock isn't right for listen to the boom (and the chime that goes with it) from the tower—" *Christ in Heaven. Christ in Heaven, keep Jeanne d'Arc safe forever.*

"I never saw one *in* a bed but O my God, it's just as bad in this bed as the other, how they do bite and the smell is awful. No I don't mind, Mrs. Rabb. No, I don't mind but look at that one—O God Fayne, have you had—actually had practice—grr—how horrible—I shall be sick, vomit—horrible. O Clara how could she. And he walked as fast as a horse Fayne said." Fayne had said the bed-bug walked as fast as a

horse and it did rather, climbing the enormous peaks of the stiff
rumpled sheet, climbing, tight and fast about his business, rather
American, rather Chicago, going on and on, not minding anything.
You would think the Mont Blanc of the bed edge where she had
squirmed fastidiously a moment since would be his absolute Water-
loo, his to be more exact across the Alps lies Italy or was it the other
way round, Hannibal rushing up to the Alp that looked insurmount-
able. This was a veritable Hannibal. But how fast he did walk. Fayne
was right. He was walking as fast as a horse. "O Fayne—splendid—I
mean horrible—O Fayne—how could you, but how splendid of you
like putting your own worm on the hook or pulling your own fish
off, takes some kind of grit to smash a bed-bug, what were you
saying Clara? But it wasn't my fault. You should have *told* me Madame Dupont told us to ask for whatever you said she told of to ask
for when you told me to ask for new rooms and where is it? Haven't
you got it written down somewhere."

"The thing to do is to put on all the lights." "Well, Pauline,
Paulet" (Clara *would* call Fayne, Paulet) "they drag in the mosquitoes and June bugs from outside." "But they may not have, we
don't know, Mrs. Rabb mosquitoes and June bugs in France, anyhow
the peril from within the city, I think is greater than without." "It's
not a thing, Hermione, to laugh at." "I didn't. I wasn't. I mean it *is*
so funny. Don't, don't please take it so hard, Clara." "But what to
you—is—funny—to—us—is—simply—" "O I know—" Hermione had
heard all this before from Clara. "I know Clara. It's serious. And
really I'm not really thinking it funny. But if you will find out what I
am to ask for, I'll go row them again. Don't get depressed Clara. It
will soon be daylight and what an elegant little bug really. He is
really no worse than a lady bug, you know fly away home. Let's
forget that he is a viper, a monster of obscenity (for he is really). Let's
forget he is a very devil and try to think of him as a lady-bird fly away
home. You know how tiny and clean they look on a huge cabbage
rose. My grandmother used to call them ribbon-roses, not cabbage
roses, but the little almost wild ones that grew over the little old—
place—at the back of their garden where we used much rather go
than to the proper bathroom. Yes, do laugh. Ribbon roses. We can't
afford to be frantic. He's only a sort of filthy lady-bug gone wrong,
turned into a bed bug. God's ways are inscrutable. No, I'm not
hysterical, Josepha. I can't possibly wake them at half past three in

the morning though our clock is a half hour fast, didn't I tell you. There the chimes again—Christ in Heaven—Christ in Heaven— No, no, no. I'm not being irreligious. It's the tune all the chimes say. Listen to it. In Rouen. All the church towers in Rouen say that simply. Christ in Heaven—Christ in Heav-en (you have to measure it out a little for yourself to suit each hour) keep Jeanne d'Arc safe for—ever. You have to measure it, make it Jeannedarc sometimes and Jean-nne-d-d-d-Arc other times to get the rhythm but you can see how it will work. *Have* you got the note book but why after all, that was easy enough. *De fer.* Iron beds, I suppose she meant. I don't suppose they like these new fangled iron beds. Poor darlings. All collected, concentrated in our picturesque big bedroom. And I don't think we can stay here for ever anyway. Yes. I think you're right. We might as well pack now. O—O—O. Tired. Tired. But what Heaven. We'll see the sun-rise—over—Rouen."

"News from home—news from home—must go—Rouen lovely. Yes, we love your city. And couldn't you, please, please, please garçon get us some hot milk and coffee, O please, please. I'm too tired to explain. No my friends aren't ill simply—well to tell you the truth—we were kept awake—all night. Yes simply eaten." "But who Mademoiselle could eat you?" "It was *them* simply. You know. The things we were rowing you about two days ago was it (when was it?) *again.* Have you got a dictionary? Creatures." "Impossible. We have none in Rouen." "Yes but do understand." O how fish-like his face was but back of it something. He was understanding the whole time and the whole time making a careful calculation, was it worth his while to risk Hell getting them extra rations and what was Mademoiselle likely to tip him. Was the older lady her mother or was she a rather subtle entrepreneuse. He didn't say, "Is Madame really your mother?" but it was written in every line of his face. What did he mean standing so thin and somehow right in his dirty apron. The garçon had stopped flicking glasses like a very fine actor in some very subtle play. The dawn rode in at the window fine and thin and outside in the narrow patch of garden Rouen lilies raised etherialized delft-blue cups to an invisible aurora. Aurora. Light lay like a crown on Rouen, light suspended in an invisible breath. Light that strode blatant from the sea-edge paused here subtly before embracing day.

Light behind Rouen hill, cut off from Rouen. So dawn rose on Agincourt . . . where was it? Where was she? This was a play subtle and so exquisite that a breath might blow it away. A play yet back of the dreariest of sordid horrors. "Don't you see. I really am serious." "Mademoiselle, could one mistake you?" "I mean seriously. *Will* you get us something to eat. I know it's only half past five. Can't you see what I tell you is the truth." "Yes. Creatures do eat you ladies. And leave them very thin, fresh at five in the morning. The thing to do is to order the—well—coffee de consolation—the night before. Say let me have my petit déjeuner at five or six simply. It must be forthcoming. I am taking a train to visit my poor old grandmother in the country and so on. I will try a little to instruct this so serious Miss." "Wh-aat?" "I mean. Things in beds. Certainly. They do eat—" "O please. Eat. Me. Hungry. Dying. Café au lait. Lots of café. Lots of au lait. No. It doesn't matter that the little breads aren't fresh. O *please—*" Did one offer it francs and how many? One, two or three? Great Milords in novels produced five franc pieces. Clara always did this part of it. One, two or three. She felt cold horror, then hot horror rising to embrace the back of her neck. The shame seemed to reside at the back of her neck and the pit of her stomach. Some symbol. Money was some symbol. French money was more than ever a symbol. "My—my—aunt—" O then one could see the look in his eyes, it wasn't the mother. "My aunt is waiting. Really will—pay—" How did one say it? "O please, please, here's two francs. Do bring the coffee quickly."

Two francs on the edge of the table. A shaft of light on the floor like light falling on an Easter morning altar. The sudden brilliance that was like the falling (oddly not the rising) of a golden curtain. Cloth of gold was suspended for a moment and then rolled a suitable background. A thin face was poised against that background. It might have risen from a pleated ruff. It might have kissed a sword hilt, a sword hilt set with brilliants, and knelt and laid the sword at her feet. A flower. Dawn. Rouen. This would never happen again. It would be always happening. This had never happened. When was it? Yesterday. "Yesterday is to-morrow." "Mademoiselle's French is charming (I will bring the small breads) but not always quite fresh."

2 "She's like a great yellow rose though I don't believe I am in love with her—" "Wh-aat?" "I mean the Correggio there is like a—like a—I mean I don't think if I were the faun I would be in love with—in love with—" "What's all this talk of being in love with, silly?" "I was talking to Clara. *She* has the Baedeker. Go look it out for yourself. It's written anyhow on the bottom. *Of* the picture. Zeus and Antiope. I said I didn't think I would be in love with the sleeping lady. She's too fat yet there *is* something adorable (one feels there might be) in the soles of her feet and the underside of her elbow that doesn't show. But she doesn't look like—" "Don't talk about pictures this way. Showing off. What's the matter with you? Do you want lunch? Are you drunk simply? Why can't you take things peaceably? This is only the Louvre." "Fayne . . . go away. Leave me alone to find it—" "Find what, impressionable?" "It whatever it—is—"

O let me alone. God. God. This is worse than Cathedrals. Let me alone. Let me find for myself. Get away. Get lost. People going away and the Louvre getting empty. Cool. Long cold galleries and downstairs the marbles like ice, cut like ice, holding something in their shapes that people didn't see, couldn't see or they would go mad with it. Not always the most beautiful things, slid thus through the breasts of the Venus de Milo from the bench in the corner (the red plush bench, shabby against the wall) showed like two thin knife edges, edges of the crescent moon. The Venus de Milo was a little heavy but if you prowled and prowled and waited for different days, little effects of shadow and light and half light caught you; depending on how empty or how full the room was, you got caught by something. That was the answer to prayer. Prayer was asking, asking. Prayer was asking for something that was so terrible and so necessary that you had no words to ask for it. When you found the words, the prayer was already a faded thing. A prayer with words was like a plucked flower. Prayer without words was growing deep, deep in the ground, in the heart of everything. If you found words for your prayer, you had already separated your prayer from the thing you prayed to. Prayer, sitting on the shabby little bench in the corner listening to the guide explaining to the party from Kansas, wasn't in words. The guide was saying "and here ladies and gentlemen in the glass case at the left" (he never varied his formula) "you have the authentic fragment of the foot, the bit of the hand and the arm and the lost apple."

How do you know it is an apple, how can you tell it is her hand or her foot? You can't but nobody ever asked such simple questions. They accepted the dogma as good presbyterians, good methodists, good nonconformists or even good catholics have a way of doing without question, without grace or without bickering. How did they come to do it? Religion of love-of-beauty wasn't this thing. But still they wanted something, looked for something. O God don't let me pity them, looking all lost towards a Cook's Guide for beauty. Let me not despise or pity nor patronize them for your ways are inscrutable and when you led the fingers of Phidias along those two crescents, you already had my hands in yours. I can't put it into words. You know what I'm saying. Before Phidias was, I am. Long ago when you struck white lightning from marble you had some of us already with you. No. I didn't ever forget. Don't let me go mad with this my first discovery. But I will—I will—I will go mad unless I go upstairs and look at Leonardo, look at Correggio, look at Fra Angelico. They are the most blatant shams. They are a curtain hiding reality.

Is Christianity then that? Is Christ the soft mist, the blue smoke of altar incense hiding the beauty of the thing itself? Is Christianity then that, at its best, a curtain, woven of most delicate stuffs to hide reality, the white flame that is Delphi, that is Athens?

O God, they don't even know about it. Not even the Rabbs. Fayne doesn't really know. Fayne reads Dante and thinks it's real when it is a circle upon circle to numb the senses, like light reflected from bright mirrors that deflects, that blinds one's eyes with its dazzle but that really hides the image. The image of truth, of beauty is in this marble bowl forever . . . a Grecian urn. Where is he, Keats of that somewhat washed out ode? Let me get to him. Hands in yours, Phidias' and mine . . . You held our fingers in yours. We are your fingers. Athene's hands wove, wove and she was the goddess of the artisan. Sculpture. Let me creep along your corridors. O God. If only I could come here at night when it's empty and speak with you . . . "Clara, yes, certainly. I was sitting downstairs to keep cool. All these pictures *excite* one somehow. How funny that just this year the Mona Lisa should be stolen. But there's that other one, you know, Madonna of the Rocks, Pater wrote about it, didn't he? No, I don't mean 'her eye-lids are a little weary' but about the background being like light reflected from under sea. A phrase like that *reveals* things . . . Napoleon's watches? Can't we do them to-morrow?" Lady of the sea. Lady of the ship's prow rising from the sea. Rose drips from wings spread rose wise, catching the sun in wings that spread out above a glacial thunder cloud riven with white hail. You stand with spread wings dropping honey-coloured petals down to us, far, far below you and Samothrace itself is here at the top of the steps—"*this* ladies and gentlemen, is the famous winged Victory"—dropping petals alike on the just and the unjust. The sun shines alike, the rain falls alike, the wings of Samothracian Nike spread alike over the just and the unjust, the seeing and the not-seeing and the almost seeing and the just not seeing. Samothrace is a small island set like a honey-coloured lump of amber in a lapis sea. Honey coloured rock that was riven to mould wings, feathers—"you will see ladies and gentlemen that the later effect of the drapery arrangement—" and the wind blowing, blowing straight from Asia, straight from Europe, you standing between, a sort of breakwater for the East and West. Let me stand between, Greeks of the islands. Mystery made formula. Samothrace a formula of God. God making islands and giving the islands to Greeks before Phidias was Greeks are and they are and will be. You can't change a static formula. "The crown jewels are in the last room, madame to the right but let me assure you—" Going on and on. Jewels. King's jewels and Louis the something or other with gems weighing down an empty head and no chin. Bourbon type with no chin, cold like fishes, lecherous. With little boudoirs painted with numberless pink ladies, with love from the air dropping blue streamers with pin-cushion pink rosettes of roses. That's art. French art. "French art is best represented by this Angelus of Millet." "French art in its essence this Fragonard, this Watteau—" Air come to light. Light come to garments fluttering in fragrance from Cythera. The breeze from Cythera (see Walter Pater) and Fragonard and Watteau and the other one, Lancret. Small world of mirrors and pinks in glasses with the stems showing. France was pinks in tumblers with the stems showing, hardy fragrance, France. Oeillets trois sous la botte and there were carts of cherries outside along the narrow crooked roofed-over little streets of the left bank. Old brocades and chairs in windows and china that would break if you so much as breathed on the window pane. Rabbits in cages under a counter chewing lupin, grass, thick tufts of green green grass, the greenest of grass under a counter piled high with purple cabbages and with blue-purple artichokes and with asparagus and with eggs in baskets neatly fitted like precious lumps of alabaster. Eggs taking on a new significance. Raspberries different, seen differently as things may seem different seen through clear glass. Things in Paris looked clear and different and a little magical with qualities defined (was that art simply, something in the air?) as if seen through a clear slightly magnifying bit of crystal. Everything a little different, was it something in the air? Climates made people. They did understand. Something in the air in spite of the noise, the raucous screams, the neglect and unsavouriness of certain streets, certain milieux. Yet different. A woman in a poor shop with a cap flung sideways brought back all the Revolution . . . "not that. No, don't let's go to the Bastille. Clara do have some more raspberries. What makes them taste like the way pot-pourri ought to smell and doesn't." . . . "Where are we going this afternoon?" "There's that little Cluny Museum everyone talked about." "Everyone. Who's everyone?" Yes who was everyone? Hermione propped an elbow on the table edge. Who was everyone? "Can't we have some of that black, black coffee. I feel—sleepy." "Bored?" "No. God no. Shut up. Dead beat." Voices all about. Then voices all going. Then almost gone and all the tables that had been crowded on the pavement empty. "Let's have the coffee outside. Everyone's gone now. Café spécial. Yes. We must have it hot, strong." "You drink too much black coffee. Abuse yourself—" "O God. Really Clara—" "Wh-aaat?" "O, I don't know what you said. No. It wasn't funny. I didn't mean to be rude. But I do. I am. I don't know what I mean. No. I don't. Fayne does." "Does what? What does Paul do?" "*Abuses* one's confi—*den*— ces." "Does she?" "Terribly. I told her par exemple that I hated statues but that she was to be sure not to tell you." "O. She didn't." "O she did. Don't stand up for her Clara. She did tell you. I could see by the way you shoved that Victory down my throat. Everybody's Victory in cheap bronze, in tobacco shops, in people's libraries, everywhere. A winged Victory on the mantel piece, height of bathos." "You mustn't talk that way—" "There you go. All for the proprietors. Like telling me not to be irreligious at Rouen. Religion. Bah—" God. God. God. God. God. Don't let any demon wipe away Paris. Paris is written in clear colours, as if someone (you?) painted in light from coloured glass. Don't let it go. Paris is a state of mind like what happens to one's mind seeing unexpectedly a clear tumbler with flower stems on your dressing table. Lighting the candles and finding the flowers, one magnolia, a flat water lily in a flat dish. Who put it there? Did Eugenia put it there? O good little old Eugenia coming to Paris on her *honey*-moon. Such a good little Eugenia with a bustle and her hair caught with a diamond arrow (I have the picture somewhere) and seeing all these things, the Bastille even. Good little Eugenia getting presents, little souvenirs for everyone. I'm not good . . .

"Well, why don't you want to go to Versailles?" "I don't. I mean I do want to sometime. Why must we go so soon? Why must we go at all . . . O all right." Versailles. O well if we have to but can't we stay in the garden. Some days, certain days a week, once a month or something the fountains play. You have to come when the fountains are playing. It's no good ordinary times. But then it's full of people. Fountains. Long corridors. Horrible to think that Marie Antoinette *ran* actually down this long hallway, screaming perhaps. Why did we come? Marie Antoinette in powdered wig with slippers too high and her stays too tight and odd little embroidered underclothes. O, it was horrible. But those poor children starving and great Signors cutting off their serf's nose. O horrible. How can things be so disjointed for why shouldn't Marie Antoinette have roses embroidered and love knots on her petticoats and stays made in Italy and tiny, tiny high heeled little slippers, rows of them. Did she pick them up and love them and play with them as if they were dolls? I think I should have done that if I had had all the shoes of Marie Antoinette to play with. Sydney Carton. Paris. London. They are always in my heart wedded, two names, how funny I had forgotten all about Dickens. Cherry trees dropping leaves and a last scene and the girl (what was her rather washed out name?) taking the coach back to London. Not that I loved Caesar less—but that was the reverse of it—not that I loved London (or Paris) less but that I loved (what was her somewhat insipid name?) Dora (no not Dora it was some one else) more. Sydney Carton so elegant and standing on the platform, all the elegance that a school girl will dream of forever. Sydney Carton. "The view is lovely from this window." Long corridors outside as well as in. The garden outside was corridors and steps and squares of water set in like squares of polished wood. The water outside and the hedges made walls and floors. It was not a garden really. They were caught here (poor people) in their own labyrinth. Going on and on from day to day, caught, not knowing they were caught. We're all, all caught, but only here and there one of us (me) knows that we *are* caught. Light above their heads, death below their feet, still dancing, going on dancing with flutes and a Venetian cello or a new Milanese flute to give rapture to the occasion. The Grand Soleil. "No. Don't let's go any further. Well if we must see the little Trianon." All the same only tiny. All the same, a doll-house replica of the big palace and huts covered à l'anglaise to play at milk maids. "Why did we come here? I think it's the saddest place I've ever been to." O sad, sad, sad. O pinks in tumblers faded and thrown on the dust heap of Republicanism. American Revolution hastening the downfall of French autocracy. Those very minute men who fired the first gun in Boston helping to nose out little rabbit white Marie Antoinette in her rose-heeled slippers. Sad thing democracy. Benjamin Franklin and America from the European angle is *not* unimportant. England sneering. France and America. The Marquis de Lafayette staying at the old house the Farrands' grandmother used to have. He stayed there I mean. All the garden of the old house (it was called the Grange) laid out in boxes, squares and rows. We had heliotrope roots and cuttings from their garden, from the Grange that was named the Grange after the estate of the Marquis de Lafayette. So I was always near, near France. Heliotrope cuttings from the Grange in my garden (though they didn't thrive, they're delicate) made me one with this. With this. O with this. Marie Antoinette running down a corridor and the heel of her slipper bent under her and she fell forward and caught her underlip. She couldn't find the handkerchief to dab at the dash of blood on her lip. Blood and foam and all the heart of a Great Sun gone down like an ocean liner in a minute. Sydney Carton. "Do you like heliotrope?" "What for?" "The flower. I mean do you like it. It smells of eternity, the sudden foam of something breaking across—across—elegance from another world. The face powder of Du Barry." "*Who?*" "Someone or other's rather vulgar mistress. I mean don't you think of things, people like that. Words darting in and out and every word related so that everything you saw and every word you say relates, weaves on to another." "What are you stumbling at?" "I mean when I said—(thought) heliotrope I thought Du Barry. Though I don't know why. I was really thinking of Marie Antoinette. But Marie Antoinette is a faded stalk of carnation flung in the dust bin of Republicanism. Liberty enlightening the world. That's us. America."

The world's good word, the institute,—that's the Institut de France. The Institute. Carl and Bertrand Gart getting books, pamphlets from the Institute, French Binomial Theorems. Mathematics is a language common to all people—dots and dashes—why don't we all speak a common language of dots and dashes and colours? Why must we be divided, hating each other, never understanding? There ought to be a sort of Spiritual Esperanto, all understanding each other but then how tiresome because French things *are* French. French things are more *French* obviously than anything American could ever be American. What is American? That's just it. Asking us to be something that has never yet been defined. I am a Frenchman. O yes then go die for it, for that visible, embodied thing you call la patrie. La patrie is visible. It has made those peonies on that cart shine with that luminous rose in alabaster light. France. France has made those peonies different from any other and our flowers at home were always *Dutch* tulips, *English* roses, O la *France* rose had to have a name, a tag to get really across to us, to make us really love it. The Seine. This is the Seine. Fancy calling the little built up island the Ile de France. Of France. Of all of France. The island of France. Islands. The island in the river where we had picnics, called Calypso's island and I asked my dear old Bert who Calypso was and he said a goddess out of a Greek poem. That was the first time I had ever heard of a goddess. "Who was she? What is one?" "What is what, Bird?" (They call me Bird.) "Why that, what you said, something about less God." "O ho, ho." Bert didn't laugh like that but how do you think of people when they laugh? It's a sort of cringing, a sort of crinkling, a sort of twisting. It's letting go. Bert let go, leaned against the rail of the bridge. (We were on our way up what we called, the mountains, for what we called, pansy violets.) O ho, ho. That is no sound for laughter. But how write laughter? Bertrand laughed. He was always immensely thin, immensely tall. Laughing. "How kind of your *big* brother to take you, such a little girl up the mountains." "Yes to get *pansy* violets." Bert laughing. "A goddess as a—god—less, a God—less. Less what, Birdlet?" "It was you who said it, not me. I didn't say anything about any less." "You did, oracle. You said a goddess—" And he was at it again. Twisting a long leg round another long leg. What was he about then. But here we are, not there. Here we are standing on a bridge over the Seine, the galleries of the Louvre to the left ladies and gentlemen and the famous Notre Dame across a little in the distance. Here we are in France. How ever did we get here? What is France? What is French? A sort of (obviously) Esperanto of the Spirit.

3 "But *who* is he?" "I tell you he is Walter Dowel. I can't tell you any more. He's very famous—" "I should judge so by his trousers." "I can't see that there was anything wrong with Walter's trousers." "Nothing wrong only they made us, the post-cards, the woman behind the bench selling post cards, the Cook's guide, the elegant late plaster cast Roman lady with the fat arms, even you, even *you*, purse proud, look wrong." "How wrong, Fayne Rabb?" "I don't know how wrong. I could tell you in a million years. I didn't know your friends, your formulas for life. But even you, I should have thought could have stood upright looking like some Cyrenian hysteria beside anybody. But you didn't. You looked dowdy and odd and fancy your thinking you could carry your mangy wilted peonies along with you through the Louvre galleries and fancy you not having French enough to get the woman's meaning—" "I knew her meaning. She only wanted a tip." "Then fancy you Miss Suavity, not having savoir faire (I think you call it) enough to get out your pennies and having to be interpreted—" "I didn't have to have it interpreted—" "Well, mama and I saw you at it and we thought it was a stranger—" "Well he is a stranger." "You don't talk to strangers—" "I mean I only heard him play a few times—" "Play? Play what? Ye gods I thought he was head floor walker in some smart shop." "No. He's I told you famous. He's the famous Walter Dowel—" "*The* famous Walter Dowel." "His grandfather invented the morse code. Telepathatic. I mean telegraphic or something. It's taken Walter in *music*—" "*Music?* That's what he does?" "Didn't I tell

you? I've been saying it all along. *The* famous Walter Dowel. Debussy's favourite pupil."

O Walter, Walter how kind of you to have asked us here. Walter
suavity, fragrance (can a man be fragrant?). O Walter you are like
great dog-wood trees, men are trees sometimes. But what makes me
so happy is that you don't seem to care, don't seem to mind our being
hot and draggled and after all not asking any odd questions, not
thinking anything odd, just greeting one as if it were at Mrs. de
Raub's without surprise, bursting into French (exquisite French) and
then going on and on, talking as if time never existed and "would you
like, Hermione, to hear some more music?" Asking her if she would
like some more music, not making any intermediate enquiries for
what was there else to ask? "Hermione do you think there is more of
the sea in this—ruuuuuuuuuuu—or this uuuurrrr—" "How can I tell,
Walter? I think the other one, no not that one, has more of the idea
but you see I don't know much about music." "No. Sit still. Don't
move. I can play things, make things come right when you are
listening." Walter. Walter. No intermediate jangling of looking as if
her face needed washing not caring that her arms were full of dusty
wilted peonies. "But *what* a lovely flat." Everything Walter had must
become by the magic of his having it, lovely. Small rooms, leading
one into another, hardly anything in them, some trees outside the
window. Seine. Clichy. "I live out here, rather in the country. Can't
stand too much noise." "We loved the trip up in the little steam boat.
It was so kind of you to ask us. It was *so* kind of you to ask us. Fayne
likes coming." "I like having them." He liked them. Walter *liked*
Clara and Fayne Rabb. Now in the light of Walter's liking them,
who (she asked in her arid little starved way) ever had? Walter liked
them. Walter found them sympathe-tic. What did he do with the
word? "You sound foreign sometimes. What is the foreign way you
talk?" "I was put to school in Munich when I was three." German.
Was he German? Du bist die Ruh', du bist der Friede. She must say
it to get near to Walter. "My mother's people, some of them, about a
third came from south Germany." German. The wind was making a
noise and Fayne sat crouched against the further wall. There was
something stronger than Fayne Rabb. Hermione had made her great
discovery. It was Walter's music.

But this is worse than anything I have ever done or seen or thought of. Sitting quite still and as if something back of me were just simply using me, using me to get to Walter. Walter with his head bent in the dusk and Fayne sobbing (yes she's actually crying) and Mrs. Rabb, poor Clara, sitting white and still and getting more white and being braver than Fayne really who was crying. I have to endure. It's almost as if you, Clara, understood what I was, am going through. No, it's no use. Things just don't happen anyhow. Walter's grandfather invented the Morse code and my father is the Gart formula and poor Bertrand. Things don't just happen. There is a sort of aristocracy of the spirit. But you are stronger than I and O Walter poor little Walter they started you when you were three. Things don't just happen. Art is sweating and going blind with agony. If I weren't so sorry, didn't feel you so much Walter, I couldn't myself sit so still here, not saying anything afraid lest for some little breath I might move in some way, get out of key with something and the message wouldn't get through. Morse code. I am a wire simply. But one doesn't really choose casual instruments. But you Walter, they put you to school when you were three and don't you see, all my life it's killed me, this that they didn't teach me something when I was three. But it doesn't matter. Things don't just happen and if I can't play it makes it better for you, for just this moment. I am crucified for you and you for the thing beyond me that is getting through to you. Is this your own music Walter? But it isn't music. Light outside, still able to see, glim and glim and another glim for someone was lighting up and they called Walter (the little children in the street—he said) *le forgeron*—laughing so charmed when he said it "they call me the *blacksmith* here." Blacksmith that was what Walter was to ordinary people. O white and strong and powerful like great white breakers. Your face is alabaster. You are more beautiful than anything one could ever have imagined. It's rather terrible Fayne crying like that. I couldn't think she'd do it. But it's worse, much worse, much more triumphant for us, quiet, who have Morse codes and Gart formulas to fall back on, Walter . . . "Are you tired?" "Walter." "Are you tired?" "Walter." "I just thought for a moment—" "What did you think, Walter?" "I don't know. That second movement. I wish you would come to Norway with me in the summer." "Walter." "I got the last bit and of course I'm going to get tea. No. Don't move. I have everything. In the dark. Hermione. I thought you might like the other half better. Which movement did you like better? Debussy liked the andante but you said it was the sea grinding at low tide and got (did you say?) on your nerves, felt (you said) wrecks and didn't you say it was like the little Mermaid. I have a drawing a friend of mine made. A man in London. Rallac. He is French. Likes London. Does fairy tale illustrations. Everyone knows him. I have a concert there next winter. Will send you to see them. I have done more work lately." "Walter." "I should get up and light the candles. Lights. We have electricity. Are your friends still here? What's happened to them?" "They went looking for your little bathroom. Fayne Rabb has been crying." "Crying? What's she been crying for? What's the matter with her? You're not crying?" "O no, Walter."

Of course the thing is terrible but it isn't your fault and it isn't my fault and it's got to be borne. Windows facing east, west and south. Southern windows. No, there is no southern window in this music. Giving us little cakes and calling downstairs in exquisite French and someone running up, his old concierge he said, going out again, coming back with a beautiful shiny loaf like a loaf in a Rallac drawing *he* said. He is fond of the Rallacs and says we must see them in London. Fairy tales and going on now, having made the tea himself and some little radishes appearing with butter on a leaf and calling it supper with red wine afterwards. We had forgotten he had strips of white chicken and lettuce leaves, always had something on hand and started calling it tea. But it was supper now with the candles making blood chalices of the deep wide goblets that must do, he said as he hadn't any proper wine-glasses. He didn't (he said) really live here, just worked here. He had—friends up the road. Would she come to see them, some friends of his. Yes, she would be glad to come to see them, glad to see any friends of his. What kind of friends? A man who made blue, blue sea drawings and drew illustrations (for pot boilers, Walter said) for Shakespeare's Midsummer Night's Dream. Midsummer. But it was winter. It was winter when Walter played. Cold and chill and the sound of the notes was the last drop of an icicle that started to melt in the spring, melting, it must melt but it decided not to melt and broke off a little crystal bead and fell down, down, down and broke with an infinitude of sound, the lightest sharp cold ice note at the top of the piano, making the whole world vibrate. Red wine. The wine was like a frozen ruby, everything static where Walter was. Morse code, going on and on and on. Everything he did was written carefully away somewhere in a big book. There was a huge book that God turned to. "Ah this was Walter playing. It's all written down here. It was the (what was the date?) about the middle of July, end of July. Late peonies. Lilacs all gone. Must have been about then for there were cherries on carts and the rabbits along the Seine on the left bank were chewing full headed lupin grass. Must have been there. Lucky to have books. My books. I am God. Look, here the candles blew askew in the wind and Walter went on and on and people collected on the pavement outside but he didn't mind even when a small boy shouted (till he was suddenly quelled by the little crowd that had collected) 'forgeron.' He is certainly writing things for me, dots and dashes, things that I and only a few people (Hermione) can read. And there is Hermione knowing all about it. Something to have a Hermione, a negative instrument. May find later use for it. Fayne Rabb? Something gone wrong? How did I make that mistake? Clara better Whet." Go on and on and on. What would God make of the page he would read, turning back, summer 1912 (was it?) long ago. Walter is still playing in the mind of God. Hermione is still sitting stiff and fearing lest she fall forward or fall sideways. Not backward. Nice little room wall with nice paper. Freshly papered. He told them all about it and how he had hesitated. He seemed to care so much about his wall paper, a sort of rose grey and his tumblers that weren't the right ones for the wine that is frozen forever. That is Walter. Fire frozen. Suppose you melt the fire that is frozen. But you can't. The thing is simply fire-frozen, frozen fire and no one can help the thing. It just is. There's no use Clara your asking him to play Chopin but he will if you ask him. Why does he do the things we ask? It seems so odd, as if suddenly you should take it into your head to ask an ocean breaker to stop for a moment and play something, say Chopin. Well, there it would know how to do it. The ocean breaker would understand Chopin. It would fall at the right moment and make of itself a miniature little lake and you would see in a miniature little lake just all that. All that, that Walter was playing. Still he was too big for this; the breaker remembered, chafed all the time that it had plunged over a rock, got caught and was now the tiniest and most perfect little play lake. It would remember that it was part of the sea suddenly and when the tide came in it would flow out again and be lost again. "Would you rather have the window shut? Perhaps we'd better. Sometimes the gendarme complains that we collect too many people." He shut the window, but Hermione was sure the thing that Walter was, still went through the window. He said he hated people but he closed the window softly, apologetically almost you might have thought. He said he loathed people and he smiled with his Byronic charm when he said the little boys shouted "forgeron" at him always. Going on and on and on. O it's so late Walter. Why did you start again. Couldn't you have let us off, let us somehow go home somewhere? Where is home? Eugenia wouldn't understand this but Clara is bearing up beautifully. Clara has something "home" about her, making Walter's little supper so sweet, presiding like an elderberry bush, Clara. Really rather like a flowering stiff wooded bush. Strong underneath. Clara. Clara not breaking. Clara even a little impatient with Fayne Rabb. Did Fayne think they were going to think of her when before their very eyes, an ocean breaker took form and white and white and white with its coat off and its sleeves rolled up and looking absolutely right with its collar loosened about its beautiful Byronic face. This is how beauty can look when God thought, "well, Helios, Apollo might take form again. Who for a father? Well someone in the background. That old Morse code fellow might do for a grandfather." God thought it all out, thinking carefully. Sometimes He made mistakes. Fayne should have been—who? What? Did it matter. The candles blew straight up now that Walter closed the window. "You must be tired." "I? I'm never tired." Why did he say that, brushing back his hair (short hair) a little loosening, pulling at his collar. God. What fingers.

What a nice little house. What a dear little lady. What an odd little lady looking so smart and somehow not at all the sort of thing you would ever in your mind remotely (ever and ever so remotely) associate with Walter. "O Mademoiselle Raigneau. It was ever so kind of you—" "Then you are—*with*—friends?" "Yes, Mademoiselle Raigneau. A girl and her mother—" "O, *and* her mother?" "O yes, Mademoiselle Raigneau." Then did Walter live here? It was all so mysterious. "Walter will be coming later." (She just couldn't say Walter. It evolved into something that sounded like the frrr of the flap-flap of an old water wheel that is going in a pond but is no good but we won't have the old thing broken up, it's so picturesque. Vrrralter.) "O but I came to see *you*. To talk to *you*. It was kind of you to let me come to talk to you." "Walter," (but you couldn't write the way she said it) "says you—help him." "O how could I help him, ever, ever dream of helping Walter." And before Hermione could finish the half bite of the excellent croissant she had begun to bite before the second half of the bite was over, Mademoiselle had begun, begun to pour out something, a long, long story, long, long story, what was it all about, her sister and another sister who had a child and how they were together in the country and how Walter was fond of her brother-in-law and how her mother was not dead but still living in their old château (which was really a farm though they called it a château) in the Pyrenees. They were part Spanish. Not really Spanish, only part and she and her sisters had played Walter's violin concerto, she herself (had Walter told her?) played the violon cello. O how odd. No, Walter hadn't told her. What a sunny small little lady to be grappling with a violon cello. Like a little lady bird climbing up, up, a huge, enormously huge sort of shiny chestnut. Great horse chestnut. France was all chestnut trees, châtaignes, they called them but it was *marron* glacé. Rather like a chestnut, like a marron glacé. Small compact and brown. How different from anything one could ever, even so remotely associate with Walter. And now she was plunged on with a history of her family. "You understand my English?" "O everything."

Tiny exquisite room. This was the "friends" up the street. All arranged. Fayne Rabb and Clara rather hurt. "But he wants me to see them alone." "Them? Are there others?" "Others than what?" "Why than this—some woman I suppose he's got entangled with?" "No. Friends of his. The Raigneaus. I don't know who exactly. People who *do* things." "Obviously."

"You didn't bring your friends?" "Walter thought there would be too many. I will, if I may sometime. I don't suppose you'd care to come to see—*us*?" What was the etiquette on these occasions? One couldn't imagine little Mademoiselle Raigneau in their rue gauche little bedrooms. "We live in such a funny part. But you see being Americans, we love it." "O yes. I know many Americans. My pupils.

Girls who have *har*-mon-y with Walter." "Does Walter teach?" "Well not really—much." Dear little Mademoiselle Raigneau, smiling and such an entente all at once flaming up between them. A big fire in the autumn burning rubbish that was the smile between them. O, don't scatter the leaves, pile them *in*, don't let the wind blow them about. They'll blow *up*—you know (they said we mustn't and set fire to the *roof*). Roof on fire, a little danger somewhere, being very careful with the slightly illicit pleasure of poking the fire. That was the smile between them. O yes that was the smile between them. They were being something funny together, not the horror, the blank starkly insane horror that stared at one with white sea-eyes out of Walter's music. Let's forget Walter. They didn't talk at all about Walter. They were playing illicitly with garden rakes, at a little barn fire, don't let the leaves scatter. They'll find out and stop us. O they were so méchantes, all the time and began talking about clothes and did Mademoiselle—O but let me call you Hermione, Walter does— like dresses? What colours? Yes. She (now you must call me Vérène—what a heavenly name, it sounds like verbena) herself sometimes liked very pale bois de rose, you know a sort of sea shell rose, do you understand? And Walter though you might think he never cares, *sees* everything. "Does he see *ever*? Doesn't he—feel somehow. I can't describe it. Isn't Walter a sort of moth that has frozen, frozen—it's all very inexact—a sort of moth whose feathers are snow crystals—O dear it sounds like a Christmas tree ornament—dear Vérène—don't let's talk about *him*."

Now they were playing together. Candles on the Louis something or other table burning with round little blobs of light. The candle flames looked round blobs of light like dandelion puffs with the sun shining on them, not clear and cold or turned knife edges away from a breeze like in Walter's studio. The very quality of people determines the way their candles burn. This was a discovery. The walls melted away and were broken and cut with heavily framed rather over-luxurious paintings. Certainly French school, good paintings, might have been in some little obscure room of the Louvre. Very late French. Vérène's father had a picture in the Luxembourg. This was really people who *do* things. Something in Vérène that though she was little and dumpy couldn't have happened anywhere else. How odd it was her notes on the out of proportion cello that were making the background for Walter though naturally you would think Walter with his height and his Byronic splendour would be making the background for her, too small, little legs really too short, chubby efficient little wrist. Vérène must have climbed trees in the Pyrenees when she was a child. Vérène, not the sort of child really of Hermione's preference and somehow wrong with Walter yet somehow filling in a gap as if lonely pine woods should be inappositely filled with rose trees or rambling peonies, great bushes, half wild, with too much sun on them and the sun above smiting down to the low bushes though really loving the pine trees. The shaft of Walter's poignant allegrettissimo was the sun far up in trees and the cold water running in, swift, swift, but water from an iceberg. Walter was water from an iceberg running in and in and in and the cello keeping up its buzzzzzz underneath was the inapposite hummmmm of many bees, bees, bees, in chestnuts filled with rose spike of pink wax flower. Chestnuts, roses gone a little riot. Low bushes not one's own kind of bushes. An odd jungle. Walter went on playing but he was quieter, more human, his face not strained, torn and white. Walter would go mad if he hadn't this stretch of low bushes, rose coloured bushes and small compact low growing trees to rest in. Walter's genius was high, high in the trees and Vérène was actually reproving him like a child. Vérène was older, she had told Hermione. "Did it matter" Hermione had asked, seeing that she wanted her to ask it. How could it matter? "I feel I'm too—old." "How mad. How silly. How could he want you other?" "Did he *say* anything?" O now what was she to answer? Walter hadn't said anything, only he had—friends up the road. "He didn't exactly say—anything. It was—in—the—air." Vérène accepted it. "But he spoke of—*you*." "Well that's different. We hardly know one another." "No. He said so. He said he wanted your advice. Do you know music?" "O, no, no, no, no, no. Mademoiselle Raigneau. I write—a—little." Music. Writing. What could one say or how could one say it? "Don't worry at me." That was the only thing to say but Hermione couldn't say it. Walter has, O it's so odd, a sort of brain. I have too. That is even more odd. It's the Gart formula and the Morse code between us. One couldn't say that. She had hardly formulated it. But there was something of a butterfly rimed with frost between them. Little Vérène would die at the first breath of frost. Walter (it was obvious) would kill her.

4 "You're exaltée. You saw him alone." "O, no, no, no, no, no. How could I see him alone?" "What's easier? You tell us he asked you to meet friends of his. You don't ask us to come along. You disappear at three, saying the friends asked you to early tea and hear music. You come home at—heaven knows what hour—and in Paris. Alone." "I wasn't alone." "Well there you are. I suppose in all decency he would have to see you back at two in the morning." "It wasn't two in the morning." "Wasn't it?" "Was it?" "Well, you ought to know."

Was it two in the morning? Odd white mist rising from a silver river, far and far and rather cold stars. Stars in France are oddly rather cold, taking on a sort of artificial glamour like diamond stars on kings' breasts. "Isn't it odd even the stars looking different?" "Stars?" "I mean over the river." "So you stood and star-gazed on the Seine." "Ever so long. He started telling me about Debussy. It was so odd. The gold fish, you know that thing he plays us and the castle under the sea, he knows all about them. Debussy says Walter is the only person who can play his music." "So you talked of Debussy. And what else?" "I don't know. Walter is making drawings, so exquisite of harps and things—" "*Harps* and things?" "O. I don't understand. He thought I might. He said he thought I might." "Understand what (at two in the morning) hanging like any street walker over the Seine parapet?" "Street walker? We did walk rather. He was making drawings of Egyptian harps and things, things like that in the Louvre. He believes he can *hear* things. Doesn't really care about Debussy. He thinks it's all written if one could only get it. He thought I might be able to get it." "Get what? Cold in your head, I should imagine." "Get—something—somewhere." "This is interesting. So instructive, strangely illuminating." "That is why he was at the Louvre the other morning. He loves Egypt." "Egypt? The last thing—" "I thought so too. But do we understand? Egypt. He means the music. The harps. Odd pipes. He says voices too. He wants to hear the voices. He cares more about that than his music."

But I care more about Greek than Egypt. Walter says it's all wrong but that I personally am all right, limited—and don't understand—couldn't be expected to understand—the *real* things. Real? What is real? Candles reflected in a mirror and our clock doesn't go here either. Clocks that go and clocks that don't go. Most of them don't. This one is like the one in the first room in Rouen before we left. Havre. Rouen. Did they really happen? "O you came to *Havre*. How funny of you." Rouen. They didn't ever seem to have heard of Rouen. "But we must go to Chartres." Must they go to Chartres? "But we're here now in Paris. How can we go to Chartres?" "Well, it was you yourself who suggested it in Rouen." "That was before we came to Paris." "Does that make any difference?" "Yes. No. Yes. I don't know what I mean." "I should think you didn't." "I mean how can anything one has suggested in Havre or Rouen, have anything to do with anything else of moment in Paris?" "Quite a speech for you. If Peter Piper ate the peck of pickled peppers then where is the peck and so on. Say it quickly, it will improve your manners." "My manners are all right, Josepha. It's your morals." "Morals? I thought you thought yourself a nereid, a nymph, a cold and icy star and all shine and luminous quality that nothing could mar or befoul." "Befoul? What an odd word, Fay." "Yes. Isn't it? Not the sort of word you get standing on the bridge at two in the morning asking the price of diamonds." "Diamonds?" "Stars, was it? Well, stars. Diamonds. Both decorated." "Who both? Walter and Vérène?" "Walter and who—is that her name?" "I told you her name long ago. Vérène Raigneau."

Vérène. Vérène. Vérène. Was it a name. Was it a person. O, yes it was a person. It was herself and Fayne and Walter who were somehow out of it, out of the picture, out of drawing. Drawing. How odd that he should draw so beautifully. "Look, Fayne. He gave me this." Fayne took the bit of paper, held it to the light. "I think he must have traced it from a book." "No. Look, Fay. It's one of the things in the big case in the Egyptian room we were looking at the other day. A sort of harp arrangement; don't you remember. They had it propped up against a lovely chair that looked quite new, quite a comfortable new chair with no back and odd arms and the seat sagging just as if it had been sat in." "Yes, I remember the chair." "Well, Walter drew the chair and the harp and put the person there in the chair to play the harp." "But he copied it, I tell you out of a book." "No. No, he didn't. You can see it's the same chair and the person playing the harp—" "It's you, I suppose." "He didn't say so . . . saying I'm too Greek and that he doesn't care for Greek things and that I don't understand. I think it's someone else or no one at all." "O, it's you all right." "But he keeps telling me I'm too Greek—not understanding—" "Does he *say* you don't understand?" "Yes. All the time." "What do you talk about then?" "I don't know . . . nothing in particular. He's quite common sometimes. He asked me if we went like all other American tourists to the top of the Eiffel Tower for the express purpose of seeing how far we could spit."

Let's destroy things. Build them up and destroy them. Wasn't that their attitude? Walter had reached perfection of a technical order. Therefore he must reach beyond it, destroy in a gesture his exquisite technique, his music flowing like water, a technique that Debussy said he himself couldn't cope with. Walter must play his music, play it the first time to let him (Debussy) see how it went. Walter playing to her, "but I want to know what *you* think. Debussy doesn't like the allegro so much either." Had she agreed (knowing nothing about music) then with Debussy? What was it all about? Why? Something in the air. Paris. Something there are no words for. Walter was right with his harps and his absolute conviction that there were things, notes, voices in the air about them. X rays, Morse code. Telegraphs and so on. We are only just beginning. People will think us of the year 1912 circa (was it?) somehow crude and old fashioned even doubting, thinking, thinking such things odd. But we didn't. Not us. Not Walter, Hermione and Josepha.

Are we ahead then of people? O this is horrible. What will people think 1922 or 1932 some great age like that, ten, twenty, thirty years from this year? They will catch us when they know that we are ahead of them. Bash out our brains. Stench of flesh roasting, roasting fumes rising above Rouen. Lilies and the Magdalene looking for the Lover. My Lord, my Lover. How odd. My Lover. You would love us all alike, making no difference, reaching us telepathically, men and women alike, both the same, simply a matter of telepathic rays or X rays or something. Christ seeing colours. Walter would be white, trimmed with blue, a terrible blue. Heat when it gets too hot becomes white, then violet. See Chemistry for Beginners. Does cold, then by the same scientific logic become something other, blue, when it becomes too cold? The cold of Walter that commences by being just cold, the soft cold of snow, soft and of the quality of a moth's breast, becomes toward the edges more cold. A cold, people can't bear. Walter knows people can't bear him that's why he hates them, hates them, apologetically closing the window. "We sometimes collect a crowd here and the gendarme doesn't like it." Shutting the window not so much against them as against himself. Byronic smile. Collar loosened. Walter shutting the window. "Now what would you like me to play you?" Asking them, waiting actually for an answer. Chopin. Chopin, the de Musset of music. Playing them Chopin.

Swans, a clear surface green lake. Nothing in the lake, no horror, no little mermaid crying for a human lover. Give me your voice and I will give you feet. The old witch under the sea asked the little Mermaid for her voice and in return she would have feet and then she could walk the earth as others and find her human lover. But we don't fortunately want human lovers. Does Walter really want Vérène? He thinks he does. It keeps him from rising up, up toward the surface of the sea. It keeps him down, down among the rose coloured bushes to love Vérène. He is kept down by this love for he would go mad (and he knows it) if he rose to the surface of his consciousness, really heard the voices he is so bent on hearing. Music. Was Vérène's cello really music? Not in that sense, not in their sense. It was music of another order. Not of the Morse code Gart formula order. Not of the order of the music of the spheres and Plato actually getting the thing down, making the exact statement, the formula, giving them numbers and figures and *design* for the thing they knew already. Plato gave them a design. Clear thinking makes a pattern as regular and symmetrical as a plotted engineer's plan or marine architect's constructed boat prow. Thinking makes lines in the air. Plato's formula.

It appears that there is a world within a world. We all live in some world (or several) but Christ lived in all. This is odd. Going on and on and on. The world of bed-bugs, of the stench of the stagnant water in the tooth-brush tumbler where she had stuffed the already half-wilted stems of the odd orange striped lilies she had some days ago bargained for in the Quai aux Fleurs. Throw the water away. Fresh water. Rinse out the tooth brush cup and find something else. But what else is there? The tea pot they had bought for their own teas at home, no not the pot, we'll need it. Bother. Orange striped small lilies in a tooth brush tumbler. That's our life here. But I don't care. I love it. I love the sordid touch with Clara and Fayne Rabb. It gives character, poignancy and point to all this. And we live on nothing. I will have all that extra money and when they write me to come back, I shall just stay on. Of course, I know I can't go back. I'd rather be a girl in a shop, rather scrub out hospital wards than go back. O, no, no, no, no. Du bist die Ruh', du bist der Friede. O God why didn't they really let me sing or something and that old Madame Terrone at Mrs. Merrick's said she would take me for nothing. Funny old thing with huge chest and odd yellow teeth and a huge démodé pompadour and a voice that made you crouch low in your chair and pray to be dead. She sang the Erlkönig and I knew I would go mad for hers wasn't an opera voice, everybody said so, but people begged her, prayed and implored but she wouldn't take their daughters. "You have a quality in your voice. I would make you a good singer but only of chamber music, you understand. I will take you for nothing. Who are you?" "My—father—is a—a—professor of—of theorems and things. I don't think I care for . . . music."

5 "I can never make out whether Walter's a second rate Olympian or a first rate demi-god." "No George." "I can never make out whether his music has got him or he has got his music." "Yes, George." "And on the other hand, I can never see whether that little black beetle of a woman has entangled him or whether he really wants to marry her." "Marry her, George?" "Yes. What do you think Dryad."

"I don't know what I think George. It seemed a matter of—of—" "Why don't you ever achieve your utterances. You are an oracle manqué." "Perhaps George, the—the—worshipper—I mean—" "Well, what *do* you mean? You seem, if I as your nearest male relative may say so, somewhat gauche, your clothes don't look right. You seem somehow more provincial than ever." "Provincial?" "Provincial. Or perhaps you prefer Surbiton." Hermione was beginning to wish she had not after all seen George Lowndes, answered his peremptory summons. "Meet me at the Cottage Tea Rooms at the corner of Piccadilly Circus, upstairs, at half past three so we can get a table." She had found the post card (forwarded from Paris to their London address and the day scratched in on the other side where George had fenced off a little space in pencil, "Friday. If I don't hear, will look."). There wasn't time to say no. Why shouldn't she see George?

"But I thought you were engaged to him" stormed Fayne Rabb "and then I thought you broke it off." "I was engaged to him." "Well, you don't after you are engaged to people and then break it off, see them again, do you Madre? What would her mother think?" This was the first time in some weeks that Fayne Rabb had mentioned (ever so distantly) Eugenia. Clara as her way was, went on sewing. Leaves from Bloomsbury sycamores drifted down making a premature autumn. "*Madre.* Tell her." "I don't know. Yes. No. Have you any, Hermione, by any chance sort of *tan* coloured sewing thread (they call it sewing cotton). This brown doesn't look right. Yes. No. I mean, what were we saying?" "You heard what we were saying, Madre. Don't you think it would be the height of foolishness of Hermione to see George Lowndes here away from home, in London where conventions are so strict, where everything is different?" "Yes. No. I mean you say you broke off the engagement, didn't you?" "Well yes. I broke it off or rather he did." "*He* did?" "Well you see there'd been a row but I've told you all about that. And I was ill but you know I never like—to—talk about—it—" "Well, why *should* you see him?" "I don't know . . . after I was well again . . . after Fayne came back again, he wrote." "He would do . . . after everything was over." "He was in Spain then, lying in the sun. He sent me yellow jasmine." "Jasmine? Pretty mangy jasmine, I should imagine." "It wasn't somehow. Something (it was dry but full of colour in the envelope) happened to it." "Like Saint Elizabeth and the roses—" "Yes. Something. It smelt of—of—" "Of what? Stutter. Stammer. Can't you ever achieve your meaning?" "That's like George. Sometimes, Fayne, you are just like George. That's how George used to go on at me." "Well, anyhow, *should* she, Madre?"

Should she. Shouldn't she. One I love, two I love. "Clara, I have found the very exact shade you're looking for." "Hermione, I wish Paulet would be as interested in her things as you are. All so neat." "No. It was mama—Eugenia who prepared my little work bag. Things I'd never think of. My mother you know. I call her Eugenia except when I'm at home. She's mama at home." "Why, pray, Eugenia?" "It's her name. My grandfather had a sort of adoration for the empress—" "Empress?" "Eugénie."

Should she. Shouldn't she. Leaves prematurely drifting down

from tall peeling sycamores. Strange scent of sun-burnt sycamores (that was a rare hot early autumn) and the odd curious cut-off feeling like being in a bird's cage, high up above the old square with the corner going on and the other corner going on. The corners seemed to be separated, odd square boat hulks stranded there, all so quiet, rumble in the distance, rumble, rumble, the eternal rumble of London. Cut apart in their little back-water. Bloomsbury.

"Well but if you have broken it finally—off—" "Well. I mean, we did. I mean he did. Then he came back and we got engaged again." "Well that alters everything." "I mean we got engaged then we—I mean he—no it was I this time—I mean *I* broke—it—off—I mean it was broken off—" "Well are or are you not engaged to George Lowndes?" But how answer that thing? "I don't know, Josepha. I had better ask him."

"We're not engaged, George?" "Gawd forbid." "I thought you felt that way about it George. Mrs. Merrick and Stephen Merrick sent their love. He expects to be back in Rome in a year or so and wants to see you. Do you like Rome? Or have you ever been there? Everything's so odd, exciting. I don't know where I have been. I don't know where I haven't. Those pictures in the Louvre transported one and I felt the same way about the Nike. The winged Victory. I told the Rabbs I didn't. I don't mean that. What do I mean? I mean seeing the Elgin marbles this morning gave me the same feeling and I didn't know, don't know whether I'm in Rome or Paris. I mean the Louvre and the British Museum hold one together, keep one from going to bits. For one is all in bits. I even like awful things, awful (I believe they are awful) like Delacroix and the Lancrets. I saw Napoleon's snuff box and the Corots. There was a little bad picture of a ship in a storm, simply awful but like one in our attic like Eugenia did once . . . but you never liked Eugenia's funny pictures. I—love—Europe."

"It's so quaint, she loves London." "Yes, isn't it odd—she loves London." "This is Miss Gart—they call her Her short for Hermione—she loves London." "O I am—so—glad. Why do you love London?" "O let me really tell you Bertie, that Miss Her Gart loves London. Such a *quaint* person—" "Yes, I love London."

"This is Miss—O did you know what *her* name is?—but you love London—" *O Walter.*

Coming across the room, bowing to someone. Someone different, out of something that never was that never could be. It was too bad about Walter, acted as if he were, as if he were something like the first aeroplane ever invented or a dug-up Dinosaur. All hushing down, fluttering down, sinking down into arm-chairs pushed aside and jumbled in little knots, islands of arm-chairs. Walter comes across the room, people fall, all turned toward him, sun-flowers to the sun. Sunflowers to the sun, whispering, whispering "Dowel you know. Only Delia in all London can procure him." Procure? How did Delia procure Walter? And where was Delia? Hermione had been jostled through crowds of people and hadn't got near Delia. Delia standing somewhere, somewhere far away, crowds and she was always interrupted, George at her elbow, "no you come here Dryad, here's another prize specimen." George produced prize specimens. They cropped up on the stairs, upstairs and when she got upstairs to find Delia George pronounced that Delia had gone downstairs and "you needn't worry about your book of etiquette, dear Dryad. Don't be so provincial." Was it provincial to find Delia, Lillian Merrick's sister Delia, all mixed up, one with another, the Merricks, school at Rome, people in the legations, poets. Everything at Delia's was like that. "Where is Delia?" It was George who had told her how to say it. "Don't be so provincial Dryad. Don't let me hear you saying Lady Prescott that way again. It's back-stairs. Everybody calls her Delia."

Where then was Delia? Delia had invited her. She had had lunch alone with Delia. Delia had said she would be bored with the crush but Walter had asked her to be sure to come. Walter had asked her to come so that he could hate them all in peace and yet play nicely. There was Walter. But she must first find Delia. What an odd Walter, like some one in an elegant Pinero revival, coming forward, one hadn't even imagined Walter (even) could be so elegant. "Huh," from George. "Old Forgeron is in fine professional form." Forgeron came forward, bowing a little. Who was he bowing to, eyes so colourless, amber and flecked grey amber. Walter's eyes were a brook's eyes, not a deep wood brook but one that has escaped from a glacier. Warmth came and went in Walter's eyes, warmth not his own, one felt, but the warmth that came to a glacial stream that runs over clear amber. Walter.

Walter would play now and this was funny. She didn't want to hear Walter play. How odd that she resented Walter, hated even Walter a little. Now she saw, felt with the consciousness of all these people who so hated Walter. Hermione had found in London what all along she knew prophetically she would find. She had sunk (with the first exquisite uprising of early autumn) under, into it. She had sunk into London as one sinks into a down cushion, into a series of excellent down cushions, all blurred, all exquisitely of a piece yet blurred. She had let go her astute hold on things of intellect (even the Elgin marbles) after her first conscientious three weeks. "We've seen all London. We've seen the Tower." This seemed to amuse people at Delia's, other odd people, friends of George's, of Delia's, who asked her to their houses. "We've seen the Soane museum." "The what, darling?" (People even in the beginning patronised, petted her.) "Soane. Sir John Soane—" "What?" "Why it's a little museum with some lovely odd things. Some odd lovely intaglios, cameos and things." "Where?" "Off—off somewhere off Lincoln's—" "Not Inn, darling?" "Well, I think so." "Fancy. The poor darling has been to Lincoln's Inn. We must rescue her. What brutes her friends are."

"Darling" had been somewhat rescued lately. Too much so. She was tired, getting blurred with it. How could it be otherwise? "I tell you Fayne that you must stay with me." "I can't. I can't leave Madre."

Fayne Rabb and Clara going home soon. Too late already. They had already out-stayed their time. Boats sailing. Grubby wharfs. Hooting of sirens. O let me shut it all out, all out in Delia's beauty.

Delia, you are so beautiful. You are beautiful with the rightness that comes with antecedents and with wisdom. Delia you are good. Delia your house is full of everyone from everywhere, you don't shut out anyone. Funny Delia. "Delia is above suspicion" someone said when someone said, "how odd of Delia to invite that *Dalton* woman here." Who was the Dalton woman? Someone crowding through chairs, making herself very thin though she was thin enough in all consciousness. There was the Dalton woman and even Walter paused, his two hands poised and then began an ironic little run up and down, up and down as much as to say, "you fiend, you fiend woman, you have driven me mad, now listen." Walter was running up and down, up and down. People were frightened but still the Dalton woman held the audience. The Dalton woman and Walter. But Walter won. The Dalton woman with a *frisson* (she would have said a *frisson*) sank into half the end of a Chesterfield that was pulled out at an odd angle and everyone began again to breathe. But Walter was standing. Walter was looking at the Dalton woman.

"O this sort of thing. This always happens," the voice was going on and Hermione turned to meet a pair of half familiar eyes, yes she had met this somewhere, rather nice with a petunia-coloured hat a little rakish over one eye and enormous jade ear-rings and odd sleek ivory-smooth white hair showing under the hat above the jade ear-rings. Odd, patrician. A petunia. Not a flower of her preference but Hermione liked to see a thing being itself. A petunia. Not a flower of her preference but with an autumn richness, no fragrance, rather heady with all but right, doing the right thing. A petunia would. The petunia seemed to know everyone, seemed to know everything. "Dear Redforth, a shocking woman. Now you watch. For two bob, our demi-god will stalk out. You wait and see if he doesn't. He told old Langstreath that he wouldn't be found dead in her house again. Shocking old snob. She had asked Dalborough to drop in and he *dropped* in the middle of the Après Midi d'un Faune. It was no après midi for poor frazzled Lydia. Her lion lept and roared and finally departed." "Sh-uuh—"

The Dalton woman and the petunia were both forgotten. Waves of cold mountain water had extinguished them. There was no colour where this was. The music was transparent. Who said there was colour in music? Someone, somewhere. People now were always saying it. Colour in music, tones, sound in pictures. Colour. There was no colour in this thing.

Back of the piano where the curtain of gold gauze shut out or lured in the most tender of silver mists, back of the gold curtain that was a gold net under the sea, to lure, to entrap, back of the curtain, no before the curtain, water welled up, up, up. It welled in bubbling sound. This was not the sea-floor. There were bits of coral to be sure—but that was the odd earring turned toward her of someone— the Dalton woman?—while the other ear (whose?) was turned to catch the music. Ears. Ears. Ears. There were ears tilted up, ears tilted down, ears side-ways. Ears were shells, were flowers, and into those ears (impersonal ears) the music poured and flowed, impersonal, everyone might listen, Hermione, the Dalton woman. Delia. This was Delia's concert. Anyone might listen for Delia being above suspicion might have anyone in to listen. Going on and on. A fountain of icy water that bubbled up from a sea floor. Arethusa was a fountain that ran under the sea, ran under the sea from Italy (or Greece was it?) straight to Sicily. Sicily. A fountain in Sicily. There were hot banks of fruit, almonds, hot grapes, petunia-coloured grapes and purple figs. Walter had nothing to do with them. He was the water simply that welled up and up. Up and up. He was the water simply. Fresh water, mountain water that ran and ran and ran . . . people were ears simply. People weren't people. Odd ears. To be washed. O *wash* your ears. You're always forgetting your *ears*. Eugenia. Would Eugenia like this music? She liked Bach. If you called Bach music then this was nothing at all. It wasn't anything. Only water, bubbling, bubbling, running, running. Water. She was the thing it flowed toward. Hermione was the impersonal thing it flowed toward. Walter was tired, his great head hung heavy on his heavy young body. The great head that was the stricken head of a wounded Hermes hung down, heavy; faster, faster, the hands were heavy, solid. How could water flow so simply from hands that were so solid? On. On. On. He had asked her to come to Delia's (though Delia had asked her anyway) so that he wouldn't too much hate the people. People. Hating people. Where was this taking her? "I would like to have a little knife, a sharp little knife. And I would like to turn and turn and turn that knife in Dowel's heart. Really. I'd like to do that and say so simply, *now you feel*." Who was saying that? O who dared say that? This is how people hated Walter. Really, really hated Walter. Who dared, who dared say that of Walter? A face was leaning toward another face, a thin highly tinted fox-shaped face with puffs of fox-coloured hair and a red mouth that made a scar and a blatant tint of red on that mouth that seemed purposely to clash with the hair colour. Who so dared speak? A face was leaning over the back of a Chesterfield and was opening tinted lips to someone who was "sh-uuhing" at it, "he's going on. For God's sake don't be funny."

Petunias. Hydrangeas. Hydrangeas artificially coloured, mauve (a word she didn't like but it expressed the other odd woman who had found the ices frizzy. "No, I don't like them. I find them awfully frizzy." What ever did the little fool mean?) and the short thick-set man with the monocle—"no not that one, I mean the other one. Not that brute, I mean the one by the window." But it seemed the one by the window who was leaning toward someone and whispering (why were they all, always surreptitiously whispering) was no more distinguished nor distinguishable from the other, the other one whose monocle was an inch thick, "ought to be an emerald, poor old Caesar." "You mean Nero." "I don't mean either Celandine." "My name's *not*—" "Well it ought to be. And what became of Dizzy's dance partner?" "You mean *Clara*?" How funny. Clara. But that wasn't her Clara. Not her Clara. Poor Clara. Would Clara have liked this? George said she couldn't bring them both. He said one or the other and there had been a quarrel at the last and Fay had been half dressed and Hermione had said they mustn't be late and Fayne had jerked at the dark blue crêpe de chine thing she and Clara had spent the whole afternoon sewing on and pulled out the whole sleeve. "Wait Pau-ul. I can sew it *on* you." But Fay had jerked it and pulled the thing leaving a slash on her shoulder. Poor lovely, beautiful, sulky misplaced Fayne Rabb. Fayne was so lovely, lovelier than all this if she would only let herself be. She wouldn't let herself, let anyone be lovely. Not lovely as flowers are. As flowers must always be. She wanted things in her own way, pulled and tore, "but you—must—feel." "But I don't. I don't, not *your* way. In my own way. O if you only knew how it went on and on and on. As if a whole book on one single page (like ancient papyrus) rolled on and on." We are here. We are *there*. We will go mad being here and there unless we give up simply, stay here and are lost, stay there and are dead. To be here and there at the same time, that is the triumph. Walter was doing that, had been doing that. "O Dowel. Excellent fellow. Starts the ghosts quivering from somewhere in Heine's inferno." "*Heine's* inferno?" "Damn, Celandine. I never was one of you élite lettrée—" "My name's not—" "Well, it should be." Flowers. Talk. How odd, how witty they all were. How could they be so perfect, all made up out of a play? Even Walter didn't see that, how lovely they were, all these people. The people took on a sudden loveliness. Was it because she was thinking of Fayne Rabb? O Fay you should have been here. "Cela—" "O don't—call me—that." "What does he call you, Di?" "The brute calls me—*Cel*—an—dine." "O—ho. Ho." That isn't how people laugh. But how write how people laugh? It is a shivering, a quivering. It's a letting go. And how delicious. She was letting go, this utterly adorable thin thing in a green gown whose hair was coming down— "Violet." "Who's calling me Violet?" "It's pom-pom over there. She's lost twenty stone since you last saw her." "O *pom*—"

The Violet of the piece was having hair pins rescued for her. "These jade things will spill." "You shouldn't wear jade hair-pins. It's pre-posterous." "Yes. Isn't it. But I won them on a bet—" "A?" "Actually. I won them, and I wear them." "You lose them you mean. Crawl under the arm-chair Teddy, that's a darling. No. That's a house-maid's hair pin." "Maybe it's De-li-a's." "Delicious Delia. No. It is quite unworthy. Now why is Delia right and why is Mrs. Shoddy Percy there wrong? They both got their gowns at Berrys." "Brute."

They didn't. They did. "Why look at the V cut as no one else does." "And the X and the Y and the Z." "One doesn't Teddy have a Z on one's gowns." "What then Vi-o-let, does one have it on?" "On?" "I mean Vi dear—off—" "Look Teddie. There's that parasite Jerry Walton. They say he killed his father." "Really? How interesting. But is it only a rumour?" "No. Solid fact. Poor darling. It meant *millions*."

O Fay, where are you dear? Look at the dear people, the funny people, the witty people. There seems no one sad at all, only someone who has broken a lorgnette, poor darling, she holds it up for everyone to see and only half the people care. O but we do care. Don't cry over it. One can see it's tortoise shell and set with tiny brilliants. Is it a crest or just your odd initials? What can her name be? O names. People. Charming people. Charming names. "Miss Her Gart, what a quaint, dear person. Little Miss Her Gart you know from Philadelphia." "From what—ever?" "A place in the Bible, didn't you know. And unto the angel in Philadelphia, write—Delia's sister lives there." "In Asia Minor did you say." Excavations, yes. Something or other about Rome. Not legations. No. Yes, I think so. Freddie's bound to do it. Came a cropper last time. "Delia."

Delia was coming forward and people were saying "Delia." They said Delia up the scale, down the scale, with grace-notes, with variations on a theme. "You are a real pet" and "won't you come to-morrow." "The Vinney woman, no one ever saw her—" and "Delia. I know you hate them—" but—"Delia, not that Oxford frump, no not really—" and "Delia. Delia. Delia à bientôt."

A bientôt, Delia, Delia, Delia. Delia à bientôt. "And that means soon, soon, Delia." "But you're not going *now*?" "But everyone is going—gone. And what is there to stay for?" "O just like you. Just like you all. Can't you see I'm tired to death. Stay Dryad." "*Dryad, Delia*?" "Yes. George says so. He says no one with any sense of humour could call you Hermione, Her Gart. He's really rather proud of you. He says we're all insane and he hopes you spite us." "Spite you, Delia?" "He says you can, will if we're not respectful. He has the greatest admiration for your—power." "Power? He's been telling me all along that my clothes look wrong, a mast and a mizzen head." "A—a—what?" "He calls me to be exact, I don't know what—a mast—and—a—mizzen head." "What is?" "What is what?" "A mizzen—ha, ha, ho." But that isn't how people laugh. Delia sank in the empty Chesterfield, laughing, surveying the wreck of her drawing room. Feathers, pomade boxes. "One feels one should find snuff-boxes people lost." "Wh-aaat?" "It's all like a play. It doesn't seem real, not this room—not anything that has happened. I love all the people—" "Which, Dryad, especially?" But she wasn't going to tell Delia. It would get quoted around and back again. They were using her as their latest little pet oracle, something odd, exotic. She wasn't having any. "I don't know" (she spoke at random) "that *Dalton* woman." "Mary?" "How could her name be Mary? Her name isn't, can't be Mary." "Why not dear? Why can't it just be. Mary means—" "O that means the mother of—mother of—" "She has two." "What?" But this was impossible. What did Delia mean by it? It was another of their cutting cynicisms. The Dalton woman with a fox shaped little face and enormous earrings leaning over the back of the Chesterfield, saying, "I would like to have a little knife. I would like to turn and turn and turn it in the heart of Dowel. I would like to say to Dowel *now you feel*." The Dalton woman. God. Perhaps (was it possible?) she had meant it.

"Delia?" "Darling?" "You don't mind my asking—" "Ask anything, darling." "I mean Lillian talked about it—seemed to—want—them." "Dear, dear Dryad—now what?" "I mean people *needn't*—" "What dear?" "I mean Lillian seemed to want them but could that Dalton woman ever—" "What? What? What?" Light coming on. Someone mysterious in the hall, lighting something. Light was creeping from the hall toward the larkspur coloured woven carpet. The carpet had the oddest of lovely shades, pot-pourri rose-colour, blue of blue and dark-blue larkspur. "The carpet is like woven petals, yet somehow right—a carpet." "Bokhara." "Bokhara. Sounds like wine coloured— petunias—" no not petunias—a hat—jade hair pins. The light was coming nearer. "Will you have the light milady," this is what George called back-stairs, "or do you prefer the shadows." The shadows? Henry James. Did footmen talk like that? "Go away." He had gone away. "Poor Dickson. He listens to our conversation. To improve his—" "*Improve* his?" "Darling Dryad, don't begin spoiling yourself by being witty. Yes. He listens. I can remember the exact inflection of poor Mary, it was only last week saying, 'don't, don't let's have the lights on Delia, I prefer the shadows.'"

6 "You're odd here, you're a great success here, but you don't dress right." "No." "I said I don't like that grey chiffon, it's too nun-ish. Maybe all right for Philadelphia." "Yes." "I said you have to have more body to your clothes. Colour." "Yes." "Yes. No. Yes. Have you heard a word I'm saying?" "No. I mean yes." "Yes, I mean no. What in Hell's name do you mean?" "I mean really, George, does it at all really matter?"

"Well, I as your nearest male relative—" George didn't like her. Not like her as he did in Eugenia's little morning room that he had said (with a snort) might almost be in Chelsea. "You don't like me here, George?" "Wh-aat?" "You don't (in London) like me." "I didn't say that. I think you're in bad hands. You keep bad company." "Bad company—Delia?" "Delia. No not delicious Delia. Delia is Hera after a cure. Juno with all the grandeurs and no fat. Delia is the immortal Artemis garbed in violet, in the violet-woven veil of Aphrodite. Delia is a second Helen come to judgment—" "You do understand, Georgio." "That's what I'm here for, Dryad." "Then who, what? What bad company? Don't you like that Dalton woman that Delia asked to meet me?" "May I ask *why* Delia asked the Dalton to meet you, Dryad?" "I don't know. It happened. The Dalton (her name is Mary) wrote Delia saying she was so unhappy—" "Again?" "Again? What do you mean again?" "I mean that Dryad. Why the Dalton?" "I told you George. She'd been writing Delia." "O well, I suppose the most discreet must have their indiscretions. The Dalton's dippy. Otherwise amusing." "Dippy?" "Her husband it appears tries spasmodically to lock her up. Bug house you know. Mad." "Is the Dalton crazy?" "Well not any more apparently than the rest of them. She's a little cleverer that's all. When a woman in that set, is clever (brilliantly clever) the husbands take quick action." "Whatever do you mean, George?" "She writes. I mean doesn't. She could if she wanted to. She's afraid of dear Freddie or Teddie or Algy. (Morris I think his name is.) She's afraid if she gets any further forwarder, he will descend and cop her." "George. You're so crazy. Yourself. Can't you tell me?" "I am. I have been." "Delia says—" "Never mind what Delia says. What do you think?"

"I don't know what I think dear George. I saw her face over the back of a Chesterfield and hated her." "Hated her? Why Dryad?" "I don't know. Something she said about Walter." "What Dryad?" "She said she wanted to turn and turn a steel knife in his heart and say *now you feel*." "Rather neat that. Old Forgeron makes one angry." "You angry?" "O well not angry, Dryad. Helpless." "Helpless?" "Well not so much helpless as hopeless. *Abandon hope all ye who enter here*. The cold irradiance of the well-cut glacier." "Well-cut?" "Yes. Perfectly tailored. The glacier à la mode." "I suppose that's funny. The sort of thing all you people repeat to one another. It *is* rather." "Thank you, Dryad. But I started saying I don't like your friends." "But who George? And why don't you?" "I mean *her* Dryad. The She of the piece. She's done things to you. You're not the same. Altered imperceptibly. Not to notice. But I notice." "Wh-aat, George?" "You and she would have been burned in Salem for witches—" "O George, George, you said that long ago . . . and that was why everything happened. Don't go on saying it." "Burnt." "You shouldn't have—you shouldn't have. You should never have said that, George Lowndes. You might have helped her." "Help her, Gawd Almighty—Orpheus or (who was it?) Orestes rends assistance to the Furies. She has a face like a Burne Jones fury. Have you seen them? In one of your eternal galleries. Not the Tate. I think the South Kensington—" "Yes. I've been there." "Where haven't you been Dryad?" "I don't—know

George." "Dryad. Piqued again. Or peeved merely?" "I don't know, George. I hoped you'd—help even now, you might help Fayne Rabb."

"Then Fayne, it's merely a matter of finances?" "That chiefly. It always has been. We would go without anything to eat (properly) for two days and then grandame would descend on us with out of season hot-house grapes. That's been our life." "Well, I can see your point. But as far as Clara is concerned you're making a mistake. You're grown up. She is. She is petting you, keeping you back. She is arresting your development. You are a case particularly poignant, of arrested development." "My dear Dryad (I believe that is what they call you) who's been talking then?" "No one. No one in particular. It's in the air. I know what I mean. I knew in Philadelphia. You expected me to stand up to Eugenia. I told you I had done it. You spoke patronizingly of Eugenia, patronized my effort as if it had been nothing. I tell you it broke my heart to break hers." "Don't talk that way. Your mother has your father. Your brother." "That makes no difference. That made it worse in a way. I was the only girl." "So am I. I am the only one at all, anyway." "I know that and I wouldn't go on this way, have gone on at all like this if you hadn't started it. Don't you remember that night in Paris—" "Nights in Paris. Nights o' Paris. O *Paris*—" "Don't be cynical, servant girlish. Paris is, has always been Paris. Athens rather. Paris brings one's mind to a fine point of illumination, of discrimination. One can see and feel and act all at once in Paris. In Paris one is one whole being, mind, body and soul as the Greeks were. In Paris I saw clearly. So did you Fayne Rabb." "I told you in Paris to harrow you, to whip you up to one of your divine frenzies that I hated Madre." "You meant it, Fayne. You haven't the courage to be straight. I hated Eugenia, loving her. But we can't creep back into our mothers, be born again that way. We must be born again in another way. You must cut, as it were the cord—" "Umbilical cord to be exact." "Yes, that simply. Here is your chance. You will never get another like it. I have kept, saved almost all they gave me. My father has been generous. There will be nothing wrong, nothing outré even in our staying on here—" "Madre has her school work. She has her job. If she misses the late autumn sailings, she's done, dismissed, finished, over." "That's all right. You're only making excuses. What anyway can you do? You only really drag her back. She's not old. People like her. She can go on, work toward coming back here. Come back here in the summer." "And you Beautiful? What of you Beautiful?" "I? I can't think, see—anything except you, me and you in two or three little rooms. I see Delia Prescott and George and Walter even coming to tea with us in our little rooms. Perhaps little rooms in Chelsea. The boats, the river. Boats hooting up the river. Down the river. Sea-gulls. Do you remember our wild ecstasy when the sea-gulls wheeled and screamed about the Nereid? And it was land then, they said only a few hours off. Do you remember the very poignant calling, screaming (or is it whistling) of those sea-gulls? But you do Fay. You do remember Fayne Rabb. It was about those gulls that you wrote that poem. You wrote about them." "I did, Beautiful. I know all that. I'd like to stay. You don't know how hard it is for me not to." "I do know." "Come back with us Beautiful." "How can I? What good would that do anybody? I'd only have to hurt Eugenia again. I've plunged in the dagger."

"I've broken her heart. She's got other things, other people. She's even altering, wants to cross next autumn if I stay on." "Then how about me? There'd be no place for me. You have your friends." "Not as I want. Not as I need them. I want a little flat in Chelsea. Delia would help me. Delia would be everything correct, convenable, comme il faut, you know all that—" "You'd use your—Delia as you call her for a screen?" "A screen? For what pray?" "For us." "Us? We don't need to be screened. What have we done or could we do to need any apology or explanation? I am burning away that's all. The clear gem-like flame. I don't want you to miss it. I'm going to write, work. You could. George took your poems to send to the Lyre, not mine." "The Lyre (or is it the Lark?) is a rotten little decadent rag—" "No it isn't. Delia says it isn't. It's quite representative and good and George has been offered some job on it. George Lowndes will have some job, help us." "I don't understand your wanting George—" "I don't. I haven't. But George says he'll help us if we stay here." "I thought George hated me." "He does rather." "Then why help—us?" "He says we're like a vision of Theocritus—though he doesn't approve." "O *Theocritus*—"

"I, Hermione, tell you I love you Fayne Rabb. Men and women will come and say I love you. I love you Hermione, you Fayne. Men will say I love you Hermione but will anyone ever say I love you Fayne as I say it? Men and women wander from caves into the light and in the caves little bare children tug at the teats of wolves. Romulus. Rome. I think never in the world will such children live, live again as live in my thoughts, my heart. I don't want to be (as they say crudely) a boy. Nor do I want you to so be. I don't feel a girl. What is all this trash of Sappho? None of that seems real, to (in any way) matter. I see you. I feel you. My pulse runs swiftly. My brain reaches some height of delirium. Do people say it's indecent? Maybe it is. I can't hear now, see any more, people. Some are kind, some aren't. That's all the division I can ever have between them . . . Hermione. My grandfather read Shakespeare—that's why, Hermione. But that's not me. That's not me. They can laugh if they want cry if they want, become rhapsodic over Her Gart, Hermione Gart or Hermione. But I'm something different. It's nothing to do with them. I'm something else. Different. You Fayne know that. Perhaps you are the first one at all to know it. I know that Shakespeare is real. *I'd count myself a king of infinite space* and that other thing—I can't remember—things like *sweeter than the lids of Juno's eyes*. Those things are real. The child in Trois Contes dancing in tight drawers for the head of John the Baptist is somehow real, even Aphrodite. Pierre Louÿs. People simper. But Pierre Louÿs (even) is real beside this thing. This thing that you allow to creep over you, to swamp you. This thing that is a convention manqué for you don't really love your mother, not in that way. If you did you would pierce through the dark nun-veil of falsehood, this nun-veil of hypocrisy. Not that nuns are. But you are. You aren't going to stay because you're afraid simply. You urge me on to defy my mother, poor soft dear and sentimental Eugenia. Eugenia is as beautiful as Clara. Even more so. Soft and holding tight to her convention. But not rigid. Clara is rigid. But her love for you is incest. Mothers and daughters don't sleep in the same bed. It's horrible."

"Peter Piper picked a peck of pickled peppers—" "Yes, it appears so. But I'll go on talking. We are legitimate children. We are children of the Rossettis, of Burne Jones, of Swinburne. We were in the thoughts of Wilde when he spoke late at night of carts rumbling past the window, fresh with farm produce on the way to Covent Garden. He was talking to a young man called Gilbert. They talked of Greeks and flowers. Do people talk that way? None I know. They are witty

but always with decoration back of it. (Nor Delia.) London repudiated the rhododendron beauty of those people. Or outgrew it. There
will be, I am sure, others. We belong here. Not in Paris. Here. Paris
is the sharp sword of perfection. Paris knows her beauty. Paris is no
slut, no prostitute. Not even demi-mondaine. People go there for
those things and find them. That sort of people could find just as
well what they go to Paris to find in New York, Little Rock or
Minneapolis. Paris is something different. France is. You say France
and something stirs in the air. Flakes and specks of electric power
take form and are directed. Paris is back of thought directing it. Paris
is, I tell you, Athens. Rome is London. New York is Alexandria.
They, Rome, Athens, Alexandria are living in these cities. The saffron clothed Chrysis climbed the wharf at Alexandria. I don't want
to be that. Nor have you that. Is Plato the only one who understood
this? O Christ also. Love is enfolding one, all of one. Light that
shoots about one's brow like a saint's halo. Sometimes I could catch
you in a mood and freeze you and keep you safe forever. Other times
you have destroyed, you are afraid. You are not whole. Not a perfect
person. Walter is. George understands things but he bickers. Trifles.
But George is kind. I love George when he is kind but I would love
him better if he loved you. Clara is stiff with some rigid family
complex. Or is it that she really did run away and have you? Is your
story right? Did she run away and are you some half-creature, really
soulless, of the wood and river? *Helen thy beauty is to me as those
Nemean barks of yore.* You are beautiful with that beauty. I have only
seen another face worthy to call itself your sister. And I don't want to
look and look at that face. That face regards me from the bright
polished door of the Prescotts' while I wait that moment for the door
to open. My own face is written on the door of my attainment. The
door that leads outward for me holds my own face engraved as on a
name plate. Hermione looks at me. There is a door leading nowhere.
That is the trip to Liverpool, the boat to New York. There is a door
of cowardice and unattainment and of nullity. That is, 'yes Madre I
am coming back with you and O Madre how happy we will be
together.' You are indecent and your mother is. It's sheer incest."

"If Peter Piper picked the peck of pickled peppers then where is
the peck of pickled peppers that Peter Piper picked?" "I don't know
Fayne Rabb but your silliness is unworthy of you. You are a Di-
adumenos, with a clown's face. You are Hyacinth mired with horror.

Hyacinth was a strong boy not a pimp. You make beauty a fool's bladder. Bladder. Yes that thing like a balloon blown up for fools to play indecent jibes with. You are the youth of the god Hermes, but you have neither wand nor wings nor sandals. You are Hermes turning from the high ladder of Heaven solely to the underworld. Hermes led dead men across Styx. You are that river."

1 "Almost thou persuadest me to be a heathen." Who said that? Who was talking? Fayne had said something like that. It was Fayne who had first said it. Was it a joke she had picked up from George or was George saying something he had heard from Fay? "Almost thou persuadest me—" George was bending down between two incredibly tall candle sticks to turn a page. What page? All France is a book. Brrr sous la livre. A livre. A book. No it was a *pound* of plums in a paper bag and the bed bug (Fayne had said) climbed swifter than a horse. No, Fayne said the bed-bug *walked* swifter than a horse, "no, no more tea cakes, thank you," and everywhere the bells were ringing, beating, ringing ("O no. Not yet. I hope to get to Italy later—"). Christ in Heaven, Christ in Heaven— "Almost thou persuadest me to be a—" George was saying it again. The candles sent up immaculate light toward a square ceiling whose corners were elegant Georgian circlets of fruit, beautiful like squares of Della Robbia quince, orange and tufts of orange blossom. "Luca della Robbia." Who was saying that? "Della Robbia. The old fellow got the essence of the Renaissance in that thing. I myself prefer it to the hackneyed Leonardo and our eternal over-patterned Botticelli." "O but I don't agree with you, Sir Know-all." "The acme of art is—" Going on and on and on and the music was coming now. Not Walter's music. There was music and Walter's music and this was not Walter's. Something not to be listened to that differed from Walter's music as the flat plaster fruits (for all their fitted-in elegance) in the lofty Georgian ceiling differed from the incarnate South, the tendrils of grape and the one tuft of blossom and the odd pine-cone. "Luca della Robbia—" It was going on. The voice that said, "Della Robbia" was going on. One could listen to the voice. It was like these other odd voices, cultivated yet containing something else, something slightly different. The voice came from the end of the divan but Hermione, seated square before the fire on a low pouffe did not turn to face its suave producer. The voice made her think of real things suddenly though she had an odd un-nerving suspicion that it was not a real person who so spoke, "Della Robbia and by God, the Baptistry—"

Voices. Notes. The voices were stopping out of some sort of politeness for George had turned. The two candles flared in exact symmetry and George (as Hermione twisted on the pouffe to watch him) stood in amazing radiance like some pre quattro-cento saint before an altar. Or was it Signorelli? Taddeo Gaddi. George brought to mind these perfect compositions though he himself was rough a little, a little too rough, something powerful and strong in old George though people had a way of sniggering, "decadent." What was decadent? Not George. Facing them with his head flung back, with his excellent throat emerging from his loose collar, George tossed back a petulant lock. Began: "Sith when I met thee in thy bark of painted sandal wood." He went on for some time in that strain and as he reached the pause at the end of what appeared to be the fiftieth line (though in all conscience it must have been about the fifth) the other protagonist began deep harp-like notes, strumming on the piano deep well ordered, well ordained notes yet futile. The producer of the notes was no amateur nor was George yet the effect was amateurish. George had hair the colour of autumn grapes, red grapes in the sun. The lights across the petulant locks of George made a picture. It was too strong, too forthright to be Italian. Late perhaps. Venetian. Tall candles and a mop of fleece. Veronese. The notes began what was presumably a prelude to the next stanza. And George discontinued.

"Odd fellow. Lowndes. Quaint fellow Lowndes." The voice was slightly patronizing. "Always think of the first time I met him. It was at Prescott's. They were handing around the fruit and old Hawky said 'George, a pear or a peach' and George said 'neither thank you, nor a pomegranate'—" It was going on. Odd notes. The hands that swung back and forth, right and left were trained, actual musician hands. What was wrong with the whole thing? O but don't criticize. Don't think, Hermione. Let it go on, on, on. Voices like music. Music like voices. No art defined here, not stark outstanding terror of Beauty. Candles that make incomparable shadows not the dandelion puffs of

Vérène's rooms on the Avenue de Clichy. The river. The Seine. The Thames. London. Going on and on and on. Other people drifting. Other people leaving. It was late, not late enough, too late. "Dryad." "Yes—George?" "Dreaming, Dryad? Did you like the opus?" "Whose George?" "Mine, dearest Dryad. I thought myself quite fetching." "Fetching yes. You seem to have fetched everybody." "Why this petulance, Dryad?" "Jealous, I suppose." "Why Dryad?" "I should like to be—somebody." "What are you now Dryad?" But how tell him? What are you now Dryad? I am something like a magic lantern sheet and on it the most horrible of dreary pictures. There is a town called Liverpool and miles of black docks. Rain. And rain. And rain. That is Liverpool. Trains hoot and trains rumble and somebody says "miss hurry off here the first bell's sounded." Climb up and up and up long stairs, nice walls, I suppose but how horrible. This is not a boat. This is not a boat. This is to boats what other music is to Walter's music. "Yes, Clara I think it so much more sensible to have come third on a huge boat than to risk the winter storms on one like we had. You *are* lucky." Fling down your bundle of flowers, your little bundle so guarded and treasured all that disheartening journey from Victoria. Boat train. Yes boat train, *not* the continent. Liverpool, the Ouratania. Ouratania. Urania. Boat. Are you a boat? Hermione climbed up from the cellar of a huge white hotel that floated on the water. Below, far below a bundle of flowers spilled fragrance on the clean bunk. Sheets like cast iron but clean. Not like Rouen. Not like Havre. Clean already as if already the sterilized breath of the sterilized States had touched them. Flowers are spilling on the floor. "Don't cry, Fayne Rabb. All the things I said to you were nothing, nothing. I never really meant them. I whipped myself up to one of my fits because you said you liked them. You're right to stay with Clara." "But you, darling?" "I told you long ago, I couldn't go back. Not go back. I have to stay. I *have* to stay in England."

Boats hooting. The very gulls drab and with soot-coloured feathers. Buoys bobbing like dead men in the stagnant water. Rain dripping. It's going thank God. Thank God. "Did you say something?" A voice she recognised, a voice she knew, had always somehow, somewhere known, a voice that seemed to mean nothing but that gave her the sense of things inexpressible behind it. "O nothing much. I was thinking of some—people." "Friends, enemies, idiots, saints or devils?" "Some of those things. Most of those things. I don't know. Yes, all of those things." "At once or at different times and how often?" "O, at once and at different times and sometimes all together and I think always." "Like when is a monkey a barber and how many times would a wood-chuck chuck?" "Something like that." "Is there an answer then?" "I don't think so." "But there must be. Now think hard. Anyhow tea-cakes help the brain. More tea?" "I hadn't wanted it." "Hadn't. We all felt that way. But after hearing dear old Lowndes and that fragrant cedar wood, we all (I speak for the committee) feel somewhat blind-O." "Blind-O—what?" "Famished. Starved. Hungry. I myself eat nothing for ten days and then eat." "Is the ten days up then?" "No. It begins to-morrow." "Why *do* you eat and not eat?" "Family. I can't stand too much of 'em. If I don't eat it annoys 'em." "What a brilliant idea. And if they don't?" "O, but they *do*." "Do what?" "George."

"So you've found each other?" It was George speaking. "Found who? What other?" "Each—the other. I've been making a most careful cal-*cu*-lation." George was speaking in poor Bertrand's sustained and careful utterance. But only Hermione would know this. George was being pleasant, charming. One could see that. "I think our rag will do the sonnet series, Darrington." The other person had scrambled to his feet and offered George the twin pouffe (due deference to the Lyre's sub-editor) beside Hermione. Hermione only just thought to look at the other person, whose voice was (had been from the first) so oddly vibrant. He flung back from his shoulders as he answered the summons of someone shaking (at him) a gilt brocade bag across the room, "ask *Her*." "Darrington, you know Hermione, don't you?" "O very well. Yes. For a long time." "Where? When? At Prescott's we may gather." "Further than that. It was well say about B.C. 325 (pre fifth anyhow) in Thessaly. Maybe Tempe."

"Then you know Darrington?" "Yes, I think so." "You can't think you know a person. You know or don't know. *Do* you know him?" "I told you, George, yes. I said I think so." "You met him at Delia's, at one of her eternal functions. You should have told me." "Why should I have told you, Georgio, I'd met Darrington?" "Well for one thing I was giving myself the express pleasure of—presenting you. I suppose your Philadelphia Book of Etiquette would state it that way." "Why worry so about me? I knew all along." (She didn't know why she was telling these lies.) "I'm sorry you were disappointed in it." "O Darrington. I say there Darrington." George evidently wanted corroboration of these statements. He put his two fingers to his mouth and whistled. Candles seemed to waver, to break, to fall sideways. A bunch of winter-daffodils seemed to come to life, to light the whole room with the glow that had till now been utterly disregarded. "I didn't see there were daffodils in that glass bowl in the corner." "There were people crowding about, Dryad. Someone should have told you." She ignored his irony lost in admiration of the whistle that didn't seem to make any difference to anybody. Most of the party had gone. The hardy representatives still lingering were evidently used to George Lowndes' vagaries. "Don't take any notice. He's always doing these things. The way really to annoy him is to pretend not to notice." A voice near Hermione, someone near the bowl of daffodils. She turned to watch this subtle analyst of George's character. George was about to lift his Pan fingers to his Pan mouth (he affected a slight whisp of grape-gold beard in those days but you would hardly notice) when hands descended. Someone's hands descended from near the daffodils, courageous little hands, fingers like thin wires, small hands really. Hands closed over George's mouth. A slim elegant shape crowded into the divan between Hermione and George Lowndes. This was just a little casual of it also, "George darling." George had removed the hands from his mouth and was gallantly in his best Provincial manner kissing them. Backs of small hands. Yes, George did it nicely.

The small slim creature quivered a small slim back, slim and excellently tailored in dark sleek very deep maroon red. A sort of very dark dahlia colour. The head bent back against the wall, and the small body curled nearer, neater into the black and gold enormous Japanese embroidered cushion. The creature turned its back utterly on Hermione. This was casual, rude really. Who was this curled, defiant (yet somehow with all the casual air of knowing what it was up to), beside George Lowndes? Hermione felt for the first time in some time, a little gasp of terror. Really terror. Did she still love George Lowndes?

What was one to do? Should one ignore the creature? Its voice purred into George's ear. "So quaint of you dearest to read *that* poem." "Why Princess Lointaine?" "Well you told me, didn't you, it was written for—me?" "Did I? Maybe. But you see I tell everybody that." "O George. Shockingly inadequate. If you are being cutting, *be* cutting." "I leave that for you, Maria della Trinità." "Trinità? Why exactly?" "You are, aren't you, obviously the World, the Flesh and the—" "Spirit, put it George." Someone had descended. It was the voice that had some time ago enthralled Hermione. The whistle had produced, like Aladdin's lamp, the slave. It was Darrington.

Two of them now. Hermione slunk further into the corner of the divan. She wasn't it was obvious, having at all her way. Who was this maroon dahlia coloured person who had outright stolen George? George had been petting her, making himself charming. It appeared suddenly to Hermione that perhaps she had been taking George too much for granted, too much her own property. Part of the past. Part of Philadelphia. Here George was something different, lionized, a person.

Maybe they wouldn't notice. But what agony listening. Did she still love then George? "Lointaine. If you *don't* mind—" "What dear George?" "There's someone in the corner, you've not noticed." "O yes, I have. I did. But is it grown up? Why do you ever let it come to parties?" The little back remained obstinately turned upon her. O who was it? Someone, somewhere? "But can't you say good-afternoon, good-evening?" "No. Mary can't. She's not going to be allowed." It was the other one now speaking. "She can't and dare not." "Dare not? Young upstart? And who are you? Imagine." "I am I. Me. Mary. I'm her latest cavalier. I'm Darrington to the rescue." O now she had it. Now Hermione had it. This was Mary Dalton. That *Dalton* woman. How odd she had forgotten.

"I can't imagine why she didn't speak to me." "She's like that." "Yes. But I met her, had tea with her especially at Delia's. The Prescotts'. George says you know them." "Mary's like that." "Yes, but I don't understand. Why? What's it all about? Do people *cut* people like in novels? Did she cut me?" "I believe so." "But I've never been *cut*. What's it about? Why?" "Don't ask me to follow the mad intricacies of our mad Ophelia." "Is she? Is she really mad then like Ophelia?" "No. Not a bit like Ophelia." "People warned me. Said she was odd, awful. George did. And then suddenly she's beside him, having cut across our conversation and he's kissing her hands in the approved troubadour fashion." "But isn't that too characteristic of old Lowndes?" "Is it?

I don't know. I knew him very well in Philadelphia. Here he's different." "Wouldn't George take on colour from any setting?" "I don't know. I was just thinking how strong he was really and how kind. I liked the way he whistled across the room and I liked the way nobody paid any attention to him." "Maria paid attention." "Why do you call her Maria?" "I don't." "But you did, you do."

Hydrangeas lifted round plum-coloured and shell pink and white balls of heavy porcelain beauty. Heavy porcelain beauty. "I'm glad you found me. Dragged me out of the corner into this conservatory. I was so wretched, miserable. It was so funny your coming across too and sitting on the other foot-stool. It was so funny. I was thinking." "One could see that, Astraea." "Astraea. Why do you call me that?" "I don't know. Does one ever know why one does or doesn't do these things? What does old Lowndes call you?" "O Undine sometimes." "Lowndes is wrong there. You have no heart like Undine." "Undine. Did Undine have a heart?" "I don't know. I think so. I move by intuition when I see you. When I saw you. You know what's the matter with me? I always wanted a beautiful mother. I should like to have had a mother like you."

8 | She shouldn't wear the violets that he sent her for she had found out in a number of little ways, whispers, innuendoes, outright comment, that he wasn't rich. He had given the impression of an insouciance that went with wealth, had thrown his head back, had grubbed in pockets for taxi fare, had said he hated good clothes. People at Delia's, the most smart (Delia had pointed out) were the most shabby. "Fenton with his Eton affectations." People who had been to Eton, to Cambridge, were allowed to slouch into rooms, to wear their clothes anyway. People wore or didn't wear clothes as they did (or didn't) in America. Each country had its standards. It was here apparently "smart" (as they called it) to be shabby. "You have to be a Duchess to dress like a fish-wife." Someone had commented on someone who was not a Duchess but who dressed like one. "It's sheer crass outrage. Putting on airs. She's making out her pedigree to be somewhat on the grand scale." "How do you mean, Delia? But she's shabby." "I mean that people here can't be shabby unless they're great. We are not obliged to accept that amount of dowdiness from a solicitor's widow. Plus the grand air. Noblesse oblige. But she isn't. We are not obliged to accept her just because she's shabby." It was all very complicated. Certain people had to be smart, others were allowed not to be. It was affectation to be too well dressed or it was an outrage not to be better dressed. Hermione had long ago given it all up. Her own little ideas had been further confused by George Lowndes. "You're too nun-ish. That grey might be all right in Philadelphia." But she didn't care now. Something in her didn't any more care. Someone had said he liked her in her slightly draped effects, the grey that flowed like water (he said) though she wasn't Undine. Someone had said that everything she wore was perfect, different from anything he had yet seen, right and smart and yet not over-done. Not, as he said, obvious. Someone had said he hated English women with that rank colour (did he mean the Dalton?) and their grabbing insistencies. Someone had said English women were harpies, were dowds, were immaculate prudes or were Hell harpies. Someone had said there were in England pas de nuances (he said it in that French way) and that he had found in her the veritable Golden Fleece. Golden Fleece. Star. What did he not call her? His phrases, his expletives were marred when judged by intellectual standards. When judged by the intellect they were perhaps trite, shallow. Hermione did not judge them by the intellect. Something seemed to flow in her, about her. She had been hurt. Someone had seen that. Before she offered any explanation. Having offered explanation, he had seen it further. "But damn. I never knew a girl who read Greek." "I don't." "I mean I never met a woman who knew remotely what Greek, what Greece stood for. You might do some essays." "O essays? George thinks I'll spoil my—style, he calls it, by essays (as far as I can make out) anything." "Lowndes has printed something?" "No. He says I'm not modern enough and I'm too modern." "What does he think he means by that?" "I don't know. He doesn't. But he wants to—to—somehow suppress me."

George seemed to have put himself out no end to damp her ardour. Always with some little jibe. "Why don't you move out of that infernal Bloomsbury? You can't live there." She had finally moved to Portman Square. But she didn't like it very much. "You must live somewhere that I can send my friends to." "But I don't want you, your friends." "You can't expect me or anyone to call on

you in Bloomsbury." "No. Not in this house. I have only my room."
"Well you have to clear out to somewhere somehow decent. You
can't stay on here." It seemed he was purposely wilful, purposely
dragging her up, away. It was just as well he did this. The fog, the
mist—crouched on the floor thinking—thinking. Rain had dripped
and dripped. November. November in Bloomsbury. December. December in Portman Square. A drawing room and a knot of bridge
playing habitués. "O Miss Gart. What? Another caller."

But this wasn't Portman Square. It was other. The Elgin Marble
room, mid-winter afternoon. Violets pushed down into her grey
long coat and violets breathed up into her face. Violets. These were
curled slightly at the edges, slightly ruffled, a little different from all
other violets. Ivy leaves about the bunch made a stiff little case, a
holder for these violets like a Victorian wedding bouquet. The ivy
leaves held the flowers stiff, gave them power, authorised them to
flow outward being held so close. Ivy. The Bacchanalias. Ivy leaves.

She had found the clue now and this was it. Jerrold Darrington had
given her the clue. This was the clue, the thing that had been for
some two (almost three) months lacking. Darrington had given her
in his odd witty way the clue. Darrington said the old Theseus there
looked as if he had fallen over board, got worn thin with sea-water.
The torse of Theseus from the Parthenon pediment did look that
way. "We'll go upstairs, look at those Tanagras." What was it Darrington had that all the others hadn't? He was different somehow.
He cared about things, didn't laugh when she said she wanted to see
some old Persian manuscripts she had read about once in America.
America even drew no smile, no cynical jibe from his store of quick
repartee, of quick and bantering cynicism. When she said "America"
she expected him to say (she was even in those days affable to all
these witticisms) "Where's that?" He didn't. It was somehow so odd.
What was it about Darrington. When she asked him he said "I
suppose it was the misalliance. My governor you know married a
country wench. Damn clever of her. She copped the old fellow down
hunting. I was born six months after though they say in hushed tones
poor Ned was a seven months' baby. Damn fool the governor. One's
people are one's damned ruin. They'll do me in yet." Darrington
spoke freely, seemed to have no prejudices yet in his speaking he

recalled other people, people who have the right to be dowdy she had met at Delia's. He was that odd combination of the old flowering charm and something other. Something serious. Something that seemed to care and care so deeply. Was it the country wench simply that had copped the governor? "My governor's a damn fool. Lost all his money speculating. Damn fool to have got caught I told him. Went to America under a nom de guerre, something like Cecil de Longchamps. I laugh myself sick sometimes thinking of that name. Poor old governor. Even yet when he can raise the fare we dash across to Paris. He used to say Jerry, don't you worry. Two thousand a year when you come of age. Two thousand a year. It wasn't two boblet." Darrington père had been unsuccessful in his little venture. "Not that I blame the old bloke. It was his getting caught simply. The people in our part of the world (the governor's Sussex Darrington) wouldn't know us. Not that the mater ever made herself popular with the county. The governor now lives on his prestige, his ancient glory. Four quarterings though what good does that do? They aren't his anyhow by rights, some shift over of my great grandmother's name. We were originally Darrington-Nortons. However we shifted it, Norton-Darrington. Now it's Darrington." Hermione was charmed with this odd light on ancient history. Darrington to the rescue.

"I'm late again." "No. No. I had to hurry out of that Portman Square atmosphere or get caught, glued tight into it and anyhow I was afraid of George coming." "Afraid of dear old Lowndes. Don't you like him?" "I don't know. He seems bent on undermining my morale recently. He knows I'm reticent, frightened, afraid to talk about things and he rushes in, tells me all the horrid things everyone's been saying." "Horrid things, Astraea?" "O not horrid. Just odd. It seems the Dalton now for instance calls me Fiammetta and whenever she does call me Fiammetta (George did what was apparently a good imitation) people burst with laughter. I don't know why. Perhaps it's really funny." "Yes, it is Astraea. There's something funny in Dalton calling you Fiammetta. I can hear her do it. I can hear each syllable as she pronounces it. That woman has some sort of power. She has the devil's own wit." "But what have I done? Why does she want to blight me?" "Fiammetta. There's something awfully funny" (though he said it seriously) "in that."

Light filtered through fog and the effect was as of some vision, some dream room, built up of dream stuff from some other planet. It was not the world this. Nereids from the Nereid portal broke the sifted yellow light with triangulated drapery. An arm lifted in that curious mellow flow of curious colour. An arm lifted and seemed about to part the gauze fog that had so suddenly descended. Voices from the other room, feet shuffling. "The curve of the Parthenon steps is perhaps the most remarkable comment on the Attic genius. You will notice from this angle that the small model in the right hand case gives in its minute way the exact proportion. Bend lower from the side and you will see the step curve. Yet from the distance they appear straight." Comment on the genius of antiquity. Darrington saw this. "Funny all this, these people. Nereids and you, Astraea. Nothing has ever seemed real before, the governor, rows at home, rowing me now, even now trying to make me respectable." "Respectable. Aren't you?" "Not as he wants, they want. Old friends, Percy Lubbock, offered to see me through the law. Couldn't stand it. They think now I'm a lost soul and I never see them except when I'm really hungry." "Are you ever, really—" But how go on with it? If he were hungry ever she shouldn't take the violets. The violets breathed fresh up into her face as she felt her throat lift toward those Nereids for some solution. Should or should I not then take his violets? Darrington had laid violets at her shrine in that same spirit as in old days people brought milk and rose-leaves to those Nereids. There was something else too that would express this. Where, where was it? Somewhere. Was it a Persian manuscript? "If you have two loaves, sell one and buy narcissus."

She seemed to hold the soul of Jerrold Darrington in her hands. He was right when he said he wanted a beautiful mother. He was her child.

9 She was telling him things (still later one afternoon still later in winter) that she would never have thought she could tell anybody, things it appeared she had not even been aware of. "Clara got so on one's nerves you see. She wanted to be autocratic and whenever I made what I thought was a pretty gesture she said I was ill-bred." "Actually said?" "Thought. It was in

the air. She was so superior to everyone. Not like old Eugenia."
"Eugenia must be rather an old darling." "No. She was cruel." "All
mothers are. You mustn't take it hard. All parents are monsters of
cruelty. They would rather one died in their clutches than that one
winged out of it, loose." "Died?" "Yes. Much rather. They haven't
the decency of hawks, not the respectability of tigers. Tigers, hawks
let their young loose to grow. Our parents feed on us like vampires
on raw flesh." "Isn't that—rather—rather—" "Strong? No not half
strong enough, Astraea. You're not free of the thing really. You think
you are. They'll come back and nab you." "O don't say that. Don't say
that—" But he said it again quite slowly emphasizing each word.
"Do you think a thing like you can last for ever? Here you are,
Astraea, in that fiendish Portman Square atmosphere. How can it
continue. If I don't marry you someone else will." "Marry me?"
"Hadn't you thought about it? Isn't it what we've been thinking of all
the time?" Lights dimmed about them made pools of rose like great
rose peonies in a half sun-lit garden. Great lights, shaded lights,
from overhead made a mellow glow and the separated little table
lamps opened as it were flower hearts toward that invisible shaded
gold light. Music from a distant corner wailed out its plaintive prelude. Something extra, something different, people had a way of
slipping up and asking for separate numbers. Who had asked for
this? Was it herself simply?

Water was about her. The cold sea-pebbles and the wind in distant
tree tops. Music. Not Walter's music. But it was not true. She had
said there were two kinds of music, Walter's and other music, but
now that Walter had returned to Paris, she must modify her statement. There were other kinds of music as many kinds as there were
winds, cloud shapes or mountain torrents. This shape of music was
something she had seen before, contemplated in her intensity, made
her own. She had heard this a thousand times and a thousand times
it had eluded her. People. Faces. Where had she so heard it? A
diamond dart that caught a Gainsborough feather dropping gallantly
over a wide hat brim recalled her. A diamond dart, faces, heads grey
and brown and mouse-brown and pure white dressed immaculately
with shell combs. Faces, the backs of heads somewhere. "I don't
exactly know—" Why did she speak? Other people were quiet. Why
must she alone speak? It was somewhere different. She was not here.
O, Darrington for a joke had asked her (was it for a joke?) perhaps to

marry him. To consider him there anyhow for the taking. Music. The pebbles that shone and glinted in the mountain torrent, tortoise shell coloured pebbles. Yes that was the real colour of Walter's eyes, not amber but tortoise shell. Hard like shell and light glazed across them. "I—have—a friend—in Paris." A friend in Paris, music.

"You mean you want to marry him?" "O God—no. Imagine him anyway asking me to do it? No, no, no, no, no. I mean the music." "Aren't you rather vague? Now just what is it?" He always spoke so banteringly with her as if each thing he said was nothing, as if the very fact of his so speaking nullified his statement. She had never heard seriousness overlaid with such indifference; she had never heard indifference stamped and moulded with sincerity. What of him was real? What lacquer? Part of him somehow wasn't there, was vague like the rose light of these great peonies that reached up toward the invisible luminous atmosphere. Hermione felt herself grey, a grey mist beside the rose warm glow of him, the thing she couldn't quite define but that seemed to draw her up, up out of some cold clear water like a closed rose-lotos bud toward sunlight. Something in him, of him, about him, that she had no words for. Was it seeing simply as God sees? Was he rose light, was rose-light about him? What he said or did would make no difference to it any more than what Walter said or did could alter the cold snow-white that was about him. Walter was snow ridged with glacial blue. Darrington was so different. "No. It's the music simply." "You think of him then when you're hearing music?" "No, no. That's just it. I don't think of him when I'm hearing music." "What then were you thinking? You must tell me." He spoke simply, sincerely this time. And in her mind, in her perception she saw again sincerely. Not rose glow and countless people and a diamond crescent catching a Gainsborough feather. Not the tea tables and the room beyond and the gay odd atmosphere and the knowledge that Regent Street outside was soft and fair with fog that flowed like a clean river. Not that. This simply. The lilting sweet and penetrating song of Solveig. "It was Solveig's song that they just now finished, wasn't it?" She knew in the moment of framing the question that it was. It was Solveig's song and a face beside which other faces in the world must be blurred and mis-shapen. A face that destroyed other faces was before her. "You see I saw Fayne Rabb first in a play. A play called Galatea. She was Pygmalion." "Yes?" "She came across a carpet, a dark carpet in sandals. She wore a robe flung over one shoulder and her knees were bare. No. That wasn't the first time I saw her. The first time I saw her was at Nellie—Nellie Thorpe—yes her name was Thorpe. Her sister took a prize in Paris. They wanted Fayne to take the prix de Rome." "Yes?" "There were other people there. Lots of people I knew, some I didn't. Fayne Rabb lifted her hand and said Koeuthoi Moi Agaiachoio—no, she doesn't know any Greek but she spoke that way. She lifted her hand simply—" "Yes and further?" "Further? It stretched before and behind. It stretches like a path on water toward the stars, a path that leads to the star Hesperus and that leads back again to the rocks and the small crabs and star-fish fastened to the low tide pools. The path she trod across the dark strip of carpet (it was a studio scene of Nellie Thorpe's and there was a good touch, a tall azalea in a pseudo-classic wine-jar) and Fayne spoke. It was Solveig's song upset me. They played it in the interval, before, after. I just don't remember." "I see." "You see you gave me Greek books to read. Not too hard. Something in you understands all this. I don't myself understand much of it. You know more Greek than I do." "And am less." "Perhaps you are less. You aren't authentic fifth or even pre-fifth. You're late, a sort of Graeco-Roman over flowering period." "I am a bit florid at times. True British roast beef." "No not that. In your soul flowering, flowering—" What was there to describe him? "Like these rose lights rather." "Pink frilled lamp shade to modify the ardour of the Attic genius?" "Yes, that simply. You are that. I burn too high, too hard. Fayne would, I think, kill me some-time. I don't see or think or feel—" She didn't know what she thought or felt for her head bent forward. Her eyes were blurred, merciful blurr that turned the room to some odd unreality like seeing a garden through a window pane, opaque with driven rain drops. The music soft and tender, nothing much one way or the other and the feeling suddenly that she was lost and lonely. "I don't really—miss—them—" Darrington was getting the bill. It wasn't that he minded her making a scene but brushing her tears away most gal-lantly she saw that waiters stirred and moved about them. They were clearing the little tea tables and re-setting them for dinner. Everyone almost had now gone. "We'll not let this go on much longer darling. You see I'm afraid your bed will suddenly turn into Zeus in the night—you're the sort of thing that would draw God from heaven—and thwart me."

10 Marry him. Marry him. Marry him? What is—marriage? Don't marry him. Marry. Him. What is— "But you can't *marry* him." Who said that? Someone had said that somewhere. In an atelier that they had taken over the Seine. They lived over the Seine in the very rightest avenue. No. Clichy. That was Vérène. Marry him. Had Vérène married him? Who would marry him if Vérène didn't marry him? Vérène married him. Vérène was the deep under-drone, the masculine bee-hum that married the stark and glittering bride veil of the Undine waters. Not waters. Walter. Vérène's violon-cello married Walter's bride notes and that was marriage of the spirit. Marry him. Marry whom? "But you can't *marry* him." Who said that? Who kept on repeating that at shorter intervals, saying it from nowhere, from somewhere. Where was it that she said it. Who was it said it? Was it dear Eugenia. Marry him. Yes Eugenia said marry because they have a house on the Riviera. No. No. No. Eugenia would never say a thing so blankly. She said marry because he wanted babies—no because he didn't want babies—no, because he has a degree from Munich and admires your verses. No not verses. He admires your intellect whatever he thinks he means by just that. Marry him. "But you can't *marry* him."

Who couldn't marry whom and what was it all about and who couldn't whoever it was marry if she (or he) so wanted it? But did they want it (he or she) and whatever was it all about? There was all this fuss about marry, marry. Do. Don't do. Marry. Do or don't. But go about it neatly. All a matter of technique, your verses.

What was the matter with her verses and who said it? It was George who had said it. He had taken other verses. Whose? Darrington's sonnet sequence. But that was Darrington. A huge large name on a page. Looks well Jerrold Darrington. O that was it. Yes, it would look well Mrs. Jerrold Darrington. Marry whom? Look well, Mrs. Darrington. Nobody making faces because she was miss-miss-hit or miss. She was damn sick of it. Quaint. She was a quaint person. They would keep on saying it. Hit or miss. Well . . . she wouldn't be a quaint . . . hit or miss. Mrs. Jerrold Darrington, a person. A person. Quaint, a hybrid. No hybrid.

Someone said she was funny but no hybrid. "Throw-back. She belongs here." Someone at a party said she belonged to England. Mrs. Jerrold Darrington. *Was* she funny but no hybrid? Did she (someone had said so at a party) then belong to England? Marry him. "But you can't *marry* him." O of course, she couldn't. Now, now she had remembered. It was in a wrong street in the wrong part of Philadelphia. Fayne looked câline from under her thick fringe. There was a basket spilling flowers. "Mama gets such adoration from her girls. It's shocking." A basket spilling flowers. "But you can't *marry* him."

No, of course she couldn't marry George Lowndes. She should have known that from the start but she had to keep him on, to prod him on, actually went to his rooms and told him she was ready, to check-mate old Eugenia. She liked Darrington. Yes, it was Darrington who had asked her. She was on a bed, a great bed (a Zeus-bed he called it) not a boat and this was London. Of course this was London. A clock striking, that little church like a cheese-box George said. A church like a cheese box standing all arrogant just in the way of the traffic. Churches in London never moved an inch for all the traffic. That was the nice thing about them. That was the nice thing about London. Would Darrington be like that? Just there, rather square-set, a little heavy (when he wasn't too hungry) with his damn-your-eyes attitude about parents and his understanding of Fayne Rabb. Would Darrington let her stay for Hermione (someone had said so at a party) was their someone out of Shakespeare and belonged here. She wanted an anchor. She wanted a haven. Would Darrington want her, understand when she told him about George Lowndes? After all, George had kissed and kissed her. Famished kisses like a desert wind full of sand, the wrong flowers, hybiscus, scarlet line of his really beautiful mouth. People said he was shockingly beautiful. She didn't want to marry—"but you can't *marry* him." No, she couldn't. She was glad though that Fay had told her. She was glad to know so exactly with such prescience that Fay *did* think of marriage . . . the room coming clear and her thoughts coming clear at the same time. Other clocks a little later took up the late one—two. One—two. Then another very far and far and far, one—two. Two o'clock and the street lamp from outside casting light across and up. Lights in London were all mysterious. Lights in the day, lights at night. There wasn't any more any day or night and now it was February and it was odd there were wedges of crocus, wedges of crocuses and an almond against a wall. An almond had blossomed against a wall outside the park. She had seen it on the way to Delia's. There was no winter in London. It was all spring. Spring. Spring.

November had even seemed a sort of acrid spring. Water dripping. Spring. Spring. Spring. The Pirenian spring. Darrington said she could, must write. He had made her translate some things from the Anthology. I send you, Rhodocleia for your hair. I send you Rhodocleia this wreath for your hair. I send you this wreath, one open rose, open anemone, twisted narcissus stems. No that wasn't it. She couldn't get it quite right. It was just as well Fayne had been so clear about it for she couldn't marry Darrington. Fayne had been so sure, so certain. Fayne had finished with—all—that. She seemed to know what she meant and said it. She said she had developed beyond *that*, wasn't that low in the biologic scale or something like it. Fayne with her clear eyes and her sullen brow. "But I'm not going to marry him, Fayne Rabb."

"But I thought you were engaged to him and I thought you broke it off." Was she engaged to him? Kisses arid but not here (in London) quite so full of desert heat and blinding wilting sand, met hers. Her mouth lifted and kisses bent and flowered upon it. The warmth of the tropic hybiscus red of George Lowndes was somehow tempered, somehow lost in this thing. The fog that drifted, that lifted, the late winter (or the early spring) bride veil of glistening, glamourous mist. "I love the mist, the fog. It seems I never was so happy." Kisses nullified her, nullified her pain, there was no pain in her heart. She had forgotten simply. In London the desert sun was modified and the hyacinths lifted simply. Mist and glamour and the annihilating beauty. George Lowndes was beautiful. Here people did not laugh at George. People asked his opinion, a little reverently. It was funny watching people reverencing George. He had done a book on Dante and Provence and Renaissance Latin poetry. Georgio in London. His odd clothes not so odd, his little brush of a beard and his velvet coat and his cravats like flowers in mosaic of maroon and green and gilt and odd vermillion. George didn't look odd though he looked more odd than ever. People seemed to understand, did not waste time commenting on his clothes. Said, "George Lowndes, odd fellow . . . he has a flair for beauty."

Georgio had a flair, had always had it. George being tender, thoughtful suddenly. "Getting enough to eat, Undine?" "O lots. Yes." "I make a point of looking up old Mrs. Towers once a week to find out." "Yes, George. She tells me when you drop in. She adores you." "Had a room once years ago in my affluent days when we crossed with my damn aunt who just won't pass out." "O George. Don't let poverty depress you." "It ain't my own exactly—" "Then whose is it?"

George seemed to be on the point of telling her something and the studio was empty. It was really empty and the floating veils of the floating laughter and people's funny clothes that yet looked right in London and their hostess, Katherine Farr. Katherine Farr whom they admired and a little despised with her huge circulation, with her one or two novels a year, all good, all a little better than anyone else's and yet not good enough for them. Katherine was so kind, had paused especially to ask her. People were kind. "I want you especially to wait on. I want you and George to stay and have some supper."

Hermione had stayed with George in Katherine's studio and it seemed perhaps the most beautiful of many, many beautiful studios, of many lovely afternoons that turned at a breath to evening and then turned (like Danaë in her sleep) to night. Mist and night and dawn took on significance. They held here personality, were people. Four o'clock was a person who entered somewhat briskly, five o'clock was announced in a hushed ambassadorial whisper. Six, seven and eight. Nine, ten and eleven. Was it the way clocks struck, muffled under mist like bells beneath sea water? The castle under the sea that Walter played to them in Clichy here took form, was something. People came and went but the people had less personality than hours, than things. Was it all haunted, here under the sea? England. Had anyone ever, could anyone ever have loved as she did?

"People come like hours and hours transform themselves to people." "Which hours? Which people?" "Well that frump on the New Era for example it seems to me must be three o'clock. A lost hour, an hour that's somehow lost, hasn't a lover." "Yes. Three o'clock is somewhat that." "I think of Mary Dalton as somehow always just about eleven. Something hectic before mid-night. An illicit extra cock-tail (but that's not the time for cock-tails). What do I mean? I don't associate her with wine but she sets me shaking as if I had been upset, as if someone had offered me a crème-de-menthe instead of early morning tea." "Rather neat that." "Katherine Farr here with her solid novels and her income and her kindness seems some inevitable but somehow rather stern hour. Which is it? Is it nine and all the day before one at a hard desk?" "Poor Katherine." "You could make her, do, into something odd, a little quaint. She might be sometimes the hours moles crawl (she seems like a mole with eyes) out thinking it is night but finding dawn. Just as dawn breaks yet hadn't the courage of its flowering." "Katherine on the whole is the best fellow of the damn lot." "I didn't say she wasn't. Perhaps that's just it. I want her to like me. I feel somehow she doesn't." "But she goes out of her way. Asked you to stay this time." "Yes, isn't that a little guilty complex? She doesn't really like me. She looks at me and thinks why don't I like the little American Her Gart? She looks and wonders. She sees I'm not very old nor very horrible. She can't say I'm actually a viper. She wants some excuse for her slight bewilderment. I'm apparently a nice girl and I'm living alone in Portman Square and it sounds a bit fishy about my expecting (perhaps) my mother soon to join me. She thinks I'm nice and I don't do things nice girls do. This for instance." "Katherine doesn't know you do this." "Yes, she does. Everybody does. Somehow everything one does here is everybody's property. I know and feel she must know. Why did she ask me to stay on here with you?" "Perhaps I asked her to." "Does that alter it? Would a nice girl do it?" "Well we were— I mean—we—" "We were engaged. What's that got to do with it? It's just the one reason according to ordinary standards I shouldn't do this." Famished and forgetting she lifted hyacinths to George's kisses.

Drugged and drunk she said she had forgotten. Drugged with the hybiscus colour, with the odd tremors that the clock made striking, striking. Clocks were always striking and the colour of the mist was different. She was sure that each vibration of each clock sent shivers, tremors through the mist. Little paths of light. The bells of Saint Clement's. Lemons. Not lemon light, silver rather, those high bell notes. Notes, bells . . . who is it in me, what is it in me, hears bells, notes? Morse code . . . Gart formula . . . Walter could you tell me? Bells made forms, notes, pictures were notes and bells made pictures, Walter said, so that he could play when she made a picture (he said) with the two candles against the grey-grey of the Clichy studio walls . . . suppressed, something suppressed that sees the very ring and quiver of the clock notes make strange pattern. O I am so happy.

George . . . and people came in after supper and the candles make exquisite daffodils in the great brown studio. One had even understood Katherine Farr in that light. Katherine. Maybe someone, someone somewhere called her Katy when she was little. Katy did Katy didn't. She was rather like a Katy did, small and compact, some little busy insect, chirping, scraping music out of its legs, not bird music, not frog music even, but music of a sort (everybody's music of a sort) understanding other people. Yes, Katherine did understand, was not surprised when she had come back, found Her crouched low before the fire. Nothing mattered. Her had done nothing to matter. After all, George's hybiscus red *did* make a warm coal glow somewhere in her heart. She had a heart. A red heart. Someone, everyone (who was it?) said she wasn't like Undine as she had no heart. Who said that? Darrington. But Darrington didn't matter. It was a pity about Darrington as she liked the Greek books. Darrington who helped her poetry. But what was poetry? George was right, had long ago, been right. *You are a poem though your poem's naught.* Why should she have questioned. Striven. George would write for them both. No. She wasn't any more engaged. Was she? Wasn't she? Did it really matter? It was something George gave her here in London. The silver of the mist tempered the heat of Georgio. She didn't any more care though of course she couldn't marry him. "But you can't of course *marry* him." No, of course, she couldn't. Ringing, ringing downstairs. She supposed she'd have to put on the lights, tidy her hair, too late to change. But that didn't matter. People were polite, didn't stare. People were all right. Even old Mrs. Towers since Lady Prescott (Delia) came to see her. Delia said the place was funny, frightfully "army." What did "army" mean or "army" matter? Delia said this was and laughed to people in chairs all about, in tiny islands. Bridge. People being discreet. Lady Prescott.

Nothing mattered, could matter. Light made the room a little common but did that matter (had she been asleep?) a knock and hot water. How funny hot water and no proper running water in the bath room. Baths but real baths not casual rushing in to wash your hands. Water in little pots with a clean towel to keep it warm. A clean towel and all as carefully set and timed as the morning tea-pot with its little fitted muffler. Hot water. Hot tea. All arranged and out of a book and somehow weird and somehow oddly civilized. Little things mattered, not the great things. Things that wracked and tore you were forgotten. Really great emotions were these things, clocks that struck and struck and left a trail of silver. A star on the sea left such a trail of silver. Star. Astraea. But she couldn't *marry*. You couldn't of course marry him. No. Of course not. Hybiscus red and . . . famished hyacinths.

A volcanic rock shrivelled, opened, cracked, fell and hyacinths were about her, shrivelled, withered as the flowers dropped by Persephone. Riven hyacinths. She hadn't asked any great thing, just to be let alone. Perhaps that was the great thing. She hadn't asked nor walked into a volcano head on, seeing it, just for the sake of the sensation. She had been so happy. She thought she had never been so happy. Candles and Katherine Farr being kind. People and faces and all blurred and nobody being a sharp sword or an angel's sword or any of those steely terrible, beautiful embodied images of stark pain. Pain had vanished. There was no pain. Pain had departed suddenly, had driven herself before it out of Hell. She had risen from Hell as Persephone from the underworld. She had crossed Styx. This was something unlawful. Terrible. This thing that burned in her hand— "the second bell's been ringing some time miss." "I'll be late. I'll be coming later," the letter slipped under her door, the letter that had been slipped under her door. Who had slipped this under her door? "Shall I come in and turn the bed down now or later?" Now or later? Now or later? Something had to be done sometime, now or later. "O now." Yes, now. She would see, Fayne would see, they would all see how she'd act about it. If she could stand up now and re-read the letter her whole life would be different. If she could re-read the letter she would be able to smile, to say yes, no. To say, no. To say, yes. Don't marry him. Who had said that? Who had ranted (it was that simply) about marriage, talked about biologic necessities? And being beyond that. Who had done it? It was Fayne Rabb simply. It was Fayne who had said one couldn't possibly marry. O *that*. What had she meant? What had she said? Why had she said it? "Did you find that extra bodice miss you was wanting?" "O yes. Yes thank you." She had said yes, thank you. She had lifted her head up casually from the vivid letter and she had said yes thank you. "Who put the letter under the door?" "I suppose it was James, miss." James, who was James? "O yes." Yes, she had given James a shilling just the other day. He would see about the letters . . . She had stood out against them, stood out against Eugenia. She had broken with them, given up her summer in the marshes. But she didn't want the marshes, the canoe sliding like a serpent to her bidding. She didn't want fire-weed spilling its flower petals. She hadn't wanted all that. She had had the silver mist, the annihilating beauty. She had felt the peace of nothingness and she supposed she must now pay. The woman pays. She had paid. She was paying. O Darrington, where are you? I sent you away. You were the one person who could understand this. "Yes, tell them I'm coming in a minute." Darrington would understand this. He had given her books and said her poems were something. *You are a poem though your poem's naught.* He hadn't said that. O yes. Now she saw it. She wasn't meant to slack and slouch with pretty candles and odd dresses and being nobody, being George Lowndes or was it Darrington? Someone, something wanted her to write. For writing and life were not diametric opposites. "Things like this don't happen in real life." That's what people said when they read novels. But they did, did happen. Things like this did happen. "Listen little idiot, when you get this I'll be married. An Englishman, a person, not one of your little poetasters. I'll write you when we get to London . . ."

11 The letter burned, vitriolic blue acid in her hand though she hadn't the letter (had not for some time had the letter) in her hand. The touch of the letter left a scar across the fingers that opened it, scar of burning acid, not of fire, scalding not searing. Scalding and searing. "O Miss Gart. You are too metaphysical." Bald headed little Chemistry professor catching her up when she wanted to apply his prim formula to the more extensive phases of life, of humanity. One and one and two, and little plus and minus signs and the acid that had broken the test tube and the scars across her wrist, tiny scars that she was rather proud of. Too metaphysical. Not metaphysical enough. Idealists said she was a rank realist and too set and defined in her outlook. Scientists told her off for being idealistic. Must she bow to either judgment? She was herself simply . . . bell notes made patterns in the air that no one could take from her. The blue vitriol of Fayne's letter had left its scar but on the whole, was she not proud of it? Scar that she hadn't turned from, wound that she had not repudiated. It was so deep, so terrible that it was almost joy to have it. It was all (had been) so terrible that it had removed itself from the first moment from any possible realm of probabilities, it was drama simply, a rather good drama. It was the second act of a rather second-rate play done by first rate actors. It was the second act (was it the third?) of a somewhat hackneyed but odd melodrama that was saved from banality by the very casual and perfect manner of the odd producers. The whole thing was in some realm in which reality was suspended while people watched themselves move, speak. They were not real. Their very unreality saved them, saved her. Had it really mattered? It had never mattered: the odd vitriolic blue that had been the burning destructive acid of the letter had almost cauterized the death wound. So deep, so vitriolic that the rest could not matter. Not even the little note afterwards so gracious, so suave in its serenity. The note from this odd person who was (it appeared) would forever be, just Fayne's husband. The man Fayne had married wrote to her. She had found the letter with a little batch of things that didn't matter and the letter itself from this odd suave person who was (would always be) just Fayne's husband could not matter. Suave like the breath of a stage producer who comes before the curtain to explain his presence. His presence being due (in all these cases) to the absence of the right hand man or prima donna. "Ladies and gentlemen, I regret having to inform you . . ." This person who was (would always be) just Fayne's husband had suavely countenanced evidently something. "Fayne is worn out with the journey. She misses her mother and has been ill somewhat. She begs me" (when had Fay ever begged anybody anything?) "to explain this. Will you come to our" (*our*, I ask you) "hotel as soon as you are able. Fayne tells me you have friends, calls on your time. I would appreciate this from you. Fayne has been a little worn . . . ill with excitement."

Answering the appeal of this person who was (would always be) just Fayne's husband, Hermione had found herself one day in April in a little odd street off Piccadilly, little odd eclectic street like going into a foreign city suddenly and it all coming back, all the odd things and little streets but this was a funny little eclectic street in which to find Fayne Rabb. Tiny cool corridor with a great mirror at the far end from which a person (not herself) paused to re-survey her. Grey person looking cool, looking right in the cool little narrow hall. A table and something, a palm in a tall basket. Baskets spilling flowers. A row under the mirror of potted shrub azaleas. Above azaleas, pink and yellow and flame red a person (not Hermione) paused to look at another person, herself simply. The person who was not Hermione turned from the gaze of the person who so simply was Hermione to answer someone, something, "yes, they're expecting me. Mrs.— Mrs.—" my God, what was their name? She had forgotten what the name was. Somewhere, somehow someone had signed a name across a page and that name was now the only guarantee that she would find Fayne Rabb. A name she had suddenly and poignantly forgotten. "O," she couldn't say "I've forgotten what their name is." These were people who had asked her. She had forgotten their name. Fayne was someone, somewhere in this nice little hotel, everything just right and someone, also just right was waiting by her elbow asking for their name, no it was her name. Hermione looked at the face in the mirror. Would it recall some name? George's name was George Lowndes, but that wouldn't do (though he had offered it to her) in this emergency. Whose name? Darrington. Darrington was a good name. The Sussex Darringtons you know. She needn't tell them that the governor had more or less eloped with a country girl and that Darrington was somewhat in advance of expectations. I mean a seven months' baby. But damn, he had said, it was barely six. Names. People. Someone might yet help her.

Someone might yet help her. *Would* yet help her. Someone from the other end of the cool little right little hall was coming toward her. Someone was coming toward her. Where had she seen him? Familiar droop of shoulders. April in London and someone was speaking to her. A tall person who bent a little and squinted a little into her eyes. A tall person who must bend a little to squint a little into even over-tall Hermione's wide eyes. He squinted a little (who was he?) and the person at her elbow waited a little and this would go on, was going on for ever. It couldn't be anyone else but Fayne Rabb's husband. Well that was that. Now he would tell her his name, tell her her own name. He did this last thing first. "I know, feel it couldn't be any other but—Hermione." He said it just right, with the exact amount of interest, the exact inflection. No one had ever said Hermione better than he said it. He said "Hermione" again and this time with a little upward inflection. "Hermione?" He was asking with a little upward inflection if it *was* Hermione but whether it was or wasn't could make no difference for he would be sure to redeem himself, to retrieve himself perfectly if it wasn't. She waited for a moment for as long as she dared wait without telling him it was Hermione. She could pretend it wasn't but that would be no good for she had forgotten his name. Had by the same logic lost Fayne Rabb. "O yes, yes of course . . ." she felt colour rise, colour across cheek bones, colour for he still held her with his slight squint. Was it a squint or was he winking at her? Of course he wasn't winking. He was so utterly right, so right in the little hall way. Probably Fay was right then and he was "a person." He spoke again in that same right voice saying the just-right thing. Now that *was* rather right of him, very nice of him, "tea upstairs as quickly as you can, for two—I must rush out—in Mrs. Morrison's bedroom."

Fayne Rabb was in a bed, a big bed, a nice bed, a better bed than Hermione had ever seen her in. Fayne was looking at someone who was not Hermione though Fayne (odd little person in a big bed) seemed to think it was Hermione. "O darling—" Darling this. Darling that. What about vitriolic blue letters and a scar across her wrist (no across her breast) that would be there forever? But there was something in this. There was something in the very poignant finality of vitriolic blue. It was a thing final, done for, finished. "Darling—" But she wasn't having any. A tall person in a wide hat looked at Fayne Rabb on a big bed. It was perhaps Hermione that so regarded Fayne propped up and wearing (for a wonder) a really pretty bed-jacket. "I like your pretty little boudoir jacket." "Is *that* all you've come to tell me?" "Come to tell you? I didn't know I was supposed to tell you anything." "Well after all—this." "All what?" "O this—all this—" What did Fay conceivably mean by all this? Fayne Rabb lifted her little hand but it was not the hand of Fayne Rabb. It was the hand of something other separated forever now from Fayne Rabb. It was the hand that had waved in its insouciance toward an azalea in a big jar. A plaintive violin was playing (inappositely) the song from Solveig. This was not that. This person that raised a little hand and whose arm stretched magnolia white from a delft-blue bed-jacket trimmed with pretty swansdown was not that one. That person had sturdy knees wound about with straps that held together sandals. Wings on the sandals. Wide breadth of strong and sturdy shoulders. Pygmalion speaking and all the world must listen. All the world must listen when Pygmalion speaks, says what he thinks, all art is this, is that. If Pygmalion could have stayed then with them, but he couldn't. He was somewhere else safe. He was safe but he was not now here. Fayne's hand was the hand now of Fayne. It waved vaguely above nice bed-clothes, it emerged from a delft-blue boudoir jacket. That was all simple. The whole thing was so simple. Vitriolic acid had so made it. There was nothing simpler than the simplest of death-wounds. This was not Hermione so this (that was not Hermione) could turn, regard the room about her. Shoes. Whose? What odd shoes on the floor. They were not Clara's, not Hermione's. What an odd row of odd shoes, pointed shoes most of them. Brown shoes, patent leather pumps, though he would probably call them something else, being, Fayne had said, so "English" and a "person." Shoes in a neat row along the opposite wall and shoes untidy along the near wall. "Doesn't your husband arrange your shoes for you? His own seem to be so neatly put together." "O my—husband—" "Yes. Your husband. Didn't you ask me here to meet your husband?" "No. I asked you here to meet me." "Well anyhow, why doesn't your— husband arrange your things for you." "Well, perhaps he thinks I should do it myself." "What an idea. What a shock for you." "Yes, isn't it. Madre always did everything—O-O-O-O—Hermione."

Small arms reached out. Were her arms then small? Hermione had thought of Fayne Rabb as Pygmalion, a little sturdy, a little strong, a little defiant. Who was this reaching small magnolia white arms out toward her? "Can't you—understand?" "Understand? Understand what, Fayne Rabb?" "Can't you understand? Can't you— make—allowances?" "For what? You seem as far as I in my limited way can make out, to have done very well indeed for yourself." "O don't be cruel. Don't, don't be cynical." But tea entered . . . Hermione was glad for tea entering. The right sort of tea with the right sort of rose buds on the tea cups. "This is lovely china." "Is *that* all you can say?" "What do you, to quote George, in Gawd's name want me to say then?" "I don't—know." "I should think you didn't." Hermione tossed her hat away somewhere, among shoes, she supposed. Her hat would land among shoes, somebody's shoes and did it matter? Her shoes, his shoes. It was obvious neither row (the neat one nor the untidy one) was ever so remotely connected with anything so indecorous as sandals. Hat on the floor. "Why are you so reckless about your hat? It's such a pretty one." "Haven't you seen a hat since you left Europe?" "Not a really pretty one, Hermione."

Pretty hat. Pretty bed-jacket. Pretty tea-cups. What after all, could be more suitable?

"But I want you to like Maurice." "But I do like him." "How can you like him when you've never seen him?" "But I have seen him." "O, you saw him? When? Where did you see Maurice?" "I saw him as I was coming in, in the hall-way." "How did you know it was Maurice?" "I didn't. He knew it was me."

But that didn't matter, that would go on for ever, that kind of conversation. It was no good that kind of talk, anyone could do it. But whatever other kind of talk could there possibly be now with Fayne? "I wanted him to like you for I insisted when we arranged about the marriage that you were to be with us." "*Be* with you?" "Yes, little fool. What easier. We've booked" (booked—Fay was getting on slowly but surely with her English) "the tickets for you." "*Booked.* Why couldn't you say taken?" "Well why should I? All I am is English." "Since when English?" "Well, I can't exactly give the moment but we were married in Saint Margaret's, West Philadelphia, about two weeks since." "Why Saint Margaret's, such a swell church, why anyhow at all in such regalia?" "O to please Madre. Some of the wealthy New York cousins coughed up when they knew who I was to marry. It was to their advantage at last to notice my existence." "What did they give you?" "O things. My gown—for instance." "Gown?" "Yes, it's hanging in the cupboard. I'm to put it on to-morrow night for the first time here and you're all to come to dinner." "Dinner? Who for instance?" "Well, old George." "George?" Famished and forgetting Hermione had lifted hyacinths to George Lowndes' kisses. But you can't *marry* him.

"How devastatingly kind of you. May I ask a favour?" "Any number, beautiful." "I would like to bring a new friend, a certain art critic,

Jerrold Darrington, poet, all those minor accomplishments that you so despise now." "O another—?" "Another what?" "Victim." "No. He's not a victim. He's been helping me with some translations, Greek, essays." "Really pretty high brow." "Yes, really. He cares about—my—mind—" "Presumably." "May I bring him?" "I don't to tell you the truth trust anyone with a name like Darrington. I suppose he's an earl's bastard and an accomplished black-mailer." "Well—he's not exactly an earl's bastard—" Someone was in the room. *Bastard.* What did that word signify? Someone was looking at them. A ghost, something. "O." Hermione had turned in intuition of strange terror not expecting to see anything, seeing Maurice Morrison standing in the doorway. Odd face, too tall, leaning forward. How long had he been listening? Hermione had turned with an odd artificial little gesture, her hand on her grey gown above, singularly erratic heart-beat. She had felt the man there. How long had he been standing?

"O Maurice." The little creature on the bed (how then had Fay suddenly become so small and wilted?) spoke weakly, "this—is— Hermione." "I know that." He came now slowly forward. The face as it squinted a little toward Hermione was again familiar. There was a voice went with it. O was it Maurice *Delacourt* Morrison the famous lecturer? "O I think I know now. Did you give talks, lectures, on art, Renaissance and several cities, Vienna, Sienese to different girls' schools, colleges—with pictures afterwards, essays?" Maurice Delacourt Morrison was smiling at her. It was odd to be sitting in a bedroom on a bed actually with the wife of such a celebrity. "We were always impressed. I mean at Lyn Mawr, you know the college—" "Perfectly." "I hated it. I suppose you hated it." "Miss Thornton, your president, was, wasn't she, somewhat of a snob?" "Yes, wasn't she? I hated the place. Was only there a short time." Maurice Morrison and school girls' adoration. Yet somehow understanding. What did he say, squinting sideways at them? "I told Maurice on pain of death not to wear his eye-glass—at least till you got used to his ensemble—" "Ensemble. But why should I get used to it?" The sort of thing you think and don't say, but Maurice Morrison suavely lifted a left over thin slice of bread and butter and bit it neatly and exactly and somehow elegantly. "Haven't you had tea?" Fayne, Hermione was glad to notice, had the right maternal-marital attitude. "Yes. But beastly. Nothing really worth waiting for—Lady Freezeworth—that atrocious woman—" He was eating their bread and butter, all rather friendly, the three of them on the big bed.

"Well, will you come with us to Dresden? Fayne tells me you have a flair, love these things." What after all could be more suitable? She had heard this Morrison talk, lecture of famous cities. From the school-girl point of view, what could be more adequate, more charming, something as we say "to write home about." Maurice Morrison and Fayne Rabb. It seemed somehow all right, most suitable. Even Eugenia couldn't mind it. He was looking at her from a distance and it occurred to her that she was behaving badly. "O it's charming, charming and so kind." What could be kinder? On their honey-moon. "O, I'd love to . . . If you'll make a list out, some little résumé of what it might cost and if I can afford it." The light softening of late spring stole upon them. He was older than Fayne Rabb, quite old, he seemed almost—almost old, like a young uncle. "O yes we must arrange it." She was standing and again a tall figure bent to smile into her lifted face. "How *kind* of you to ask me."

He saw her to the door, saw her out of the door, all grown up, like a nice half-strange, very young uncle. The right voice, the right gesture, not insisting too far, letting her run away into the dusk without overdue protest. "Yes, Fayne tells me you like running wild a little. I won't insist then on the taxi."

12 "But dammmm-nnnnn." The expletive broke china, would break china if it went on thundering and re-echoing in the little side-room where George had drawn her, drawn her out of the crowd so he might expostulate (as he put it) sanely with her. The expletive hung like wasps clinging to the chandelier that hung a little too low, dwarfing the small room with its great elegance. The little room off the big room in the little right hotel where the others were waiting, clustered about palms, waiting for Fayne who was their hostess and it was funny her being so late but she had stayed upstairs to talk with Maurice's mother and they had gone on talking and they were trying on all the pretty things and she was putting on her wedding gown and her bride veil just to show them. "Da—" this time it stuck in

George's throat and Hermione was afraid it would swell there like a frog swelling and burst George Lowndes. The "da—" became finally a low rumble of mmmms and nnns and the same feeling that another host of buzzing flies had joined the already thick group about the ornate mirror. The mirror was at the back but it reflected itself and George looking at her in another mirror across the narrow corridor. The mirror across the corridor and the back of her reflected head and George's side face was broken from time to time by people crossing. Darrington. Darrington looked rather like a head-waiter in his evening dress. His face was too heavy, too Flemish for the collar. Was that the country girl his governor had copped or who had (was it?) copped his governor? Fayne Rabb made people seem common. Her odd curious stone like, marble lift of flawless feature. Fayne's features were flawless in the right setting and facing George now straight she knew, felt inwardly that she was really grateful to this Maurice who had so set Fayne in the right place. Fayne with fair skin, with magnolia white skin but looking right, with curtains half drawn more beautiful than any one could possibly imagine. "Don't you think Fay is looking better for the change? I felt her mother, poor Clara, was responsible for that strained look, for that constant nervousness and her odd erratic furies. She seems perfect in this setting." George was sitting beside Hermione on the narrow bench against the wall. Narrow, hard little bench, half furniture, half wall decoration. George slid forward, disconsolately. "You don't mean to tell me that she's really married?"

"Married. What do you mean George, really married?" "I mean she told me something utterly different." "Different?" "She said this was a trial trip. That she and Maurice there weren't going to—ah—experiment till they knew each other better. That she was really fond of Llewyn." "Llewyn? What's John Llewyn got to do with it?" "Did you meet him? Do you know him?" "No. Only here. I used to hear him lecture in America. Rather scathing. Browning in lavender gloves. It was he (Fayne tells me) introduced them." "Introduced them—exactly." "What do you mean, exactly?" "I mean it's Llewyn that she's in with. The other person is only a sort of mari—mari—" George's French deserted him on most important occasions—"well, ah, complaisant. I mean a complaisant husband who isn't really married." "Married? What do you mean, really married?" "I mean that simply. I mean he never—ah I mean they—" "O George what *do* you mean? Can't you just say it simply?" "I mean there ain't no damn use your thinking you're going to Dresden with them." "But I've arranged everything. He's even got my ticket." "He damn well has—well, he can damn well keep it or—" what George murmured was lost in his velvet coat sleeve. He seemed to be biting at the cuff like a bad-tempered organ monkey in his little jacket. "George don't eat your buttons. There'll be food soon." "O God damn, why did I ever come here?" "To see, as we all came to see, Fayne Rabb in her bride things."

Fayne, it appeared, had thought she had kept them waiting long enough for she came in, drifted across the mirror that reflected (had reflected) Hermione and George Lowndes. Fayne looking odd in a fashion-plate bride veil and a fashion-plate bride-train and yet wasn't it right and proper, though she pulled her veil off instantly and old Mrs. Morrison took it reverently, already seemed to love her. Fayne Rabb with relatives, in-laws, someone who was (someone said) related to a baronet and the rest of them, all of them who had so shone in Hermione's little constellation cluster, looked odd, looked insignificant. George looked a little odd as if he needed to be explained and evidently someone had already thought that for old Mrs. Morrison was fluttering toward them "but my son tells me you have written *such* a work on Dante."

Old Mrs. Morrison said it rather clearly, rather loud, in a loud clear voice so that the relatives (the one who was, it was whispered related to a baronet) might understand why George came in a velvet jacket. O yes this is Mr. Darrington (she had got that also, she was explaining Darrington) "not Kent, the Sussex Darringtons." Darrington seemed to have more of a sense of humour or of proportion for he wasn't having any of the patronizing chaff of the relation to a baronet. Hermione found that Darrington in spite of the chin that rose slightly too roundly Flemish from the collar, stood the test better than dear George. He knew the answers to all this, in spite of (or because of) the governor's odd position. "Yes. Sussex. Beastly bog. Sheep and sky-larks sounding like corks popping." Was this desecration or merely the right answer? Putting someone (the relation to a baronet) in his right place. People. Odd funny people to see about Fayne Rabb. They had dwarfed herself and George ("And which did you say she was engaged to?") and Hermione was supposed to be engaged to one or both, George or Darrington, and her little cluster, her tiny constellation went dim and lustreless beside that conflagration that burned about Fayne Rabb. Fayne in her white robe, the moon. Her chin thrust out arrogant. Hermione had seen her look more beautiful though she liked her in that dress, it made the right marble lines and the arrogant full but firm little breasts and the line that the dress brought out of the perfect narrow hips. Hermione liked to see Fayne look right. Even the relation of the baronet must respect this.

"And this is her glove." It was old Mrs. Morrison. She was holding it up like some holy relic while Fayne's constellation seemed to be forming and tying itself about arms and tying bare arms about its own immaculate dinner jacket. "This is how they do things in America." She was explaining the finger cut off at the knuckle. Odd thing, a white glove (when had she ever seen a long white glove of Fayne's?). "The finger is cut off, you see—" Old Mrs. Morrison paused in rapture, "for the *bride's ring*."

The glove, the ring. They would be leaving in a few days. Now they were going in to dinner. Going in. Yes she would wait, going in. Who was meant to take her. But there was no arranging this thing. George had her, tucked her hand into his velvet crook of his velvet monkey jacket, "I'd beat it right now, Dryad. Only I don't trust you with 'em. As your nearest male relation."

"As your nearest male relative, I tell you this won't do." "But George, you have been arguing round and about it and it seems such rank futility. Fayne is married. I will have (if you are so dead-set on your conventions) a chaperone—" "Chaperone?" "I mean she's married. Her husband asked me—" "Husband?" But they had been going on and on with this, it seemed they had been going on and over and around this for years, centuries. It seemed some barren desert and the sand, the hot arid arguments of George blasted, withered her. "Don't you see? He's that very famous lecturer." "Lecturer be—" "Yes, yes, yes. But I mean even Eugenia, even my mother must know all about him." "Did you ever hear of your mother going to Bruges or Ghent or Little Rock or Athens, Iohio, with any one on their honey-moon?" "Well, no—not exactly on their—" "Exactly." George seemed to think this finished matters. Each time they got to this point in the argument, George seemed to think the matter finished but Hermione would begin and would continue. It seemed with that slim shape in beautiful white satin to recall her that George was some rankly gross little organ monkey with his wrong velvet jacket. They all looked right, especially the husband. Waiters would do what these people said. There would be no jumble and quarrelling over tips and people trying to bully one though on the whole people were inclined not to. But the *feeling* that they might. None of that. Fayne seemed to rise somewhere in the dark street, to rise a white star, a white folded lily. Her dress wound about her stern small figure like lily leaves, a lily-bud still budded. "Don't you understand? They're not really—married."

When they got to this point of the argument, Hermione said, "but what difference can that make (if it's true)—" and George answered "It wouldn't. Only the whole thing has been cooked up for this precisely. It's the Llewyn person that's concocted it." "But nonsense, Fay hardly at all knows him." "She told you that, did she? She was anxious to impress me and told me something different." "O George it's all so mad and so unlike you. So unfair, simply." "Maybe it is. Maybe it isn't. But I'll be there at the station." Climbing weary stairs to her room, her lovely room that she had thought so beautiful, her room full of sound and colour, that in early spring had been filled with bell-notes like angels' feathers ruffling wind, ruffling, little petals . . . such childish images, such sentimental things and she had minded. She had slept in this room, wakened in this room, had letters pushed under the door, Darrington's letters, all those faithfully funny little letters when he was being funny simply. "Well, I don't mind Astraea, if it's Zeus but no one else, I warn you." She was to have Zeus for a lover. No one else. The Zeus-bed, the bed (so clean) that Darrington said might at any moment become Zeus or the Bull that carried off Europa. Letters under the door with her early tea, to be devoured in dim light sitting up in bed. Letters and jokes that had made cyclamen trail of colour in the dim room. "You Astraea, *are* that Rhodocleia—" *I send you Rhodocleia for your hair*. The room was different. All the trail, all the built up tenuous memoirs had been blighted. Can a white lily-bud blight with its devastating beauty all the garden?

"Then you have decided not to do it?" "No. George decided." "What then exactly happened?" "I went to the station as arranged with bags and baggage and found George had waited, seen me, seen the things coming through, countermanded the order, got the ticket back from Morrison—" "All while you waited?" "Most of it before I had arrived. I don't know how he did it."

Could she see Fayne again after this? Fayne's last word had been with odd theatrical little lift of brows, "O I hadn't realised it had gone *so far* with George Lowndes." The husband was all suavity but she saw, they let her see, what they thought of her. Whispers. Innu-endoes. Burning scar of blame that wasn't right though George had kissed her. George being (as she had never seen him) rude to every-one. "Her mother cabled—" He had made that up and other things but shame had burnt across her. A wilted, worn Hermione lifted her tea-cup, smiled at Darrington. "I don't think I can stay now in London. Everything looks different and my room's changed." "Changed?" "I mean it used to be full of light, rose colours. All your letters. If I go across to Paris will you write me?"

13 There was no separation in this. She was in Paris but there was no separation. Things existed in different planes. She had moved into a train, out of a train, into a boat, off a boat, onto a train. The real life she was living might have been the same anywhere, Shanghai, New Orleans or Rotterdam. It only hap-pened she was now in Paris. She moved instinctively (knowing Paris) to the Rue Jacob, the right side (being the wrong side) of the river, their side of the river but in a different hotel, not one of the old ones, not talking to the same people, "but where is your aunt? Where is your cousin?" She wouldn't tell them that her aunt was in Shanghai or Amsterdam. She wouldn't have the heart to make up stories. But she must make up, all the same, stories, other stories, "waiting for a boat. Yes Mademoiselle Moore gave me your address. Yes, I knew Miss Moore in Philadelphia." Books, note books, addresses from some one, from some one else, all people in Philadelphia (unto the angel in Philadelphia, write . . .) that she had forgotten. She had forgotten all those people, had made a point of quite forgetting. How odd she had never "looked up" as they say, anyone, all the little sheaf of letters, introductions, having Fayne Rabb, seeing Walter, had been enough. George too asking her to see people. The same street. "Yes thank you madame. I am very tired." Yes the room was pretty. Yes Miss Moore was a great friend. Yes she had been at school with Miss Moore's sister, the other Miss Moore. Yes she knew Miss Mira Thorpe. Yes we were all so proud of Mira Thorpe, she had taken the prix de something or other and yes she knew Miss Thorpe, the other one too in Philadelphia. Yes she would stay until she heard from her friends who were due over, maybe one week, maybe three, maybe all the summer. Yes she liked her petit déjeuner in bed, in the morning, about eight, no not later. Yes she knew this part of Paris, had been here before, yes it was last summer.

Was it last summer? It seemed impossible. Late last summer. Not a year past. Not a year past, it had seemed many centuries. Centuries with painted emblems like heralds' banners. All the months had banners, painted signs, emblems of time spent and time lost and time perhaps forgotten. Emblem banners, all lost, all taken in a moment in some unfair badly arranged tournament. Fayne had taken all the banners simply. Fayne had entered unfairly pitched lists and had simply walked off with everything, George with his vermillion and orange lilies, Darrington with his rose light and his streaks of flaming passion. Lilies. Lilies. There were lilies in the street. Muguet. It was muguet everywhere. Why was it muguet everywhere? It is, don't you know, mademoiselle, have you never known, mademoiselle, the first of May. We have muguet. She bought muguet. Why did she buy muguet? She walked swift and erect and reckless past the Institut de France. The world's good word the Institute. The Institut de France. She belonged to the Institut de France because Carl Gart had had books from there and she had torn the wrapping off and helped catalogue the books. Other books . . . the hounds of spring are on winter's traces . . . Poems. *You are a poem though your poem's naught.* To the left ladies and gentlemen we have the famous Notre Dame. The Isle of de France. The island of France, all France. Islands. *All the world's a stage.* Muguet (why?) tucked into her light spring jacket. "Hello Her-*mi*-o-ne."

Who the—? It was a voice. Someone who knew her. Not as bad as she had expected. "O hello." It wasn't as bad as it might have been, in fact it wasn't bad at all. "I didn't know you were here." "Well, I don't know myself that I am. I mean I rushed off from London, only stayed there to see some people, love Paris, London hateful." Hermione had learned this early. You must say you hate London to most

Paris-Americans. "Awful place. I only stayed because I have some friends there." "George?" "O yes, dear old George. But he's coming over. They all are. Walter's due to give another concert." Not a bad sort, looking younger than she was, a pretty flat the right side of the river. Hermione had heard all about her, had been once to see her, crowding in for a moment one day when the Rabbs were busy. Pretty flat. Pretty apartment. Woman too old to be young, not young enough to be old. Didn't seem old. What was the matter with her?

Hermione stopped to look straight into Shirley Thornton's eyes. A pretty name Shirley. But she had never seen her. Why had Shirley Thornton who didn't know her, stopped her, called her Hermione? What did she want of her. Shirley Thornton standing in the full glare of May day splendour looked thin, peaked, the right sort of clothes, a hat shading her almond shaped eyes. Her skirt tailored and fitting beautifully. But come to think of it, Shirley hardly knew her. Didn't know her. Why did she speak, why had she spoken to her? "I wanted to write you last year—I was busy—" Had she wanted to? She had forgotten all about her, had particularly not wanted to see her. Shirley had taken one of those precious hours, when hours were very precious. Hours. Did they exist now any longer? What was life? Muguet. "Yes. I was so casual. George so awfully anxious I should know you." Why had George wanted Hermione to know her? Hermione had not stopped to ask, nor cared to. "Come to see me. Soon. You have the address?" "Yes—Shirley." "You didn't seem to remember me." "O I did, I did perfectly." "You seemed lost, vague, uncertain somehow. That's why I spoke, called you Hermione." "Yes." "Do come. George will soon be over. We'll all dine together."

. . . That odd spectacle would in no way leave her. That spectacle of George heaving a summer overcoat toward a departing train, pronouncing, "sic transit gloria mundi." Hermione didn't want so simply to see George, to dine à trois with George Lowndes and another, someone who wore the right clothes, lived in the right street, had the right food, hung the right pictures, boasted even the very right piano, the baby-grand taking up more than his share of room, making the rest of the room all the more cosy and compact for his unwieldly baby bulk and the bulk of the things he stood for. Hermione recalled her little visit there with Shirley, talking about something, talking about nothing, wondering if she would be too late for the Rabbs at the little Rue du Four crémerie where they always had their supper. Rue du Four, the wrong side of the river, not caring what the girl had said or who she was, having come because George sent her for some reason, making polite adieux, writing that she couldn't come again, was called suddenly to London. All the same it was part of that wrong side of Paris life that now escaped her. Escaped her? But it never did. Little rows of communicants were passing in the streets, set there to remind her. Little rows of little girls with long trains and veils . . . God, God, what a farce and she wasn't (George said so) even "married." Bride's veils, muguet and the parks a paradise of chestnuts. That year the pink and rose shell chestnuts broke across her like shells from some forgotten paradise. Shells from some sea. Aphrodite. But Fay wasn't. O if she only were, if she only had been, if Hermione could have fallen at her feet, O Fay, you're grown up now in your bride things . . . a lovely mother. O Fay, let me be your first child. But she hadn't. Couldn't. But it wasn't true, couldn't be true what George had told her. How she hated George Lowndes. Why had she anyhow presumed his tale true? Fayne carrying on a "vulgar intrigue" (it was George's phrase) with this Welshman, this fascinating Llewyn that they all knew, had known (but O so distantly) in Philadelphia. Llewyn with his Oxford affectation and his brilliant pronouncements on literature. "Browning in lavender gloves." It gave one a new idea, destructive, dominant, domineering. Fancy Fay having met him by accident, somewhere (where?) and his falling for her. Little Fay rather wistful with her hatred (her then hatred) of all men. "But you can't *marry* him." But it wasn't true. George was vulgar, base. George had betrayed her. It was George who was vulgar.

No, she mustn't stay here. Mustn't go round and round things and throwing herself on the bed to think things out. No. She mustn't. What should she do? Where should she go? Not the Louvre. Lovely corridors and Fayne's pronouncements coming back. Why did they all make such amazing statements, nothing sacred, they were all so brilliant. Pictures, statues, poems, people. They made their brilliant statements. Browning in lavender gloves. They had everything at their finger-tips, such very clever people. Clever, even George couldn't stand up to them. They chaffed George. They found fault, quite sternly with his Dante. Poor old George. They hadn't spared him, frayed his blatant banner of scholarship, ripped it to pieces with their brilliance. O that was the right setting for Fay. Fayne Rabb was as clever as any. She was far more brilliant. Fayne with her conflagration. No, no, no, no, no Fay was something different. O why do my tears flow like some damned leak in the roof? Not proper tears just coming on and on and making one uncomfortable. Am I ill then? It's being alone and muguet hateful in a tumbler like those striped orange lilies they had bought at the Quai aux Fleurs and never enough tooth-brush tumbler to put flowers in. Muguet. What made her think of Shirley? Seeing her that day (some ten days ago?) when she first bought muguet. Muguet. The first of May. She must go and see her.

14 "Thank you so much. Yes I do like lemon. Yes in England everyone has milk, never lemon. They say it is so *Russian*. No. I simply stayed as I had friends there. Yes. I know. Yes." The baby-grand strutted forward, nosed with his baby-grand grand manner into the very table, dwarfed them, the chairs, the book case crowded with untidy layers of books, magazines. Shirley had everything. It was something to have everything. Shirley was very kind. Quite kind. It had been rather casual, bouncing up the stairs, rushing in at tea time, but she was alone, said she was glad to see Hermione. "You see I seem to know you, knowing people that you do." "Yes. Yes. Yes. Yes. What people?" "Well there's George Lowndes." "O, of course, George Lowndes." Did this Shirley love then George? George kept coming up, coming back. "That's a portrait of him." Shirley was waving a tea spoon (a Florentine little lily on a disproportionate stem handle) toward a portrait. "O yes, I saw it when I came in." George had all the while been squinting slightly at her back, squinting ironically, with hand lifted and a more than ever ornate vermillion and speckled gold mosaic cravat. "I told George I'd keep it here though it's really his, belongs to him." "O yes." But Shirley needn't go out of her way to explain. Why did she explain. Did people accuse *her* of things too? Had she kissed George, had George kissed her? Did people lift well-bred eye-brows and smile and say in well-bred voices, "O I had no idea things had gone *so far* with George." Is that why Shirley liked her, wanted to talk to her? Did Shirley really like her. Wasn't it that Shirley wanted to find things out, was trying? But Shirley seemed not so much to want to find out things as to (with an interrogation) impart them. "And what really is the girl like he's engaged to?"

"Engaged to? But I didn't know he was engaged." Hermione had been under a vague half-impression that it was she herself who was vaguely half-engaged to George Lowndes. "O. But I thought he'd told you." "O no. Never." "But how terrible of me. He wrote me in the strictest confidence." "O but—" O but. It seemed somehow rather odd now. If George were engaged, really engaged, he should have told her. Had he told her? He mumbled, murmured, had a way of hurling sonnets at her and asking her opinion. Was that his way of telling? Had he told her? She remembered one evening, the most beautiful, it seemed now, of all the many beautiful London evenings. But London wasn't real, London was a dream. London had been destroyed, marred, blasted. The castle beneath the sea, the very sea, the little Mermaid, all the dream and half-mystery, the glamour of the drift and drift and the cold annihilating beauty. London. Where was it then in London? Hyacinths were reaching up to kisses . . . kisses that at last hadn't hurt her. George was speaking to her—"my damn aunt just won't pass out." "O George, don't let poverty depress you." "It ain't my own exactly." "Then whose is it?"

Had that been his idea in asking Katherine Farr to ask her to stay on alone in her studio before supper? Was that what he wanted? Just to tell her. "O George didn't exactly *tell* me but he hinted." "Well, I thought it odd. He said, always said he was your nearest relative—" "*Male* relative." "Male relative. I thought from that you were quite intimate."

Had George then deceived her? You don't kiss people like that, you don't kiss them at all if you are "engaged" elsewhere. Engaged, what an odd idea. The whole place was mad, obsessed. And Shirley now continued. "And Walter." "Walter?" "I believe finally the two parents have consented. You know marriage in France is a grave ceremony—" Shirley was speaking blankly to a blank wall. The black undeviating surface of the baby-grand. "He gave me lessons for a time. Harmony—" Harmony. Vérène had said once, "Walter gives lessons in har-mony to American girls, my pupils." "Are you then a pupil of theirs?" "Theirs?" Hermione looked into almond shaped odd eyes that were almond shaped no longer. They were wide, staring, glassy like a crystal gazer's. "Theirs. Vérène's." "O little odd Vérène. No. Not from her. No I never had much faith in Vérène save as a house-wife." "*House*-wife?" "Well isn't it that exactly? It's so exactly right and she's so pretty. Walter needs a mother." "Mother. *Is* she pretty?" "Well. I thought so." "*Did* you? I can't say that I ever thought her—pretty. I think she's funny and she helps out his music—" "*Does* she?" "O I don't know. I don't know anything of music." "Walter said you listened." "O—*that*—"

Was she a spectator then? Was she to be always looking, watching, seeing other people's lives work out right? Hermione seemed to herself suddenly forgotten. As old maids must feel turning out lavender letters, letters gone dim and smelling of sweet lavender. Was she then lost? It seemed suddenly that she must clutch, find something. Herself was it? "I don't seem to understand this sudden fury of engagements." "O it's natural." "I suppose so—" But it wasn't. It was somehow queer and twisted . . .

No, no. It wasn't twisted. Walter wasn't twisted. What had gone wrong, gone wrong with everything?

But there was one thing to hang on to. These letters that she had swept up from the hall table, the letters that she had picked up from the floor slipped under the door, the letters that she was taking so for granted, as much now of her routine of life as her early morning chocolate or her tooth-brush, became by some turn of events, something super-natural, sub-normal, something that must spell escape, regeneration, beatitude. For wasn't that just what separated them, separated her now from this slightly ageing (poor darling she was only thirty but Hermione was taut with her youth's arrogance) Shirley? Wasn't it just that separated Shirley from Hermione? Shirley was odd and now in the light of the numerous mad engagements Hermione just a little pitied her. Thirty was getting on somehow, someway ageing. Yes, thirty must be an awful age, all done for, labelled, even Vérène saying in a new little, hard little manner, "but we all thought George was going to marry poor Shir-lee." Vérène was little and tight and suddenly one had lost faith too in Vérène, too busy to care more than smile, lost in a dream, lost in a vague happiness that made her eyes fill with tears and it was too dreadful to be pitied by Vérène. But why pity them? Why pity Hermione? A white staggering Walter stumbled into the little boudoir where Vérène had asked her to wait as "I am seeing some people, dull ones, you know who offer their con-gratulations." Hermione certainly didn't want to sit through French visits of congratulation and Walter had escaped, fallen into a little chair that must, it seemed, break under his beautiful massive body, mopped his forehead. "God, this getting married's horrible." Had he said that to Vérène? But one expected a man always to feel like that. Then smiling, all alert as Vérène came in to tell them of another gift and the dress won't be late, it's, it's— ravissante. O it was all ravissante. Ravissante. But God Hermione was like Walter in this. She didn't want to be married, all satin like Fayne Rabb, all a snare, not even married and now Vérène who was already— But one mustn't be horrible. Perhaps she wasn't. Anyhow what did it matter and was marriage always a sham, a pretence like this was? Ravissante. But the letters that at first she had so taken with her tooth-brush, with her morning chocolate became by a turn of events, different. Letters were different now, might mean something. Letters in the light of Shirley just turned thirty might mean something. Must mean something. George at Shirley's and George was vague like a magic lantern picture, all colour and no body. He didn't matter. Even his little jibes didn't any more matter. It seemed odd Shirley having him so much there, lost, it appeared, in intimate talk. Had George then come to explain, to make it all right, to get things on some kind of basis with this Shirley? But what anyhow did that matter? Letters that had meant nothing now began to mean things. "Streets. One goes through them with one's eyes shut and one's eyes open because there at Piccadilly Circus I bought some violets. Piccadilly. I go down Regent Street sometimes and do you remember the crocuses you wanted to see at Hampton Court? Only Americans see these things. But you just aren't. Do you remember that vale in Thessaly? But of course you don't. You have other things more precious to remember. Thanks for the Correggio. Funny but it is like me a little. Isn't it hot now in Paris? O tell me what the places look like. Chestnuts. I may be coming over later if I get that reviewing of the Guardian. Jerrold."

15 Darrington got his job, came over. Paris suddenly became (with the coming of Darrington) Paris. Space existed as space, Paris as Paris. Vérène someone little and tight that Jerrold had to be taken to see. Vérène being charming, in Vérène's eyes it was all right now. Hermione was no longer (not that she ever had exactly been) in the same catalogue as "poor Shirl-ee." Shirley herself being a little vague, lost talking on and off in bright spurts about Pater, about Landor. Darrington finding Shirley clever, sparks flying, George making a little mew-call from the divan in the corner. "Ain't you ever, Dryad, going to speak to me again properly?" "I can't see that I, George, haven't." "What's the matter? Why so stand-offish, Dryad." In the light of Darrington's arrival, she could afford to sting out at him, "don't you think, George, it was a little, just a little—odd—" "Odd, Dryad?" "I mean if you were engaged all that time—to—kiss me." "The odd thing is not to kiss you, Dryad." "No. I don't like it—" George had pulled her down beside him where he curled half hidden by the very grand baby-grand. "Listen Dryad darling—" "O George you might—you might have told me—" "Dryad develop-ing a Puritan conscience—" "No. No that isn't the argument. It doesn't—seem—right—" "Well, Dryad as I never see my—ah—fian-cée save when surrounded by layers of its mother, by its family portraits, by its own inhibitions, by the especial curve of the spiral of the social scale it belongs to, I think you might be—affable." "Would you be affable if I were engaged to—to—Darrington?" "Are you?" "I didn't say I was or wasn't. Would you?" But George's only answer to that was a crude drawing her toward him and the baby-grand with its baby-grand manner scowling its disapproval. O it looked hideous, servant-girlish as she saw them in the polished surface of the very grand baby-grand. A little distorted, a distorted vague Hermione pushing away, a distorted heavy George. It was ugly, a lacquer carica-ture in a polished surface. This was what love was, would be, a heavy ruffled shining and yet hard picture. Someone pulling at something, one or the other pulling, the other (or the one) pulling. Pulling and pushing and all the beauty of virginal line and the glory of independ-ence shattered. Pulling, pushing. Grand piano. There . . . even though it had been America and Her was caught, glued in her domesticity somehow had more line, more beauty, more reality than this thing. This lost, somehow, already smirched Hermione who was

H.D.
96

(in the highly polished surface of the baby grand) pulling away from a monkey in its velvet jacket.

Lillian Merrick. The school at Rome. No. This couldn't conceivably go on forever. Eugenia with her many letters and these last ones, "We may be coming over so your father thinks you may stay. Be sure to see Mrs. de Leinitz and don't let your summer things be shabby. You hadn't enough last year and I can't imagine how you're managing. We love to hear all about your friends and your good times. I am glad Mrs. Walter Dowel has been so kind to you. How fortunate you are in knowing these brilliant people." Brilliant people. Yes George in a red monkey jacket, Fayne with a white face painted like a circus rider, Fayne doing her little "stunt" balancing on toe on a white galloping stallion and holding two clowns (Llewyn and Morrison?) balanced on quivering buttocks. Not hers. The buttocks of the great white horse, and Fayne Rabb pirouetting in white face and white frilled petticoats, Fayne turned from Pygmalion with strong sturdy thighs and staunch young shoulders into a parody of womanhood. Doing her little prize stunt for the world to see. "But you can't *marry* him."

No, one didn't marry. One did stunts. But she wasn't any longer interested in George. "Don't rumple and ruffle my dress." "Since when Dryad, have you begun to worry about dresses?" "Since this minute."

Hermione emerged from behind the shelter of the very grand baby-grand piano. "Shirley, we never ask you to play for us—" "Gawd, don't ask her—" Shirley looked up an odd twist to her fine straight eye-brows. A white flame of pain crossed her eyes, dark eyes, wide apart staring like a crystal gazer's. Why had George said that? Was he being rude simply? But now his rudeness seemed insanity, seemed blatant cruelty. His rudeness, his casual approach to both of them, for she was sure he had kissed, had long been kissing Shirley. Don't marry him or her—just go on kissing them. Well, what anyhow did it matter. Wide flame of pain in the almond eyes of Shirley flashed, went, and the almond eyes of Shirley were just odd almond eyes with a little glow of passion. "O George is like that. He thinks I play so badly." Play badly? Was that it? Was that the thing between them? Hermione knew there had been something there. Something that had drawn her near though so straightly separated, from Shirley.

"O but you don't—I'm sure you don't. I know you do play nicely." It was Darrington. For a moment pain swept away and Hermione loved Darrington. Darrington who was making her write again, who was bringing almond eyes back to their normal level of just rather odd blank kindness. Shirley was very kind. Little suppers, tea at any time, people coming and going. It must be lovely to have such a charming flat, a place you could see people, not crowding odd hours in at the Louvre, in restaurants, in tea-shops. It was exhausting never being able to talk properly to Darrington. Shirley was very fortunate, clever too, that was what was wrong really with Shirley. She was clever.

"The trouble is you're too clever to be a real musician." "O?" "I feel it. You could write. Criticism. The two don't go together."

What was lies, what was truth in all this? But this wasn't true. This table, this chair, this supper, this coffee after supper, this cigarette. But was this true, just this, this smoke wreathing up and up in the rose-shaded light of the lamp casting its again shaded glow through the half drawn curtain of the inner room beyond the wide French window. Was this true? Was this smoke curling up and up and the numb beatific column of its beauty quite true? "I'm glad I've at last taught you to smoke properly." The voice at her elbow as part of the vagueness of the cigarette was true in the same sense that the smoke was true. Darrington's voice. Darrington's voice had always been true for it had always (from the first) been vague, been apprehended through a sort of trance state as first apprehended in that vague drawing room somewhere (London?) where George had made pronouncements on sandal wood and thy painted bark. Whose painted bark? "O George I thought you'd written them to *me*." "What made you think that Lointaine?" "I thought you'd told me you had." "O but I tell that to everybody." So George had apparently. Told that to everybody. But George Lowndes with his stark beauty, with his brush of beard, with his velvet jacket, with his now accepted scholarship and his little recognized position wasn't true. He had suddenly projected himself out, become a certain person with a certain reputation and something had departed. Was he a cigarette simply that had been smoked out? "I'm glad Astraea that at last you're dedicated." "Dedicated?" It was Walter asking the question, Walter resting his great weight heavily in the low garden chair with the light from within and the shadow from without struggling across his alabaster features. O God. Again pity wracked her. Pity rose and spoiled the dream, the drift and drug of the thing, this smoke that curled up, up in Vérène's garden, that was reality. Pity cut across like white hail across a smoke-blue lilac bush. Pity was white hail that slashed and tore and rent her. Pity. For who simply? Could it be for Vérène all smooth and small and dark opposite Walter, presiding in her own little garden (their own little garden) over the excellent and exquisite al fresco little supper? Could pity blight with its arrogant assumptions this place of peace, this garden, this far and far and far slow rumble and pulse and beat of light that was far Paris. Could pity so arrogantly enter this demesne? "O Vérène darling, Shirley (I saw her yesterday) sent a message to you—something—I've half forgotten—" "Was it about coming in on Monday?" "Yes. That was it. I said I was due out here this evening. She was having some people in and asked—me—" (Hermione had almost said—"us") "to meet them. When I said I was dining at Vérène's she said, 'give her this message for me. Say Shirley's sorry but she can't possibly come Monday.'" "But she promised—long—ago—" "Why worry with her?" It was Walter, alabaster rose and shadow. Walter spoke seated massive and great in the low chair. "Why, Vérène, have you been so concerned about her?" Vérène said, pouring coffee that she didn't know, had never really liked the girl, but as she was one of Walter's pupils— "*Was* she? Did she ever do anything?" It was Darrington who asked this, evidently half out of curiosity, half to fill the gap, and Vérène said before Walter could anticipate her, "nothing."

Walter said, "I shouldn't exactly say that Vérène. She had ideas." "What sort of ideas?" "O, things that you—wouldn't—follow—" And someone laughed, was it Vérène simply, blind in her arrogance, full and blown open like a summer rose? The wind had ruffled her petal, the lordly king-wind had stooped from the North, had swept down from the cold irradiance of glaciers to embrace her. Vérène might laugh proud in her little moment. Rose that the wind must pass.

"O I thought her rather odd—her eyes—charming—" Hermione said this. She had thought her odd, began to see her as charming now that she was wreathed about with smoke, with lilac-blue that was the odd and prevalent image of the vague sensation of rest and of recognition Darrington's voice brought her. It had been that way from the first. Darrington had been a voice before he was a presence. He was a presence now, permeated as white wine with alcohol. Alcohol was crude, a poison without the white wine. Darrington's voice was the distillation of pure aether. What was his voice? Again it broke across her musings. "Old Lowndes, it appeared, was one time thick with her."

The thing that Darrington said was not exactly the right thing to say on the verge of George Lowndes' engagement. But that was the nice thing about Darrington. He said the wrong thing in the right voice. There was something piquante, engaging in his manner. He said these things deliberately, one felt he knew he said them, not crudely like George, with his "for Gawd's sake don't," when they had asked Shirley to play for them. Walter said, "yes, we thought here, she was going to marry him."

Talk about Shirley, about nothing, about something. It appeared suddenly to Hermione cruel, petty, unmitigatedly mean to talk this way about Shirley. She supposed, with a little shiver of apprehension that this is the way they would (obviously) go on about her if she stayed hanging on much longer, alone, not with her people, a bit of drift-wood. But there was Darrington. "Darrington to the rescue." There was Darrington. But she must do something—do something. Smoke of cigarette. Let me smoke, forget. Let me forget simply. What was it that she wanted to forget and was forgetting? She tried numbly to recall the thing she was forgetting. Walter spoke anticipating her thought, her half remembered image, "funny that girl marrying." "What girl?" It was Vérène asking. "That friend of Hermione's. Fayne Rabb."

"Mademoiselle is dead." The maid said this simply. She made no gesture of apology. Something was lacking. People didn't say in French, "Mademoiselle is dead." They didn't say in English "Miss est morte." "Mademoiselle est morte." That is what she said. Was it possible that Hermione had mistaken it. Was she saying, Mademoiselle is out, or had she forgotten her French, did morte mean asleep or gone away to the country or married or engaged or writing a grand opera? It might, it appeared mean any of these things but it couldn't possibly mean what the word meant in the dictionary. Hermione had never to her knowledge heard this word, pronounced so blatantly. Morte. Or was it Morgue? Morgue, a place for dead people. The idea did not enter her head. Her heart stopped beating. "But Mademoiselle asked me here for tea; it *is* Sunday?"

The maid in her ordinary voice assured Hermione that it was Sunday. Hermione assured the maid that she had been asked for Sunday. They continued in their odd detached way to argue for it couldn't be true what she said. Shirley wasn't dead.

Shirley wasn't dead. It was impossible. There were a thousand things she might have said to her. Shirley with eyes gone wide like a crystal gazer's. Hermione had suspected something terrible. What was terrible? Was marriage—no it was death—terrible? "But we thought she was going to marry George." Little May day communicants going to church in long veils and long frocks and white slippers and hands crossed over prayer-books. Brides of God. Little wise virgins. Virgins. Shirley was a virgin. That was what made them laugh, asking why she didn't marry George Lowndes. Soon they would laugh at Hermione who hadn't married George Lowndes. "But of course you can't *marry* him." Marry. No. Dress up and parade like a vulgar midinette in a bride's veil and let your mother-in-law (by proxy) hold up the long glove with the severed finger. "But it's for the *bride's ring*." Let them all do that. Chestnuts had never been so glorious. Trois sous la botte. Livre. But that was muguet. It wasn't a pound, it was a book. France little book like in the revelation for her to devour simply. Bitterness of things too sweet. O broken singing of the dove. What was it all about? Was this why she couldn't go to Vérène's and Walter had said why worry so about her. Wide rose, Vérène, with little intuitions, with a conscience. Did she know this was about to happen? Monday. This was Sunday. "But this is—Sunday." Hermione repeated it to the maid who was standing ghouling at her. "She asked me to come Sunday." Still the heavy figure with its impassivity blocked the door way. Black beetle. That was it simply. Black beetle. Insensitive. Grasping. Did one tip people? What for? She didn't want to go in. "What, whaaat did Mademoiselle die of?" The face looked at her. Face blurred. Vérène pitied them all. All brides of God. Little communicants. Wise virgins. But she was with God. Afternoon spoiled. Late for tea. She had hurried but she needn't have hurried. She was too late anyhow. "What did Mademoiselle die of?" Faces blurred. Fayne Rabb. What was it all about anyway? The maid leaned toward her whispering.

But who killed her? Walter was looking at Vérène, Vérène was looking at Walter. The letter lay between them. Shadows in the room. "How dreadful for you, Hermione." Someone was saying it was dreadful for Hermione. Someone was breaking the silence that lay between Vérène and Walter, the silence that became tighter and harder like an ice floe that becomes harder the harder the river presses on it. Someone should say something. Someone did. It was Darrington. "But poor Hermione rushed out to tea. I was to meet her there. I met her coming back—on the stairs." Someone had met someone. Who? Darrington had met Hermione. "Darrington to the rescue." Someone was thinking in all this of Hermione. But Hermione looked at Walter, looked at Vérène. Walter though he did not turn his head, felt Hermione. He felt Hermione staring as he had felt her in his music. He knew Hermione was there though he was looking at Vérène. Must they all feel sorry for Vérène because Vérène had done it? But had Vérène done it? Who had killed Shirley. The letter lay on the floor. Walter was twisting one great hand with great strong fingers. Fingers that had begun at three, tiny fingers, going on and on and Walter had that kind of power, detached power. It was detached power that had killed Shirley. Walter simply. It was Walter's music. "But how was—I—to—know—" Walter was asking this of the void though Vérène as usual thought anything addressed to the void by Walter was meant for her. She would mother Walter. O don't let me see her mothering Walter. "It wasn't—your—fault—Vrrralter." No. Don't let him know it was his fault for it was his fault. The letter said so though she had not read the letter. She had found Walter reading the letter as she stumbled in to Clichy. She had rushed to them . . . a letter had reached Walter. What did the letter say? It was on the floor there. Pick up the letter, someone, it's shameful lying on the floor—no, I didn't see her. She was lying on the floor. Anyone could look at her, inspectors, horrible people for she was outside the law. She couldn't be cremated. She had killed herself. She had left another letter asking to be cremated. Did it matter? But she couldn't be. All these letters, meaning nothing, meaning everything. They had all killed her.

George had killed her certainly. It was Walter saying it, "But we thought she was going to marry—George." George must be blamed, scape-goat. He was a scape-goat. Kissing them all. Let all the sins of all the kisses be upon him. For this was a sin. Kisses that had killed Shirley. Vérène was making it right, was trying to make it right. "She should have married—someone." She should have married. Then it would have been all right. Then she wouldn't have been a virgin, gone mad, simply, like Cassandra. Shirley was like Cassandra smitten by the sun-god. Music. Walter.

Music could kill people. Love could kill people. It was Hermione who had killed her. Hermione on May-day might have reached her. Shirley looking wan and odd, seeing that Hermione was unhappy. Shirley had seen this. Hermione might have reached across, said simply, "I am so unhappy." Hermione hadn't done this. Hermione had killed her.

"But I killed her." "You are mad, dear child. She fell in love with Walter. The letter made it all clear. Vérène asked me, as someone from outside to read the letter. I read it carefully. Dementia. Suicide in the family. She was obsessed with the idea of some white after-life, words like that. I can't remember. It was a touching document. She died of love simply." "No. I might have helped. I was so immersed in my own idiotic little petty hurt, I couldn't see her. She asked me to come to her house that first day, May-day, in such an odd voice. If I hadn't been so immersed in myself, so shattered with the web of myself, I would have seen her. Myself had wound round myself so that I was like a white spider shut in by my own hideous selfishness. I should have been a bird, a sort of white star or bird winging up and up and up—I'm not religious. The Rabbs said I wasn't. I should have been a sort of saint, a sort of flaming thing loving my martyrdom. I should have been white and clear and like a sword at the head of armies or a banner in the hands of soldiers. I should have said love is like this, see I have loved and I am a banner, a star. It would have hurt me to have said that and I didn't want to be hurt. I was too small. I let my own petty pain wind about me. I let myself be obscured by myself and I became a white spider hidden in web, a mesh of self. A grey hideous web, I can almost see it. Fayne Rabb killed her."

"Killing and not-killing have nothing to do with it. The letter made it all clear. She had been in love with Walter for some years. She couldn't go on any longer with it—" "It isn't true. It's all lies. No one of us is in love with any one of us. What is love? A circus dancer with a white horse balancing to a fanfare on the back of a black stallion. Circus dust, spectators. What is love? A monkey in a velvet jacket reflected in the back of a polished hand-organ, embracing a white satyress. What is love? A parody—smoke wreathing between lilac bushes, another in a crinoline or a bustle, a dart catching a feather in a gallant hat, a march, a drum, a beating, a forgetting, a memory, I send thee Rhodocleia for thy hair—" "Astraea." "What is Astraea? What are we all? You are the only one that said a kind word to her—" "Astraea, you exaggerate. You were very nice to her, always." "Nice? Sheer nice as anyone might have been nice. I, with my flair for rightness, my spirit, my wings. I the thing that Walter said drew out his music, the nymph, the Dryad. I the Spirit you all talk about sat and watched another topple—topple—fall—" "Astraea. This is all wrong, morbid of you." "I have lost faith in the thing they loved so. Walter saying I drew music out of him. What is music to a soul lost?" "It isn't lost. Her soul isn't—" "Plato says we are servants of the gods. No servant can neglect his work. To kill oneself is to drop out, lacking in service." "The gods won't look hard on her, Hermione." "Maybe not. It's me, I'm thinking of. What have I been doing? Where have I been? Wandering in a maze. Hermione this. Hermione that. An angel, a saint, a poet, a child. I am none of these things."

"You are all of these things." "I'm tired of this. I'm sick of my own attitude. What is Fayne Rabb beside this thing? It was so clean. They said she had planned it all so carefully. She left money for the maid's taxi fare, just the right amount so that she should rush out with that letter to the Dowels. So clean. Not anything horrible. So clean under her breast. All gone. That is true love. That is true marriage. Fear gone. A white bullet—" "Hermione. This thing has upset you. Hermione . . ."

Voices down the street. Voices down the hall. Fatigue so great that she held her head up under it, above it like a drowning man gasping,

gasping for breath. Herself, the immaculate image, the saint, the spirit, had been shattered for her. Forever. A white bullet had so shattered it. Intuition and fine feeling had not been fine enough to sense this. The very proximity of this other spirit. The very nearness of this authentic sister, tangled in a worse web than she was. Herself had wound about herself blinding herself to the soul's unhappiness about her. Life had been cruel she had thought. It was herself simply who had been stupid in being so deceived by sheer appearances. Fayne on a white horse led the fantastic circus. Parade round and round a room, parade round and round a world. The whole world was girded by this fantastic procession. Monkeys in velvet jackets jibbered at her. None of the world escaped them. Venice, Prado, Spain, Holland, Dresden— Names came and went like lights flashing on a white screen. Was there no reality in all this? Names and fantastic backgrounds. America, the wilderness, the rockies. How could Americans cope with all this? How could they cope with so much having so many racial strands and counter-impulses? America had killed her.

"I know she was alone too much. She had got away from home. She was, we thought, so happy." She had got away from home. Shirley had escaped and this happened. Would this happen to them all, to all of them? Darrington might help her to work and she could have something, claim something out of all this. Spain in the Californias. Strains of Dutch and Latin in their make-ups. Coming back to Europe. Flaming out like marsh-lights, brilliant with no roots. Here and there, trying to get lost. Henry James lost in Sussex marshes. One after another but she wouldn't be lost. Henry James wasn't really lost. Not Henry James, not Whistler, not Sargent. Lost yet not lost in London.

France was a book of beauty and of terror. Rising up to the highest attainment, Walter talking of notes in the air, beyond the air, harps. It was Walter who had killed her . . .

PART II

1 Darrington came across the room. Candles made a smudge in the distance. How far away was the other side of the room? It wavered and fell. It fell and wavered. Perhaps next time it really would fall down. "Jerrold."

Darrington came across the room. He sat on her bed, their bed. She hadn't really gone to bed, just piled the cushions behind her back and sat up and sat up and listened. Darrington came as he had always come at her voice, coming toward her, his head bent forward, his yellow French book half open in his hand. "Jerrold." "Darling." Darrington called her darling, had always called her darling, had been calling her darling forever. "Where—am I?"

"You're right here, here right enough. Thank God we got you out of that damned nursing home." "Yes. I forget. Keep forgetting. The funniest thing was when they stood at the end of my bed and told me about the crucified—" "Hush. Hush darling." "Jerrold." "Darling?" "Are there any men left, any at all in the streets, not, not in khaki?"

"Keep quiet. Don't talk. Don't talk about it, darling." "I can't think. Can't think about anything else and yet all night (is it night?) my head has been going round and round. You remember that girl I almost forgot." "Which girl Astraea?" "That American girl that crossed with me—when just was it?" "You mean when you first crossed, two years before the war." "Yes two years before the war. Where was it?" "Where was what?" "Someone, something got— killed." "Hush darling—don't talk about killed." "I don't mean the nursing home. I don't mean the horror of the nurses. I can talk of that now. I don't mean their taking me into the cellar—while—it— was happening. I know they took me into the cellar. I know the baby was dead. I know all that. I'm not afraid of talking about it. Really Jerrold." "Hush. Hush darling." "I mean long ago, something happened long and long ago—the other side of a chasm. Someone. Something. A silver bullet—" "Don't talk of bullets darling."

"Read Browning to me." "What just do you want dear and the room's too dark; can't turn on the electricity till the raid's over." "Read anything—your voice—it was always your voice—sometimes in the worst times, I hear your voice. I wouldn't have minded if they hadn't been so horrid to—you—" "Do keep still. Don't fidget. Now rest there." Darrington pulled the cushion to a flat plateau, lifted her by the shoulders, pushed her into the down cushions, "now don't talk."

"What shall I read, darling?" "That thing about Fortù—Fortù, was it? The Englishman in Italy, you know what I mean. It takes me back to Sorrento, to Ana-Capri. It makes things come right. *Gaudy melon flower.* I said those things over and over and over before—it—before it arrived, I was going to say. But it didn't. I used to think I would keep all Italy, the melon flowers, the gold broom above Amalfi. It wasn't England I loved having it. How could I have loved England? God—God—God—" "Stop talking . . . stop . . . stop, darling." "I can't stop talking. I've been quiet for weeks, all those weeks in that filthy place. They didn't kill me anyhow. Their beastliness at least made me glad for one thing. I was glad, so glad it was killed, killed by them, by their beastliness, their constant nagging. The Queen brought Atkinson's eau-de-cologne. But would eau-de-cologne mean anything to anyone who was having a baby, *having I say a baby*, while her husband was *being killed* in Flanders? They got exaltées, those nurses and their cheeks flushed with ardour and they said . . . O Mrs. Darrington, how *lucky* for *you* to have your husband when poor Mrs. Rawlton's husband is actually now lying wounded . . . and Mrs. Dwight-Smith's husband is MISSING. Their cheeks went pink with almost consumptive joy and fervour while they drove and drove and drove one toward some madness. Why isn't Mr. Darrington in Khaki? What is khaki? Khaki killed it. They killed it. Italy died and cras amet and I send you Rhodocleia for your hair and swiftly walk o'er the western wave, spirit of night. Italy died with it— *Why isn't Mr. Darrington in khaki?* Good old ecstatic baby-killers like the Huns up there. What is khaki?" "Hush hush—" "Another gun. Perhaps we'll go this time—read Fortù."

> *"Fortù, Fortù, my beloved one,*
> *Sit here by my side."*

"Go on, go on reading. Don't let anything stop you. Go on. It will make things come right. Go on reading. Don't let anything stop you. After all percussion or something only broke all the upstairs windows last time . . . they may do better this time . . ."

> *"Pomegranates were chapping and splitting*
> *In halves on the tree . . . straight out of the rock side*
> *Some burnt sprig of bold hardy rock-flower . . . great*
> *butterflies fighting, some five for one cup . . ."*

"Butterflies fighting makes me forget. Funny my being alone. And it was gone, all Italy was gone. Amalfi was gone . . . Amalfi's gone with that crash. They're trying for Euston station but they've got Amalfi . . . the things one didn't know were real, until shattered by unreality . . . guns, guns, guns, guns. Our own gun makes more noise but it rattles nicely, just over us that anti-aircraft . . . Amalfi. They've got Amalfi this time. The zeppelins and the anti-aircraft guns are both shattering Amalfi. Butterflies fighting, some five for one cup . . . did you say some five for one cup? Somewhere butterflies are fighting . . . but what butterfly can fight against this thing any longer? I should never have dreamed five butterflies could fight some five for one cup. And why did we come here? Because that plaster Flora was spilling her plaster basket of plaster rose rosette roses like the one (almost) on the long road to Ana-Capri. Do you remember why we took these rooms? That was why. No. Don't speak. Hold me closer. They always try for Euston. It was because that plaster Flora spilled her plaster flowers and we remembered she was just a little like the one in the Signorina's garden. Oranges were in flowers . . . winter blossom and winter Hebridean apples, gold winter oranges above Mediterranean water. My grandfather said of all the things he wanted to see in Europe (we always spoke of Europe in those days, not France, not England, not Germany, just Europe) was the Bay of Naples. The Bay of Naples . . . . . . that was near enough. I can't get any exaltation out of bombs bursting. God knows I've conscientiously *tried* to do it. Perhaps it's because I'm not English, not European. I feel Europe is splitting like that pomegranate *in halves on the tree*, Europe, all of it that I so love . . . how long have we been married?"

"Why do you ask that? It's almost three years now." "One year before the war. Italy and coming back just in time and everything broken, everyone scattered . . . everything different. Italy . . . is Italy different? But it can't be. Italy would be the same if all the Huns of all the universe (who exactly are Huns?) should over-run it. Things now are like Gibbon. The decline and Fall. This is history, I suppose. Go on reading."

> "*. . . about noon from Amalfi . . . his basket before us*
> *All trembling alive*
> *With pink and grey jellies, your sea-fruit . . .*"

"Yes. And lizards everywhere. Flowers burnt out of rocks, like volcanic embers. Those red anemones. O yes. Everything will come right. Everything has come right. *Open my heart and you will see engraved inside of it Italy.* But I love France too. But Italy is to France what a red ember is to a polished gem. Yes France is a gem polished and cold and flawless and beautiful I can't think of men dying, only of France, la patrie a polished amethyst or some eighteenth century cameo. No, no Hun (what is a Hun anyway?) should break and steal and plunder. A pity though it's happened. That's because I'm not English I suppose. We always spoke of Europe. I love Europe."

> "*Meantime, see the grape-bunch they've brought you,*
> *The rain-water slips*
> *O'er the heavy blue bloom on each globe*
> *Which the wasp to your lips, still follows*
> *Still follows with fretful persistence:*
> *Nay taste, while awake . . .*"

"I did taste . . . but it's gone. They've broken it . . ."

> "*Next, sip this weak wine*
> *From the thin green glass flask, with its stopper*
> *A leaf of the vine.*"

"It was you who taught me to love those things, Capri Nero, Capri Bianco, cigarettes, the pear trees against Solaro were a mass of blossom and there were prickly pear and cactus. The small goats scampered before us and there was that singular goat-herd (for a long time we thought we'd dreamed it) piping under that one clump of cool willows. Cool willows and below, so far below that one could for a breath have flung oneself down, the sea. The sea. Thalassa. Yes, it was Greece, not like Tuscany. We had Greece, having Italy."

> "*The wild fruit trees bend . . .*
> *All is silent and grave;*
> *'Tis a sensual and timorous beauty,*
> *How fair but a slave.*
> *So I turned to the sea . . ."*

"So I turned to the sea. Do you remember? I went first. You were heavier. You were surprised and I loved plaguing you. You had only seen me in London and in Paris and you had no idea what I was like really. You found what I was like really. I think it frightened you. Open my heart and you will see engraved inside of it Italy. How could I have known, loving France, loving England that I would love so much better, Italy? France is a polished gem, a priceless intaglio, England is a great wide rose spread just before its falling, Italy is a live ember burning the hearts of men."

Now why must he do this? Why must he do this? She might have known he would do this, clutching her in his arms, the moment she was happy with him. Everything had come clear talking of Italy. Images smudged, as it were, on a square of thick glass were smudged out by this Sirocco rain they read of. Italy and the talk of Italy had washed out the black, dark grey and khaki-coloured images. Khaki images were splashed like mud across the clear window of her mind and now the clear images of beauty, the gaudy melon flower, the rock islets showed clear. She looked through her mind into a far country. Pays lointain . . . pro patria. She looked through a clear glass far and far and just before her as if the wall of the room had parted, she was looking through between columns (the two sides of the enormous book-case) into a fair country, rocks, the silver lentisk, the white plaques of sea-rosemary, a flute in the distance and the lines of Theocritus. Why must Darrington now spoil it? Hadn't she had enough? Months and months of waiting and now this. Now this, this curious weakness and this reward of weakness; the mind clarified past all recognition, herself gazing through her mind into a fair country. There was no wind. The sea so far below gave no sound. A boy far and far and far was pulling a boat and colours familiar through cheap water colours all their lives took vivid form, were prismatic colours seen through crystal. The walls of cone-shaped Vesuvius and the jagged edge of Capri, the wall that was Capri was rising out of the sea, an island, a Greek island, the island where Odysseus heard the Syren voices. Little plots of earth set like bright rugs on the vertical island mountain, were bright marigolds, and clumps of early winter flowering irises. Irises, white, yellow, blue and lavender. Marguerites growing in enormous balls of white flower made the immaculate white walls a shade more subtle—shell grey. Oranges were flowering and against citron flowers great globes of ripe fruit, rocks and the crevices and the slopes of trees and flax flowers laid like rugs, true gardens of the Hesperides. A church bell (a cathedral bell) was ringing and it was Easter. "Do you remember that odd poor Christ we said looked like Adonis?" Darrington remembered, but he didn't really care as she cared. He was living in the present and its terror.

Why didn't he go then if he felt like this? He said he would wait now for conscription, he was dead sick of hypocrisy and can't his "gov'nor" try to get him into a snobby regiment for the family kudos. Family. Kudos. But she was sick, so weak that she only wanted him to go, to go away somewhere, somehow quickly. Everyone took it out on her, would do when she got a little stronger. Nurses bending over her . . . watching her . . . asking . . . no, no. It was impossible. There was no such criminal cruelty in any world, never never in England. She had dreamed a horrible dream and reality was different. Reality that she looked at, propped on the heavy cushions while the guns went on, went on, went on, was something very different. Guns dropped sound like lead-hail and if the guns were quiet they might hear some more pertinent manifestation. One like last time, an enormous shattering, breaking and tearing . . . guns over-head were better though they dropped lead hail that beat and seared her brain, brought pain back to her consciousness. "O Mrs. Darrington. Everything's arranged beautifully. There is at the moment, only one other—in—your—state." Only two of them. Only two of them waiting. But the other woman had a husband in France so they were nicer to her. O God. Why isn't my husband in France? Guns, guns, guns. Let him at least have the decency to leave me, let me lie here listening. I love listening. Maybe the next one will crash on us. Then I will go simply through the two tall columns (two upright edges of the enormous book-case) into a land that claims me. Patriotism. "There was that Austrian poet at Corpo di Cava, do you remember?" Darrington remembered but there was an odd wide glare to his eyes. He was thinking like those nurses of the cellar.

"Darling wouldn't it be better—in—your—condition—" "No. No. No. I can't go downstairs with all the other people. At least it's cool here and so quiet—" "*Quiet?*" "I mean with you—yes—quiet—" She wasn't with Darrington really, not here. But how explain it to him? His eyes went wide, vacant. He didn't dare think about it. O God don't let his eyes go vacant, then he'll spoil it, then he'll bend and kiss me. Why can't we be happy? Why can't I just remember?

"But you don't care?" "Darling. You—know—I—do—" Guns were quiet. Tea steamed into her face and she drank the fumes of the tea like some drug fiend, the scent of drug. Tea smelt of far sweet hours, of afternoons of all the happy little times they'd had together. Darrington had made the tea while she lay listening. He was nice, did nice things. She supposed he really did care, had been sorry. It's so hard for a man to say such things. He knew it hurt her to talk about the baby. She supposed he had cared. He wouldn't have let her go through it, almost a year and her mind glued down, broken, and held back like a wild bird caught in bird-lime. The state she had been in was a deadly crucifixion. Not one torture (though God that had been enough) but months and months when her flaming mind beat up and she found she was caught, her mind not taking her as usual like a wild bird but her mind-wings beating, beating and her feet caught, her feet caught, glued like a wild bird in bird-lime. Darrington hadn't known this. No one had known this. No one would ever know it for there were no words to tell it in. How tell it? You can't say this, this . . . but men will say O she was a coward, a woman who refused her womanhood. No, she hadn't. But take a man with a flaming mind and ask him to do this. Ask him to sit in a dark cellar and no books . . . but you mustn't. You can't. Women can't speak and clever women don't have children. So if a clever woman does speak, she must be mad. She is mad. She wouldn't have had a baby, if she hadn't been. Darrington had said he would "take care of her." Did they always say that? Darrington had said he would take . . . but he was, he had made the tea, had brought her the tea. He had been reading Browning and the words had cleared her mind, swept away horrors like clean rain on a mud spattered window. Darrington had read her,

> Next sip this weak wine
> From the thin green glass flask, with its stopper,
> A leaf of the vine.

Words had fused with her horror and the memories that weren't real, like a drug. Words were a drug. Darrington had given her this drug.

Darrington had given her words and the ability to cope with words, to write words. People had been asking her (just before the war) for poems, had written saying her things had power, individuality, genius. Darrington had done this. Therefore she must remember, try to remember, try to be things she had been before the war—no before *it* started. The world was caught as she had been caught. The whole world was breaking and breaking for some new spirit. Men were dying as she had almost died to the sound (as she had almost died) of gun-fire. Guns, guns, guns, guns. Thank God for that. The guns had made her one in her suffering with men—men—men— She had not suffered ignobly like a woman, a bird with wings caught, for she was alone and women weren't left alone to suffer. There were always doctors, and mothers, and grand-mothers. She had been alone . . . alone . . . no, there were nurses. No there weren't nurses. Nurses had all run upstairs to get the others to bring the others . . . babies were crying . . . ghastly mistake . . . some doctor . . . and guns . . . but there were guns in France and she was in France for women didn't suffer this way. She was suffering for two, for herself and Darrington. Darrington had refused suffering . . . "O no, Jerrold. Don't let them push you in now. Wait decently for conscription."

Unmarried men were going, had gone. They would soon get Darrington. God, God, God, God, God. Why hadn't he gone? Why didn't he go? People's faces—"O Mrs. Darrington. It's so funny. You're the only woman here whose husband isn't . . ." Isn't? God. But it was true. Guns. Guns. Guns. Thank God she had suffered to the sound of guns and the baby wasn't . . . dead . . . not born . . . still born . . . but it didn't matter. "Darling but—you—don't—care—any—more."

2 "Jerrold, but I do care." By a super-human effort, she lifted her face to his and smothered under his kisses, she went on with it, "yes, I do care awfully," for what did it matter? It didn't matter. It wasn't real and what she was doing had no reality, no meaning. It was one with drab walls, walls of drab men that stood between her and—guns, guns, guns. But Darrington would go soon, would go to France soon, so that she could lift up her face to his and let his arms (khaki arms now) hold her close, close, "being away from you has made the difference. I see what you are now, have always been." She would have to go on with it, no matter what might happen for his arms were khaki arms now and soon he might be dead, dead—what a relief. No, she mustn't think things like that. Had she thought it? No, she hadn't thought it. She had never thought it. "You've made everything so lovely here. I never realized how huge the room was. Dinner was so charming with the white wine." White wine? Where had it come from? White wine. Delia had sent her some white wine, saying she looked peaked, Delia being heavenly, everyone being heavenly because of Jerrold being in Khaki, they were being nice to her though everyone was gone. Did they think she wanted another baby? Were they being nice to her hoping she might have one? Was there nothing else in the world? Men and guns, women and babies. And if you have a mind what then? But there were men with minds, must be men with minds, feeling as she did and it wasn't so bad, now Darrington was in khaki. Going to France soon. She must keep up. "Where did the white wine come from?" "O Delia sent it, delicious Delia, done up in uniform, hateful meet-ings—" but she mustn't be horrid about Delia. They were all busy, all the pretty drawing room turned into a red cross section and she knew she ought to have gone on making swabs but it was so horrible, not seeing swabs but what they were meant for, and talking, how they gossiped and Delia working so hard. Poor Delia something had gone out of her. Delia however hard Hermione might try to think it, wasn't the same. She had lost her soul somehow in this mess, this work room, this lint, this cotton wool. But no. It was Hermione who was horrid. How horrid to hate them, all the women who went on talking as if they were enjoying it, and the worst of it was one felt they *were* enjoying it. It was horrible of her not to but how could she help it? How could she help her vivid mind not seeing? Her mind had been trained to see. Cultivated. For just this horror? Women talking, picking cotton, making bandages. O God, don't they see what they're making them for? Am I the only coward? But I'm not. I had a baby, I mean I didn't—in an air raid. I know what pain is. They don't know. They can't see. But for Delia's sake (delicious Delia) one must go on, go on, done up in a dust cloth and an apron, with one's nun's face. But she wasn't a nun, all the rest had clean faces, her face wasn't clean. It was smudged with gun-powder for she had been under fire—wasn't a dressed up nurse, was a real casualty. "O Mrs. Darrington, we hear your husband—" What had they now heard? But they hadn't. They had mixed her up with someone else. Her husband wasn't better, wasn't worse. Her husband was just the same thank you. She had unwittingly said the right thing. They thought Jerrold was wounded, then someone whispering and they let her alone for they had found out that she had had a baby in an air raid just like Daily Mail atrocities. Novels were right. Even newspapers. She had had things happen in true journalese style, she Hermione who had drawn music from people, who was a child, they had said then, a spirit. Where was that? Who was a child, a spirit? And when had all that happened? Jerrold had gone back now. Hermione had gone back now to the Red Cross Unit that was Delia Prescott's great drawing room . . . where Walter had used to give concerts . . . where gold gauze had been the first Liberty gold gauze curtains Hermione had then seen, where Delia had always had wedges of winter hyacinths in the round sort of marble basin in the other little room off the big room where the tables were crowded now against the room wall. Jerrold had gone back. Hermione had gone back . . . Delia was resting by her. "O is that you Delia?" Must talk to Delia about something else. She couldn't go on hearing their callous appraisal of how someone "took" something. People all "took" things like that. But she hadn't. But they didn't know she hadn't, she would go on pretending. But she might get across to Delia. Delia, delicious Delia, who wasn't (nobody could accuse her) delicious in that fawn-mud uniform. "Delia." "Dryad." Dryad. She would scream simply. Delia had forgotten herself. She had called her Dryad. People now didn't call her Dryad. She had been Dryad in the old days before the earth opened and left part on one side, part on the other.

Thank God at least she was on this side of the chasm. She hadn't thank God, gone (as Jerrold wanted her) to America. "Jerrold was mad wanting me to go to the States." "Poor Jerrold." Why did Delia say poor Jerrold. "Why did you say that Delia?" "I don't know. After all he *is* in it and there's George out of it. I can't know how he does it." "But George is American." "That doesn't matter, Dryad. He's here with us." "But we're American." "That makes it twice as hard, people sneering (and they're right) about the dove-cote." "Yes they're right, but it isn't our fault, America's not in it." "They make us feel—it—is—" Delia must work five times as hard as anybody, Americans must suffer five times as hard as anyone else to show—to show what? An *American*. What did they mean by that? They said it so often nowadays. "Lady Prescott —" Delia tired to death trailed her weary khaki across to another table. Lady Prescott's unit. Delia.

Henry James died of it, their great American, and they said Americans didn't care. Didn't care. Some didn't. But when they did, O Gawd, as George used to put it. George. How could he go on wearing the same spotted speckled mosaic of cravats? But poor Georgio. One never shoved anyone into it, couldn't. Not even Darrington. Guns, guns, guns, and how small they looked like a little pack of hornets, so near and so small, a whole flotilla of little planes this time and how brave of them. How low they were flying, people talking of poisonous gas and people straining upward and all in the daylight, you couldn't say they weren't remarkable, extraordinarily brave, extraordinary super-human courage to fly low over London in full noonlight. And the crash that followed and would follow and all of us blinking up into a lead-grey light that was the full noon glare, how could they do it, and all of us really marvelling that they were so brave really, English people, so surprised, all of us were so surprised that noon seeing them fly so low. We all said they must be "us," we all said hearing the stifle and the low growl, "no, it's them." We all marvelled saying "baby killers," watching one, two three, all flying in a neat formation. "Those beasts. Baby-killers." Yes, that was true. How odd that the most blatant of journalese should be true, the most banal and obvious things were now true, the war had made things like that true. Hermione had never read, listened as little as she could until this became true. "Baby-killers." The most obvious and low level of horrors, O Gawd, and prose and poetry and the Mona Lisa and her eye lids are a little weary and sister my sister, O fleet sweet swallow were all smudged out as Pompeii and its marbles had been buried beneath obscene filth of lava, embers, smouldering ash and hideous smoke and poisonous gas. Was London still there? It was hard, would be hard to find it. Some of them might be left, there might be an afterwards and then some of them would get to work and dig, dig deep down and unearth all the old treasures. There was no use remembering the treasures, the cold, sweet uplifted arm of some marble Hermes, the tiny exquisite foot and bird-like ankle of some Aphrodite. Those things were being buried and all they could do was to watch, to stand in little groups and knots and after all with the volcano belching its filth over them, they were all one, must be all one, fear, terror, the obstinate courage that refused its terror made them one, facing bright hawks in an odd grey poisonous noon that swooped and swooped and we all said, "it can't be them, it's *us*, it must be, flying so low," but it was *them*, insinuating themselves, what courage, what dastardly beauty of destruction. "Baby-killers." Gods, men, flying high, flying low, "ours" were as brave of course, better, braver, better altogether, but not so tight, not so hard, not so devastating in their cruel cynicism. Baby-killers. Little Willie, big Willie, newspapers making all life on one level, but how could we help it? How could we help it? O thank God, I'm here, didn't go back to America. How could we help it. "Delia."

"What darling?" "How can you—go on—with—this? You're looking more and more ill. It's killing you." "It—has—killed—" O God. Hermione was forgetting. So many were dead. She had forgotten that Tony whom she hardly knew was out of it, "gone west," but he was away so much, the house always seemed Delia's property and Delia was above suspicion though people had a way (as people did in those days) of a little pitying Delia. Women would, of course, Delia being so beautiful, so chaste in that odd American-Greek manner in spite of what people said, when Americans were like that, they were high and pure and divine and Delia was like that and Lillian Merrick was like that. Tall and cold, new England, that was another name for a transplanted England that was more English than England, more

H.D.
118

Greek than Greek. Delia was like that. Lillian was like that. Her—
mione had forgotten Tony, there were so many Englishmen (had
been so many Englishmen) like that and Tony was so often in Africa
and so often he was running across to France. France. Tony was in
France for good. Hermione had forgotten Tony. "Delia?" "Dar—
ling—" But what could she say to Delia? She couldn't now say chuck
it, they're exploiting you, they're killing you, they're beasts, devils,
they are more cruel than the wasp-devils who fly low over London
and at least have their courage, their panache, what are these devils?
Nothing. They don't even have children for the other devils to kill.
We are in it. Killing and being killed. Who are these? Obscene rows
of suppressed women, not women, but some of them have lost sons.
O, don't let me be cruel. I am so muddled. Poor Tony. "I never—
knew—Tony." "He was like that, Hermione. No one ever knew him.
He said I was aloof and—" "Cold, Delia?" "Cold, darling. Yes, how
did you know?" "It's the sort of thing they say." "*They* say, Her—
mione?" "I mean—Jerrold."

3 O put it on, put it on, how funny I look, like a doll now. I
am a doll but it will amuse him. He said Merry Dalton was
so "cute," he said cute like that not knowing it was so silly,
so full of silly school-girl silliness to an American. English people
picked up American words, used them in such an odd way, "cute."
He said little Mary Dalton looked "cute" and Mary (they called
her Merry now) was setting the pace for everything. Poor Merry.
Hermione had suddenly got across to her, saw her in one tremen—
dous instant. But it was wrong Merry sympathizing with the Irish
(though she was half-Irish) it was all wrong. But one was so tired of
this disciplined death, this row of people one loved gone, all gone,
nice people who did the right thing gone, one might as well find out
how the others lived, for one couldn't believe that Delia's, that Lady
Prescott's red-cross section represented the whole of life. Being
good, being good, rolling, unrolling lint until her fingers ached and
she knew she would go mad but anything was excused when one's
husband came back, "no. I won't be here for another ten days, five
days, three days, (what was it) my husband is due across." Husband.

Husband. But this wasn't a husband. One might as well sleep with a navvy from the street only there weren't any, they were all soldiers, but this person was as strange, more strange to her than Captain Ned Trent whose father had been *the* General Trent of Ladyburg and Captain Ned was an Irish rebel and had reacted from the right thing to this extent, the police might call at any moment and it was all going round and round and round. "You are more beautiful than Merry Dalton," he had said, "but you haven't her charm." Was that it? Dash eau de cologne across black lidded eyes, make up, funny thing, how different she looked, it didn't look right, she looked hectic, ill with the bright stain but the others did it and Jerrold said she must brighten things up, make things hum, it was his last leave, he was sure it was his last leave. The old house, the big room, faster, faster, they could dance, pull the rug up, they could dance 1918, they could dance. 8,8,8. It was nineteen eighteen. 1918. Let them dance. Darrington had his commission now. Let them dance. It was bad form, shocking. Really Merry shouldn't have brought old Trent. Everyone knew what he was up to. It was shockingly bad form but he was such a gentleman. Yes, he was a gentleman like all the others, like Tony Prescott but he had got tired of good form and his father at Ladyburg and he was kicking up a little bit of a row and they couldn't shoot him because of Ladyburg and Darrington only a lieutenant really ought to be saluting and how funny for Trent was a real officer and a gentleman throwing bombs at the English in Ireland, not getting shot, all very complicated, can't shoot him, his father Trent of Ladyburg. Boer War Captain, a real soldier beside whom all this was bluster and obscene belching of volcanoes and ash and O God it was funny the taste of it, taste and smell, might as well sleep with a corpse as sleep with Darrington. The red made her eyes darker, brighter, make the red make eyes brighter, dark, dark rings, fatigue, looking dissipated, just fatigue, O God, might as well sleep with anyone as sleep with Darrington. Over the top and the best of luck. They were dancing. Merry had her little head thrown back and Jerrold bent and kissed her. You let them kiss you. They would be going back. The boy in the corner had lost his arm but he was still in uniform. He was wild and shy by turns, had never seen anything like this, Darrington had brought him, seemed puzzled, they seemed *ladies* but couldn't be, couldn't be, ladies don't dance—that—way— But he adored Darrington. Darrington had brought him and this was Darrington's wife—widow. She had almost said for Darrington was dead. If only there was someone she could tell about Darrington, would the boy know? She wanted to get to someone, make someone understand. The boy wouldn't understand. Even the war and the lost arm and the terrors of the trenches would never change him, there were nice women and there were women who weren't nice. But he must change. She must change him. Hermione wished she hadn't made up, wished she had her own pallor to confirm her, wished she could get to the boy, reach him, put her arms about him, pull his tired head on to her shoulder, be a mother, a god, a saint. She wanted to cry, O look you are real, the others—but the others were real too. You couldn't call Lady Prescott's war-workers real. You really couldn't. Merry Dalton whom she had always hated was more real than that. Merry was real since she had found her name, since Captain Ned Trent had found her name, Merry, for them. Irish, half Irish. You can't go on for ever being English. Let her rip. God. Let her burn. Troy town. Over the top. Over the top. Troy town and Delia a sort of Helen, Delia preserving Beauty. Let Delia preserve Beauty for Hermione was tired of beauty, tired of herself, of being reviled, she would fling in with the rest, see, feel, see, hear, Captain Trent said she was as beautiful as Merry and he loved Merry. All going. All gone. The boy leaned forward and lit a cigarette with a child ennui from the smouldering ash of pretty Louise Blake who had suddenly appeared, a friend of a friend of a friend—pretty, was she? Hair drawn tight up from squint oriental eyes. Looked as if she might be a magazine ad for some arcane scent, Fleur d'orient. She was Fleur d'orient. "I've found a name for you at last, Louise." "What—ever?" "Fleur—fleur d'orient. Florient. It's a name of a powder I think." "I don't want names of powders." Louise was a little hurt. She did so look like an advertisement of some rather obvious slightly risqué powder or scent. American. Something had flooded something, the river no doubt their studio, everybody had pneumonia and bad drains. Louise had come through the floods and the drains with the most chic of pre-war prettiness. All of them looked odd now, different beside Louise with her pre-war chic. How could Louise manage? How could anybody manage? Were they all like that or like Delia? Hermione wanted to be like both. Had to be like both. She was younger than Delia. Delia couldn't understand exactly.

Now looking at Louise, Hermione wished she hadn't made up,

couldn't do it like Louise. Louise must really help her with some clothes. She was tired of the old old gold and green that swept away from her shoulders. For a breath her body would be bare. Half a league—half a league—half a league—Captain (pre-war) Trent had known that, known all about it. They said he had heat wave, sun stroke, wouldn't shoot him but the police were after him, all the same and Merry, poor pretty Merry (why did one now like her?) had taken him on—taken him in— But could it matter? Hiding him. Pre-war romance. There is romance. Dance for the candles flicker, the boy with one arm leans forward. Louise tilts back a dark head. Florient.

A goddess is a god less—where did that come from? God and goddess, God and god less—what was going on, round and round and round and there were no two ways about it, you had to be in it or out of it and going on and on and on at Delia's was stagnation, was not her work, was not her world. She didn't believe in it, didn't believe in those hard lipped women (O God forgive me) who worked like that not knowing what love was, not knowing what life was. It was different with Delia but Delia was noblesse oblige and Delia anyhow was older, was that other generation, like Lillian Merrick, just old enough to be a very young mother to her or an elder sister. Delicious older sister. She had never had one. They weren't, it appeared, delicious. Relatives weren't. But Delia was a sort of older sister but you couldn't keep it up, half here, half there, half seeing that Delia was right and being sorry that they had lost sons and the other half saying but damn, damn, damn, why did you let them go, why did you let them go? You have lost sons but what have they lost, what have *we* lost? Sweet life, sweet life that was over sweet, life, life, life . . . is life so light a treasure? How do you feel when the guns go, clutching at life? Life, life, life, they wore it like a white flower to be tossed away. O but you gave them life. I know, mothers, mothers, mothers. But I am a mother. I mean I am not, was not. Don't let them get you. Who is that boy, French? Someone was asking if the boy was French but everybody knew he wasn't and someone else said "I thought he was Windsor dele Terre back from Rome." The boy in the blue wasn't dele Terre—(half English whom they had all, in the old days, known) but another boy, a stranger, speaking American, in horizon blue, speaking American. "An American fighting for France." He was an

H.D.
122

American fighting for France. There were all sorts of Americans. The room going round and round and round and the boy wore his light flower, his life so lightly pinned, so lightly to his horizon blue coat, pinned so lightly. O God don't let the flower fall out, the flower of his life, who is he anyway? He was a friend of Louise's, an American fighting for France, permission leave. God, look at them wearing their flowers so lightly. Who are we to be good or bad. What is good or bad for a woman? One thing. The boy with one arm seemed to protest by the very fine slender line of his attenuated child shoulders that there was one way of being good for a woman. Through the smoke, the cigarettes, the glasses ringed on the table and the glasses (little islands of glasses) on the carpet, one frail boy seemed to protest. He was a child really. He had had a nice mother, a young sister. He was too much a child—O God, let me not see. Let me dance on the walls, for Troy is burning, Troy town is down. Where is Delia? But she isn't so beautiful. Americans can't stand such glare, such strain, they're too slim, go out like lamps. Something that had made Delia beautiful was gone. Delia would go on, go on, and then some day they would be surprised when she stopped going on. She was too brittle, Americans were, to stand too much of this. Race. But there's a different physique, you couldn't stand too much if you were an American. You saw it all, saw them all, Troy town and the flutes were playing. They were dancing on the walls of Athens; let the Spartans in, for what is life, sweet life that was over sweet? Life is a white flower, a red flower, to be worn becomingly, to be tossed away. Horizon blue. An American fighting for France.

Who are we fighting for? What are we fighting for? Well anyway I'm Darrington's wife, they'll give me a little pension. O God, why don't they all go home now? Can't they see that we're all tired but they seem to love staying, the boy with one arm, looks and looks and looks . . . what does he see against the wall? What does he see between the books, the other side of the curtains the uneven, untidy rows of books are making? Does he see what I am seeing, what I used to be seeing, the days long ago, 17, 17, 17. Seventeen was long ago but even in seventeen Darrington had plunged in suddenly from the north of England, from his training camp, had plunged in, running his hands along the books as if they were some sleek cat's back, running his hands over separate books like so many loved kittens. He never took books out now. He said Browning was a bore, he was of course, was he? Fortù, Fortù, my beloved sit here and the gaudy melon flower. What was the boy seeing looking at the books? Was he seeing the books or beyond the books? Going on and on and on. Over the top, certainly, and certainly the best of luck. Napoo fini. Fini la guerre. Napoo fini everything, Fini la guerre, nothing. It would never be. Might as well dance, who was one anyhow to prate of virtue? Going on and on and on, only I wish Florient wouldn't sit on Captain Trent's lap, after all he is a gentleman and he treats us somehow (some of us) like what the boy with one arm would have called "ladies." Gentlemen and ladies, ladies and gentlemen, let me show you the prize secret of the universe, an elephant with two trunks, a fat lady with a beard, a duck with two heads. Monsters. Were they all monsters? No use living in two worlds, got to choose, going on and on but how can I choose, Darrington (lieutenant Darrington) is my husband. Did you know? Look at me, look at me, tall thin emaciated child with one arm, I know, I understand. I feel. I am. I am all those things you stare at. Don't stare. Don't stare. Over the top . . .

"Why can't we have some more drinks?" "Drinks. Drinks. You know as well as I." They were bickering like a navvy and a pub keeper's wife. Life was like that. You wore life like a white flower to be tossed aside. But she had so tossed it. She had given her life. She was already dead. She felt so sorry for those others who weren't dead. If only the boy would know that she was dead too. If only he would stop staring at the books, thinking he was the only one. "What, another raid? O damn. I did want some sleep. Best clear out before the damn thing starts." It was late. Let them stay and they would stay all night. O go away. Can't you see how I'm dead, tired, dead tired. Can't you see I'm dead—tired—dead-tired—tired—dead—go home.

It seems to me I can feel her wings. She is somewhere. She endured. She spills rose petals from her wings and the petals drift down the marble steps of the temple, not of the Louvre, no, I suppose they've wrapped her up in excelsior and put her in the cellar. Certainly they would. All the Louvre galleries empty. I had never till this moment thought of all those empty galleries. Must have been the boy in blue, the boy blue, little boy blue—horizon. On the horizon. The far horizon. She stands on the far horizon, though they must have locked her up in the cellar to keep her out of harm's way, they did *care* the French. Did they care? O they did care. One felt that, one felt that they (who were left of them) cared. Cared. Pro patria. "What were you saying, darling?" Darrington said, what were you saying and when he said "darling" she remembered that Darrington had wandered bare-foot under the olives, silver olives, olive silver Sirmio. He had loved olives, olive silver, O sister my sister, the hounds of spring are on winter's traces, will you yet take all Galilean but this thou shalt not take. No, no. This thou shalt not take. It was standing, tall and unimpressed, waiting only for a moment to float downward. It was standing on a niche of the Acropolis, that is where it was, it wasn't in the Louvre any more, it was standing on a ship prow, somewhere a ship had her standing, Nike of Samothrace was standing. "Victory."

"What were you saying, darling?" "Darling" brought something with it. It was that Naples faun that held the wine jar or was it the marble bronze of the moss-green Narcissus? Was Narcissus still standing in the Naples gallery, with his naif yet so sophisticated gesture, his hand lifted, his head bent forward? Bronze that had been burned as they were burned beneath lava, smoke, ashes, dust, death, years, obliteration. Self of self was so buried. Who had said "darling"? Hermione leaned standing against the table, leaned standing and leaned staring. Who had said what? Who was she? Where was she? Moss green of a small bronze that had been unearthed and was still unpolluted? Should she be the same underneath, after it was all over? Would she be the same, herself the same, a statue buried beneath the kisses of the war, no, beneath the kisses of her husband? Did husband, "my husband" make it any better? What was she going to do, say? What would she think? Her thoughts were not her thoughts. They came from outside. But everyone was like that now, exalté, hungry, it was wonderful not wanting to eat, not worth it, exaltation. Exalted. They were exalted. "Mademoiselle could not drown her exaltation in the dead sea." A French man had said that but she couldn't now remember. Someone was coming toward her. "Jerrold."

"How did you think the party went?" "Has it gone?" Why did she say that? It was a sort of cheap rejoinder, not worthy. Voices in the street. Someone might be returning. People had a way of straggling back for forgotten cigarettes, cases or lost papers or bits of uniforms, "I say Darrington, my word, I've left my" (whatever it was) "with you." Did they make excuses to come back? People, people, people. People loving Darrington. Did they love Hermione? Darrington's laugh. If only she were more robust, stronger. People loved Darrington. Boy in Blue, boy in khaki. Why do you love Darrington? All the men loving all the men and who could blame them, "you people don't understand a thing about it." No, they didn't understand, knew nothing of the war, scrounging bread off Fritz. Did they really scrounge bread, why did they say such horrible things, "the whole place stank of Fritzes." One came to accept such statements, over the top. You see, Troy town was down. Town, down. You see there isn't any use struggling against Darrington for a world away, a world away, a world away the Winged Samothracian Victory is waiting. O if I would die and be out of it. What good is the food after you do get it, waiting in line with filthy devils, really hungry people who do care, do awfully care, after all, we've fed our faces all our lives and the things are so filthy when we do get them, they're no use. Over the top of Troy town. Someone *had* returned.

"Who's scratching?" "I don't know. Don't let's open." "But we can't leave them there. It might be Captain Trent." "Damn. Trent's business isn't now ours." "Why not?" "Are you mad? He's an Irish rebel—" "So's Merry." "That's different."

4 One had to admit it was different when one opened the door and saw her standing like a stage-set, all perfect, like a good curtain call, her strange mauve and old gilt gown making a picture of her. Merry was tall (though she sometimes seemed so tiny) standing against the velvet black drop curtain that was the black-black of the raid-darkened hall. "O, it's Merry." She was standing and now in a moment something in Hermione took fire, took flame. Something flamed up in Hermione like the white flame, the white flower boys wore now (invisible to but few of the rest) fastened to their blue or dark-blue or horizon blue or fawn

brown uniforms. Merry. "O it's Merry." And in speaking Hermione felt something flame up in her, a ghost, a ghost of long ago and a strange poignant hurt that Mary (it was Mary then and Maria della Trinità) had given her. Her name was Princess Lointaine then and Maria della Trinità and that was long ago across a chasm and George Lowndes with his kisses, his scape-goat kisses was out of it, but you couldn't say Merry was. Names, people. People, names. Merry came from across the chasm the other side, gold daffodils, someone reading poetry, things that weren't any more true. Names make people. People make names. Her smile was the same jasmine white ghost thing that that flower was, that invisible flower that boys wore pinned so lightly. The flower of Merry's smile was ghost-jasmine, she wasn't alive really. Was she alive? How had she got there? Why did she stand there? She hadn't rung the front bell downstairs. "How did you get in?" "Some of the people from the top-floor were rushing back from somewhere." "O it's those munition workers doing night shift. They have the top floor." But why tell Merry that? Who were girls having the top floor, doing night shift while the rest of them danced and the glasses made islands and the boy with one arm stared and made her heart leap and fall down (a fish half dead that leaps on dry land) and her soul reach out, reach out saying look my white flower is as white as yours but she hadn't, didn't say it. "Wh-aats—up?" It was Darrington. Merry walked forward. She walked as an actress who has had her cue. She would, it was apparent, fall forward at the right moment into one of the big chairs. Her cue would be step to right, stagger unsteadily, fall gracefully. But she hadn't spoken her lines yet. Darrington was standing. Hermione was standing. Take two paces to the right, pull the curtains that are already pulled for there is a faint rumble (a stage rumble) far and far and far. Stage rumble. It reminded her of a melo-dramatic Civil War play that she had seen as a school girl. Rushings, uniforms blue and grey. "They are firing on Richmond to-night." That play was called "Shenandoah." What was this? On leave? Permission. Take your choice ladies and gentlemen for we can't choose the parts we play but we can name our own show. Call it "Permission." Damn good show. They are firing on Richmond to-night. Troy town was obviously down. "Whaat-s—up?"

"Rather tired, that's all." Merry sat in the chair, she didn't stagger but this didn't seem right. She had come to say something, wasn't saying it. Why did she stare white and white, jasmine-white? "Old Trent?" Darrington was a brute. You could see that Darrington was a brute. It couldn't be possible that he said it and it hadn't happened. They were in the wrong play. They are firing on Richmond to-night. This was the wrong play. They should be wearing crinolines, being Southern ladies, all made up crinolines, *on with the dance let joy be unconfined.* Soldiers weren't real. There were boys wearing flowers but they were different. Darrington wore no flower. He would not be killed. You could tell when they would be killed for the flowers were white and ghost-white and white and jasmine white and the fragrance of the flowers reached you across dead Fritzes, across bread scrounged, across scrounging and billets and tight places and Mademoiselle in the family way. There were flowers and soldiers. The boys were flowers. Darrington was a soldier but why if he now felt it that way couldn't he have gone in the beginning? Captain Trent (prewar Captain) was at least a real soldier not this pretence and was it true that Darrington had got the gas-helmets when he was a runner (a private, Private Jerrold Darrington 171892 and the rest of it, how often she had written it) was it true that he had got the officers out of a "tight place," someone said he had done something decent but he was a runner and got somewhere and there was a gas attack and they sent him back for his commission. Maybe it was true. Private Jerrold Darrington and what difference now? What difference now? She liked him better then and the men (navvies) had called him Jerry and now things were different and things were different and the things were different. "Old Trent?" Who exactly was he? They are firing on Richmond to-night.

There was death and they had died a certain death and Jerrold hadn't. Had Merry absolutely died? She seemed in a state of just not-understanding, for so little she would understand, what was it that was lacking? The story was all right. The story had body, continuity, unity, all the things the right sort of impossible story would have. All the stories now were of a low level of art but they made good stories. Life is, isn't it, damn bad art, but who had said that? It was the sort of thing Darrington used to say but didn't any more say. Darrington with his "to the chaste all things are unchaste" and Darrington to the rescue and his Theseus like a sea-rock with the weeds still clinging and his Astraea like a star, a child . . . where was that Darrington? There was a chasm, a split, the volcano had so split them and across the other side candles were flaring up and George was reading and it was George saying, "almost thou persuadest me to be a heathen." People didn't say things like that, anyway they were silly things to say, but why should they? Why be démodé, it wasn't à la mode any more to be witty, it was Fritz and Fritz and such vile repetition and his breath breathed into her lungs was that curious death and that curious emanation. He had been in a gas attack for his breath breathed into her lungs bit and burned and she coughed violently after he had gone, thank God that time, he had been hurried up north again, up north, his commission and a little pat from some-body though he was only 171892 for all he was a navvy with the navvies, Jerry, a navvy but rather nice coming back rather brown, rather nice if his breath hadn't been filled with gas, making her cough, making her cough. Cough. Across a chasm there were can-dles and daffodils and the hydrangeas that had lifted porcelain blue and wedgwood blue and delft blue and porcelain white and porcelain Sèvres china, Dresden china pink. There is always a tulip on Dres-den and sometimes an iris. Flowers on china. Merry was like that, French rather, the Irish were when you came to think of it, after you had had your full dose of England. Merry was like that. Merry already looked different, it took her no time at all to recover. The jasmine had faded from her lips. There was the old pre-chasm red and fox-red though now it had faded to the burnt pale hectic colour of fire swept leaves. She was burnt out, pale in her burning. But there was no jasmine. She was not yet ghost. Merry was sitting there and talking quite naturally. These stories were so natural. "They met us at the corner and Ned said I was to leave him. I don't know where they took him." This had happened before. It was always happening. Plain clothes men like some odd, old pre-chasm detective story. Sherlock Holmes. Doctor Watson. All, all those incredible, impossi-ble things had come into life. Life had found its level and those things were on its level. "He asked me to come here. He said Her-mione will understand." Hermione looked at Merry. She did under-stand. Merry was no ghost jasmine. Colour came back, blue eyes, that looked blue, blue, blue, the delft-blue, the porcelain blue of conservatory hydrangeas. She was not a real flower, not an orchid though her mauve and gold gave her quality, gave her frailty. Was she frail? Didn't she burn simply where life burned? Didn't she cultivate Hermione for the life that burned about her? What did Merry see in Hermione? "What are you staring at, seeing?" Merry was staring, her eyes staring. Blue. Blue. "You look—odd." "I feel odd rather. Nothing the matter. Odd simply." Hermione was odd. She wasn't in it, wasn't out of it. She didn't love Merry Dalton, didn't hate her. She couldn't condemn poor Trent, though she couldn't wholesale admire him. It was stupid and the guns had stopped. There was something in the uncanny odd quiet of it, the streets quiet, no (however distant) rumble, no whistles nor rumbles, things you don't think, in London, you are hearing but which (in London) you miss when they stop. As if a heart stopped simply. "Something's stopped." "It's the guns." "Yes. It must be." Darrington was pulling the other couch out from behind the screen that shut their enormous room into sections. The other big couch would do for two of them. Which two? What was this? What was her mind doing? People thought like that those days. Thoughts came from outside like swallows suddenly appearing, wheeling, appearing, wheeling, turning. Spring and the swallows of her freedom. Birds. "O Merry. Yes do stay." Darrington was already beginning to remove bits of himself, a belt, bits of things, a belt. The leather belt lay where he flung it among the ring of glasses. Ring. A ring. Ring around a rosy. A ring. A ring. A ring. Brides of God. What kind of a bride? Of God. What kind of a God? O yes, pretend. Don't think. You are so tired, take Merry into your bed. They can arrange it after you have gone to sleep. Swallows were dipping and wheeling and this world was not real and she had left her husband on the rocks at Capri . . . swallows had reeled and Odysseus had turned that corner for the Syren voices . . . voices . . . voices . . . almost (not quite) Hermione could hear voices for the food wasn't worth eating when you got it and "O do stay Merry. O of course, it's too late. You can't go home now and you can't sleep in the kitchen. There's an extra munition worker in the little old room we used to have at the back. Stay here." "How wonderful. How beautiful." Darrington went on undressing. "O yes. If you want one." Merry didn't want a night dress. She pulled off the mauve and old gold and she was gold and mauve underneath. "I don't take up much room." "I don't take up much room either and the couch is wide. Are you all right Jerrold?" Jerrold out of delicacy seemed to have removed bits only, rolled in his great coat. He was simply "rolling in" as people

130

did nowadays. People didn't sleep, pulled off bits of things and Hermione pulled off bits of things. Darrington seemed to be asleep. "Who'll blow out the last candle? But it must be almost day. Good-night."

As in a dream she could hear them the other side of the room, but why wake? Mary was a slut, a little fox-coloured wench out of some restoration comedy. Hermione had always known Merry was like that. Or wasn't she? Delia had asked Merry to see her, Merry then being wistful (when wasn't she?) and saying, "poor Mary Dalton wants friends, new life, that terrible contretemps with" (whoever it at the moment was) "and all her frail spirituality threatened." American women were like that, so good that they couldn't, wouldn't see. Delia was like that and Hermione was half like that but she wasn't going to let her sterilized New English-ness do her out of the show. It was, all told, a damn good show. A very good damn show. Sleep with her arm above her head and listen if she wants to for what she hears is nothing, a sort of sweep of swallow wings, the swallows of her redemption, the swallows of her freedom. Of course if Darrington (she called him Darrington so often in her thoughts) knows I'm awake it will be a little awkward. Swallows sweeping, sweeping but what god had sent her this, this clue of her redemption? It was better than being dead. Death was a freeing but this was better, this death in life, this ghost in life, this life in death. O Delia, delicious Delia you have only a half-knowledge, this is the true knowledge, the white-half of my knowledge reaches up, up to the sun of its attainment and my roots rooted fast here, here in the present, here in this mire. My husband wasn't like yours (or like pre-war Captain Trent) an officer and a gentleman but I'm glad for that for if he had been he would have gone off at once and my life would have been so clearly on the rails, a poor unhappy and good woman. I'm now none of those things. I had that child . . . no. I will talk of it. You Delia never had a sign of one. O delicious and beautiful sterile lovely goddess, beautiful in your goodness as I might have been if God hadn't given me this mystic knowledge that I'm already O so comfortably out of it, dead simply like the boy who looked at the books, whom I couldn't, didn't dare to comfort. Florient. Perhaps she'd do next. People, faces, people, ghosts. They're lying in the mud in France, in

Flanders and I'm in a warm bed. Warm bed. I know you all. I feel the wind over your faces and I know the mud about your feet and Jeanne d'Arc was the same, white lilies, white lilies are growing from the trenches, there are lines and lines of lilies across France. Lilies are flowering across France and some few (some very few) in London. We see our death. We take it. We find our grave, O trench wide grave, O bed here narrow enough grave and this other whose smile was for a moment almost the jasmine-white of the redeemed, changed and crept from her bed, crept from her redemption, crept from her fate. Could thou not watch with me one night? Or was it one hour? Anyhow, anyway it worked either way for they had only just "got" poor Trent. Who was he anyhow with his own fiery and self-chosen crown. Trent's crown dripped red roses, bombs, the English. All wrong but it wasn't the deed it was the motive and his roses were red roses dropping, dripping over her, over her. He had sent Merry back to Hermione saying Hermione would be kind, "I like that woman." He said he liked her, a woman, he said he liked her, told her she was beautiful, not with the charm of Merry but staring at her and now they had him. A tight place in London. There *were* tight places, it seemed, in London and lilies grew up and up and the room was full of their glamour. Across the room, there was a mud bog but filled with nothing, seeds fallen by the roadside. Some fell by the roadside. Some fell upon good earth. Trenches were good earth and the seed fell there and grew and grew and grew. Some brought forth sixty, some thirty, some hundred. A hundred. 1900. Hundred. 1800. Hundred. 1700. Hundred. What was hundred? 500. But you thought of 500 as B.C. Numbers held charm, power, you could think in numbers. 500 B.C. wasn't so far away. She might have lived it yesterday, it was nearer than to-morrow. All this means that I'm still listening . . .

5 | One didn't marry. One did stunts. That was it. That was right. For what had her marriage been, all told? Certainly not a marriage. Racing about Italy and being called Signora, nobody ever thought she was married anyway. Some people were like that. Never got the credit for anything. Anyway Mrs.

Darrington and a pension. But he wouldn't die now. He wouldn't die now. They didn't die when they were cast by the roadside. Darrington was dead now. He wouldn't die. There was no white flower any more to be hoped for but what was this? What was this? "Darling. You've slept late." Someone was kissing her, brushing her face like a nosing puppy. Who was that? Late and far there had been sounds of flutes, olives and olive silver Sirmio so this was somewhere else and someone else but it couldn't be anywhere else. It was Italy. *Open my heart and you will see.* It wasn't anywhere else. There was a plum tree that shed its flower as the irises raised their trumpets, their horns of gold. Gold and fleurs d'or semées. Flowers of gold were strewn upon her banner but they had taken it. Soldiers were fighting and her banner was lost. "Why don't—you—get—up?" O if now she opened her eyes, she would remember and she wouldn't remember for she would never open her eyes, was dead simply. "Open your eyes, open your eyes." "How sweet you look Jerrold, where's" (for she had never really forgotten) "Mary Dalton?" She sat up and made pretence of wakening though really now she thought she had been asleep, dead-drug of sleep, such sleep as she had not hoped for this side of the grave. "This side of the grave. Isn't that Landor?" "What precious?" "Fields of asphodel . . . something or other this side of the grave?" "I don't know, why do you ask that?" Darrington had arranged her tray for her as he knew she liked it. O if now he would go, this perfect hour had come, an hour that flowers with the old flowers, the wild cyclamen, the wild olive spray she plucked to wind with it. This is us, she had said, you and me, you the cyclamen, me the olive. "Do you remember that little wreath I made and for fun put it on a round stone and said Hermes, Hermes." "I remember your saying Hermes and the round stone. How could I forget it?" "I don't know. It seems—seems—right" (but did it?) "to forget things now." This was wonderful. She had died simply. Mary Dalton was gone, not even a scarf, a lavender scarf that she could make an excuse to come back for. "Why did Mary go before I got up?" O this is marvellous. I don't care that she's gone or that she was with him. I am, it is evident, a most immoral woman. Signora, most little signorissima. Signora. Signorina. "Do you remember how they would always *issimo* us, you and me." "They liked us." "Yes. They liked us." She liked them too for a moment, drawing them back, drawing them up to the top of the pond of filth, the mire where they had lain, regrettable, dishonourable little souls, hers and his, disreputable and regrettable. "I'm glad it's over." "Over? God in heaven what do you mean over?" Hermione sipped her tea. She hadn't slept so well for months, this side of the grave she had slept, slept, slept. "I'm glad the party and the raid's over—" "And my leave, precious?" "O Jerrold—" She could talk like that. She could balance the fine cup (one of their relics) and dispassionately look at Jerrold. "I saved that cup for you. Wouldn't give it to Merry." Hermione looking at Jerrold, believed this. There was seriousness, a look she had almost forgotten, some deep root somehow of love, some devotion. Had she regarded his love too lightly? He was younger. His love had been that rapture of some wild young thing and she had liked him, loved him because he was wild and didn't do the right thing and hated his family and wouldn't (in the beginning) take a commission as his gov'nor was simply after family kudos. He had hated them, held out against them for they had tried to spoil his writing, hadn't wanted him to write and perhaps she had mis-judged Jerrold. "I never seem to see you any more." He was looking at her, his eyes were clear and cool enough in that half-light. The room was dim with a clear blurr of darkness and Jerrold in his uniform, just shaved, fresh, right, somehow the right lover if not the quite-right husband. Husband. Husbands. "Why did we ever get married?" "Well there was no particular reason for it but it saved my life, precious." "Saved your life?" "I mean I would have been pitched in sooner if I hadn't been." "That's so. That's why we got married." There was a reason for everything. "And I couldn't have stood going back to America and I couldn't have endured people being horrid though they were anyway." "They always are horrid." This was someone else. Something had flowered in the night. Jerrold's hands were cool, his eyes were wide and undeviating. "I'm sorry dear, for all the hurt I've brought you."

"My dear, you never brought me any hurt. What ever?" He found a cigarette now, lighted it. Her little hour was perfection upon perfection. The waves of clean smoke came over and across her knees drawn up a little and Jerrold found her feet, two long feet which he caught like a hunter in his wide palm. Her feet beneath the clothes were held, caught and his hand was strong, Saxon, strong, a strong hand beautifully modelled, beautiful like his own feet, those statue feet that had pressed so clear and flat and right with the arch curve on the dark trodden paths that wound through olive and along the rock-edged cytisus bushes of the hills above Solaro. Feet, hands. What was more gracious than this? Had she no heart? No conscience? "I'm afraid I'm rather odd. I didn't mind—Merry—" Jerrold did not turn. Was he used to this sort of thing? Had it happened before? Had Merry been "near" him before? It didn't matter? Did it matter? If she could drop her head across the bed clothes and cry it would be all right. She couldn't. She saw that Jerrold Darrington was clear and right and shaved and clean and in the right clothes and his new routine had thinned him again and his cuff was elegant. The cuff that rested across her knees with the new "grip," the hand under it. He was right. Was she then wrong? "My clothes were so shabby and worthless—" He wasn't listening. Was he thinking of someone else, something else? But did it matter? Did she care really? "I suppose I am a sort of Undine, George used to say so." "What did you say, darling?" "I said I suppose I must be rather terrible." "You are, dear." "Terrible. Terrible. How am I?" But he was wandering now about the room, finding bits of things. He said, "you'll be ready. We must clear off now in twenty minutes" . . . and she wanted to answer something, couldn't say it, had no words to say it but if she could wait here with her chin on her drawn up knees, remembering the feel of his wide palm about her feet, she would manage to find voice, to speak, to give him that word, that message, that signal before it was too late. She mustn't lose all the things that had made her one with classic beauty, Italy, Solaro, the lizards on the sun-baked steps of the House of the Faun and the avenue of cypresses of the road of the dead at Pompeii. *There are no fields of asphodel this side of the grave.* She wanted to reach out and the time was short, he was buckling his belt, was bending, searching, looking for his little odd things, the thin book he carried, what was he now reading? Did he read nowadays? She never now could ask him, he was sure to flaunt the old things at her, bruise and tear her with some frivolous, silly or destructive jibe, make fun of something sacred, something deep down that she hadn't known she cared for till he took it, turned it inside out, spat on it. *Swiftly walk o'er the western wave*, for instance though she didn't care for Shelley, didn't ever read him. What had happened? What was done, was now lost? *Swiftly walk o'er the western wave spirit of night.* Could she manage to find one, one line, one verse? O God, let me remember for words are like the bubbles of clear light on the surface of this mire, this mud pond, this vast wash of débris and death and filth that is our present. The porches of the Temple of the Sun and the little houses of Pompeii held their power though lava swept them and though ashes debouched filthy. A centurion was found standing, waiting at the entrance, at a gate-way, the Roman Legions. Ave Imperator. Senatus Populus. Was she like that centurion, a Keeper of Beauty? Must she stand while the filth burned them fell burying them and must she stand watching the filth, the lava, all the burial of all the beauty? If she could reach, speak to him. She must reach, speak. What should she say, speaking? She spoke, not thinking what she was saying, not knowing what she was saying, "there are no fields of asphodel this side of the grave." There are no fields . . . fields. What is a field? A field is a plot of grass and it is strewn with flowers. There are small sweet pulse, butterfly weed, little thyme heads. Butterflies wing across them, tiny butterflies. You can take a field and spread it like a rug across the floor and you can step on the field, stepping out of your bed. You can stand on the field and you can watch the mark your foot makes, you can see your foot ringed with blue thyme, or with cyclamen, or with gold pulse. This is imagination. Imagination is stronger than reality. For outside is fog, mist and the room is cold but your foot is stepping on a carpet and if you find your stockings you will be thinking all the time of a gilt gauze peplum and the fall of the marble as the sun shines on it and you may stoop down and gather the broken cyclamen where your foot stepped and lay them at the feet of the marble Nereid. The room of the Nereids. The room of the Nereids where Darrington had sought her, found her, where Darrington had brought her violets and across the room of the Nereids the London mist had woven a garment, a veil, the veil of Aphrodite. Now look this is the veil of Aphrodite. It isn't one lover but if your lover leaves, you stoop down and pick the broken cyclamen and make a border for the veil. Darrington can never be torn from the veil of her Loves. The veil of Aphrodite. She would take that veil and at the last lay it at a shrine but it is hard weaving with Troy town down and my husband has been faithless. No, I am not a Penelope. I know I am not. People reach over, Captain Trent but I won't go to him, couldn't because of Merry, anyhow he's now locked up. The veil must be woven subtly and one flower cannot disown another. Fayne is the very sea-blue edge. The edge of hyacinths is (though I had forgotten her) Fayne. This isn't everything. I wish my garters matched, this is this and this is this and both wrong anyway. Can't find warm underthings, does it matter? Put on extra outside jacket. Hat over face. Hat over face. Hat far down and chin only showing. Glass smudged with mist, too many tumblers, will hurry home after the train, wash up tumblers, open window, a little rest, peace. Books, will try to drag some books from shelves, Darrington doesn't now want books.

"There are no fields of asphodel this side of the grave." "Damn, you might have thought of something cheerful." "O but I am. I do. I only said it as a joke." "Joke. You all take this bloody war as a midnight revel." "We—all?" "Yes. The whole damn lot of you. London gets more randy every time I hit here." "Is it that—" But why ask it, why say it? Why say, isn't it you that's randy? Death ringed their nostrils and there was no taxi and they almost ran the length of King's Road, making for Euston, not like other leaves, the taxi, the rumble and luxury of it and the smoke in her throat and her eyes stinging with fog and feeling that she was ugly, hopeless and her hat jammed down over her eyes and how odd to look really pretty (would she ever?) again. Trains rumbling. Trains. Rumbling. Smoke to be breathed in layers, breathed in and out, like cotton wadging. Cold. O it was cold that winter. Cold. Winter. There are no fields . . . cyclamen was lying and broken horns of cyclamen in that smoke and rumble gave an added fragrance. Trampled flowers smell sweet. Was this the end? Was this the end? Hysteria but suppressed. Hysteria suppressed goes to the head like wine and you make pictures, patterns and she was quiet and she felt her eyes clear and staring. If she could now cry? Was this the last? Broken cyclamen, the sweeter for the crushing. "Don't you know—I love you?" Faces, people, men, officers, red tape, men, men, men, dragging bundles, dragging packs, hat tilted, swank, officers. Trains. Smoke. A lover. A lover. No one would ever think it was a husband. "Over the top." Why must he say that, standing in the window? She wasn't a soldier. Over the top . . . going, going, going, going . . . Jerrold.

6 Hysteria suppressed goes to the head like wine, but all the same this was more than she bargained for, for the thing about her wrist was real, she knew the corner of the street, the name of the street, the name of the other rectangular street and she knew where she was but a gold circlet had clasped her wrist, just one gold circle, just the circle of fingers, not hurting, just catching her wrist as she lifted her hand to straighten her hat, for she thought out of the fog someone looming toward her looked familiar, but it wasn't . . . anyone she knew. All the same this was a very clear thing, not anything she had made up. It might be that I'm hungry. We are all hungry. Is God hungry? Did God being hungry have hallucinations like they had or was this something different, quite other, out of another world? For it was outside herself . . . what happened.

Hermione turned the corner (on the way home from Euston) in the fog and noted the names of streets and thought, yes I promised Mrs. Lechstein that I'd stop in for she was worried and asked me if I thought we could manage to put some of Lechstein's things down in our cellar. They always seemed to hit near us, near her, but we were safer as we were the other side of the great square where the little plaster Flora had spilled her plaster flowers and that is why they had come here. She and Jerrold had come because the plaster Flora was like the real Flora (but was it a robed Ganymede?) but you know the one in the Signora's garden at Amalfi. The one that spilled things, fruits or flowers, girl or boy, and the oranges had dropped petals and star-blossoms and the scent was paradise. So every time you (or she) saw the plaster Flora, blossoms spilled, they did really but in imagination like the carpet that had spread (this early morning) under her bare feet, the feet Darrington had for a moment caught in his hunter's palm and she hadn't found the words for Darrington. A message, a signal that should have flared, didn't flare and it was over the top . . . over the top . . . was she over the top? For this thing was real and she looked at her wrist pulling back the sleeve that had slipped back into place. As the wide sleeve had fallen from her uplifted arm (as she lifted her arm to straighten her hat, thinking it was someone looming out of the fog, but it wasn't) a space had been left free, free against the chafe and rub of thick sulphur fog and that naked space of meagre wrist had been caught for a moment but it wasn't imagination. Someone, something had caught her wrist at the corner of Guildford Street and Old Queen's Square, that old street, for the Lechsteins lived two houses below and she was remembering that Milly Lechstein, now that Isaac was gone, wanted to keep the statues safe, treated them all like so many babies. Milly Lechstein loved the statues. Isaac was gone. Jews loving beauty. No country. Like Hermione no country. But she had a country. She had a husband. This thing out of the fog that placed a bracelet about her meagre wrist . . . my husband . . . the gods, you see, were alive. The mist was full of shapes and odd looming creatures and you never knew in the darkness (day dark or night dark) what might or mightn't loom up at you. This place was blanketed down and it was wrong about their treating the war like a mid-night revel. It was wrong and it was the other way round, the war was treating them like dolls and puppets and painted dolls and she had painted her cheeks but had managed to smudge it off afterwards and she was glad it smudged off for out of the mist someone had caught at her, caught at her. She was no Penelope. Cassandra maybe. She had known he was there. But he had never taken form before, never taken her wrist, caught it, made a circle of fire about it, so that even now with her arm hanging naturally, under her coat, she could feel, feel . . . did it mean Darrington wouldn't come back? What did it mean? *There are no fields of asphodel this side of the grave.* But there are. There are. Must go in. This is Milly's and I said I would. But I don't want the responsibility for the things, can't have it. The statues are live things to them, they love them and Isaac is gone into a sort of kosher regiment, but all the same in it, gone, in it over the top . . . I must have it now, must see it now, the bracelet. But when she pulled out her thin wrist as if to examine a wrist watch that wasn't there, small wrist bone showed, flesh looking phosphorescent under that half light. Night and day. Night and day. Death and life. And Lechstein's famous statues . . . "Milly. Yes. I know it's too early or too late for lunch or tea. What time is it? Let me have something. You darling. How right and simple they all look. I'm glad you didn't send them away. Keep them here. Don't go scattering the things all over London. The risk's too great. Yes. No. No. Yes. Gone back. Yes. Yes. When is Isaac due over? Gone back. No. Nobody's fault but we don't want them smashed. Don't be so nervous for the statues." War. War. War. Statues. Imagine it's going on, going on . . . in France. All London a night club. Over the . . . over the . . .

He looked at her in a curious quizzical way and she had seen him before but where had she seen him? He loomed at her across the room, out of the room among the statues, someone not in khaki, not in horizon blue, coming simply toward her, had he been there all the time? She didn't seem to notice things. "Have you been here all the time?" He smiled at her. Where had she seen him? He was a stranger but she had seen him. Was it at her own house at one of those ribald parties? She couldn't remember, facing him, while Milly bustled with some trouble below stairs and bells ringing and he was looking at her. Things had happened, were happening, were going to happen but he was like a mist of gold dust, flower dust in that meagre room furnished with nothing but Lechstein's statues and the few low stools, the low stool she was seated on and another or so and nothing in the beautifully proportioned room, big room full of statues and the day and the night merged here, was it morning or afternoon? He was speaking to her and she had seen him before and certainly at one of her own parties and he was asking her to come out to lunch as he believed Milly would forget them, wouldn't remember them, she was always in trouble, it would be someone to collect a bill and he had only come on business. He was asking her to go out to lunch with him and as Milly came back, he said he believed it would be all right and he was paying Milly, it appeared, for the statue, someone's bust, some friend of his, a commission from long ago, but he had been away and would she see that the thing went straight to Cornwall? He was paying in a lordly manner for a statue and one did pay for Lechstein's statues sometimes, it seems, and he went on talking and how had he got there? Had he been there all the time? "Isaac wants to do your head," and Hermione smiled at Milly but she couldn't imagine what a head of hers would look like now, now that she was gone . . . over the top. Had she a head? Milly was appealing to the other person, "wouldn't it be interesting," and he was assenting of course, he was politely assenting. "I must take Mrs. Darrington out to lunch. Promised I'd not be late," as if it was arranged but she had not come here to meet this person, what was his name, Vane, now she remembered, wealthy, heart trouble, dabbled in the arts, helped Lechstein. She had met him here at Lechstein's and she had had him among others at her house, their house, over the top . . . Vane. Cyril Vane. Wealthy. How marvellous to be wealthy. "Yes. I promised Mr. Vane." What had she promised? Milly was tactful, thought they had arranged to meet, had they arranged to meet? Why had she turned into Milly Lechstein's this morning, why had that swerve made her mount the steps and the gold bracelet, all in a dream and now she was seated in a restaurant, where was it? Late in the afternoon, over coffee, coffee, good coffee. Her clothes were shabby but there was something Victorian and "genteel" about it for the right kind of woman looked shabby now and Vane with his distinction and his pallor might have been an officer, a wounded officer on leave. Everyone rushed about, made a fuss, how were they to know it was only heart-trouble and he had never been in it? How were they to know that his words came right with no merging and blurring of filth, no "Fritz," no "that's the stuff to give 'em." People didn't talk that way, not officers and gentlemen, only Darrington, but after all, he was her husband and she was no Penelope. "Quaint of old Milly to call you that." "Me? What." "Shouldn't have thought she could have so far penetrated—" "Me?" "Didn't she? Or did I dream it. Morgan le Fay."

7 Then staring in the mirror she saw herself, saw herself, yes, she was somehow dehumanised and he was seeing it and Milly Lechstein had seen it, saying in that funny way, "you look like Morgan le Fay, Mrs. Darrington." Milly called her Mrs. Darrington. What did Cyril Vane call her? O obviously Mrs. Darrington. He would call her Mrs. Darrington. Who was Mrs. Darrington? Mrs. Darrington was a bit of earth and someone, someone else had stepped out of Mrs. Darrington. Mrs. Darrington was a trench, wide and deep and someone else had stepped out and was out and wasn't Mrs. Darrington. Across a room that swam in a delicious haze, a haze that was made of gold on pale gold, the wine gold, the odd straw-gold of the head opposite, sleek head bent forward, head undimmed by powder, by explosive, by gas, by green and green and red flares falling across wastes of barbed wire and dead Fritzes, head bent forward, some god had set a head there in a restaurant (imagine it but I know you can't quite realize it) in that odd 18, 18, 18. Do you know what I mean? In 1918 there was one head, gold head, a tall stalk held up a gold head though the head dropped forward with odd pre-chasm affectation, a head on a frail long stalk, like some great yellow pear but heavy on its tall, very tall stalk. A head that was gold that caught glint of gold from the light reflected down from the rose-lamp and the wine had been gold and now gold from within and gold from without made a sort of halo, a sort of aura of light as if they were on a stage (all the world's a stage) and the spot light had them, the spot light in all that dreary waste of London held them and so held, so caught, Hermione must dutifully consider, look, see what it was that was held, consider what it was, lift her glass to it, far and far and this was something pre-chasm, wine didn't any more do things to you. But this did. This was pre-chasm, something different, they thought he was wounded, an officer, wounded and they had brought out this—pre-chasm. You tasted grape and grape and gold grape (can you imagine it?) and gold on gold and gold filled your palate, pushed against your mouth, pushed down your throat, filled you with some divine web, a spider, gold web and you wove with it, wove with it, wove with the web inside you, wove outward images and saw yourself opposite smiling with eyes uptilted, smiling at something that had crept out of Mrs. Darrington, small, not very good, looking at you in a glass, tall, very tall, not very good, divine like a great lily. Someone, something was looking at something and someone, something was smiling at someone. Wine went to your brain and you knew there was no division now and there was someone, one left, just one left like yourself who was dead and not dead who was alone and not alone. We know each other when we see each other, people like us. We were two angels with no wings to speak of, with the angelic quality that comes, that goes, that will come, that will go. His was youth and his own thwarted health, making him look gold on gold with that odd pallor that made gold on gold ray out almost visibly from his forehead. He was wealthy and his clothes were pre-chasm and it was obvious to anyone looking at them that everything was all right for he was a gentleman, therefore he must be an officer, therefore she must be—but why go on and on and on and on with this thing? Cigarettes made her one with every beauty she had forgotten, days and days and nights. He was talking of Rome, he loved the Spanish steps, he had always wanted a little room, two rooms, something small and something (as he put it) 1860ish. She could see the 1860 candelabra, the light and glisten of it, the many facets of the candelabra and the old arm-chair and the tall blue blue vases on the over-ornate mantel. And then all redeemed by elegance and marble of that regal period and then the almond blossom from the campagna (in February) would bank up against that mirror, that other mirror where she could almost see herself looking, smiling . . . candles.

Go back further and you saw him, Etruscan with his thin face. His face was thin and his shoulders that broad thinness that you see in Egypt. Egypt, a honey-lotus looked at her and already she had forgotten the dead body, the Mrs. Darrington she had left long ago, on a bed, on a wide grave. Someone had stepped out and put a foot upon a carpet and someone had broken cyclamen horns and cyclamen fragrance had assailed the nostrils and cyclamen had dripped across roofs, across station platforms, the frail incense of it had wavered and men, men, men, men had lifted heads, sniffed this rare thing; men, officers had lifted heads but that was the other side, the other side of the river, of the Styx, where they all were, all drift of ghosts and she was this side, had simply by her own acumen, discovered this side and the odd thing was there was someone this side with her. Of course, she was a little drunk, wine went to your head for the food was good enough of its kind, but food wasn't food, it was odd things, fricassee that didn't taste of anything but the coffee was black, black. The cigarette was the incense and the wine was the wine and the body opposite her the sacrifice. She could eat that body, devour it, it was gold, it was honey-comb and the wine was good and she was quite happy, had never been so happy. A wreath crowned her head, violets and he was talking, talking, saying nothing, talking the way people, charming people, used to do, about Rome, about books, saying things that Darrington had forgotten, saying things . . .

He would go on saying things. He was a lump of amber and Hermione had only to look and look or to rub her palm across that smooth surface and electric sparks would answer her, warm her, light her. God sends things to people. He had caught her wrist. Was this God? or messenger of God? Was this some manifestation of the force that caught her wrist (with Darrington gone) . . . it was Cyril Vane. Hermione had seen him before. Had not seen him before. He had been one of a little group, had come, had gone, seen him somewhere else as they did, drifting in and out. Gold. Like a great pear. "Has Darrington gone back yet?" She would tell him Darrington had gone back and then he wouldn't come to see her. But she would tell him, "Yes, he's gone back." Vane would pay the bill, Vane would wait for her to reach, scrubbling about for bag, for gloves, Vane would say good-bye somewhere, somehow, not coming to see her for he wouldn't as Darrington was in France. She didn't want to see him. She didn't want to see him. She wanted to wait, to wait, to watch and to reveal herself to herself watching herself. She would go home, wash the tumblers, get down books. "Thank you for taking me out this afternoon. It's been the greatest pleasure."

But it had been a moment, a dream, a yellow lotus of forgetfulness and it couldn't hold on into the room, into the smoke, into the lack of coal and now into another leave . . . another leave . . . how they came back, how they came around and the sort of half-state, the sort of Limbo that she was in, that she managed to maintain, not seeing people, reading, sewing a little, had to be broken . . . another leave . . . and she was caught back into her body, caught back into the body of Mrs. Darrington, the person she was, it appeared, still, caught back, held into it, like a bird caught in a trap, like a bird caught in bird-lime, caught and held in it, all the time remembering her Limbo, the state she maintained through weeks, going on and on, not at Delia's any more, but digging out her books, determined to remember, like the Centurion, to stand guard over Beauty, one soldier over Beauty, while the lava fell and fell and the ashes rose higher to suffocate. Darrington said, "well, why did you?" and she didn't know the answer to that for she had said, "go ahead" and that meant only one thing for Darrington. How was she to know after it happened, after it kept on happening (Florient had the big room on the second landing for the county dame in the Air Ministry had had to leave London) that she would so care? Did she care? It was worse than caring. It was like having a body and being dead, mercifully, and then someone coming and saying no, you aren't dead, you are only half-dead, crawl back to your body. Conscientiously she had crawled back to her body, after she had winged out, gold, gold gauze of wings, winging up and up against a rose shaded light (she remembered) and now back in her body (not even comfortable Limbo) and she had been so happy. "I never thought—" "You never thought. Well you might have thought—" He was right. She was wrong. She had not thought in her pride, in her habitations, in her frank terror of this newest of the new Darringtons that they would (as one used to say) "carry on" to that extent, but why shouldn't they? Did people in the house know? That was what wracked her, people in munitions, all the people, good people, though she had repudiated good people, repudiated Delia and the Red Cross work and the munitions, still you had to think, had to remember, but Darrington was an officer, so everything was excused him if he wasn't a gentleman and it went on and it went on. "You're upstairs so much of the time—" "What did you expect when you so sweetly gave us carte blanche?" "I don't in the least know what I did expect—" "I should think you didn't. It's obvious that you only wanted to get me out of the way—" "Out of the *way?*" "One can't be expected to believe in the entire altruism of your scheme." "Scheme?" "Obvious—" Darrington was huge. He seemed to loom huger and huger each time he came back. He was so huge (but they go that way) that he would soon, it appeared, burst. Horrors of his bursting . . . yes, it was rather good of Florient after all, to take him on, a bargain is a bargain, "no, I don't want him, take him," for she wasn't going on with this sweet to sweet to sweeter, saccharine stuff of Merry Dalton, never never that again. Let it be daggers drawn, she wasn't one to clutch at that hulk of flesh that had been Jerrold. Hulk of something that was like a bloated great zeppelin but women seemed to like it. Rent him out, lend him about, military stallion. Florient was the right note, chic, pre-war chic, Paris, rue gauche, knowing all about it, he wouldn't break her, pressing upon her, O let it rip. Let him go, he had gone but what an agony, herself was like a wound, a burn against herself, within herself. Hermione in Mrs. Darrington turned and festered, was it the spirit simply? Trying to get out, trying to get away, worse than having a baby a real one, herself in herself trying to be born, pain that tore and wracked and what was there to do? Yes, my husband's due again . . . keep it up, one spark of pride. She had nothing against Florient, little bitch, but Florient might have thought of the munition workers. That was all she had against Florient done up in fresh rouge and looking pretty at that. The sort of thing absolutely for him, the sort of touch absolutely. Pre-war—no she wouldn't say it. She had nothing against the sheen and lustre of Florient with her lips the right red and her cheeks the righter red, peony made up, peony on a lacquered Japanese screen, thin and tall and with that Sienna slant to eyes. Sienna, Siamese slant to eyes. Yes, Darrington couldn't have done better, had he got her the room or was it true that she had had to move, had had to find somewhere to go, that the horizon blue officer had known Miss Aimes who had the house, that it was *he*—who had got her the room? In their house? But there were rooms, everybody knew there were rooms, they were free to anyone who could pay the rent. There must be no mystery. Let it be all in the open, the house was turned into a "house," that simple, by the coming of Florient, the house, her house that she had found, had taken (because of Flora spilling petals) was a "house." Her house was a "house" now and she didn't care, didn't think, for what did it matter? She couldn't any more go and watch Delia being white and white and the smell of blood on the bandages, she knew she was mad, it was all over everything and no one saw it. Out damned spot. What was there to do? Soul beating and tearing, why don't you get born? "You're quite wrong." "Wrong?" "I mean I haven't. Have been alone here." "Who can make me believe that?" "No one. Nothing. It's the truth. Truth will last—" "Your truth is a—" If he said anything disgusting now, she would tear at his throat. Her hands were thin, were fine but if they met in his bull-throat one or the other would go for her hands would never, never come out of that throat. Her hands were quiet. She was quiet. She was looking at Darrington and it appeared she would soon go—soon go mad. "Darling—" Why did he say that? "What's come over us?" She didn't know, couldn't say. Something had apparently come over them and she was tired and she couldn't go on getting colds and the coal had at last utterly given out. Wrapped in a coat. Feet drawn up. Looking at each other like two Russian peasants in a Tolstoy novel. Life was Russian. Life was damn bad art.

Now he said, "is it true Vane wants you to go off to Cornwall with him?" It was another day and she was so happy spreading her fingers to the unaccustomed luxury of the fire that she didn't think, couldn't think and Darrington, Jerrold, had brought her winter daffodils. "He never came here while you were away. Only lately." "Lately?" Darrington was different, he was looking at her, eyes wide and staring, not the mad badness of him but wide and somehow lost, lost in the room, looking around the room, their room, that he hardly ever came to now, asking her about Vane. "What—does—he—want?" "He doesn't want anything. He's just sorry—" "Sorry? You told him?" "No. Things get about. You can't expect them not to. He asked me if I—liked you." "And you told him?" "I said I had liked you, loved you. That you were different." "And he said?" "He said, 'you'd better wait till the war's over and give the lieutenant a fresh chance.'" "Why did he say that?" "I don't know. He doesn't really like me. He wants to—save me." "Damn right—" "Right?" "To save you. You'd best hop it. Clear out. You can't stay here another flu epidemic. You're most all in now." "Yes. We—all—are." "Astraea—"

Trampled flowers smell sweet. "Do you remember the spray of violets that were growing, by just that miracle at the base of the broken white marble foot, that hadn't been dug out yet, leaves brushed away, a foot that had been there, had been standing. So Beauty is still standing, a broken foot—" "You are obsessed with these things, sister of Charmides." "Charmides? I don't remember." "Surely you do, Astraea. That poem of Wilde. He loved statues." "Yes, Charmides. Statues—" "You never loved, cared. We were never married." "Married? But Naples?" "The wind from the Bay was as married, more, than I to you, Astraea. The rock cytisus was more your lover, not as people love." "Was that my fault?" "Fault? Your misfortune I sometimes think, seeing others, knowing the red wine of ecstacy that you've missed." "Missed? Have I missed anything? I smell the locust blossoms that fell along the quay, the smell of salt weed and the honey locust blossom and the atrocious guitars with Verdi, their Bella Lucia which weren't atrocious. Things are what they are in proportion to their setting. Love is what it is in relation to its surroundings. I loved you, loved the wrong sound of guitars that weren't wrong. Things change and love is not to be measured even with an angel's rod. You are wrong. I loved more than all these people." "I tell you, frankly, (we were always frank) you do not." "Do they know that ecstacy of the senses when a phosphorescent eel or some globe shaped sea-monster turns and makes a cone of light in the shadowy tank of the aquarium? There are senses and sets of sense vibration that they don't know. I felt with senses that you don't know—" "Don't argue. You can't argue of Love. You don't know about love—" Let him go on. Broken cyclamen, trampled flowers are sweeter. He loved her very much and his self had opened to let self out. His other self, or sleeping self opened before her eyes. It was hidden like the fleck of colour in the tulip bulb, that fleck of colour that was his life, his soul. It opened before her eyes but it couldn't go on opening. They were severed, had been severed. It is to their credit that they recognized that severance, saw it, stood up to it, dared it, challenged it. "You won't forget—" "Forget?" What was forget. Things are part of you as the threads of a deep sea creature, its threads of feelers are itself. Butterfly antennae are the butterfly body, more subtly, more intrinsically than the soft moth-belly of it. It was her misfortune (sometimes her questionable strength) that she felt outwardly with her aura as it were of vibrant feelers rather than with the soft moth-belly of her body. She felt knowing her limitations, more than they felt. Knowing her limitations, she realised that the tender feelers of her being were in danger. Butterfly antennae to be withered like the soft forward feeling of a moth's breath. Breath of a moth, of some soul . . . "Does he really want you?"

"I tell you yes. At least he doesn't want to go alone there." "If I go west, then he'll marry you, look after you." "O no. I don't want that. I don't think so far. If you come back I come back. You will be different after it's over. This is no test of courage. I'm sorry I couldn't have done more, helped further." "There is no help, there was none. Louise knows my needs. I love her. You don't know what I mean by that. I love her, she adores me." "Obviously. Do you want to marry then?" "God help me—no. Not Louise . . . wait for me."

8 So she waited. She was in two parts. Part of her had got out, was out, was herself, the gold gauze, the untrampled winged thing, the spirit, if you will or if you will the mere careless nymph, the careless lover, the faithless wife. The faithless wife had wings of gauze and now she knew better what love was for Cyril Vane was tall and gentle and not heavy and not domineering like her husband. Husband, lover . . . the 1860 thrill. I don't yet quite know how I did it, it was partly that he helped me, seeing that it was all lop-sided, it was brotherly of him, rather dear of him at the last bursting into my room after he had said good-bye saying he would—come—back. She had come away out of the ruin of London, escaping raids, escaping cold and colds and the horror that was around them. She had poise here, power. She was re-established. It was Vane who was her husband, more her husband, thoughtful, always right. She had reticences with Vane . . . a "nice" woman, over-romantic, tenuous, poetical and this was her right husband. Vane was right and Darrington never had been and that was why looking back, looking back across the weeks, across the few lovely months that she felt tremours, sadness, wistful longings for that other who was so very far from perfect. "What, another letter?" The letters came now more and more frequently from France. Letters from Darrington from France. Letters, it was right to have letters. Whose were the letters? Postman seeing letters, all the letters, it was right that she should have letters. Hermione hid the letters from her husband as if they were from a lover—it was so mixed, lover, husband. She should have obviously married someone like Cyril Vane, great house, everything clear and clean and beautiful, walls lined with books, her own room and everything right, the house-keeper dignified, everything right. People like Vane didn't have to explain things. It was people like Darrington that had to bluster a little, say "the gov'nor you know, four quarterings, but all faked." Faked or not faked you did not hear of Vane's people, nor his quarterings. People, faces. She was right here, face looking at you is right face for you Hermione. Your face now belongs to you, skin with a hint of burnt-honey brown, hair drawn back and fastened with broad band. Face looks at you and your hands though thin are firm and strong and fasten the velvet band and your frock is smooth and your hands are clean and your sewing bag is right and you don't care too much now about reading. You lie in the sun and your face nozzles down into tiny bell-flower, tiny white bells of heather, so sweet a smell rising up, rising up from the edge of the cliff and below you, there are further shelves clotted now with primroses, thick with clotted blossom. Shelves flow like veins of lapis and those lapis veins are simply hyacinth but seen from up here they make just such a deep blue line like a crack of lapis in a shelf of emerald. Was there ever such green? Flowers that are (it must be) rose-campion, little flowers along the edge of a field; the fields are small, small, simply imagination come true. This is reality. Heady gorse, thick with its yellow makes ridges and lumps of pure gold and I must be somewhere else. I haven't died for I am substantiated, there is no breaking out of myself, I am myself. I can walk, run, lie on the grass for there is never anyone about here and it's odd the place being haunted and Vane getting it cheap and a bore Fletcher, the house-keeper keeps saying she hears noises. She'll leave, that's the next thing and I hate cooking and we are so far from anywhere and no one has been here since the—war. What is the war? There is a thing you mean when you say "since" and "the." What is the war? People, faces that don't matter. That is the war. The war is people and faces that don't matter. The war is Louise with her Sienna slant of eyes and the carnation embroidered Chinese shawl and her standing and looking and looking and standing . . . the war is some boy who was swept out in the column for the whole column was swept out and they said it that way as if the whole column being swept out was the reason for his being swept out and that that explained it. They didn't seem to understand death, didn't know it when it faced them, was this bravado, or sheer stupidity? But I can't cope with England. I can't cope with all this. Cornwall is Phoenician and that boats tipped their sails toward this very rock and certainly if I went high on the carn at night, I should see things, images, ghosts. Funny old Mrs. Fletcher the housekeeper hearing things, says she can't stand it much longer. Loneliness. She must be . . . lonely. What is loneliness? Loneliness is a room full of people and Louise in a carnation embroidered shawl and the crowd going round and round and round and having to keep one's head up. Loneliness is a crowded room and the guns making a row and people, people, people . . . a gull wings up and wings around and screeches at me. His nest must be near here. I'll find it.

Gulls crawl into my arms but I'm not alive. It's rather odd suddenly being dead, being out of it and the others alive, somewhere, no, dead somewhere and I alone alive. Loneliness of Eve in paradise. That is my loneliness. Gulls crawl into my arms for I am too happy to cry but if I could cry it seems to me I would be happier. I don't care about anything, about anybody. This place seems to have been made for me but what is wrong? Paradise won too soon, beauty in its perfection come too soon. I hate myself for not caring any more about the lilies that grow with each minute across the length and breadth of France. Each minute that the clock ticks, each minute that my heart beats, some boy is flinging away a flower, a white flower, one alone on top of a hill, one alone in a ditch, but one can't go on remembering these things. I forgot them long ago and I for-got them for if I had gone on thinking, remembering (Americans don't care, don't understand) I should have gone mad simply. I felt it coming up, rising up against my skull. I felt a lily-bud push up against my skull, it wasn't imagination, it was reality, (like the bracelet that day, going to Milly Lechstein's) something I *saw*, not something I imagined, vision not dreams. In a vision, I saw myself grow up against my self and knew in a few days the white lily bud would strike the top of my head which is my brain, which is my skull. Then, if the lily-bud had struck the top of my head (the metal layer that was my brain) it would have withered simply. My soul would have withered as simply as a lily itself (any French lily) seared by a cannon flare. Lilies that fall and lie fallen, the lily of me grew up and up and up because I let the head go, the right and wrong of the head and Darrington helped me, Darrington said do wrong for to do wrong is to do right. What is right? What is wrong? Wrong is plodding through days and dying in London, dying in London. Right is saving myself, my life, for what? I am lonely in this paradise. Look at me bird, you hate me. I found you, I got you. I don't care how your parents screech and wheel above me, you are old enough to leave your nest and you fill a hollow of my arms. There is some hollow of my arms you fill. You fill it completely. I know I have stolen you, ruined your happiness, but why shouldn't I? I am priestess, infallible, inviolate. I am chosen. No Penelope. Cassandra? Madness rings me. I see in rings, in circles, light is advancing in a spiral. Light struck from the wall. Gulls. Crabs in sea pools. The wild orchids ring rocks. Make sacrifice. The white bull that lowers after me seeks to slay me. The fox crawls out of his hole to watch me. We are alone. Phoenician, left over, this coast has reality but the rest is hollow nothingness. I am sorry that I can't any more believe in the reality of war-fare. Jerrold.

"Jerrold, I must tell you at once. Let me know how you feel about it . . ." But before she could hear from Jerrold there was some oracle to be placated. She would find what the oracle said and she would follow the oracle whatever Jerrold said. She would ask Jerrold first, tell Vane afterwards, consult the oracle in between times but whatever the oracle said, must go. Oracle, there are thousands of you. Antiquity lives here. Witchcraft . . . but I won't try anything like that though I could try it . . . I know I have knowledge. It's come here to me, the knowledge that I have knowledge. I must make some demand, find out something for things like this don't happen (only in war-time) and Cyril said he would be careful, would be careful . . . careful. They always say that,

Darrington said that. Vane said that. "Careful." What is care? Cassandra. Am I then Cassandra? What has Vane to do with it, long body, slim and cool and different . . . what has he to do with it, always thoughtful, never domineering? He has had nothing to do with it for he says always he has been careful but what is careful? There is God in one and God out of one and now that God is in me. I feel no difference between in and out. Something had happened to me, whatever the oracle may say, I know already something has happened to me. But I'll ask it, for inside and outside are the same, God in and out, all gold, gorse, pollen-dust, gold and gold of rayed light slanting across the low spikes of white orchid and fragrance in and out, the same wind that blows across waters blew sails here from Phoenicia and perhaps I was a gypsy, Egyptian, having children as priests, priests having children with priestesses. This is no ordinary thing, war-time, things happen and the white bull shook and lowered at me but I must have the answer. Gull in my arms fill my arms. Sacrifice and sacrifice and now they will hate me, the birds will hate me, not all the birds. Go away sea-bird, I must find a land-bird and now in my room, I'll wait and ask . . .

Layers of life are going on all the time only sometimes we know it and most times we don't know it. Layers and layers of life like some transparent onion-like globe that has fine, transparent layer on layer (interpenetrating like water) layer on layer, circle on circle. Plato's spheres. Sometimes for a moment we realize a layer out of ourselves, in another sphere of consciousness, sometimes one layer falls and life itself, the very reality of tables and chairs becomes imbued with a quality of long-past, an epic quality so that the chair you sit in may be the very chair you drew forward when as Cambyses you consulted over the execution of your faithless servitors. Cruelty and beauty and love of beauty is the common heritage of the whole race. Everything is to each but it is only in developing one's own genius, one's own mean personality (which is one's innate daemon) that we can reach the realization of some sphere which is for all time, eternal, flowing as water, colourless, transparent which falling imbues the very common chair you sit in the very ordinary book you lift and open with some quality that is one with the Revelation of Saint John the Divine or the orders of Sappho. Colour there is in this sphere world, colour of the red anemone, colour as seen under clear water, colour as sea-coral seen through crystal. World falls over your head and you are embedded in the world; you are its only imperfection, a fly in its clear amber; you are its only imperfection yet your very presence giving quality, point, perspective to this otherwise so measureless luminous body. Fly in amber, Hermione stood in her room, a very fly enclosed in clear substance and she asked of swallows wheeling and swirling before the small open window if she should have it. Her heart ticked, dared not tick, knew the moment she had made the poignant demand of something outside (you may call it God or Plato's circles) that it would answer, that its answer would be infallible. The door was shut. The window was open. The window faced east, faced the semi-circle of terraced stones that was the Druidical, that was the almost classic amphitheatre that the opposite carn made for the receiving of the sun's first rays, for the receiving of the dew of the sky, for the receiving of the round globe of the moon that floated above it, would fall and embrace the very curve of the hillside like Artemis the thigh of tall sleeping young Endymion. Classic images here blend with Druidical surroundings, the round stones placed in their circle of seven, the very obvious flat altar stones higher on the carn and the enormous great ivy-trees, rounder than a huge, huge arm, trees of stock of ivy like a body, were the body (obviously) of some God. Dionysus. Druid priests. Ivy. The crown of the sacrificed. Things in the air, several layers of mysteries and all the time the knowledge that England was a cloud and she was looking down at England and at the war and at all the poor dark cloud of people from a height, so high, so clear an atmosphere that breathing it, she felt her very lungs gross and porous, great porous gross wings, beating inside her hulk of bone and frame of white bone covered with parchment flesh. Her body was like some mummified thing come to life and the breath in her lungs was pure spirit, the breath was part of the outer circle, the circle that had fallen, that had fallen some days ago (what was it, two days, three, must count exactly) when even the remote possibilities . . . how did one think of these things? The whole pain and worry had been eliminated. Her body was like some coffin merely, a thing of bone and fibre, a cocoon for the enfolding of a spirit.

Body now with clean hands, having lain all day on the rocks, having floated across the aquamarine surface of the tide pool, the one you own, your own pool that Vane even, had not gone to, body that has been cleansed in sun, in sea are you ready for its welcoming? Hermione asked this, waiting, knew that the answer was already premeditated. That God had prepared the answer as he had prepared the question in her own mind. God was the answer and the question. God was the lover and the beloved. God was the union of God with God. "If a swallow flies straight in, now without any hesitation, just in here to me, I'll have it."

Classic images here blend with images of Christian beauty. Hermione bent to scrape up the little blue object from the floor. The thing was round and blue and hard, it appeared like any lapis-blue small song-bird clasped in the hand of some Florentine bambino. All images blend here as she bent for it; she bent and took the creature into her hands, into her heart, she was bending, accepting the inviolability of God's Testament. Why should God ask this? She didn't know. She knew in the dark sub-consciousness an abyss of unimaginable terror, the pain, the disappointment, the utter horror of the last thing. Swimming on the surface of her mind was something other, different, of some other category than sheer crass experience. Experience had nothing to do with this thing, nor logic nor love even. It wasn't because of Cyril Vane that she stooped and swept the hard small blue thing from the floor, sweeping it up, its little crab claws sticking like insect claws to a dark leaf. She picked the little creature off the floor and images blend here, Undine, Morgan le Fay, some Florentine Madonna, some nymph whose beauty had been violated on some Delphic shelf. She was good and bad and remote and impossible. You don't go off to Cornwall in war-time and have babies. You see the manifest impossibility of the thing? Another thing . . . but she would not think of that. Something would happen, must happen, for God so simply had admonished her. God had swept one of his birds inward with a touch of his finger, one of his souls inward . . . "all rather awkward of course, but I'll hear from Jerrold." Awkward. She hadn't any more to speak, to feel. She had forgotten Vane.

But she must remember Vane. After all, it was his child, if it *was* his child for how could you say, lying on the rocks . . . it might just be the sun-self loving her. Daemon or angel. The sun was neither good nor bad. Apollyon. But she didn't accept all of revelation, all that wasn't in keeping with the other, "thou shalt love the Lord thy God" . . . God had swept across her white clean body and maybe it was the sun-set. People had children like that, daemons or goddesses or devils or mage women. Women in caves, there were caves all around these hills and there had been ancient sun-worship and the stones were still set tilted toward the sun-rise. Things, you see, never die and layers of life were all co-existent, in harmony for that shelf of the coast was empty (in 1918) and she was recalled to another element. However she must remember it was Vane's child . . . "it was odd. I just put it up to the birds. I know you sympathise a little with my notions, with my birds and following them and finding nests. I thought you'd like to know what I did, what happened." "What did you do? What happened?" "I went to my room and the birds, swallows, were wheeling outside. I shut the door and opened the little window and I said simply, if a swallow flies straight in I'll know—I'll have it." "Did one?" "Straight in—" "Um-mm—very pretty notion." "But you—see—I mean—it isn't just an—idea—" "You mean?" He was looking at her. He stopped stuffing the bowl of his pipe, held the pipe in that long hand, that beautiful hand, now so useless as all of him now was. There was something greater, other, some lover that swept across clean bare limbs that made all one's soul at one, that loved Morgan le Fay, Undine, and the Madonna alike and called one other names of far distant gods for gods had always (even God) loved women. Light of some Mithraic festal, she knew all about it. Babylon. Assyria. Things alien to her own cult of classic images were yet suddenly all blended, all at one, good and bad alike, welded one in the mystery. Mystery had stooped, had embraced, had welcomed her. Vane did not understand. His hand was lifted, the long white finger like some musician from some temple playing his flute note, arrested in a moment, not playing the flute note and the sacrifice was ready, unpolluted, covered with sea-salt. Vane was seated on the broad couch, a yellow French book (they always had yellow French books) open at his side, his feet rested on the beautiful rug. The room was lined with books . . . piano . . . tables . . . books, books. Hermione had opened a page from a book of Life, a book that was open, that was about one. Mysteries were written in the air and you asked answers of the mysteries and were granted them. "Yes. I mean, it's some days. It's some . . . days." How go on explaining that some days mean nothing and that some days was no indication. Only if you happened to—*know*. "It's some days—I mean it's pretty certain—" How tell him that it wasn't the "some days" that made it pretty certain but something else, something so different, so other. How explain while he still waited, his hand lifted, his pipe lifted, not furthering the sacrifice. Was she not even to have the sympathy, the interest of some brother priest? But did she now want it? In a flash it seemed his perception could in no way reach her. God had answered swiftly. God would sustain her. The very finger of Vane's hand as it now fell, was as it were the very thumbs-down to his own predicament. It wasn't a feeling that a door was shut on her. It was that he had shut a door to the entrance of himself into this fair country. It was a country from which anything might emerge, from which he obviously had no right of entry. Was she alone then? Heart rending, human heart-ache said so. Human heart-ache . . . but she was not human, the body was a mere parchment case, painted nicely, nicely set and fitted. Vane said "why worry till you quite know? In any case it would be pretty awkward."

9 | Painted case that had been so hieratically perfect for its receiving became (like the very larva of the future butterfly) now a jelly of vague unrest, of vague forebodings. Painted case so lovely and so calm and so inviolate if only you could stay a painted case, if only all the artificial glamour and hieratic spiritual fervour could be maintained. Did Madonna hold her own against this glue in nothingness, this inchoate mass that you become once you take——full hands for taking? She slept alone, was alone, had been. Jerrold wrote, "do everything to keep well. I want you to keep well. All I want is to look after you. All I want is to look after it." But what did that matter? It was fore-ordained that Jerrold should so write. Who was Jerrold? At best some secondary Joseph, at worst some oaf of erotic maniac who had bartered his wife, who had so sold his honour. What was Vane? At best some tall half-sexed Gabriel or Michael, some angel of annunciation, some spirit who had appeared and made what was ordained, what was to be, reality. O

Angel of Annunciation, "then you will—help—me—with—it?" She asked the question standing before him, already the weight of her own undertaking heavy on her, the weariness of her own pilgrimage seeming to stretch out and out before her. There was her own little money, the little sum that had seemed so smug and secure but that the war and Jerrold away and Jerrold and his leave-extravagances made now almost nothing, a drop, enough to keep from starving, not enough to go into a proper nursing-home—what did the Virgin Mary do on this occasion? O ask the arch-angel Michael obviously for God having ordained this would not leave one of his prostitutes no, one of his concubines (a wise virgin anyway) empty, forsaken. It was quite evident that God wouldn't but on the other hand was it God or some mage of wickedness for she didn't any more think (had she ever thought?) that Vane might be its father. Morgan le Fay you must summon your magic, become mere scheming wizard, witch for you must be assured that this, this thing that is God's, this thing that is the child of some sun daemon will be looked after. Of course, God, her Lover, would look after her, all the same it was the Angel of the Annunciation, when you come to think of it, who was responsible for the fiasco, wasn't it? I mean he came in all that glory and a dove entered (but here it was a swallow) and love entered and the glamour and the beauty and the hieratic loveliness and the beauty of the moment and the joy of her own realization of her acceptability of God, entrapped her. Well, anyway she was entrapped for God. It was not like the last one but now she began to wonder even if the last one had not been some rapt and perfect cycle compared to this thing. Darrington's image came before her as she watched Vane. She was asking Vane now for some guarantee that he would look after it and she recalled Darrington, Jerrold with his "lie down darling" and "eau de cologne is best at the nape of the neck and the wrists where the veins beat." Darrington had lifted the wrists, bathed them in the aromatic sweet stinging scent, recalled her to mountains of flowering oranges, rocks where gorse lay heady and sweet and where the red anemones made the earth a veritable Aetna, all the earth, all that volcanic earth where anemones like poppies were blood stains and foot prints of the dead God. Adonis, Christ died along the slopes of Solaro that pre-war Easter. Eau de cologne and the merciful numbing of consciousness brought those things back, had brought them back, in the first year of mad London. Guns and war and blood-anemones and then the annihilation that smarting of the fragrant scent brought to her. Darrington had been at least a veil, a sort of clod of earth for her numb roots that had reached down and down and deeper than she had then known. Only now she realized with the recurrent symptoms that Darrington had been earth beneath her, mud if you will, slime but substance, rich substance for her down reaching roots, substance so that her flower head might lift the higher into this thing. Darrington had been mud, earth so that she might lift to this Mithraic entity, this god in the sun, this being that had trapped her. She was caught and the recurrent symptoms made her realize that she was not so neatly a painted box, a neat coffin for its keeping. She was being disorganized as the parchment-like plain substance of the germ that holds the butterfly becomes fluid, inchoate, as the very tight bud of her germination became inchoate, frog-shaped small greedy domineering monster. The thing within her made her one with frogs, with eels. She was animal, reptile. Animal, reptile, she still held to the letter of convention. "Will you look—after—it?" "Look after it? I only want the war to be over, us to get some way on firm ground—I only want your wishes in the matter." This is not what lizard-Hermione wanted. This is not what eel-Hermione, what alligator-Hermione, what sea-gull Hermione was after. She wanted what an animal wants, what an eel wants, what even a bird must have. She didn't want the letter of the covenant. Vane offered that. "You know I only want—have only wanted—" He would say it again, he only wanted her wishes in the matter. But could he know her wishes? Gabriel of the Annunciation, cold and calm and proffering the lily, what do you know of god-head?

Morgan le Fay. I am witch. I have made this thing. There is, can be, no such room as this in this world, therefore this room is not in this world, therefore we are in some other world. Mrs. Fletcher gone, how wonderful, all the slight pretence, the slight as slight pretence that things are "all right" and Mrs. Fletcher polite but I'm glad she's gone for she took off just that edge, "madame, would you like a hot-water bottle," took away the reality of the non-reality, "madame your hot water's ready," and the gold film that lay over the house was a little desecrated by her presence. The house was itself now, sunk on its haunches like a lion, tame now, knowing its masters, its lovers, knowing its keepers, its children. Hermione and Vane were children of the old house, the house that was haunted that Mrs. Fletcher had so at the last hated that she had burst into agonizing tears and said she never had known of a gentleman's house where foxes stole the bacon. Foxes. No hunting. Tracts of moor, tracts of bushes, an adder, great hieratic creature curled in the hollow under the little out-house and Mrs. Fletcher finally deciding that some devil dwelt there. Did he? Someone, something lived in the great house, someone, something smote the beams and some note far and far sounded like some harp, some note, some string of notes, so that Vane seated at his table lifted his head and said "do you hear something?" Hermione had heard something but it was a breath of hearing like the sound you hear as a child in a sea shell of the whole sea. Monks had been driven from this cliff edge by daemons or was it finally that the daemons had been exorcised by monks for now the little church was gone too and the rocks still held the print of waters, of waters, of waters—— you might, you did climb down to find Vane staring from unutterable height, white face, moon face stupid against a cone of sky, and waves that walked in . . . walked in . . . waves here and feet. It was evident that this was rock ledge of Laconian Artemis, some Artemis of the sea, some statue ought obviously to have been there. The house now crouched like a lion feeling its young turn under its supine belly.

"I love the house, Cyril." "Do you?" "You know I do. Why did Mrs. Fletcher hate it?" "People do. They can rarely rent it." "Have you bought it?" "I will if you would like it." "Like it?" Belly of a supine lion, she was Morgan le Fay and she had made this house, this interior, how could she then so like it? "I mean I don't know that I exactly *like* it—" "There you are. You're like Preston, all those people who were here last summer—" "Didn't they?" "They were angry with it—it felt it—" "It would, somehow." "I don't quite understand the knockers, that's all." "The knockers? But they're the easiest, the simplest—" "People say so—"

The "knockers" knocked according to Cornish tradition, things it seemed to Hermione quite in tradition, not odd there at all, things tradition said out of the forsaken tin-mines—Phoenicians had come here . . . Mithraic . . . inimical . . . not to her inimical. "I don't understand having a child. It seems to me that I must be having a colt, a frog. It seems to me I must be having a dragon, a butterfly." Why did she say that?

Morgan le Fay drift in to dinner in an old long semi-precious frock, drift in and seated at the head of the table, queen it over the long room, the odd coloured strips of oriental tapestry, the books and books and the luxury of the great fire making things dance and sing and the beams dance and quiver so that the fire-light is the very quivering of those gold strings that sounded, that they had both heard sounding sounding, leaving almost strips of light in the air, quivering air-strings of vibrant metal, strings, harps. "I think it's much better since the Fletcher left, more at one, more a piece." Chatter a little and let this precious red goblet that Vane must have to-night, bring some human colour to your gill-white pallor, Morgan le Fay for they will find you out, and swiftly, they will find you out and swiftly. Chatter a little, laugh, make him think for a moment you have forgotten. "Chilly. Funny and it's only August." Outside the deep sea full and sweet and fertile, lay and lifted to an odd sky that was not as other skies (it was 1918) and years were odd things then for the stars wheeled differently, years wheeled differently, hosts of spirits ascended to heaven but here and there daemons watched and sat and guarded mysteries for God, even God who demanded the sacrifice of spirits wheeling toward heaven, knew his people, his odd witches, his eternal guardians of the mystery of wisdom. Wisdom was an adder that had lifted a lithe head so that Mrs. Fletcher on the way to the little out house had fallen screaming into the low prickly gorse, had had actually to be rescued ignominiously, had sobbed and wailed in hysteria of repression, "but gentlemen's houses—" Gentlemen's houses were free of adders and raised heads to greet Hermione. God keeps his little secrets. God, you have made me one with you here and the farm girl came regularly, laid dishes, took away plates, cooked their own farm-fowl in their own rare red tomatoes, vegetables, odd red and rich things, different, eating. Hermione eat and don't sing. Remember some of the testaments of the wise, try to recall wisdom for you are one of the children of Wisdom and God has told you one or another of his little secrets. Hermione, lift the goblet and sip the red wine and smile and be suave for God has told you some of his little secrets but you are in a world of men and men can blight you, men can ruin you. Morgan le Fay try to collect all the little threads of magic for God will take care of you only if you take care of yourself. Men, men, men, men. There were thousands of men. War dripped its rose-red petals, life upon life and love upon love and lilies rose up across the broken trenches. Guns creep nearer, nearer, will the guns prevail? Morgan le Fay drink deep, breathe deep, don't lose your little witch-like pathos and your witch-like beauty. Not beauty as the world sees it but beauty as Mithra might see it. Morgan le Fay . . . "what's that, Cyril?" "I don't know, the usual—" "Is it some big—boat?" "How do I know?" Guns, guns, guns, booming in the heavy stillness, guns, horror, listening, all the reality of the witch-world broken in a moment. "O Mamm I must be off. It may be, like last week, another bit of wreckage." Gone. Little Hezzie from the farm had gone. Adventure. Guns. Boats. Even here, Morgan le Fay . . .

Guns, guns, boats. It kept happening. In the heavy August night, guns, guns, boats. Morgan le Fay smile and draw your invisible veil across your invisible eyes and look through the veil at odd inimical creatures, buff creatures, buff creatures, mud-coloured creatures with high boots, polished boots, polished so that you could stoop and grin, grin back Morganlefayishly from polished leather. Has guns, guns, guns broken even your solitude, house like a lion? Will the "knockers" knock across the waste of years, of wreckage flung here on these rocks? Spars floated and bits of wreckage and barrels and kegs were washed up along the cliffs at the bottom of the garden where the shelves had been for so long impenetrable. Where Hermione had actually climbed down and had actually stood where (she was sure) no one had stood, had ever stood, boats now nosed in and nosing polluted clean sand, sand across which Artemis had stepped, taking the shape of wave on wave for her sandalled foot. Guns, guns look, Morgan le Fay, morganlefayishly through your veil drawn to make you invisible and hide yourself and look again. Men, men, men, men, men. Where had these men come from? A great car was drawn up outside the house, outside the empty ruin of the ruined shaft of grey stone that marked the ancient Phoenician tin mine where the knockers came from; Cornwall, Land's End, motors of the barbaric, like the Roman great cars rolling serenely over magic, over roads made for Phoenician donkeys. You are new, you Romans with your great chariots, Romans, great men with great shoulders. What do you see here, Romans? Romans in great cars, Romans left great cars to prowl about the house, to post little groups of Romans along their coast, to accost Vane with all deference but with a hard finality. His house. Their house. There was need of something. Was it of their house? Romans accosted Vane politely, did not see her, Morgan le Fay, concealed Morganlefayishly to mock and jeer at Romans, men, men, men, men. Were they part of men, men, men, men? What was Vane doing in his gold and slender inviolate youth? There was no more youth like this. Youth now had wings, slid across the layers of the air, slid across ether and prowled in the very bowels of the mid-earth. Youth no longer walked, held its slim inviolate beauty up toward sunlight. Youth wheeled in mighty armoured chariots, youth lay on the metal decks of hideous gun-boats, youth slew and was slain . . . the house was desecrate.

Nevertheless, she knew her own terrain, she prowled up toward the carn height and lay in a hot sun that fell and lay and almost lifted her in its pollen dust of weight massive beauty. The men, men, men, were invading their slopes, were desecrating the rocks, were spreading their magic of desecrating wires and were stopping at their kitchen door for water, for fire, for directions now and again from little farm-girl Hezzie. Hezzie looked upon these barbarians as desecrators. These "foreigners." Hezzie close in the magic of the house, held them at bay, held on to the magic of the house for things like this had never been done, never "had ought to be." Things that desecrated, that brought back things. Men, men, men and the strange human heart ache. Must she go back to men, men, men? Men could mar or make her. Men could not. Men could do nothing to her for a butterfly, a frog, a soft and luminous moth larva was keeping her safe. She was stronger than men, men, men—she was stronger than guns, guns, guns. The luminous body within her smote her. It was soft and luminous and the colour of the gold sunlight that fell over her. The body within her was a mysterious globe of softly glowing pollen-light. It would give light in the darkness, she was certain, it would give light in the darkness, would, she was certain, glow pollen-wise in the darkness if the rest of her should be darkness, mysterious glow-worm within her would give light, show her the straight path . . . and many there be that go in thereat. Straight is the road. Narrow is the path. God is. God is . . . mysterious light that would show her, straight and narrow the road to her redemption. She was stronger than men, men, men, men, guns.

But was she? "I can't stand it." She didn't know what she couldn't stand. She was ill, tired, she wanted something, she didn't know what she wanted. Vane looked at her with that odd quizzical expression, the same face that had met hers coming straight toward her through rows of statues,—statues, the odd and lovely and sometimes twisted things that Lechstein made, that were statues, statues. The same quizzical, slightly frigid, slightly imbecile stare of the well-bred annunciation angel. He didn't understand. He couldn't. "I must go to London. I must see a doctor." He looked at her as if she were somehow not very well bred, "there's a doctor in Penzance." "No, you don't understand. I must see my doctor, the one I—saw—before." Now she was back with it, now she had the clue. She saw, seeing Vane not Vane but Darrington. She saw her old experience. She wanted something that would bring her near to Darrington.

Long ago, seeds were dropped in Egypt's coffins and thousands and thousands of years passed (we all know this) and seeds brought to the light after thousands of thousands of years, sprouted, germinated, were sheer seeds of grain or barley, or of "some other grain" showing after thousands of thousands of years the inventiveness of God. Barley, grain or "it may be of some other seeding" came to light, some tiny green tips of two upward praying Akhnaton-like sun-hands, little sprouts of grain, praying toward the sun, little twin hands, the same always. The utter uninventiveness of God showed here. Seed dropped into a painted coffin was the same seed, the same germination that had always been and Hermione was now sister with every queen, sister with every queen, sister of Cleopatra, of the mother of Jesus, of Caesar's patrician parent, of every char-woman. Seed that held the globe of the sun, that pollen-light within her . . . "it's as well you came. You couldn't have carried it another two weeks." Ether, all the horrors, all the old fears, all the tempest of terror and this, this note of her choice, even now God gave her the choice, take it or leave it. Draw your ugly old clothes together again, smile in a crisp professional manner, "but my husband is now in France and after the last disappointment—I—want it." Did she want it? Why did Hermione stare in well-bred, well-feigned correctness (it was the right note, babies in war time) at the woman whom she rather dreaded, the same woman, Lady Hewlett, who had helped her, friend of Delia's, the old horror of the other time, why had she come back to look at her horror, to regard it, why was she doing this? Why had she come from Cornwall, why had Vane come from Cornwall? There seemed no reason under the sun, in the sun for anything but this thing. She followed it with what little brain she had left and seeing the clue, the gold thread she dared see the labyrinth. Horror was still about her but Darrington wrote, had constantly been writing, "have your child, keep well and I will look after it." Secure still in her Morgan le Fay little witchcraft, she could look at Lady Hewlett and smile and need not apologize for looking shabby (it was the right note in war-time) and say with mock fervour "O isn't it all splendid, he writes constantly they have them on the run." Fritz. Who was Fritz? A cypher in the riddle, a damn bad joke, something you had to grin over, brighten over. "Have him on the run." Smiling, husband so right, not dead (why wasn't he, posthumous baby) has Fritz on the run. "Mrs. Darrington with great care and a little discomfort—" O yes, that meant wearing that hateful brace, but what did it matter? God had given her the choice even now, it was a mangy sort of choice for she couldn't help it. It was like "yes I joined the army as a volunteer." What was it? She didn't know what it was. She must be very careful.

"Well, what did the doctor say?" She wouldn't tell Vane what the doctor said. She would smile at a painted annunciation angel who was now nothing, no one, someone who would conceivably help her. She said, "O things seem to be going jolly well." Affectedly, using a word she never used, smiling at him, being an imitation of something "county" that he must have hated. Smile at him, let your lips curve over your hard skull for you were a queen two thousand of years ago and it's still *noblesse oblige* and queens' children are very precious children. Horrible . . . for a queen. Are you a queen, Morgan le Fay? Yes for God lacks in inventiveness and once a queen (there is no escaping it) always a queen. I was a queen. I can smell the rush of water seeping down, then sweeping down from inland mountains, crossing sand-wastes, dragging trees and bushes along with it, Nile river. Nile river, great river like great inland American rivers, like no European rivers. Rivers were her kin and she was kin of rivers dragging silt down from high plateaus and from rock precipices. Little ugly room (she had borrowed Doris Redfern's little flat for Doris was away now with her medical corps) and Vane looked wrong and she felt down, down a sort of despising of him for his wrongness, for his wax-annunciation angel look in the midst of all this clutter of books, papers, a general untidy efficiency about Doris' flat with her medical books and her piles of pamphlets and her tables and chairs all utility proof, firm and yet clean and high, a little box of an office of a flat. Vane had looked right in the great Batenburg Square room with its high ceilings and its elegant Georgian decay, and he had been right in the old house, crouched like a lion. He said, "then aren't we to be together in London?" and she wondered where and how they could be together and thought how odd it was that places could change people and Vane seemed hyper-critical, leering, critical of this high up little clean box of an office that she had crept into, suddenly sinking to her lowest, being meagre, not noble, finding rest in this matter of fact, familiar, professional atmosphere after the gold and pollen and the weariness of the inhuman loveliness of Cornwall. Fox-gloves were beginning, had put forth great ruby spikes and she was weary of this loveliness, *noblesse oblige*, she could adapt herself to other circumstance, already felt lighter, better. Why tell him? She knew what Vane would say, would intimate if she told him. Why be uncomfortable, why be braced together? *Noblesse oblige*. Queens' children are so precious and queen not so very beautiful. "Then what do you think best? Had I better—" Better? What had he better? This was no moment for lawyers, papers, documents, hard cold facts. She wanted her veil woven subtly, secretly, anyhow did she care a damn now about Cyril Vane? Hypercritical, sensitive face that wasn't really sensitive. Bad copy of a bad copy—Carrara marble, late honey coloured marble but with no authentic line. He was, had been, authentic in Cornwall. But she didn't want to marry him. Why this marry? Marry? Why marry? Head bent forward. All the quality had gone, the quality of youth, the gold pear, the gold quattro-cento page, the saint, the young Michael. She hated Cyril Vane intensely. If he felt anything, he could say something, not this "the right thing" touch—marry—lawyers—*noblesse oblige*—I am not going to stoop to you, wax angel.

10 God singularly lacks inventiveness and she found herself in the woods, in the forest, in the little old cottage that Delia had lent her years and years ago, again in the little old cottage and Delia being kind, not knowing what had happened, saying "of course take the cottage, Jerrold has been writing me, we must all take care of you." No, this is no cheat. Morgan le Fay, you must, by your witch-craft make things come true and this cottage is small and pure and clean like a little built-up Hansel and Gretel hut in an old-fashioned operatic stage-set. Songs sing and I am alone and the woods bank the house and flank the house and there is a great waste of stubble and stumps opposite the house for they have cut down all this slope of the hill for air-service, wood, wood, woods, guns, guns, guns reaching even here in this remote Buckingham valley, so remote yet so near London, remote, far away but you can borrow the farm donkey any time and drive in to the station, five miles away for they all knew Delia in the old days, "how is Lady Prescott, is she never coming again to Chissingham?" Delia a sort of goddess in the machine, very much still in the machine, being ground and ground to pulverized nothingness in the machine, look using you I have used the machine, am greater than the machine. O stretch your limbs on the couch, pile pillows back of your head, balsam pillows, gone a little thread bare, boards showing cracks, little summer-house, not a house at all, how heavenly of Delia to really let me have it. Balsam pillows back of her head and she was alone, only Marion Drake from the big house a mile away, Marion their one neighbour in the old days, who (Delia used to wail) spoiled everything, would make a garden party of their week-ends, not understanding really happiness, umbrellas, striped red and vermillion against the beech trees, walls covered with exotic creepers. A garden a mile away and Marion Drake being friendly as far as her ambulance work in the five mile away Twickham would allow her. Thank God for that. Thank God. Marion Drake's caught in the machine but my husband's an officer if he isn't a gentleman and she will plunge in here once a week at any rate sensing my "condition." Lie on the long couch, pile balsam pillows behind your tousled head, thank God for this security and all the wood you want, scrape it up yourself for the cuttings are free to anybody but the farm people actually have enough wood and I will burn beech boughs, and beech leaves and make songs in the fumes of smoke . . . of smoke . . . God lacks in inventiveness for this happened in Arcadia (or was it America, the same number of letters, she counted on her fingers, and they look the same) and we wore a bear pelt and worshipped trees, tree boles and knew that men weren't worth anything except for this and after this, kill the men, queen bees, let your workers sting the useless males to death. Lie with your head propped up by the balsam pillows (I remember that very summer and how we all shredded off needles for these pillows) and let the breath of balsam go deep down, deep down for you need all this Morgan le Fay. Don't sing, eat. Gather twigs and burn them. Pray to your near gods for God lacks in inventiveness and this has happened—this has happened.

Marion Drake, nice name, name like twist of brown coloured silk, silk that runs from fawn brown to dead leaf brown to adder-skin brown, one into the other without perceptible break in the subtle brown-brown shade of it. Nice brown taste, nice brown feel about her name, "night candles are burnt out and jocund day" but I have no reason to think of that. I don't like Marion Drake meddling, why can't she let me alone? I'll have to rake out clothes, rake over clothes, can't go up there to tea in my old garden smock, why not? These things are more comfortable now, can't do it, will have to find some back-wash of pseudo-artistic finery as Marion writes in the little note (left under the butter and eggs basket) that she would be disappointed as the girl (who is she?) has read my lyrics, has never met a "poet," wants to meet a poet, has been to Greece. Why Greece? What Greece? Greece is a thing of rocks that jag into you, every Greek line of poetry breaks you, jags into you, Hellenes the supreme masochists, *hurting*—how did they manage it? A line, a word, the name of a flower, the name of every flower, hyacinth—but that's smoke blue, like clouded semi-precious stone. What shall I wear? The girl has been to Greece. There's that old slate-grey blue thing that I can pull about a bit but it means spending the morning sewing and I wanted more wood, sun lies heavy on the rough brambles, berries are almost over, frost makes a veil, the bride of God, the dead bride, Persephone veil over the bushes, over me, Persephone in Hell. Greek dead. I am a Greek dead. Not a dead Greek. Hellenes are the supreme masochists . . . and now she saw that the girl was a Hellene and this was odd for she had been so webbed over with the Egypt sand and sun-dust, with the quattrocento angel and the wax loveliness of the annunciation that she had forgotten (it appeared) stark colour, blue colour, colour of a jacinth, a smoke blue translucent stone that was one phase of Hellas. But Hellenes were masochists and when she looked into two blue eyes across the little extra festive bounty of Marion's tea-table (the girl had driven some ten miles over from Krissenden) Hermione remembered her name, Hermione, my name is Hermione. Hermione was the mother of Helen, or was Hermione the daughter of Helen? Hermione, Helen and Harmonia. Hymen and Heliodora. Names that began with H and H was a white letter. H was the snow on mountains and Hermione (who now remembered that her name was Hermione) remembered snow on mountains, sensed the strong pull-forward of sea-breakers, sensing the foam that was white and the white steed of some race chariot. And white steeds, white flowers, white rocks looked at her out of enormous eyes set wide in a hard, clear, slightly semitic little face, clear skin, wide brows, hair twisted in two enormous coils and that odd commanding look and that certainty and that lack of understanding and that utter understanding that goes with certain types of people, Delia's sort, people who were simple and domineering, never having known anything of scraping, of terror, of the wrong thing, of the wrong people. Hard face, child face, how can you be so hard? The smile froze across the white large teeth and the white perfect teeth showed the lips as hard, coral red, clear, beautifully cut and yet the child was not beautiful. Each feature was marked with distinction, with some race clarity but taken all in all, she was not beautiful, repellent a little— "How charming. You have really been to Hellas?"

Hellas, Hermione, herons, hypaticas, Heliodora . . . did names make people? Was it saying "Hellas" and not "Greece" that was to save her? Speaking herself frigidly (slightly repelled) to this young old creature who had everything (Marion said so) Hermione was repelled and for the same reason strangely lighted, concentrated, brought to some poignant focus. O this was it. This was to be her undoing again, again, again . . . she was not to be let drift and merge into the forest, into the cold green, into the cold shadows and the shadows that smelt of grape-blossom though there was never grape flowering in this Buckinghamshire valley forest. Trees smelt of green grape flowers but she was to be recalled, repelled from her musings, brought back; Morgan le Fay smile your little odd twisted smile for another will replace you. Smile and plunge back home into your little forest and say I'll never see that hateful hard child again, hard, pedantic and so domineering for you are doomed Morgan le Fay. Don't think you can get out of it. Smile and waste your brain . . . try to waste your brain . . . you have no brain . . . where have I put my Greek Anthology?

Weave, that is your métier, Morgan le Fay, weave subtly, weave grape-green by grape-silver and let your voice weave songs, songs in the little hut that gets so blithely cold, cold with such clarity so that you are like a flower of green-grape flowering in a crystal globe, in an ice globe for the air that you breathe into your lungs makes you too part of the crystal, you are part of the air, part of the crystal, and the air in your lungs and the voice that rises to some impossible silver shrill note in this empty little hut is a voice of silver, you are nothing, a blur of nothing, only the air in your lungs and the beating of your lungs like wings and the high impossible note make you one with beauty, with reality though you are nothing, ugly dark blue mis-shapen gown, stooping to gather twigs, to light the fire, breathe in the fumes of the smoke and you are one with the forest. Gods, daemons. This is your character. Your voices, your lungs (breathing air) chain you to people, you have lungs like people, air is free to all. On the just and unjust. Air. Air is a deity. To-day he wears silver sandals, the frost of sandals is in his breath and when he kisses me I am taken with his winged heels to the top of Olympus and I stand viewing all Hellas. Hellas? Hellas? What of Hellas? O, Hellas was yesterday at Marion's and that stark note of command, that demand-ing of me all that I have—what is the girl, she must be foreign, English people never care like this, don't read everything, she picked my brains, how tired she left me. Morgan le Fay build your pile of branches, blow high your smoke . . . breathe in your enchantments with the forest smoke, sing silver . . . silver . . . for you are doomed.

What is the matter with me? Why can't I get away from people? I am in several pieces, it's true, but I gave up the stark glory of the intellect, I chose finally this thing. *O sister, my sister O fleet sweet swallow.* I might not have had it. I chose it and I am taking the consequences of this choice which was the great choice, which was heaven. Unless you become as a little child, unless you become one with a little child, I have it and I am it and I don't see why I can't be let alone anyhow. Cornwall was some ledge of enchantment and Morgan le Fay fell under a druid altar and a god watching the sunrise, waiting for the sun-set so discovered her and sent his bird, the bird that came in, *the sound of a child's voice crying yet* and I said yes, soit, so be it, bowed my head like Magdalene, like Mary and said yes and I know that God makes me one, one with trees, with the sea, this is my terrain, even as a baby I used to crawl away under the bushes, the great white rose bush was like a forest to me then and I made nests of twigs, pretended to be a bird, a great swan with my nest and the kittens were the cygnets. Nests and birds and the kittens whose fur was like down and the colour was right, brown cygnets, rather ugly for beautiful swan, that was me, great swan of four years under a white rose bush. Eugenia (I called her mama then) loved roses. Pull off the thorns, it is more polite, strip them carefully if you offer them to anybody, for it shows you have been brought up nicely and everything you do wrong reacts on your parents. Who had brought up Darrington? Or Cyril Vane? Thorns. Für bei den Rosen gleich die Dornen stehn. Toute épine a sa rose. It works both ways. But it was all right. I ran away. Vane said he would "look after me" but I ran away. I couldn't sit night after night and see him not understanding, well bred annunciation angel in Chelsea, in Saint John's Wood. We would have had a pretty house, everything I wanted and the romantic scandal but all patched up, poetical, and his family so wealthy . . . I couldn't have stood it. Except ye become as little children. O he might have tried to understand, just to have said, "good for you, splendid, you are risking your life again like any soldier" but he wasn't a soldier and Darrington was only an imitation one though she didn't hold that against him and he couldn't be expected to understand. Für bei den Rosen gleich die Dornen stehn and after all there had been that beauty of pre-war Italy, pre-war Easter in Sorrento and the oranges that year had an unearthly fragrance. Freesias bordered the garden paths and she found violets to weave a crown . . . wound into her hair so funny at night and Darrington called her Aphrogenia. Aphrogenia . . . *a blossom of flowering seas . . . and a goddess and mother of Rome.* Rome. The campagna. The Pincian Gardens, it was about this time, early winter that we went there. Tea in a little underground passage, very chic. Italian officers (pre-war) in blue cloaks. *O sister my sister, O singing swallow* . . . all the same I don't see why they can't let me alone. I am Morgan le Fay (am I?) and I belong to trees, woods and I have every right to my security in this little hut with its delicious cold and its delicious isolation and I don't want to be disturbed, worried by the pedantic wretched child. I can't think of her as grown up. "Dear Mrs. Darrington" (she would call me that) "it meant so much to me to see you yesterday. I'll send the car over to fetch you. It will be too far for you to walk," (O bother her, bother her, bother her) "there's no time for an answer. The car will call anyway. I'd be terribly, terribly disappointed. You can't understand. I never met anyone before who knew the Greek Anthology" (bother her, damn her, I don't) "it meant everything to talk that day of Mallarmé" (Mallarmé, had they? Tuerons la lune) "I beg of you. I am so very lonely."

Let her be lonely, bother her, there is no such thing as loneliness with a great grey fur rug over your knees. No, there is no such thing as loneliness curled into one corner of a mammoth car, there were no cars like this, how did this come here, great car like a conqueror's chariot and the wind through the open hood and the world outside made perfect, perfected, and made proportionate to perfection. What do I mean? Why do the trees look so different for they do. It must be just the sheer human perspective but this is luxury and we have all forgotten luxury, we have lived in ditches, for years and years and our lives were light things, pinned lightly to our coats, our brown, fawn brown and horizon blue jackets, tunics, they called them, flowers to be worn lightly, to be tossed away. I have lived so long with trees, with trees that I don't know what to think, feel like some captured hamadryad under this pelt, this great pelt, how primitive the wealthy are, how primitive this is, rolling on and on and on and the roads are all narrower than they ever were when I walked them, scrambling over the ditches, catching a cluster of red berries to stand in the corner of the clean little hut. All the roads are different. I have no time to remember that that corner held the great orange shaft of late autumn lily that had escaped from the nearby cottage and this is the Tinkers Arms where I stopped that rainy afternoon for tea. Solitude, splendour with a little book in my pocket, tea steaming, "yes, I am here for a few months, my husband is in France. I know Miss Drake." The country, the country, every inch of it was measurable, English country, being kind to her, why were they kind to her? They were kind in Cornwall, here they were kind to her. Morgan le Fay, great autumn lily wandered from a garden, what are you doing, lover of luxury in these woods, orange lily, glowing with fire, kissed of the fire, in some wood, some beech forest? What are you doing, Morgan le Fay? Drag the pelt over you. It's getting late. Soon real winter. Prolonged autumn with dark evenings. Sense of mystery in England. England is all a mirage, love it—love it as you love a dream, a place for ghosts, for phantoms, for throw-backs, Morgan le Fay. They were always kind to you in England, I don't know why, for people say it is a hateful country, why were they so kind? Morgan le Fay, smile Morganlefayishly . . . "yes, I loved the drive over. No, not cold." House full of odd things, chippendale, old hall, was she living here? Don't ask. What is the weird child doing here? Why didn't she say something, say "my father paid a billion billion pounds—for that car," why wasn't she communicative, say, "I bought this dress at—" but where had she bought the dress? Hermione couldn't quite "place" the dress. Where had she found the dress, it was too old for her, her shoes weren't right. Who had dressed her, head pulled forward by the huge coils of braided hair, tea brought in, she was clumsy with the tea-cups. "O let me help you," but what a thing to say, never met her but once, asking to pour her tea, that hieratic ceremony. The child held the huge tea-pot in small unbelievably fine little hands, hands too small, too small for anything, head too heavy and hands too delicate, too small. Head and hands don't match, what is the matter with her? Her head is too big, her hands are too small, her eyes are far, far too blue . . . "do you—

do you—paint?" "*O paint*—" The girl put down the heavy tea-pot, turned eyes that were far too blue on eyes that were grey and green and somehow coming back (Hermione felt this) to some indoor perspective. "Paint—what made you ask it?" "Your hands—I don't know—something in the way your eyes stare—" O lovely room, last stray bit of sun, like a gold gauze of fine web falling, filtered through trees outside between drawn beautiful curtains. Little waif, are you a le Fay too? What is this family that seeks its own, brothers and sisters, lost people? Vane had been so dear in Cornwall, was it her fault, her own lack of patience that had lost him? Sister, brother. What were these hectic relationships, this Louise-Darrington alliance, for instance, what did it know, what could it know of these things, these inevitable kinships of the spirit?

Stark colour broke across an old room, gone dim with light fallen to gold-grey, fallen to grey with the hint of gold that under clouds at sun-set throw over grey water, gone to grey water . . . the room was filled with grey water from which odd knobs and handles and the flank of a candle-stick emerged, streaked in the water-grey like metallic gilt sun-fish, flicking here and there fin or under-belly, flicking colour, metallic from and-irons, the claw foot of a table, the reflected fire-light in a polished bowl and the stark upright shafts of hot-house carnations (she had not noticed them before) white wax spikes that glowed now, gave uncommon frost and winter and artificiality to the interior that up till now had been just the web and comfort of a big country room with the firelight and the inexpressible comfort of the great arm-chair after the camp-chairs, deck-chairs and the low crude (but so dear) foot stools of the little cabin shelter. Carnations. "How did they get there?" "What—where?" "I hadn't noticed the carnations till the sun faded and they glowered out wax-white, taper-white, I hadn't noticed the scent, now it comes over me, so spiced, so cold, so hieratic in this room that smells of logs, of tea, of comfort, of pot-pourri, I noticed that when I first came in." "We always have carnations—dada loves them." "O dada." Then there was a dada. Who was this dada? My dada paid a billion pounds for the car (but she hadn't said it). Which car? An emperior. He was Tiberius obviously. "Is your (if you will forgive me) 'dada,' Tiberius?"

Was it possible that the child could laugh? It seemed so. High, clear, the voice of a boy laughing over a fish that has fallen from his line that he with some arrogant and unexpected gesture has caught back, flung into the net as it was just escaping. The laugh lit the room with the same metallic glamour, the slight note of discord, like clear tropic fish beating up out of grey water. "You don't seem altogether— English." This was the sort of thing one never said nowadays. She oughtn't to have said it. "You see, being myself really American—" would excuse everything, every lapse and the faux pas of intimating anybody wasn't English in this time. "O but we are—we aren't—" "I thought so. I mean I thought you were—you weren't. What (if I'm not being curious) *are* you?" "Dad has boats. Now not so many. A hundred have been lost. We were always in Egypt in the winter—" "You were born then in Egypt?" "No—nearly though in Naples—" "Ah—Naples—" Under trees flowering with the locust blossom, that sweet honey and salt of the sea and the salt and the weeds lying against the break-water and the odd wrong songs, the bella Lucia and the atrocious Verdi. "Naples—" The word prolonged into the odd interior, the grey water from which the fin of a brass candle-stick, the flick of the back of a cigarette box or the bright ivory worked on the polished idol she just now noticed, made eccentric Chinese, tropical odd comment on the very greyness. Pot pourri-like incense and the heady sharp stinging sweetness of the staunch white taper of the hot-house winter carnation . . . room full of subtlety yet strength, odd comment on the world, on the war. How had she ever come here? In the room against the sheer north grey and the more obvious erratic Chinese, tropical glint of fish-fin that was the candle-stick and knob of something that was the crystal glass knob of something that was the crystal substance of some delicate jelly-fish, more obvious European, classic colour obtruded. Naples? Names, people, names. Naples. Atrocious sound of Verdi, Bella Lucia. Blue, blue, blue. "Why is it that one immediately thinks of stark blue, thick blue that you can cut with a knife when one says Naples?" Someone from somewhere had switched on a light but it didn't matter and the light was modified from where she sat by the heavy idol on the table, by the sprays of tall upstanding stark wax-taper of the white carnation. Someone was moving forward, gathering up the tray but it didn't matter. It was the sort of someone that would do things like that so they wouldn't be noticed, could go on talking, even about Naples. "Stark, stark blue. Why is it?"

O this is terrible. At last after all these months. I have found perfection, have fallen into a beautiful chair, have sat throned yet at peace, doesn't the girl know what is the matter with me? O this is too much, too much. The run over in the great car, the warm rug about my feet, the feeling of the world coming back, yes the "world," houses with carpets on stairs, windows with curtains drawn, wine in different shaped glasses, stems of glasses in a circle on white damask and flowers in the centre of the table, made artificial by the stiff upright symmetry of them. Flowers on tables and curtains drawn and the right side of the right person at the right dinner at Delia Prescott's, all those things came back when I sank in this chair, smelt the translucent fumes of tea that was real tea, tea a ceremony, Chinese . . . what was it? All that had come to Hermione in her corner of the room, in her great chair and now all that was going. Didn't the girl understand? No, it would be like Marion, wrong kind of delicacy, never to have told her about the baby and after all, here is this child, perhaps she knows nothing at all. O impossible! Yet staring back into eyes that stared and stared (now that she was just leaving) Hermione asked herself if perhaps she wasn't in some net of wrong enchantment, must pay, it seems for everything, but this was too much to pay for beauty and seclusion and the trees going past the open car window all in proportion. Paintable. Things seen in perspective become things to be grappled with. Art. Isn't art just re-adjusting nature to some intellectual focus? The things are there all the time, but art, a Chinese bowl, a Chinese idol, a brass candle-stick make a focus, a sense of proportion like turning the little wheel of an opera glass, getting a great mass of inchoate colour and form into focus, focussing on one small aspect of life though really it is only a tiny circle, a tiny circle. You get life into a tiny circle by art and that was where Morgan le Fay was wrong with her craft for she would say all art is man's mere imagining and see, the shell by the shore, the one petal of a water-lily is a sort of crystal glass, a bright surface and you yourself staring at it, may make things in the air, pictures, images, things beyond beauty beautiful. But there is where Morgan le Fay was wrong. We are strung together, we all have lungs, must breathe, breathe, breathe, we men and gods, rather we men and demi-gods for Morgan le Fay and Circe and Cassandra and the Oreads and Hermione were only half-people, half gods, demi-divinities like this child whom now half-god Hermione saw was also one of the half-people. O what good did motor cars do anyway and having Tiberius for a father if you had to stare this way? Now sinking back in her chair having almost said good-bye, Hermione must ask her.

"What is it in your eyes. I'm awfully sorry (will the man mind waiting another ten minutes?). I can't go home all alone without knowing. You will I am sure forgive me. I want to know what it is in your eyes for they have looked at me and looked at me, seeming to want to tear something out of me like evil-minded urchin opening up a chrysalis to see the unborn butterfly. I am sorry if I have been uncomprehending. It's true you wrote me you were lonely. I have forgotten for a long time the meaning of that word for I am—I am—" but she couldn't tell her that. It occurred to Hermione suddenly that the child might hate her, turn against her, consider her beyond the pale, a woman with a fine leashed intellect (for the child adored the intellect) having so far forsaken the snow-white arcana of Pallas, so far as to fall . . . fall . . . fall . . . there were other islands. She wanted to tell the child about those other islands. "There are other haunts, not of the intellect." The child said simply staring with the eyes that weren't now blue at all, gone grey as if a film of ice lay with devastating blight across a space of blue and heaven-blue gentians. That was the trouble, that was what unnerved. The eyes were glazed over like the eyes of the blind. There was something odd, unseemly, difficult. Hermione wanted to get out, get away, hold on to her web of gauze, continue the melting loveliness into her own room, take it back with her to spread it like thin honey over the plain wheat-bread of her plain days. She wanted to eat the gauze with her spirit, make it her own, take it back, treasure it and let flecks of it brighten days and days . . . for days after all were days and sometimes drawing the water from the little well, wandering up to the distant farm for her supplies, waiting at the post office for her notes from Darrington (Darrington was writing, writing to her) she felt days as days . . . heavy lead-winged days that had to be endured for at the end of days and days there were worse days . . . worse days . . . days of fire and slaughter . . . madness, no, she daren't think, had morganlefayed it, made herself a dream in a dream to sustain herself, to sustain the small le Fay. What was this staring at her? Was it another child, child of her mind, her spirit? Did God increase his burden . . . to him that hath . . . shall be given . . . but she didn't want this mad child vamping her. She couldn't stand perils of the intellect. She wanted to escape the mind and all it stood for. She wanted to take from this girl not give to her. "I know. I suppose you wanted to paint. It was like that with me—only music—" What was she going to say, where was it going to take her? "I shouldn't think too much, wait a little—wait a little—" The girl said surprisingly yet not to Hermione at all surprisingly, "I can't wait much longer. I've thought it all out. I can't have what I want, paint, the smell of it, boxes of paints, freedom—I'm going to kill myself—it isn't exactly anybody's fault—but I can't stand it." "Can't stand—what?" "Everything. Nothing. All things. Nothing at all. Myself chiefly."

11 She was too young to talk about self, self, self—what was self? Self was a white carnation in a tall, green tumbler, (you can't kill your *self*) self was a lotus-lily folded in the mud, self was the scent of pot-pourri across the fumes of beech bark burning in an elegant room and the polish on the floor and the net of gilt that was the sun, that was the curtain before the window that caught the sun, self was the sun caught in a drawing room curtain, caught now in a curtain that was too heavy. Hermione looking up from her tea-cup, jerked herself violently back from the contemplation of self, a lily bud folded in slime, of self, the scent of white wax carnations . . . this is different . . . "I almost thought I was back again in Buckinghamshire . . . time is so funny now . . ." catch yourself back Hermione, you are getting more and more lax, don't seem to understand time at all, it's a sort of madness, a sort of drug having a small le Fay and the girl even now doesn't seem to realize it and it's three months since I saw her in Buckinghamshire and I must move out to Richmond soon, in a few weeks to be near the nursing home . . . "I am going out to Richmond in a few weeks, be sure to make me remember to give you the address. It isn't fair to talk this suicidal talk till I get better." Time was so funny. It got funnier and funnier . . . what was self? What was time? No need asking what truth was for jesting Pilate never stopped to find out, no one would ever find out "what is truth?" The girl would go on staring at her and staring at her. If she woke up dead, after the baby, after the chloroform (is that the reason she wanted the baby? Legitimate suicide, she understood why the girl wanted to die, but with chloroform) if she woke up there would be no peace—there are no fields of asphodel this side of the grave. There were certain problems you had to settle this side of the grave, might as well settle them now but she hated the girl in the great London house in her governess-like blue clothes, in her wide room, in the beautiful great drawing room, "is that really your portrait," for it occurred after staring mesmerized at something that at first had seemed a subtle bit of colour but that had turned out to be pearls painted, carefully painted pearls that had given back a cheating semblance of glamour and the thing had turned out to be a portrait and all twisted and all wrong eyes had looked at her. Eyes had looked at Hermione from the wall of the enormous drawing room and mesmerized she knew she would never, never escape those eyes that looked and looked and looked. Those eyes said to her what she had just said, they asked and asked, "what is truth?" They were devouring wicked eyes in a face that was smooth and sponged clean of any character. Eyes that were the wicked eyes of a Roman judge, that were the excruciating blasting cynical eyes of a Nubian torturer (only they were blue). What were the eyes? Hermione almost asked whose were the eyes, for they did not any more belong to any-body . . . they looked at her night and day . . . demanding.

Her eyes were the wicked eyes of a child, some wicked, excruciating son of Darius splitting open a chrysalis, now so soon of itself to be split . . . it was more wicked now even than in Buckinghamshire for now the chrysalis was so near, only a little while. "I must move out to Richmond, then you will come to Richmond," but she was asking it as a sort of duty, hating the girl, hating the eyes that split her open. Why didn't the mouth speak, beguile the eyes? The mouth was too perfect, a little too wide, but in shape too perfect, but it had to be wide, that perfect mouth to cover that row of beauty. Hers were straight, beautiful, like a young lion's teeth, not cruel like an old lion, like a young lion, teeth that could worry bird feathers—teeth that gave back the authentic sheen and shimmer that those pearls painted on that parody of the child throat did not pretend to give . . . teeth . . . pearls. "That picture isn't—like—you." But now she was being rude, holding herself in so many layers, so carefully housed, self and self and all confused and blurred by the cocoon state she was in. Self. What is self? Self is a lotus bud slimed over in mud. Small le Fay, you are more a self than I am, but I am giving myself to you to make a self. Are you giving yourself to me to make a self? What is a self? She was too young to say that. She had said months ago in Buckinghamshire that she couldn't stand anything, most things, what things, herself chiefly. She had said that. She was too young to say she didn't like herself. Beryl. Her name was Beryl. It was impossible, had from the first been impossible, that her name could be anything but Beryl. It might be—it might be—what might her name be? Beryl, Beryl, Beryl. Yes, her name was right. Beryl was her name. Beryl. She was nothing but a name, nothing but those jewels staring at her, making Hermione into something that wasn't Hermione. Hermione was a cocoon, a blur of gold and gilt, a gauze net that had trapped a butterfly, that had trapped a thing that would soon be a butterfly. Hermione must stay a net of gauze, not be beguiled by eyes into some open rock-hewn wind blown spaces of the intellect. You see the intellect is Greek and if you are having a le Fay, a small le Fay, you must not be Greek. Let the intellect sink like a great white god, Pallas, or Helios, God, intellect into the ripples of self. What is self? Self is a great stone, a mill-stone, the intellect sunk and self is the ripples of sub-conscious or super-conscious gold over and over and over. Beryl was a lode-stone, a magnet, a devastating cruel daemon who would not let it rest, would not let it rest . . . "but *why* do you prefer Propertius to Homer?" There was no answer to that, they didn't blend, you never said the two in the same breath. But there was an answer. There always was an answer. Intellect would never let her go, never would let go. "Propertius offers me red wine in a goblet—lets me forget. Homer—makes—me—remember—"

You can't go on with this, you can't go on with this. Names were stones, were jewels, Catullus, a red lump of uncut slightly dulled over, dimmed over garnet as if the froth of wine had left its dim froth of scum on a red stone but he was not transparent, even translucent like Propertius, but he should be. Verses, carved and hammered, the Sapphics of Catullus, were small garnets giving back light, but you see what I mean, the feel of Catullus in the throat (the very u, u, u, of it, the stress on the u in your mind) makes the heavy froth or scum of grapes that blur over the texture of pure red and make it a blood stone, semi-precious but a weight about your throat—O weight of beauty about thin throat that rises, Morgan le Fay to escape—to escape—there is no escape—blue eyes say so, the eyes of some Persian magnate's horrible boy child, eyes of a prince, the Beryl eyes of Beryl, Beryl. Beauty is Hell—should one say that at her? Hysteria. Don't let me get hysterical for she makes me see things, the scum rises, floats and finally my brain looks out and I can't let it, I can't let that happen or I will go mad and the le Fay will be queer—odd—a monster not a small thing, amber and gold, floating to life, borne here like a golden willow catkin down a stream—down a stream— "Yes you should read it, learn Latin (it's a pity you hate it) just for cras amet—" O God. Where do these things come from? "I know I'm indulging myself—" what a word, what an idea—"but may I have more—tea. Those sandwiches are so delightful"—words, what words—they were talk-ing of Catullus, "I don't know why I like, why I dislike. I am no critic of letters." Letters. Cras amet. Someone had to love these things. *Poetry like certain other of the things of the spirit will die if it is not loved.* Someone—somewhere—had said that. Where? Who? Wila-mowitz Möllendorff. She remembered the name. But he was Fritz. Fritz. Over the . . . top. Over the . . . top. But they were. They were over the top. People didn't stare like that unless they were over the top and now it occurred to her, "Pindar is too like Bach. That's why I hate him." But was he? There were other lines, the violets of Ion, other lines of Pindar but on the whole say Pindar is like Bach and dismiss him. We have no time, no time. "Anacreon of course is our Herrick." Yes, of course, Anacreon, Herrick. "You know snow white blossoms, what do I mean, white blossoms, plum, no, cherry, floating against dawn. Anacreon. Dawn. Eos so like Eros. People, names. Every Greek name is of course a person. Names are people and hold light and seem to gleam with light within themselves. Especially when they are stones. Don't you think so? I mean, I am sure you see it that Aphrogenia is simply froth and foam of the sea but Aphrodite comes out clear, is crystal. Words, people. Names. Of course, the Greeks must have gone mad saying those words. The very names induce a sort of hysteria. And in the end they had to be conquered for who could stand up against swords, fighting with names like that, your heritage. Sappho, Anacreon in your veins, for the race is to the race. I mean every Greek held all that as every drop of water holds all the sea. Greeks. Names. I must have another sandwich."

This thing would prolong itself and clocks were striking. Hermione was in a world of mystery for a great house on Curzon Street is always mysterious. Thank God we were not born on Curzon Street for Curzon Street (say it, you will see what I mean) holds mystery. Clocks were striking, striking, silver and one not as far as the others with chimes. It sang its silly silver song and sang it again and a third time. "One quarter's missing, like the moon three quarters full." Ah that was herself, that was Hermione. "A most awkward shape, the shape of the three quarters striking but the chimes are pretty—" Silver, silver, answering silver, silver. Was she dead? Was she enchanted, under the sea in this house on Curzon Street? "Are you—alone?" No one about, nothing. Catullus filled the room for his name lingered and clung like the very wine lees against the marble (in the far corner) of some second rate 1880 French goddess. A sort of small Fragonard Clytie by way of the Luxembourg. The small wrong goddess was right here and like the wax white carnations brought the taste, the character of the owner of it. Dada. Tiberius. Hermione could smell the scent of his excellent cigars, could see the lilt of light (blood-stones, Catullus) in his super after-dinner port. "Port. Do you like it? I was thinking of Catullus" —but she wasn't. Chimes, silver. Enchantment. Why did the girl stare and still stare at her?

The eyes would still stare at her the other side of—the other side of— Styx. There *was* another side and this was the great discovery . . . another side in fog, in mist, with wounded soldiers sitting in their odd-smoke-blue uniforms along the benches that now in Richmond Park were all marked "for the wounded." In 1926, 7, or 8 some great distant era, people will forget benches, that benches were marked in parks "for the wounded" and you couldn't sit down on them, not Hermione even dragging a heavy skirt that swished against inadequate light ankles through the long grass through the gardens. Richmond Park. It was a heaven, an aura of world. The world has an aura, just as they say (odd Indian mystics and illiterate people say) people have them. And the aura of the world was visible to Hermione (and to some soldiers sitting in smoke blue hospital uniforms on a bench) visible, tangible, walking through the late winter mist, it was the aura of the world and the world had melted away (not to everybody, to Hermione, to blue soldiers on a bench in Richmond Park). The whole world had melted, had become an aura and Hermione thanked God, thanked someone (she couldn't remember who it was—a man called Vane?) for having injured her, wounded her so that she, like soldiers on a bench perceived a world outside or inside the world, part of the world, as the moon-nebula is part of the moon, part of the world and yet not part of the world. The world's great throb of guns, wounded pulse beat was silent. You see the world was dead. It had died with beat, beat, beat of pulse, that was beat, beat, beat of guns that was going on, had been going on all the time across a narrow strip of water, in France to be exact (have you heard of the war in France?). People forget so easily, I think it was 1919. I don't remember. Only feel with Hermione how odd it was that her ankles like a deer's were too frail to hold up an awkward bulk of body that was Hermione's small le Fay. Hermione looking bulky and unseemly as any char-woman slid past people, past houses, seeing nurse maids that were pulling mis-shapen children, crowds of children, all mis-shapen in the sulphur fog and nothing was real, nothing but the slightly meagre herds of deer, the deer, the deer whose ankles were her ankles and she understood the deer sliding along the hedges of the distant far edge of Richmond Park and the great trees dropping last, last left-over leaves that were already over; there was no real autumn, no real spring, crocuses were darting up in the sulphur spring light, little rows of blue and saffron crocuses and bunches, clots of cream-coloured crocuses that came up, that came out in the yellow sulphur light like odd planet colours, like colours seen through some spectrum, like observing the sun aura or some star aura from a long way . . . crocuses weren't stained glass, radiant in rain washed colour. They were hectic blue that was fire hectic flame blue, like blue given off by burning chemicals, waste of a world and the flames of the waste were hectic fire blue and odd cream white and soft, soft white all blurred in the sulphur that was part of the aura, the edge of the aura, like the edge, the corona of a sun eclipse.

The earth was eclipsed and in the eclipse as in ordinary sun eclipse we (Hermione, soldiers on a bench) were permitted to see the odd penumbra, the light that the earth (wasted dead eclipsed earth) gives out. It was our so great privilege. Most people, it seems odd, never saw it, just as most people (it seems odd) never felt the sudden end of the world when the guns (the world pulse) stopped that soggy autumn day. Long ago. *That* had happened long ago, but still there were soldiers sitting on a bench, what a pity, what a pity when that glory (armistice) happened, you couldn't do away with the consequences, just be glorious and done with. Blue soldiers witnessed that it took a long time to be resurrected after you are dead. So did Hermione. What a pity, what a pity, Madonna had all that weary and mis-shapen time to go after her glory of the angel and the wax lilies. We never hear about Madonna and her weary waiting and all that and we never hear about blue soldiers on a bench. But I suppose it's all right. Only some people, char women, tobacconists, evil deck hands felt it. Hermione felt it. Some people who knew that the beauty of things is a snare and you don't get glory in a sudden moment. Soldiers sat on the bench and watched people. They watched people and saw Hermione sliding by ill-shapen and with her clothes pulled wrong and her bulk too heavy on her thin ankles. They sat on a bench making remarks, common, bitter ugly.

But blue eyes, evil eyes, were calling her out of that nebulous world into which she had so softly fallen, blue eyes were dragging her ashore as one drags the mercifully almost dead to land, blue eyes were working their horrible first aid and were calling, calling to something in Hermione that was lost, that was forgotten, that had slid away, been taken away just as the guns, helmets, bombs, gas masks (what not) had been taken from odd smoke blue soldiers on a bench. Hermione was defenceless and blue eyes called her back to war, to fight, to resist, to appeal. "What do you think of Middleton?" O stuffy books. Couldn't she let stuffy books alone. Books were books, part of the old world, part of the people who didn't understand that the world was dead, its heart had stopped beating, guns, guns, guns, you never felt their throb and tremble till they were gone as you never feel the heart beating in you, till it is gone and you are dead. When you are dead, there is merciful quiet and you realize all,

all your life you have been slightly listening, slightly asquint as it were mentally, listening, waiting, listening and a little afraid all, all your life, lest it should stop, should stop and you not know it had stopped. It was like that when the guns stopped but most people didn't know, were still alive (they called it) not drawn out of life, out of the pulse and beat and throb of it like blue, smoke blue soldiers on a bench watching people pass, saying crude and ugly things but all the time at peace with great peace knowing they were dead, not listening any more, not waiting any more; pulse stopped beating. It was so marvellous and nobody knew. No one at all seemed to know but you can't tell them about it, any more than an Indian mystic (or some illiterate mumbling person) can tell you about your aura; it is blue, it is grey, it is opal clouded with amber. Amber clouded with opal. That would be a lovely aura, some little sempstress in a corner working, sewing, with pricked rough fingers might have it and a great lord who commanded men, men, men, guns, guns, guns to move up, across to men, men, guns might be sodden illiterate green or grey striped with a nothing of blue-smear, no real blue like a convolvulus petal that has been crushed, smeared on an asphalt pavement. That is how it is with auras, with illiterate people seeing, sensing, not actually seeing (but it was only the illusion of mist) that aura and Beryl had not seen it. It was just that kingdom of heaven and being like a little child, accepting everything, like the soldiers on the bench, like Hermione, honourable wounds, dishonourable wounds, it's all one to God so long as you are wounded . . . because she loved much. So it was like that and Beryl with voracious eyes and brilliant intellect was talking of Middleton and Hermione propped up in the one big chair that her room boasted must answer, find an answer . . . Middleton? Who was Middleton? "O yes. I think his horse play is legitimate—Aristophanic—"

She had said the right thing by accident, her brain seemed to work that way, automatically but she couldn't go on expecting the right answer, like throwing dice and expecting double sixes every other time . . . why didn't the girl go? Brain went on (she had tested it) on a rail all by itself though brain was (she had tested it) a white marble statue, a bronze heavy thing that had sunk, had sunk, irrevocably like the precious cargoes of Corinthian plunder that had sunk . . . had sunk . . . "didn't they want last winter? I mean winters, and winters ago, to drag Lake Nervii?" Yes, Lake Nervii. Where had that come from? Outside Rome, she and Darrington had walked the whole way outside the gates proper, walked up and up and up through winter olives and on and on and on through winter olives (there were violets, winter violets) and winter was a clear hard spring with almond blossoms like clear hard shells flung against a blue, blue, blue that wasn't a dome but simply a waste of space going on and on and on . . . olives. "I remember last winter—I mean winters and winters ago—a winter in Rome and how we walked, my husband, Jerrold Darrington and I, miles and miles and found the lake. We didn't get to the opposite side though they say there is a whole area there, almost another unexplored Pompeii." Hermione had determined to sink into her own self-made aura. Herself had woven herself an aura, a net, a soft and luminous cocoon but somehow daemon eyes drew out of her all these things, all these other things. Was the girl a witch, some bad thing, some evil thing? Why did the girl draw these things out of her, things that came automatically, a sort of superior intellectual psycho-analysis, going on and on and she wanted to drift, had been drifting, had not thought of the galley sunk in Lake Nervii for years and years, did not believe she had ever thought of it since that winter day, winters and winters ago. Why did the girl do this? How did she? "What in God's name is the—" She couldn't say "*what* is the matter with you" though in another layer of her consciousness she sensed something that was wrong, something that was dangerous. Eyes don't look normally out of faces like that. Small chin, small Eros chin, mouth more than a child-Eros, a mouth that was a youth Eros, perfect bow of slightly too wide mouth but lips narrow, coral— "Do you remember the shop, that special one at the top of the via Quattro Fontane, just this side of the entrance to the Pincio? It was a common window. I don't know why I remember it. There are so many of those obvious striped Roman scarves and coral." Lips were coral lips, smooth, lips were Eros lips, the mouth was too perfect though the nose plunged forward dangerous, too large, ploughing as it were a way before it, but the nose in this light was put on, rightly placed, giving too much character to the characterless child face. There was too much character for that baby chin, that breadth of chaste arc eye-brows. The nose gave too much character and the eyes spoiled all the effect of peace, and of non-entity.

Eyes and nose were wrong or was it perfect small chin and perfect mouth and chaste nymph eye-brows wrong? Something was wrong. Two faces, one on top of the other, both Greek, neither Greek, each spoiled by each. "No. I have never been to Syracuse."

Syracuse, Syracuse, Syracuse. Why do you say that name? Hermione. Your name is Hermione not Morganlefay, what a pity, for Morganlefay was such a comfortable person, don't you know what I mean, aura like a willow catkin, aura and flower of self blurred over, not really flowering, shining like penumbra of the harvest moon, glowing a sort of yellow, the heat the willow catkins give off in the spring, the colour of the blobs and blobs of willow dust reflected in silver, a silver reflection of gold aura of willow catkins, that is the aura of Morgan le Fay. What a pity that a name, just a name spoken (Syracuse, Syracuse) does something, it's odd how names (Greek names like that) never lose, never have lost their potency. And it's rather horrible. For if you say Syracuse it's like a knife and it's like a crescent moon and it might do terrific damage. You must be careful how you use these Greek names. People are right, nice comfortable people in comfortable houses, these Greek names are dangerous, don't have any Greek about, it's a sort of white gun-powder. It's right not to encourage people, children, learning Greek, gun-powder white or black is gun-powder and we're tired of fighting, all that happened in 17, 18 or was it 19. It might have been just 17 a long time ago in Syracuse, 17 B.C. or A.D., something of the sort for the name Syracuse breaks down the centuries, there remains nothing but the name, white gun-powder, powder made from temple pillars riven and split and ground to dust. Those columns had to be riven and split and ground to dust. Those statues had to be riven and split and ground to dust. Out of the dust, the most minute electric distillation was contrived and gun-powder resides in the words, the electric shimmer of the sun on those shafts of marble, the sun and glint of the sun on the uplifted forearm of some Hermes set against a background of livid green-black laurel. The sun and glint of sun on marble remains in just such words, in Syracuse for example. Take a poster with "see sunny Italy" and read "Syracuse" in a dark tunnel of a railway station and shut your eyes for in a moment the whole station may explode; that's the way with those words but they bide their time. Treat them carefully, speak to them, speak them (if you

dare) softly, intone, sing or chant or whisper them. But know—
know—know—that they are full of power. When the gods will, they
will rain those words again on us, poor earth, poor penumbra of an
earth, not worth destroying.

It's too late now, Morgan le Fay. Don't try to be too inappositely
feminine. But I must be. I am having a small le Fay. This is evil and
bad of some one, something to send this fantastically wealthy de
Rothfeldt girl to me. If I can do without a husband (O put this foot
stool under your feet, we—*we*—I ask you—must be so very careful) if
I can do without a lover (O eyes, O glamour, O small crescent moon
or words of some such ilk) if I can do without anybody, I can do
without anybody and I want to prove to myself that I am strong and
that I am alone like Madonna was (like a charwoman was, like the
mother of Caesarion was) alone. We are always alone. Why not
make the best of it? Was it some sun-god on the rocks that had sent
Beryl, for people don't come like that out of nowhere, not in 1919,
asking to talk about poetry. Dear Madge or Kate or Doris, they were
all wearing plough-boy boots, O it was all right, it was splendid of
them. I adore them for it, on the land, sleep in the barn, don't get the
consideration of an ordinary sweaty plough boy and I love you for it
or else more people like Merry, that dreadful Merry in crêpe de
chine lavender cami-knickers, nothing in between, over the top,
either you were a plough girl sweating in thick boots or you wore
crêpe de chine cami knickers, not at all Hellenic. How I hate those
cami-knickers, something worse than the plough-boy girl with his
(her) so honest and so terrible fervour and his (or her) horrible
carrying on and his (or her) hands ruined like Honore Trent's who
had done such lovely drawing, great blue, blue, blue spikes of larkspur thick with paint, fit for things like that and her nails (she had
written) were split at the quick and she was tending horrible pigs
while the farmer laughed at her . . . no, people have forgotten. O it's
perfectly honourable of them and brave of them of course, it's bad
taste (not done) to remember, such a silly time. Honore Trent. "You
know I know a girl who used to do beautiful paintings, just flowers,
perhaps you'd like to meet her." For she remembered that the de
Rothfeldt girl, Beryl, long ago in Buckinghamshire had talked about
paint, wanted to paint, Honore might put Beryl on the right track,
but where was Honore? "I mean you would like her"—just spoke for

the sake of speaking, not thinking, for the word Syracuse, like a knife, like a sword, still like a thin and blighting cymiter.

12 An arm pushed back. "I don't know what's happened. I waited a long time. There are green dog-woods sweeping over the bed and that photograph on the mantel piece is Jerrold, my husband—husband—husband—you see he is my husband—he wants to look after it—he says he will—husband—but are you—what are you—khaki arm—are you a husband?" The arm pushed Hermione back, she was pushed back and inappositely the arm that was an English khaki arm pushed through green branches of American dog-wood and the heavy scentless blossoms swept like white ivory and heavy froth of white on sea shells over her crumpled coverlet. "Have you no fires here at all?" "O we did have once—no coal now—I am a newcomer. I came only a few weeks ago to be near St. Mary's nursing home—" "I know all that. Have you—no fires here?" The face above her was the face of a stranger. How had it got here? "How did you get here?" "The people next door said you'd not been moving about for some time—hadn't heard you. My patient next door, it appears, got used to you, listened—" "Next door? Where am I?" Next door. That was Lilian and the Grex girls and stealing lilacs and the dog that had puppies and the several kinds of butterflies and "you know my grandfather always knew them—all their names. We had a glass case of them hanging over his desk—and the bald-headed eagle—" The face was a strange face but not strange for it appeared over the top . . . over the top . . . the face appeared over the top—khaki, neat collar, nice collar, elegant cuff. "What is this on your cuff?" "It's wings—air service—I'm out on special duty—epidemic—" Face that neither smiled nor scolded, just looking at her while the arms held her down, while the hands, thin hands, brown hands smoothed the coverlet, "I'll send the nurse in here . . . my next door patient's better."

"No. But don't go." Hermione realised now in a moment a great gap. There was a gap. A gap that must be filled. Her hands reached up

and her hands clung to khaki—it must be Jerrold, they all looked like
that and it was Jerrold and anyone would do but no one would do,
never the man in the next room whom she had smiled at once on the
stairs and is that what had saved her? Was it Morganlefay who had
smiled that had saved her? You never know what will, what is going
to save you. You sneak through life, up and down stairs and the wall
paper was a funny bright rose-salmon but she had rather liked it, on
the stairs, brightening the stairs, clean little house, little house where
they had taken her, let her have a room for a few weeks while she
waited as Beryl had run her out (she must be all right, "yes I have a
husband") in the motor car. Little house that had been rather funny
and clean and full of people that hadn't mattered, that Hermione had
seen through a mist, through the gold gauze that was the aura of
Morganlefay who was waiting, of Morganlefay who would morganlefay it to the very bitter last end, smiling at someone on the stairs
that hadn't mattered, that now mattered. In life you never know who
will, who won't matter. They descend, they fall, they rise, they swim
in and out of your life for life is the swaying up and the swaying
down of great forest branches and clinging to life, to Jerrold, to khaki
shoulders, Hermione realized that at last, at last she was lost, for
clinging to khaki shoulders she realised that in all those months
(nine now almost) she had had no one, no one's shoulders, that's
wrong. But of course Morganlefay would be like that, run away, be a
queen in the forest; it can't matter if men don't want you, Undine for
a small Undine wants you. No one wants you. No one wants you.
But someone does. Someone did. Someone was lonely, a little man
who had been in munitions who had the room next door. Had no
one ever, ever smiled at him that he must treasure a ghost smile, the
smile of a mere outsider, a half-creature, an Undine, an Oread? Do
men get so lonely that they must love an Oread? There are women,
women, women, women in the street, on the stairs, in railway car-
riages brushing past you, brushing past you on the stairs little man.
You are a little man. Why did you smile and why did you listen? Woods bend, woods bend. The arms were strong but thin and
pushed her away, away. O don't you push me away. If you push me
away I know that's the last. I know then that I am pushed away
forever. Don't push me away. I'm married. "My—husband—is—in
France." Khaki. Khaki. It would save her. It must save her. The
wings on his wrist were wings. He wasn't a man. He was more than a

man being less than a man, being an angel. Less than a man he was a man, he was an Angel. Azrael. He was a doctor. Doctors have to do things like this, shutting down eyes. If he put his fingers on her eyes, she would shut them, never, never open them. If he put his fingers on her eyes, she would shut them, never open them. She wouldn't let him. Her hands slid from smooth thin shoulders and slid down to wrists and clung to fingers. "My—husband—is—in—France." The thin fingers drew away, drew away, drew away, if he pushed her away now, the one man to whom she had clung, toward whom she had reached in all these months, she would be dead—float down the river—be quite happy. Man, men, men, men, men. Guns, guns. The guns had stopped or was it a heart? Trees wafted great branches and if he pushed her away she would be lost but she could be lost for the twisted little man who had been in munitions and hadn't wanted to go home and had kept on his room here perhaps he hadn't a home, what is a home, who was gruff and common had heard her not moving. Were one's last moments then of so, so great importance? The little man in the next room was a sort of little Buddha, he increased, great in magnitude. He had heard her open her cupboards, heard the rattling of the curtain rings, heard her spilling out her tooth brush water. The little man had heard her pull her chair forward, had heard her drop her book or heard her scraping in the far corner (which was to him the near corner) for slippers on the floor, heard her move and walk out, not heard any more . . . had he nothing to do but listen? "Why did he listen to me?" Had she said that? Had she thought that? More than the little man who was nobody (who had been in munitions in the next room) was this one. This one was more than the other one for he answered questions, did not ask questions. The little man in the next room was a sort of cherry-wood carved Buddha who watched but this was a different kind of god. He answered all your questions. "Why did he listen?" "He listened as invalids have nothing to do but listen"—had answered her question not scolding her, not pushing her away, holding her shoulders, smoothing out the bed clothes . . . "you must be—very—careful—" Now if he scolded her she would go away, drift away. It would all be very simple. He might scold her and she would drift away like cutting the cable—of—a boat—of a canoe. Canoe drifts under dogwood blossoms and the boughs of trees arch over water, the salt creek, we can go on and on and on, then leave the canoe and tramp

H.D.
190

that half mile inland for the water lilies. Water lilies had grown near salt pools, across dunes . . . sand. "Why must—I—be—so—careful?" Of course one must be, the boat might upset at a breath, don't let the paddle tangle in those weeds, dangerous, it's scraping pebbles . . . dangerous . . . canoes—water lilies just beyond—"Why—must—I be so—careful?" Pushing her down, pushing her down—she would drown in water lily petals—just the way to drown—"you must— remember—" Remember. Mnemosyne the mother of the muses. One, two, three to nine. Nine muses. You must be very careful for the nine muses dance, clasp hands in a ring—mustn't miss the dance, ring, nine—nine—nine— "Why?" Ask it. Ask it for you have—forgotten.

13 "Pity you had that set-back." It was Darrington. Hermione saw Darrington sitting in the arm-chair drawn close to the bed edge. This was really Jerrold, the brown face, the close cropped head, the stick that he held in his hand, elegant stick, he was a visitor here, elegant stick that made all nothing, dispersed all the past, the khaki upon khaki, the boom of distant thunders with a wave of a magician's wand. Darrington was Darrington again. Darrington was Jerrold, thicker a little, heavier, but Darrington with his coat cut modishly with his shoes, with his trousers, something that took her back, in spite of herself, because of herself, something other, something different. Darrington played with the stick, his hands were firm and white fleshed at the knuckles, his hands were finer, whiter than the burnt brick of his still somewhat foreign face quite warranted. Hermione propped aloft, regarded the white knuckles, remembered sonnets, canzoni, songs, letters . . . things Darrington had written. "How's Louise?" "O Louise?" Darrington lifted heavy eye-brows and his hands stopped fingering the ebony stick, looked across at Hermione, smiled across at her and smiling, his smile with a conjuror's magic brought back camellias, white and red, red rosettes and white rosettes that they had gathered, scraped from the clean sand of the paths to lay on the stone of Shelley, to make a circle, red rosettes, white rosettes across the stone, across the words carved in the tomb of Shelley, "*nothing in him that doth fade but doth suffer a* *sea-change into something rich and strange.*" All the black and tumult had faded. Hermione saw the reader of the Vatican, white statues smiling and Darrington (then) standing among them, a brother. Well they were both battered. Hermione would not be able to face white sisters, clothed only in their impermeable beauty . . . she thought of swollen flesh . . . her own . . . Darrington was no better, no worse, hardly now other than she was. They met in a smile, in the cut of his new clothes, in the affectation of his slim ebony stick. The world must recede, the black tide must recede . . . there must be, there was the pendulum swing. It had swung back to pictures, to ebony sticks, to a watchet-blue (he called it) swansdown edged bed jacket she was wearing. "How's Louise?" But Darrington had smiled away incongruous question. He said (and the words came strange from the face of this new-old Darrington) "when are you going over the top?"

Over the top . . . Hermione had to stop, to draw herself in, to drag herself back. Over the top . . . of what? She remembered swiftly "O after my little set-back, they said it might be later . . . earlier . . . they didn't know. It might happen any day now."

But that that was going to happen was nothing to her now. Something had happened, more strange, more miraculous than anything that could ever happen. Darrington was with her, beside her, a Darrington had crept out of the brown lean khaki, like a great moth, elegant in shape, still a little foreign in his bronze but all different. Who ever said clothes made the man—did or didn't make the man? For clothes made Darrington smile with an old pre-chasm smile. The smile Darrington smiled had nothing to do with rows and rows of livid dead, with barbed wire, with the flare of red or green blazing above broken trenches, with the drone of planes, with the sudden flare and drop of bombs, with "over the top" (though incongruously he had just said it) with "Mademoiselle in the family way" (though she was patently) with "scrounging" (though she had. Beryl had brought the exquisite bed-jacket, everything) with "going west" (though she had, patently, had come back again, had been dead, was now alive) with "that's the stuff to give 'em." Darrington smiled a smile that erased all that, the smudged out image of the war, of terrible things that had happened, of Louise and Florient and Merry.

"O Merry. Where is she? I have quite forgotten." Darrington went on smiling. He reached toward her and his hand found hers and his kisses found hers . . . "Forgotten . . . never see . . ." He had forgotten something, they had all forgotten something. Darrington and Hermione were wedded in this new understanding. He had forgotten. She had forgotten. He was going to take care of her and he had come back and he was so happy and everything was going to be all right. Forgotten. Merry was forgotten. Louise was forgotten. O far and far and far, pre-chasm things came back, the smell of the ice-cold corridors of the Louvre on a summer day and the hot sound that was "deux sous la botte," the little boy who pursued them down the rue du Four and the carnations, the pink spice-sweet little garden oeillets that Jerrold would buy from him. "Do you remember those pinks you used to get me? Sops in wine you used to call them. Wine pink. Pink. French." Darrington remembered and thinking of wine pinks, fragrance was about her. England was gone. Faces, people, people, faces. "Little Vérène, poor little Vérène . . ." "Vérène?" "Didn't you know? You've forgotten . . . so had I till only the other day when Delia came to see me." "O delicious Delia . . . is she still?" "No. Tired but smiling through it. Lost. Gone. She's still alive." "That's something." "But Vérène . . . most hideous of calamities . . . Walter . . ." "O forgeron. Poor beast . . ." "Beast, yes. Like a great white sacrificial ox. Great white creature, spending his time playing for wounded poilus, odd things, red cross (or the French equivalent) concerts. He was born you know (an American) in Munich." "All rather complicated . . ." "Yes. Vérène's mad."

It seemed so long ago. That they should still be holding on to life with such tenuous threads and Hermione pulled threads to get something of that pre-chasm into her speech and all the pre-chasm was as she recalled it, worse even than their own particular and unique Purgatory. Other things. Other people. Things that had existed in one dimension, that couldn't any more so exist. You couldn't any more move on a straight line, you advanced in a spiral and as you grew nearer to the higher things (nearer to the higher? What muddlings) you grew more vague, no, more distinct, but a distinctness in vagueness that was most tantalizing. Get across the chasm, for those things had existed. Get across the chasm for this thing that holds you in its arms is pre-chasm, a little heavier but kisses that she had lost, that had been blinded, blotted out in a dark cloud. Get across the chasm to the other side for there are dreams still the other side, ivory, bronze. Dreams dwell in ivory and bronze, the Narcissus of the Naples gallery. "Do you remember the blue-fire phosphorescence of the huge blue deep sea sort of jelly fish that so fascinated me in the aquarium?" "Aquarium?" "Naples. I seem to be in two sets of perceptions . . . blue green of phosphorescent fire and static bronzes. That Narcissus, you remember. Two sets of clearly defined perceptions. We'll never any more be able to see anything straight on—clear—" "But we do, darling." *Almost thou persuadest me to be a heathen.* She did see things straight for a little moment, but she knew it would soon slip from her. She couldn't go on seeing things in different dimensions all the time, "steadily and" (was it?) "whole."

"Vérène's I told you, mad. You don't seem interested." "I am. Only aren't we, all? What's odd, incongruous—" "O, I don't mean like that—like we say it, she's mad, you know. I mean insane, insane, locked up." "Where—how—why—I don't understand." They were drawing things out of the depth, pre-chasm to observe them. Things she had for years forgotten now came back— "How did it happen?" "I don't know. Delia told me and it seemed like the end of a story. A story I had read, put aside, forgotten and then years and years afterwards (five years?) found again, finished, done for. It made me feel something was finished—the old régime I suppose—all the old beautiful intensity, the France we loved—Vérène so smug. She's not now. O poor little ignorant smug little tight closed, wide open French rose. So smug, so secure and always so sure that everything would come right once one was married—do you remember?" "It links on somehow to that queer girl—" "Shirley yes. Also pre-chasm—a clean bullet, finished." "And the other queer creature?" His breath was on her face. His ebony stick had slid to the floor. "Be careful—I get— tired—" His breath was on her face and it appeared in one sudden moment of illumination that this was not right. Vérène went mad since she couldn't (it was evident) march with events. Shirley shot herself since she couldn't march forward. Wasn't that it? The wave had lifted them to the crest. One must roll in, on with the tide, with the times, or be crushed under the wave, ground to death in the trough and the great drag back that would be the inevitable aftermath of the war and all it stood for. All those lovely years. Vérène, delicious Delia, all the funny people, someone with a monocle at Delia's, someone saying someone was like Nero, some girl who spilled hair-pins, hydrangeas and the smoke blue of odd conservatory colours, George with his *almost thou persuadest me to be a heathen* and the upward drift of candles in Vérène's elegant Clichy apartment. Walter and the great drone of the sea. But Walter was out of it, always above it, he hadn't been caught, not actually, he was the inapproachable glacier and he would go on being that. But caught in the flow, Vérène without volition to sweep onward, caught and frozen (Hermione had always known it would come) by Walter's distant, beautiful aloofness. Vérène and Shirley, victims—victims— wasn't she the greater victim? She and Darrington? No, no, no, no, no. She felt sensing the wave push back of her that she would land, finally, safely, be thrown, advancing, going on, be thrown by the very impetus of the wave strength up, up on dry land, onto a new post-chasm world. Strike against the wave, the advance of the wave and you are doomed . . . Morganlcfay.

Kisses held Morgan le Fay and she was Circe, Calypso to those kisses. She hadn't strength against them. She was smothered and kisses recalled her to worlds away, pre-chasm. Would she go on with Darrington? She felt the kisses and she felt herself numbed, pollen dusted over with the kisses. Kisses brought back people, pictures, a honey-coloured Correggio nymph, the wide wings of the marble Nike. Wings of marble, islands of yellow stone, amber lights against rocks where the sea weed caught sunlight in its translucent surface. Ivory of small winged Erotes. Some Dionysus with a head band. The Nereids— "Do you remember those violets that you used to get me?"

He remembered the violets. He remembered everything. They remembered far and far back as if the years of terror (five was it?) never had been, had been some fulsome nightmare. Clear out of the years of terror the past rose, rose and cleft the years of terror like white lightning, a black storm cloud. The past, images of the past that had all the time been there, that had been buried under the stench of lava and molten metal, of guns and broken trenches, of earth mounds that were graves, the very substance of volcanic furious, the past, all the past had been there, all the time, white, in clear images, people, things, all the people, all the things and in some moment of rapport, holding her close, forgetting (both of them) all incidents of mere Louise, Merry or Cyril Vane, they conjured back the past, at one in a rapt intensity. The past rose and broke across the present, broke across the five years of dark disaster like some dancer that steps half-naked before a black drop-curtain. The past seemed safe and secure and the war was but a curtain that had fallen, "you will come, you will come back—Astraea?" He had conjured the past with a wave of his ebony stick, she had renewed the past with the white swansdown on her blue bed-jacket. Watchet blue, he called it. It was the colour of the blue eyes of Fayne Rabb.

Almost as if her thoughts had been his thoughts, though she had never spoken of her and the days of odd upheaval stood between them and this was the first time that he had been allowed to come to see her since——almost as if her thought that had risen like the half-naked dancer, gracious, sinuous, before the black drop-curtain, almost as if his thoughts had been her thoughts and as if the past was a very visible embodied image, Jerrold Darrington said, "yes, Phoebe is a pretty name for it. But one's name's a little awkward sometimes." Darrington was looking at the very beautiful small doll with black hair that lay asleep in a wide basket. He said, "why don't you name its other name, Fayne Rabb?"

14 "I don't understand." Hermione was facing Darrington. The room in the little Soho hotel that he had asked her to, was narrow with the window (top floor) overlooking a narrow side-street, overlooking the narrow debouching door of the Temple Theatre opposite. The room had grown narrow, it appeared, while she regarded it for at first the room containing Darrington had contained Italy, the slopes of Monte Solaro, anemones blooming pre-war Easter red and the blood red of the foot steps of Adonis that had been the atrocious wooden image that they had carried to the songs of pre-Hellenic old volcanic southern gypsy chanting. Christ had died and Christ was to be born again. Red anemones had flowered against the dim shabby paper of the narrow room and red anemones had fallen beneath her feet and had burned the very soles of her feet as she had stepped tentatively out of her bed cold mornings, mist cold early spring mornings, mornings over Soho like a bride's veil for she was that in her renewed love of Jerrold. The narrow room with the stained sulphur coloured paper had been wide tunnel toward enchantment. At the end of the now narrow room, like vision projected by an enchanter's magic, there had been the white cone of Vesuvius, the shale that had been the other side of Vesuvius, the side that sloped toward Pompeii, that was shale and scattered vineyard when seen from Herculaneum. The room with its narrow sordid proportion and its one narrow meagrely curtained window looking over the Soho back street had been wide and marvellous, a small concentrated space, like the tube of the Indian mystic, self-made from which, or at the end of which, he projects images of marvellous reality. The wall paper, Hermione now observed, was the mustiest of faded mustard yellow. The wall paper, Hermione saw it for the first time, was faded with a smudgy uneven spottiness that let show through the mustard like spots, the egg-stain like spots of singularly mal-formed tuberous yellow rose buds. The room became a room in Soho and the paper sordid as she saw it. The room shrank. "I don't understand you at all. You go off on a vulgar escapade with Vane. You have this child—" "I thought we had talked all that out before. I thought it was arranged that it should—be—yours—" "How could it ever be mine? How could you ever be mine?" "Then why did you ask me to come back here? I might have—stayed—with—" She might have stayed with Vane. But she didn't say it. She didn't even think it really for she could never have stayed with Vane. The room shrank to its mean proportion. "What are we going to do anyway about it?"

"I told you I had Beryl arrange for the baby at that officers' wives' farm home for a few weeks—" "A few weeks—there's always afterwards."

Afterwards—afterwards— But why hadn't he thought of that before? Was the strain too great—was Darrington some monster simply who was sent to persecute her? "I tell you I love Louise." "Why didn't you tell me that before I came back?" "I didn't want to hurt you." "Rot. You'd hurt me enough. You hurt me long ago. Why didn't you say simply you were going to carry on with Louise—" Hermione heard the words, listened to herself speaking the words. "You go at once and register that child as Vane's."

Register the child. She had not thought of registering the child. There had already been preliminary taken for granted registration of the child—Mrs. Jerrold Darrington—baby, female—Phoebe Fayne.

There had already been that. Why begin again? Why begin again? What was Darrington after? What was it all about? "Why hadn't you seen this before—made it clear sooner?" Her words like white lead came from her with the force of something beyond Hermione. Hermione, worn past endurance, found words that she had never dreamed she had the strength to utter, forming somewhere white bullets, white searing lead, in the inside of her now cold head, and white bullets, white searing lead, projected outwards, out and out and out into a void where Darrington was, where Jerrold was. Someone was standing before her, someone who had nothing to do with Jerrold, some odd, uncanny and evil metamorphosis, evil and evil and bloated and dull as that very Cretan Minotaur. Minotaur sent to destroy the Athenian youth, to destroy beauty, Minotaur of wickedness . . . Hermione no longer recognised this creature, herself one white frozen heat of flame repudiated some obscene creature who suggested obscene and evil things. "Register it? But that's the merest legal formality. You said it was to be yours. I have your letters. You urged me on to have it. You let me go through with it though I was crippled with the last one and you let my friends (my bloated millionaire friends as you call them) see me through the added expense of the pneumonia and that dreadful set-back that meant that double nursing and impossible delicacies. You let me do that and you asked me, comfortably out of it, out of this world, to come back to Soho."

Trampled flowers smell sweet. But there is a murderous ox foot, a cloven devil foot. Was it the war simply, that walked forward that would crush with devil horns and great brute devil forehead the tenderest of growths—Phoebe. Phoebe. Don't say her name out loud, Hermione. Keep Phoebe Fayne out of it. It was you who were wrong drifting into this, tired and having no proper place to go to and it was better (far better) for Phoebe to have that officers' wives' home (what a cheat) in the country to go to for a few months until you could arrange, Beryl arranging it, Lady de Rothfeldt so kindly arranging it, officer's wife . . . pneumonia, very ill, husband only just returned but a cheat. A cheat. Husbands didn't return like this with a bit of a uniform, his old tunic with a dash somewhere of a bit of ribbon as a smoking jacket. Jerrold was all in bits, trousers and jacket didn't go together, Jerrold was all in bits. "I will look after you," and "now register it as Vane's," didn't go together. Jerrold was a Minotaur and there was only one thing now to do about it. Dodge him.

"I'm just waiting. Was just waiting. They said I must be careful. I'm going out to-morrow. I have to go to Richmond. You have to register them in the district where they were born—Richmond." "See that you do then. See that you do then. It'll be evidence to divorce you . . ." Divorce? Was she hearing, seeing? She was mad simply. This word that they had none of them used (Vane had so suavely brushed it) was brought out in a fervour of brutality against her. "Divorce *me*?" "Of course. It's the only way to do it. I as a returned officer can prove your infidelity—" "*My* infidelity?" "Well, Louise and I—that will be overlooked. You are, aren't you, the offender?" "*Offender*?" "I mean—well you know what the law is in England? You can't divorce me as you have been unfaithful—" "*Unfaithful*?" Words out of the Daily Mail meaning nothing. Where had he picked these words up? What did these words mean? Words out of the Daily Mail mean nothing. Unfaithful wife, returned officer husband, lover, baby . . . words out of the Daily Mail meaning nothing.

"But what about you? What about—?" "O well—that—you can't *prove* anything." "Prove anything? But I have your letters. Details. Your writing me all the details . . ." "Look here, Astraea"—even now, even now, *Astraea.*

Nothing in him that doth fade but doth suffer—but doth suffer—suffer—suffer—sea-change. You suffer toward sea-change but there was an end to legitimate suffering, this suffering of Hermione's was illegitimate. You don't take more than your share of suffering any more than you take more than your share of happiness—wheels within wheels—the labyrinth but Theseus (was it?) had the clue, walked straight on, straight on, labyrinth of London upon London and the war, black abysses of pockets of blackness into which you wander feeling the crash of a plane, sensing, feeling the blue body crumpled—an American fighting for France or the brave fawn-coloured young body ground—ground—don't think. Labyrinth. How marvellous to be of it, in it, one of them, one of the Athenian youths and maidens sent—sent—Athenians. Hermione stared at the wall, waiting for an answer for the wall was mustard coloured and the map that she had pinned there now some days ago, a map fallen from one of the Weeklies now became something other, somewhere else, another pocket, another world. "That map's rotten—cut up into Balkan states and all wrong." Map pinned to the wall, sketched in map from London Weekly that she hadn't thrown away, had pinned on the wall, map of the Balkans, difficulties, marked off in dark lines, cut into dark thick lines, political, meaning nothing, but a map from a modern weekly (last week's?) and the problem of the Balkans and the map was nothing but it covered a space of the mustard paper and the map was a map of Greece, all distorted by political black lines and dotted lines, the sort of map, you remember we had with our weeklies in that odd spring, never to come again, mist like a bride's veil over Soho, and she would talk of the map, thus dodging the Minotaur, thus dodging Darrington. She would pretend not to have heard Darrington, would go on talking as if the registering, deliberately of Phoebe as illegitimate was nothing, could be nothing, though she was Mrs. Jerrold Darrington and how difficult to explain, "you see I am married but this is someone else's child." But Darrington was mad. The whole thing was impossible, all the letters, he was mad, shell-shock, dissociation (she must make excuses for him) but it was wrong, Hermione knew it was wrong. Hermione had had her share of suffering and if she took more than her share of suffering the world would topple over for you can't arrogate virtue to yourself, you can't suffer more than Christ—and she had suffered. Dead, resurrected but she had come to the wrong place. She belonged in heaven after Phoebe—and she wasn't in heaven. Heaven had been open to her and she had walked straight into Purgatory or Hell even, this hell of Darrington cowering over her, a little now cringing to her. This was worse than his bullyings. He was cringing to her. What had happened? What had Louise done? Drugs, sleep—evil—drinks—the wrong kind—abuses—turned his head—come back—he was so nice a week ago. It had all happened in a few days. Turned into a monster, a Minotaur when Hermione had thought he was one of the youths of Athens, he, as she, lost alike in a labyrinth, alike in the end to be saved, but he wasn't to be saved—Astraea—how dared he call her that. He was mad obviously. Astraea was a name that went with al fresco suppers and the odd pear tree that had plumed itself so extravagantly like a white swan against the upflung hills of Ana-Capri. Astraea was shining over Amalfi and Astraea was the very heart of the orange flowers, golden with that tight whirl of still smooth petals, texture of the orange flowers so much more ivory smooth than any camellia even, even than the wax smooth and ivory stiff gardenia. Elegant. Things of the senses beyond the drift of people

and the stuffiness of trains and the Italians with too many children—
that remained apart and untouched (then) in grubby cheap little bed-rooms, in bed-rooms on the rue gauche that were youth—
youth—simply.

"The map is rotten." It was Darrington again saying it. And now the
map took form before Hermione's dazed eyelids. Her eyes seemed to
see nothing. Were open, staring like glass eyes, saw nothing, grey
glass eyes, but her eyelids seemed pricked with luminous light,
seemed to burn, to glow with some light within—*eyes and they see
not*—her glass grey eyes didn't see anything, would never see anything. "Of course, Jerrold. I understand about the baby. I'll go at
once and register it—naturally—as it should be—" Dodge him.
Dodge him. Register it as it should be as it could not possibly other
be. Phoebe Darrington by all the laws of spirit, by all the most brute
made laws even of brute matter. Roman law. She had heard once half
heeding about Roman law—the child born—he had come to see
her— She couldn't get the exact wording of vague but exactly recalled
Roman law. But she would—she would— "Of course you know if
you make any false statement—" Darrington speaking. False statement. False statement. What now was coming? False statement.
Hermione turned eyes from the map on the wall and grey glass eyes
saw now Darrington. They saw Darrington—they looked at Darrington—yes and they see now—her eyes (horrible) saw Darrington—Minotaur with bull throat, with head bent forward. Minotaur
that was about to brutally destroy her. No. He couldn't. For her eyes
were pricking, with painful realization behind the eyelids—eyelids
were white orange petals, other eyes, gold rays behind the eyes—
Astraea . . . "of course you know if you make a false statement it's
perjury and—five years penal servitude."

15 Penal servitude had her by the throat, drove her on. The
flurry of snow was ash that spring (do you remember?)
and penal servitude had her by the raw edge of her skirt,
dragged at her underclothes, grasped up like a slimy hand from fetid
water, Dickens, all the horrible things one read about, in London,

come true, London come true, Dickens' London, "my lords and gentlemen" but I thought we had gone on, gone on. They always screamed that they had done away with Victorian things, in London. Grey ash drifted against a grey ash face lifted to grey ash drifting. Penal servitude had her by the hem of the skirt so that she stumbled heavily climbing up the bus steps and the curved steps of the swaying bus (that she used to run up blithely) were the steps of a lighthouse that swayed and swayed. A sort of lighthouse built on a sort of bell-buoy sort of thing, swaying like a bell buoy in a storm when the bell rings and rings. Once in Venice there had been a summer mist and the bell buoys were set loose . . . and bells sounded across Venice as they sounded now in London. Penal servitude. All the bells of London sounded penal servitude for if you have a husband who is an officer and a gentleman he comes back . . . and screams why did you, why did you, like a clock ticking, like a heart beating . . . penal servitude. Captain Darrington. Yes. I am Mrs. Darrington. Penal servitude made Hermione one now with the faces that loomed up out of white ash out of mist of snow and snow of mist, looking up at her from the circle of Piccadilly. Daffodils shone like suns through cold mist. Penal servitude was daffodils in Piccadilly . . .

"Poor, poor thing." "Yes . . . Delia!" "But what a dreadful experience for you my dear. Did you say it was her sister?" "Yes, her sister." "But you my dear . . . with Jerrold just back. What a dreadful sordid little thing to have to happen to you." "Well . . . no . . . you see her husband was in the army." "Yes. But even so. Esprit de corps is all right. But you my darling. After your own terrible experience." "I only wanted to make sure Delia, before I told poor little Winnie what to tell her sister . . . after all, I know nothing of the law (why should I?) if it *was* straight." "My darling . . . no law, no judge in England would condemn her." "Then . . . penal servitude?" "Her husband must be mad." "Shell shock probably . . ." "Shell shock . . . people of that class get hysterical."

To walk carefully because the paving stones were egg-shell, to walk carefully so as not to put down a foot, down a foot too heavily. To walk carefully toward something that was something that was something . . . another bus . . . to Richmond . . . with the same flurry in her face and streets, people, people, people, streets and I am one now with every felon, with every thief, with every Whitechapel beggar who reached out toward a baker's basket for we knew how tempting (do you remember?) the butt end of a brown loaf could look sticking from a basket. I am one with felons, with thieves, with "sick and in prison and ye visited me." Sick and in prison, I was visited, Delia was an angel. There are everywhere angels. It started with that bracelet clasp that day I met Vane at Lechstein's studio. A bracelet to clasp my wrist, to say there was something behind the mist, beneath, beneath are the everlasting, everlasting . . . "come in, Mrs. Darrington." "I hate to trouble you. Yes, I did manage to get Phoebe's registration through this morning. So impressive . . . Phoebe Darrington. I must just look at Phoebe." "Phoebe is doing herself very well these mornings. She *will* eat soap though." "O?" "Loves soap though. Really you must tell her not to eat soap though." Phoebe was sitting up in a basket. Take her away. "I just came to look at Phoebe. No. No I mustn't touch her. You see I've been in a bus (I couldn't get a taxi to the registrar's). London is so germ ridden. And I want to ask you . . ." ask you, ask you. Don't let me look at Phoebe. I am a beast in a cage. The thing is so soft. It would be better to put hands round a throat . . . don't think, don't look. "I'd rather walk downstairs." "*Down* stairs." "Our house is a wreck still, these furniture van people are so shocking. No labour . . . of course that's to be expected. My husband and I were talking it over. It's such a bitter disappointment . . . we do so want the baby. But could you possibly just as a special favour keep Phoebe for a few days, just a very few days, longer?"

Downstairs it was "such shocking trouble with the furniture van people . . . all their old officials and these new ex-service men . . . but they will do the moving sometime. In the meanwhile (O it is such a disappointment to us) *could* you keep the baby?" Tears come to ash eyes sometimes or a sort of thing that is blinking that is not tears, that people think is tears, that is not in the least tears, that is the blinking of eyelids over eyes because grey ash has drifted into eyes and there is a little flick and sting of the ash powder against sensitive dragon-fly great pupils. "No . . . it's really all right. I have been quite fit. You did such wonders for me." People, things, things, people.

These people had spikes of delft blue hyacinths, of wedgwood blue hyacinths, of hyacinths sticking straight up, growing out of moss, moss set flat on a round earthen pot and hyacinths growing out of earth in a square of a window. England is like that. There is always a square of a window, and looking with the flick of ash powder against her heavily pupiled dragon-fly eyes, she saw the square of garden and the flurry of ash, and knew that here was not ash, that here was petals drifting. "That pear tree was just coming out when I was upstairs." "The blossom's almost over." "Yes . . . but it's years and years . . . and yet the pear tree is not over." "What, Mrs. Darrington?" "It seemed so funny . . . I mean all the other with the furniture vans and all that. I suppose having one's husband come back sets one back . . . I mean it takes one back, all the old books." Books were toppling out of a book case that a crash and a brrrrrrr and a bang had set sideways and Louise was Florient dancing. "Florient was dancing." "Mrs. Darrington?" "I mean those flowers—*flowers* are dancing. I was glad to see them . . . those few hours before . . . before . . ." "Mrs. Darrington . . . we will keep your little Phoebe." The nurse had returned, had consulted another nurse, the secretary sort of nurse was standing. "O thank you . . . *thank* you so much."

Those people, said Hermione to Hermione, don't know what they have done. Sick and in prison and ye visited me. For if they had said "take the little girl, we have no room for the little girl" it would have been walking on and walking on in the snow, with snow and petals drifting and walking on and walking on in the snow. It would be like the worst, the very worst imaginable melodrama, Way Down East, or something that here they call East Lynne. Don't people see since the war, in the war, that Way Down East and East Lynne was true, are the only truth? And beggars saying, "kind lady for Gawd's sake, a penny,"—are the truth and things like Jean Jean sent to prison and taking a loaf of bread because he or someone else was starving are the truth? Dickens with "my lords and gentlemen" and "dead my lords and gentlemen" is the truth for how could you go on? How could you go on? You would have had a baby in your arms and stumbled . . . and there is always a river. Melodrama is so awfully funny . . . so terribly funny. Here I am sitting on the top of a bus and it might be anywhere with light snow drifting and little pink almonds all along the fronts of brick houses and behind rusty laurel hedges putting out pink fingers . . . Eos the dawn. Eros. Someone, somewhere makes me think of Eros.

"Yes. More tea." Don't you see that if you go on having tea, then having a wash and changing, everything comes right? In Soho there was no point in ever changing . . . "I would like to stay here." Rugs under her feet shot up convolvulus tendrils. An atrocious statue in a corner put forth white hands, said "come unto me all ye that are weary." A footman passed across convolvulus and did not trample out the fronds of blue and hyacinth blue and delft blue and rainbow blue and Canterbury bell blue. Eyes that were as blue as any blue looked at her. "I mean . . . I will stay. I'll send back to to . . . to the hotel we stayed in for a few clothes. I'd like to stay here with you. Does it suit to stay here with you?" "Mama is away. Jacko is away with mama. I am alone. You can have the little room next my room . . ." then in an agony lest life should slip, lest the footman should step through the bluest of blue convolvulus blue that was the very blue of Bokhara, lest the tray should slip and the little cakes should fall onto the carpet and melt the carpet that was ice that was a film of pure ice, lest the legs and tables and legs of tables should slip and jumble together . . . Hermione held on to something. Hermione held on to this thing. I will wait till the other footman takes the cakes in little baskets (both look thin, both must be "invalided out"). I will wait as they are thin and invalided out and I am thin and invalided out. I will wait as there is esprit de corps between me and the other footman, until the other footman has gone. He has gone. "Has he gone?" "Gone?" "The other footman?" "Yes. Did you want something?" "Yes. I wanted to say this." Fumes of amber tea melted with fumes of convolvulus blue fragrance. The room was chill with a fire burning at the far, far end, like the far, far blaze of a star, Aldebaran, some Eastern great star or Nineveh so simple. "I want to tell you." "Yes." "I make a bargain with you. If you promise never more to say that you will kill yourself, I'm going to give you some-thing. If you promise and promise that you won't any more smuggle in those frightful and dangerous . . . things . . . I'm going to ask you something. I want to make a bargain with you." "Yes." "I want to tell you something. Can you bear me to tell you something?" "Yes."

"The little girl is not my husband's little girl . . . do you understand these things?" "I *hate* your Jerrold Darrington. I am so glad." "I want you to promise me to grow up and take care of the little girl." "Do you mean—do you mean—" A light is shining at the far end of a long, long tunnel. The glazed eyes of Beryl, the wicked eyes of some child Darius, the eyes that prodded prongs into the eyes, the eyes of intellect turned glazed with knowledge, cold with wisdom, were a wide child's eyes, were the eyes of an eagle in a trigo triptych, were eyes of an attendant angel on an altar. The eyes were wide eyes, bluer than blue, bluer than gentian, than convolvulus, than forgetmenot, than the blue of blue pansies. They were child's eyes, gone wide and fair with gladness. "Do you mean . . . for my own . . . exactly like a puppy?" "*Exactly* . . . like a puppy."

Appendix

Asphodel à clef: Brief Lives of the Persons
Behind the Fictions

Like Huxley's *Point Counter Point* (1928) and Lawrence's *Aaron's Rod* (1922), *Asphodel* is in the tradition of the roman à clef, originally an aristocratic subgenre that invited the reader to open aesthetically locked doors with the keys of privileged knowledge and to savor the piquant tension between the invented and the real. H.D.'s circle of friends was especially given to writing in this form, an extension perhaps of their personal politics and intrigues. *Aaron's Rod*, for example, contains an unflattering portrait of H.D. as the self-absorbed Julia Cunningham, and other characters in that novel represent Aldington, Cecil Gray, and Dorothy Yorke. In 1926, H.D.'s friend John Cournos published *Miranda Masters*, a novel about the H.D.-Aldington marriage and the lives that intersected with it; and Frances Gregg and her husband Louis Wilkinson coauthored *The Buffoon* (1916), a lampoon of John Cowper Powys and other literary figures, including H.D. who is maliciously caricatured as the American Eunice Dinwiddie. It is worth bearing in mind that at the very time H.D. was creating *Her* and *Asphodel* with a cast of characters derived from present and former friends, several of those people were likewise busy fictionalizing her.

The following is a list of the characters of *Asphodel* arranged in alphabetical order; the name of each character is given along with a chapter number indicating his or her first appearance or mention in the novel ("1.1" means part 1, chapter 1). This in turn is followed by a brief biography of the person upon whom the fictional character is based. The list also includes significant figures alluded to or discussed in the novel. These biographical capsules are designed to provide dates, facts, and contexts that will help orient the reader and encourage independent research. I have allowed the events of *Asphodel* and H.D.'s pre-1920 biography to dictate the kind and amount of information in each entry, telescoping the data accordingly. There is a minimum of overlap among the entries, which are designed to interlock with and illuminate each other.

A few characters in the novel seem to lack clearly identifiable historical counterparts, either because H.D. meant them to be typical (or perhaps composite) rather than referential or because information that might lead to their unmasking has not yet turned up. These characters are omitted here. A few identifications are tentative, and I have indicated this where appropriate.

H.D. herself provided biographical keys to some of her novels: the typescript of *Her* contains her pencilled list of the characters and their historical counterparts, and she included similar elucidations in letters to Norman Holmes Pearson. I believe that a knowledge of H.D.'s life enhances the experience of reading *Asphodel*, yet such knowledge does not "explain" the novel or account for its aesthetic strategies; nor should *Asphodel* be unquestioningly accepted as thinly veiled autobiography, as some biographers have tended to do. However faithful it may be to the events of H.D.'s life between 1911 and 1919, *Asphodel* is a highly experimental work of fiction created at a certain point in H.D.'s development, with all the clarities and distortions that this vantage on her past may have introduced.

I would like to acknowledge here the generous assistance of Louis H. Silverstein, who provided essential information for many of the following biographies. I also wish to thank Charles Timbrell and Caroline Zilboorg.

Louise Blake (2.3): probably Dorothy (Arabella) Yorke (1891 or 1892–1971), an American who grew up in Philadelphia and as a young woman travelled with her mother to various places in Europe, settling in Paris in 1914. Interested in the arts, she was among H.D.'s circle of friends in London during World War I. In 1917 she stayed at H.D. and Aldington's apartment in Mecklenburgh Square while they were away, later moving to an upstairs room in the same house. An affair developed between Yorke and Aldington when he was home on leave from Officers' Training Camp after receiving his commission in November 1917. In letters to H.D. from the front, Aldington affirmed his continuing love for her but also said that he desired "l'autre" (Yorke). His relationship with Yorke continued throughout most of the 1920s, after his separation from H.D. Under the name "Arabella Yorke," Yorke translated Emile Dermenghem's *The Life of Mahomet* and Renée Dunan's *The Love Life of Julius Caesar*, both published in London in 1930. (For further information, see *Richard Aldington and H.D.: The Early Years in Letters*, ed. Caroline Zilboorg [Bloomington: Indiana University Press, 1991].)

Mary (Merry) Dalton (1.5): possibly based in part on Brigit Patmore (1882–1965), who was born in Dublin and christened Ethel Elizabeth Morrison-Scott. Her mother's family had been landowners in Ulster, but Brigit rarely mentioned this fact, preferring to express her love for Ireland in the form of enthusiastic support for Irish independence. In 1907 she married John Deighton Patmore, grandson of the Victorian poet Coventry Patmore, and settled in Putney. A member of London literary circles before World War I, Brigit had met Richard Aldington and may have been his lover before either knew H.D.; the two may have been involved again at some point during the war (when Aldington was married to H.D.), though this is not certain. In the late 1920s Patmore and Aldington formed a relationship that lasted nearly a decade. In addition to two novels published in the 1920s, she wrote a volume of memoirs, *My Friends When Young*, which her son Derek Patmore edited and published in 1968.

It should be noted that certain aspects of "Merry Dalton" do not seem to correspond to Patmore, even though Merry is an early version of Morgan, the Patmore figure in H.D.'s *Bid Me to Live (A Madrigal)* (1960). "Lady Delia Prescott" in *Asphodel* (1.5) may also be based in part on Patmore, inasmuch as Jerrold and Hermione first meet at one of Delia's parties, just as Aldington and H.D. met at one of Patmore's.

Jerrold Darrington (1.7): Richard Aldington (1892–1962), born in Hampshire and raised in Dover and its vicinity. With Pound and H.D., he was one of the original Imagist poets and went on to a prolific career in letters. He and H.D. met sometime after her arrival in London in the fall of 1911, finding a common ground in their love of poetry and Greek art and literature. In 1912–1913 Aldington joined H.D. in Italy where she was travelling with her parents; their visit to Capri remained a cherished memory for both. They were married in London in October 1913. Their marriage, which was emotionally and professionally nourishing early on, became strained during the war years, especially after Aldington's enlistment and his affairs with other women, and they separated in 1919 after the birth of H.D.'s daughter by Cecil Gray. They began to correspond again in 1929. In 1938 H.D. obtained a divorce, as Aldington wanted to marry Netta Patmore, Brigit Patmore's daughter-in-law.

Phoebe Fayne Darrington (2.13): Frances Perdita Aldington (b. 1919), H.D.'s daughter by Cecil Gray, registered by H.D. as Aldington's child. In 1928, Perdita was legally adopted by Bryher and her husband Kenneth Macpherson. Married in 1950 to a literary agent, Perdita Schaffner has described her European childhood and her two mothers, H.D. and Bryher, in several delightful memoirs, including "Pandora's Box," published in H.D.'s *HERmione* (New Directions, 1981). Her family nickname was "Pup."

Walter Dowel (1.3): Walter Morse Rummel (1887–1953), born in Berlin of German and American parents. His mother was a daughter of Samuel F. B. Morse. A distinguished pianist, he was a champion of Debussy's piano music and played premieres of the *Douze Etudes* and some of the *Préludes*. He also composed his own music and collaborated on projects with Pound, H.D., and Aldington before the first war. H.D. met Rummel, probably through Pound, in America in the summer of 1910. His devotion to mystical thought intrigued her. He married the pianist Thérèse Chaigneau in 1912, divorcing her some years later. From 1918 to 1921 he was involved in a professional and romantic relationship with Isadora Duncan, performing joint recitals with her in various European cities.

Katherine Farr (1.10): probably May Sinclair (1863–1946), prolific British novelist and writer on philosophy, feminism, and other subjects. Pound, who had met Sinclair after his arrival in London in 1908, introduced H.D. to her in 1911. Sinclair became a strong public supporter of her poetry and in 1927 published an intelligent appreciation, "The Poems of 'H.D.'" (reprinted in *The Gender of Modernism: A Critical Anthology*, ed. Bonnie Kime Scott [Bloomington: Indiana University Press, 1990], 453–67).

The Farrands (1.2): probably the Ashursts who, according to H.D. in *The Gift* (New Directions, 1982), owned "the best house" in the area of the Doolittle home in Upper Darby—"about two miles away or nearer, if you went across the fields" (103). In a note in the typescript of *Her*, H.D. described the Ashursts as "'business people'—litt. [*sic*] type."

Clifton Fennel (1.1): possibly Joseph Pennell (1857–1926), born in Pennsylvania, American illustrator who settled in London and became noted for landscape and architectural views. Influenced by Whistler, Pennell wrote a biography of him (1908).

Bertrand Gart (1.2): Eric Doolittle (1870–1920), H.D.'s beloved half brother. He assisted his father at the Flower Observatory and later succeeded him as professor of astronomy at the University of Pennsylvania.

Carl Gart (1.2): Charles Leander Doolittle (1843–1919), H.D.'s father, born in Indiana. He became professor of astronomy and mathematics at Lehigh University in 1875 and later took a similar position at the University of Pennsylvania, where from 1896 he directed the Flower Observatory.

Eugenia Gart (1.2): Helen Eugenia Wolle Doolittle (1853–1927), H.D.'s mother, born into a Moravian family in Bethlehem, Pennsylvania. She married the widower Charles Doolittle in 1882 and bore him several children. H.D. later recalled her mother's gift for music and painting. In the 1920s she lived for extended periods with H.D. and Bryher in Europe

and travelled with them, becoming a third mother to H.D.'s daughter
Perdita.

Hermione Gart (1.1): Hilda Doolittle (H.D.) (1886–1961), born in Beth-
lehem, Pennsylvania, moved with her family to Upper Darby outside Philadelphia in 1895. She attended Moravian schools in Bethlehem and later the
Friends' Central School in Philadelphia. In 1905 she enrolled in Bryn Mawr
College but withdrew the following year for personal and academic reasons.
After her engagement to Ezra Pound was broken off, and he had left for
Europe, H.D. met and fell in love with Frances Gregg and went to Europe
with her and her mother in 1911. Except for short visits to America, she
remained in Europe for the rest of her life. In 1913 she married Richard
Aldington. A child by him was stillborn in 1915; a second child, by Cecil
Gray, was born in 1919. She spent the months of the latter pregnancy first in
Cornwall, then in a cottage in Buckinghamshire, and finally in a nursing
home in London, where Bryher helped her morally and financially through
an illness that threatened her life and the baby's. H.D.'s first "imagist"
poems were published in 1913, and she soon became noted for short, intense
lyrics of Hellenic quality. Between 1913 and 1919 her publications consisted
chiefly of poems and translations of Greek choruses. She was assistant
editor of *The Egoist* in 1916–1917, and helped Amy Lowell with the 1915,
1916, and 1917 volumes of *Some Imagist Poets*.

Isaac Lechstein (2.6): probably Jacob Epstein (1880–1959), British sculptor
influenced by vorticism and African art and noted for his portrait sculp-
tures. His prewar work, such as "The Rock Drill" (1913), was admired by
Pound and other modernists. In 1917 Epstein was living with his wife
Margaret Dunlop ("Milly Lechstein") in a house-cum-studio at 23 Guil-
ford Street, a block or so from H.D.'s apartment in Mecklenburgh Square.
He was called up for military duty in the same year and served in the
Artists' Rifles. In 1918 Cecil Gray posed for Epstein, but the plaster was
later broken up; Gray also posed for the hands of Epstein's "Risen Christ."
Epstein made three heads of Gray's friend, the composer Bernard Van
Dieren (see Richard Buckle, *Jacob Epstein: Sculptor* [Cleveland: The World
Publishing Company, 1963], pp. 82, 104).

John Llewyn (1.12): John Cowper Powys (1872–1963), English writer and
lecturer. He met Frances Gregg in 1912 and fell in love with her but, being
married, urged his friend Louis Wilkinson to wed her. Because of the
suddenness of the marriage, Wilkinson agreed not to consummate it for a
year (see Oliver Marlow Wilkinson, "The Letters of Frances and Jack," *The
Powys Review*, no. 19 [1986]: 43–57). Powys accompanied the couple on

their honeymoon to Europe and, with them, met H.D. in London in April 1912. She agreed to travel with the couple to Brussels, but Pound aggressively intervened and prevented her from going. The name "John Llewyn" may also contain an allusion to the writer Llewelyn Powys (1884–1939), John's brother.

George Lowndes (1.1): Ezra Pound (1885–1972), born in Hailey, Idaho, moved with his family to Philadelphia in 1889, soon settling in nearby Wyncote. In 1901, while an undergraduate at the University of Pennsylvania, Pound met the fifteen-year-old H.D.; they were engaged, and disengaged, at least twice between 1905 and 1908. In the course of their romance, they shared ideas and literary discoveries, and Pound introduced H.D. to Balzac, Ibsen, Morris, and other authors. In 1908 he left for Europe, published his first book of poems (*A Lume Spento*) in Venice, and in the same year settled in London where he soon acquired a reputation for bohemian flamboyance and American bumptiousness. In September 1912 he helped launch H.D.'s career by editing some of her poems and placing them in Harriet Monroe's *Poetry* under the nom de plume "H.D. Imagiste." Pound met the Englishwoman Dorothy Shakespear in 1909 and by 1912 was unofficially engaged to her (she is the "fiancée" George Lowndes refers to in 1.15). They were married in 1914. Around this time, personal and professional clashes led to a cooling of Pound and H.D.'s friendship, but they later resumed correspondence, and H.D. recorded her abiding affection for him in her memoir *End to Torment* (New York: New Directions, 1979).

Miss Moore (1.13): probably Louise Skidmore, a friend of H.D.'s from Philadelphia and Port Jefferson, Long Island, who recommended a "rue Jacob pension" when H.D. went to Paris in May 1912 (H.D., "Autobiographical Notes," entry for 1912 [Beinecke Library]).

Maurice Delacourt Morrison (1.11): Louis Umfreville Wilkinson (1881–1966) formed friendships with the Powys brothers while at Cambridge University. Between 1905 and 1919 he lectured in America, often in Philadelphia, and later was a University Extension lecturer for Oxford and London universities. He wrote several novels and a study of the Powys brothers (1936), some of these works under the pen name Louis Marlow. He married Frances Gregg in 1912, and they had two children. Frances obtained a divorce in 1923.

Clara Rabb (1.1): Julia Vanness Gregg (d. 1941), the mother of Frances Gregg. A widowed schoolteacher, she and Frances lived in North Philadelphia when H.D. came to know them.

Fayne (Josepha) Rabb (1.1): Frances Josepha Gregg (1884–1941), H.D.'s companion in Philadelphia. H.D. met her around 1910 and fell in love with her, later writing that Gregg "filled the gap in my Philadelphia life after Ezra was gone, after our 'engagement' was broken" (*End to Torment*, ed. Norman Holmes Pearson and Michael King [New Directions, 1979], p. 8). H.D. and Gregg were introduced by Pound to London literary circles in 1911, and Gregg had a minor career as a writer, publishing poetry and prose in *Poetry, The Forum, The New Freewoman*, and elsewhere. Although hurt by Gregg's sudden marriage to Louis Wilkinson, H.D. remained in contact with her in later years. Gregg was killed with her mother and daughter in the bombing of Plymouth in 1941.

Vérène Raigneau (1.3): Thérèse Chaigneau (1876–1935?), a distinguished French pianist (H.D. makes her a cellist) "known in Parisian music circles for having organized the Concerts-Chaigneau (which promoted old and new music with participants such as Jacques Thibaud, Lucien Capet, and Marya Freund) and as a member of the Chaigneau trio, with her sisters Suzanne and Marguerite—violinist and cellist" (Charles Timbrell, "Walter Morse Rummel, Debussy's 'Prince of Virtuosos,'" *Cahiers Debussy*, no. 11 n.s. [1987]: 25). Before World War 1, she performed with Walter Rummel, Harold Bauer, Pablo Casals, and others. She and Rummel were married in July 1912; they divorced in 1925. Chaigneau apparently suffered a mental collapse around 1918 and was institutionalized. Her father, Ferdinand Chaigneau, was a successful painter of the Barbizon School whose painting *Cattle by Moonlight* hung in the Luxembourg at the time of H.D.'s first visits to Paris.

Rallac (1.3): probably Edmund Dulac (1882–1953), noted artist and illustrator and friend of W. B. Yeats. Walter Rummel and Thérèse Chaigneau knew Dulac and his wife and stayed with them in London in May and June 1915 (see Colin White, *Edmund Dulac* [New York: Charles Scribner's Sons, 1976], p. 76). In the same year, Dulac did a striking portrait of Rummel. *Stories from Hans Andersen* (London: Hodder & Stoughton, 1911) contains illustrations by Dulac, including several evocative ones for the story "The Mermaid."

Beryl de Rothfeldt (2.10): Bryher (Annie Winifred Ellerman) (1894–1983), daughter of the wealthy British shipping magnate Sir John Ellerman. An admirer of H.D.'s poetry, Bryher sought an introduction to her in 1918. The two became friends, and Bryher provided support to H.D. during the later stages of her pregnancy. After an initially intense emotional phase that lasted into the early 1920s, she and H.D. settled into a lifelong companion-ship punctuated by intervals of separation, living in London and Switzer-land and travelling widely with the help of Bryher's funds. Bryher's diverse writings include poetry, autobiographical and historical novels, literary and film criticism, and memoirs such as *The Heart to Artemis* (1962), which contains an account of her meeting with H.D. and their life up to the outbreak of World War II. She founded a film company with her second husband Kenneth Macpherson and published the review *Life and Letters Today*.

Shirley Thornton (1.13): Margaret Lanier Cravens (1881–1912), born into a wealthy family in Indiana, went to Paris in 1907 to pursue her musical interests, studying piano with Ravel, Harold Bauer, and possibly Walter Rummel and Thérèse Chaigneau. Rummel introduced her to Ezra Pound in 1910, and she became Pound's friend and secret patron. Probably through Pound, H.D. met Cravens in May 1912, if not before, and visited her at her Right Bank apartment. Personal frustrations, depression, and a history of suicide in the family led to Cravens's suicide on June 1, 1912. Cravens had invited H.D. to tea for the afternoon of June 2, and H.D. learned about her death from the maid at the apartment door. Cravens had not married.

The mention of a "Miss Thornton" (1.11), president of "Lyn Mawr" when Hermione was there, presumably alludes to Martha Carey Thomas, presi-dent of Bryn Mawr during H.D.'s enrollment. This Miss Thornton should not be confused with Shirley Thornton.

Nellie Thorpe (1.9): Nellie Thorpe is the character who introduces Her-mione to Fayne Rabb in *Her*. Nellie's sister Jessie (who is called Mira in *Asphodel*) is said to have won a Paris art prize. In the typescript of *Her*, H.D. identified Nellie as "Mary—(?) (friend of Frances [Gregg])." Nellie Thorpe may be modelled on Mary Herr (1885–1960), a lifelong friend of H.D.'s from her college days. Mary was in the Class of 1909 at Bryn Mawr and majored in German and English. Susan Stanford Friedman has written that H.D. met Frances Gregg "through her college friend Mary Herr, probably in 1910" ("Hilda Doolittle [H.D.]," *Dictionary of Literary Biogra-phy*, vol. 45 (*American Poets, 1880–1945*), ed. Peter Quartermain [Detroit: Gale Research Company, 1986], p. 120). H.D. maintained an affectionate correspondence with Mary and made a point of seeing her when she visited America in later years.

Barbara Guest claims, however, that H.D. and Frances Gregg were "introduced by Nan Hoyt, a mutual friend. Hoyt appears in *HERmione* as Nellie Thorpe" (*Herself Defined: The Poet H.D. and Her World* [Garden City, NY: Doubleday, 1984], p. 22). In her article "Hilda Doolittle and

Frances Gregg," Penny Smith mentions an Amy Hoyt who was a friend of Frances Gregg (*The Powys Review*, no. 22 [1988]: 48).

Captain Ned Trent (2.3): probably Captain James Robert (Jack) White (1879–1946), son of a famous British general of the Boer War. White helped organize the Irish Citizen Army in Dublin in 1913, worked with the Red Cross in France in World War I, and engaged in various pro-Irish activities. He was the original of Jim Bricknell in Lawrence's *Aaron's Rod* (see Harry T. Moore, *The Priest of Love: A Life of D.H. Lawrence*, rev. ed. [Penguin, 1981], pp. 364–65).

Cyril Vane (2.6): Cecil Gray (1895–1951), a Scottish composer and music critic who was among H.D.'s circle of friends during World War I. In the spring of 1918 H.D. joined Gray at his house at Bosigran Castle in Cornwall and by August learned she was pregnant with his child. They grew distant after this point, and later attempts on the part of H.D.'s friends to persuade him to contribute to the child's support were unavailing.

About the Editor

Robert Spoo is Assistant Professor of English at
the University of Tulsa and Editor of the *James
Joyce Quarterly*.

Library of Congress Cataloging-in-Publication
Data
H. D. (Hilda Doolittle), 1886–1961.
   Asphodel / by H.D. ; edited with an
introduction and biographical notes by
Robert Spoo.
   ISBN 0-8223-1240-9 (alk. paper). —
ISBN 0-8223-1242-5 (alk. paper : pbk.)
   I. Spoo, Robert E. II. Title.
PS3507.O726A93   1992
813'.52—dc20   91-45620 CIP